# The Flight of Swallows

AUDREY HOWARD

# The Flight of Swallows

HODDER &
STOUGHTON

First published in Great Britain in 2009 by Hodder & Stoughton
An Hachette Livre UK company

1

A CIP catalogue record for this title is available from the British Library

Hardback ISBN 978 0 340 895429
Trade Paperback ISBN 978 0 340 89543 6

Typeset in Plantin by Hewer Text UK Ltd, Edinburgh
Printed and bound in the UK by CPI Mackays, Chatham ME5 8TD

Hodder & Stoughton policy is to use papers that are natural,
renewable and recyclable products and made from wood grown in
sustainable forests. The logging and manufacturing processes are expected
to conform to the environmental regulations of the country of origin.

Hodder & Stoughton Ltd
338 Euston Road
London NW1 3BH

www.hodder.co.uk

# The Flight of Swallows

# I

She could hear James wailing as she waited her turn outside
the door to her father's study and beside her Robbie began to
whimper in anticipation. Her other three brothers had run past
one by one, heading for the wide staircase where Kizzie waited
to comfort them. She held Robbie's hand, doing her best to
assuage his fear; after all, Robbie was only six years old and
inclined to be timid. Who could blame him?

At last the study door opened and James, seven years old, a
year older than Robbie, scuttled into the passage, holding his
hand to his behind. His pale cheeks were wet and he cast an
agonised glance at his sister.

'James . . .' Charlotte whispered, doing her best to convey
her sympathy, but the boy did not answer, speeding as fast as
he could towards the foot of the stairs. He had left the study
door open and a male voice sounded from within.

'Come in, Robert,' the voice ordered and Robbie's whimper
grew louder, turning to cries of blind terror. He clutched at
Charlotte's skirt, unable to move. 'And be quick about it,
child. I am a busy man and have no time to waste.'

She remembered last summer when they had been waiting
in just such a situation as this. There had been a butterfly
against the window at the end of the passage that looked out on
to the garden at the side of the house. It had been beating its
wings frantically against the glass, such lovely colours of
smoky brown, flame and pale grey, the flame and grey spotted
with white. It had been trying to escape and she had known

exactly how it felt but there had been no escape. For her or the butterfly! And today was the same.

'Go on, darling,' she whispered encouragingly to her little brother. 'It will soon be over.'

'No, please, Charlie . . . don't make me . . .'

'Darling, you know I can't—'

'Charlie, please . . .'

Charlotte Drummond hesitated, then, the child's terror bolstering her own courage though she was sadly aware that it would make no difference to what was about to happen, she stepped bravely into her father's study, her small brother cowering beside her.

Arthur Drummond stood, feet planted apart, on the rug before the good fire, his back to the arched fireplace with its cast-iron fire basket and fire-back and pretty tiles on either side. Above it was a large mirror which reflected the back of Arthur Drummond's sleek head and the snug room that was exclusively the master's domain. Though it was the beginning of the century and new styles were rapidly encroaching in most upper-class homes the Drummond household was not one of them. The house had been in the family for genera-tions, but not until Arthur had married the daughter of a wealthy coal owner had it been modernised to the Victorian fashion which still prevailed. The room was dominated by an enormous leather-topped desk on which stood a heavy silver inkstand, an ornate well-polished brass and frosted glass lamp, a silver cigar box and a photograph of a very pretty lady in a silver frame: the children's dead mother. Beside the desk was a side table well furnished with decanters and glasses. A globe atlas was set in a brass meridian ring on a stand and on the walls hung prints of hunting scenes, horses and dogs. There were two deep and comfortable leather armchairs, books lined three walls from floor to ceiling and a cheerful carpet of reds and blues covered the floor. Most of his wife's money had been gambled away but the comfort remained.

In his right hand Arthur Drummond held a thin, whippy cane with which he casually slapped his right, booted leg. He wore riding boots and pale buff breeches with a well-cut, three-buttoned, cutaway black frock-coat, for he was about to mount his expensive, well-bred horse and join the meet at King's Meadow, the home of one of his many acquaintances. His silk top hat waited on the desk. He was tall, handsome, lean, with hair the colour of the glossy brown conkers with which his sons played furious duels. His eyes were the same shade but where his hair gleamed in the firelight his eyes were flat, with a strange pin-prick of light which Charlotte, with sinking heart, was aware boded no good.

He frowned as his son and daughter entered together for they, and his other sons, knew the routine that attended a punishment. One at a time, boys first, in order of age, and lastly Charlotte who, as the eldest, was considered to be the ringleader in any wrongdoing or if not the ringleader should have put a stop to whatever it was before it began. She was expected to listen to the woeful cries of her siblings before submitting to her own chastisement.

'What is the meaning of this?' her father asked politely, as though questioning her on some trivial incident that should not have occurred. 'You know I will see you after Robert. And for goodness sake, stop blubbering, Robert. What a cry-baby it is.'

'Father,' Charlotte quavered, 'would you allow me to re-main with Robbie . . . Robert . . . during his . . . his . . .' She wanted to say his 'beating', which was what it was, but her father was already irritated by her behaviour and that word would only make it worse. 'He is so frightened, and really, he took no part in the . . .' She paused nervously.

'Yes?' Her father's voice was silky but menacing.

'He just happened to be there when the boys – after all that's what they are, no more than boys, and climbing on to the roof of the . . . well, it's a boy's trick, isn't it and—'

'Are you questioning my judgement, Charlotte?'

'No, Father, but their ball had—'

'That is enough. Not another word. Now I would be obliged if you would leave the room and wait in the passage.'

'But, Father, Robbie is—'

'I will attend to Robert, if you please. Now leave us. I will deal with you later.'

Charlotte's heart plummeted as she pried Robbie's hand from her skirt. She looked down into the tear-streaked, woebegone face of her little brother. The child was ashen and Charlotte felt that streak of stubbornness, which she was not aware she had inherited from her father, spring up within her. A storm of resentment against the unfairness of what her father was to do. Well, perhaps not a storm for no one stormed against Father, but a surge that she subdued, since it did no good. Nobody could stand against Father. She could remember her mother who had died when Robert was born which was perhaps why Robbie was as he was. He had never known the comfort and protection of a mother's love and always appeared to be searching for something he had lacked despite the love she and Kizzie lavished on him. Jean Drummond had been a gentle little woman who had, like them all, been intimidated by Arthur Drummond and who, it seemed, had made no fight to stay alive after the birth of her sixth child. Charlotte had been ten years old and quite devastated by her death, as had the three older boys, Henry and William and John, but at the same time the tragedy had been somewhat alleviated by the arrival of Kizzie, who was to help the nanny in charge of the new baby. Without Kizzie Charlotte often wondered how they would have survived. Not that they were in any sort of danger but she had filled a void left by their mother; was always there when she was most needed – as now – and in fact was considered by Robbie, who had never known his own mother, to be her! She was a bulwark behind which they might hide, a shield to guard them, though she had no power to stand between them and their father. *She was just there!*

Charlotte stood in the passage, her hands to her ears, doing her best to shut out the sounds of the swish of the cane and her brother's distress. Six of them, which was moderate in view of the twelve the older boys had received.

Like James, he ran past her and scuttled up the stairs and Charlotte waited for the call from her father. It was her turn now!

'Come in, Charlotte,' he said pleasantly. That was the trouble, he was always pleasant. Sometimes she almost wished he would rant and rave, show a flash of human temper, but then he surely must know that his children's naughtiness was really only high spirits, which they indulged in when he was not there and certainly not enough to merit his rage.

'Now then, Charlotte, perhaps you would be good enough to explain your recent show of defiance. You know it is my belief that children should be punished for any wrongdoing and to climb on the roof of the conservatory where they could not only have fallen through the glass and seriously injured themselves, but also damaged the building and the rare plants it contains shows a considerable lack of judgement and you, as the eldest, should have restrained them. One of the gardeners could have brought a ladder and climbed up to retrieve the ball and I would have thought you had the sense to see it. Do you understand?' He paused and hit his boot with the switch and Charlotte realised that he could not wait to begin but she could not help herself from speaking out.

'But, Father, the boys were—'

'It is you we are speaking of, Charlotte. Not your brothers. They have been disciplined and now it is your turn. You must learn to think before you act—'

'But, Father—'

'And if you interrupt me once more I shall be forced to take further measures.'

Charlotte had some knowledge of what those further measures might be since she had suffered them before. The last time she had been unable to sit down comfortably for a week!

'Now, miss, bend over, if you please.'

He indicated the leather chair which was already pulled out from the knee-hole of the desk where he attended to household and estate matters. Where he interviewed the butler and housekeeper. He nodded to Charlotte, that curious expression in his eyes deepening. Obediently she leaned over the back of the chair, praying to the God of her childhood that it would not be the worst sort of punishment that she had suffered in the past. She prayed in vain.

'Lift your skirt and petticoats.' Oh, gentle Jesus, please not my drawers.

'Pull down your drawers, if you please. This is a—'

Without pausing to think of the consequences she stood up and whirled about, her skirt and petticoat dropping into place and whirling with her. Her father recoiled in amazement, for a moment not quite knowing what to do because none of his children had ever defied him. *Really* defied him. Then he lifted the switch as though to hit her across the face with it but just in time he collected himself. It would not do to have his daughter going about with a weal across her cheek.

'What do you think you are doing?' he demanded in that cool voice he could assume.

'I'm refusing to . . . to . . . bow to your ludicrous and pointless order; pointless because it will do no good. We are punished for the slightest transgression, ones that we do not even know we are committing. How natural it was for the boys to try to retrieve their ball which was only on the very edge of the roof of the conservatory. It hardly seemed worth it to call the gardeners and Robbie and I were merely watching. Does that deserve the thrashing you have just meted out? Well, you will not thrash me. I am sixteen and will not be exposed to . . . to . . .'

'How dare you question my judgement,' her father hissed. 'I would advise you to obey me at once or you will go to your room and be locked in there for—'

'Very well, I would rather be locked up than be beaten on my bare . . . my bare flesh. It is indecent, disgusting . . .'

Charlotte watched with horrid fascination as her father's face turned a dangerous crimson, the colour of it appearing to leak into his eyes, then just as suddenly he pulled himself together. His daughter was almost as tall as he was, a strong and healthy girl, and he did not wish to struggle with her since it seemed in her present mutinous mood that was what she would do. Fight him! She had a splendid figure, deep-bosomed with a slender waist and hips and long legs. She was lovely, as her mother had been lovely, her hair a warm tawny shade, a mixture of her mother's pale brown and his own chestnut, but where his eyes were brown hers were a deep and startling aquamarine. She spent a great deal of her time outdoors, walking, playing the popular game of tennis and her smooth skin was tanned. She had a full, peach-coloured mouth and perfect white teeth and very soon he knew he would have no trouble marrying her to some suitable landed gentleman, perhaps even titled!

It seemed there was a stand-off. Charlotte was breathing hard in the attitude of a boxer in a ring or a gladiator facing an opponent and he was somewhat at a loss as to what to do next. None of his children had ever refused to bow down to the punishments he meted out to them. The boys appeared to have inherited their mother's meek and gentle ways, though he had seen signs of defiance in Henry, the eldest at fifteen. It was strange really because he wished his sons to be obedient and at the same time to show some spirit, having no idea that it was he who had made them as they were. Afraid of him, disliking him, wanting to defy him but unable to pluck up the courage to do so. It had been left to this daughter of his who looked quite magnificent as she glared at him. Still, he could not have this, could he? He must make a show of authority.

'Go to your room and stay there until I give you permission to leave it. I will have bread and water sent up to you and that is all. Talk to no one. I am to go out now and cannot spare the time to deal with you but when I return we will resume this . . . this discussion. I will consider the punishment you deserve and sincerely hope that you will have become calm by then.'

He turned his back on her to show his utter contempt, or so he would have her believe, but the truth was that for the first time in his life as a husband and as a father he had been defied and was not quite sure what to do next. He needed time to think and the hunt at King's Meadow would give him a chance to do that. The weather was perfect for hunting, a crisp winter's day, the frost of the night before almost gone. The meet at Armstrong's place was always a splendid affair and a day's hunting would put this problem in its true perspective.

Five miles of hard riding, the hounds in full cry, everybody too absorbed in the chase to notice that Arthur Drummond was somewhat distracted. He had to negotiate deep ditches, choose the right place to jump winter hedges crisp with the last of the frost, and keep firm hands on the reins of his hunter who was inclined to be spirited. Jupiter, he was called, bred from a famous line of Arabs said to have been brought back from the Crusades.

By the time the fox was dealt with, a young lady, a house guest of Drummond's, had been blooded and the riders were making their cheerful way back to King's Meadow, he had forgotten all about his recalcitrant daughter.

★    ★    ★

Charlotte sat on the edge of her bed and stared out of the window at the stretch of lawn sloping down to the small lake in the middle of which a fountain sprayed in a shimmering, sunlit haze. Across the garden ran a path to the wood that edged the property with a hazel thicket and dense oaks beyond. Malachy, the gardener, was busy at something on the edge of the woodland, and from almost at his feet, causing him to look startled, a rabbit ran out and bobbed across the lawn. Rooks rose in a black swirl and went trailing off across the deep blue winter sky. Denny Foster, the under-gardener, came striding round the corner of the house, calling something to Malachy and with a nod Malachy stopped whatever he was doing and followed Denny to the back of the house, probably to the kitchen for the hot chocolate Mrs Welsh, the cook, provided for the servants' elevenses.

There would be wood violets peeping through the winter grass under the trees, the violet roots sending up little green trumpets of new leaves and the elm trees were just breaking into blossom. She had seen them yesterday as she and the boys had been having what Robbie called 'adventures', the games the older boys had devised just before the terrible event that had caused so much distress this morning. Sometimes they were swashbuckling Royalists about to take arms against the Roundheads; sword-play which they practised to get used to sudden ambuscades, or an attack when you were carrying despatches. Their imagination was vivid, garnered from the books they read and she sometimes joined in though she preferred to watch the birds, investigate growing plants, pick flowers when there were any to pick or just daydream, as her father would call it.

She sighed deeply, wondering how her brothers were. At least they had Kizzie to comfort them, and as if her thoughts had conjured her, the door opened slowly and Kizzie's rosy face peeped round it. Her usual beaming smile was not in evidence.

'Ista orlright, chuck?' she asked in her broad Yorkshire dialect. 'Tha' pa's gone off on 'is 'orse. 'Untin', Willie ses an' won't be back while dinner. Them lads is upset, especially our Robbie though Harry reckons 'e don't care. Poor mites'll not sit down terday nor termorrer more like. 'Ow about you, lass? Did 'e . . .'

'No, Kizzie, he didn't beat me, though he tried. I'm afraid I refused to be thrashed so he sent me up here today. By the way, it's bread and water for me.'

'Gie ower, great daft loony!' Kizzie's red cheeks became even more colourful in her indignation. 'I'm fetchin' tha' summat ter eat right now an' it'll not be bread an' water. Bread an' water be damned. Tha' was only lakin'. All bairns lake an'—'

Charlotte stood up and put her hand on Kizzie's arm as the young woman advanced into the room. 'No, Kizzie, you know he'll find out. He always does and then you will be in trouble as well as me.' She was trying for a bit of humour but she was close to tears. 'Do you want your "bum" smacked, which is what I was threatened with, or, worse still, do you want to be dismissed? Think, Kizzie, because I couldn't manage without you.'

Kizzie's face softened and she put her strong arms about this girl who had come into Kizzie's life when she was ten years old and Kizzie four years older. Her mother had just died and the nanny the family employed could not cope with six children, one of them a newborn baby. Kizzie, whose full name was Hezekiah, loved and mothered them all, despite being only fourteen. She had come from a big family who lived in Overton where her pa worked on the land. Eleven of them in a tiny cottage, Kizzie being the eldest. Her mam would miss her, she said sadly, but there was no room for them all, and not on what Pa earned. It was either into service or the pit as a pit brow lass and so with Mam being related to Mrs Welsh, the cook, she had got the job at the Mount. Her relationship to Mrs Welsh was very vague, Mrs Welsh being second cousin to Mam's auntie, but Mrs Welsh was a firm believer in knowing where those who worked in the house came from and Mrs Banks, who was housekeeper, agreed with her.

' 'E's addled, that pa o' yourn, an' I don't care 'oo 'ears me say it.'

'Kizzie, be careful. If my father heard you, or even realised what you are thinking he would dismiss you on the spot.'

Kizzie shook her head sadly. 'Aye, lass, I'm afeared 'e would. 'Appen I'd best keep me gob shut. But tha' must eat summat. Tha' pa'll not be back while ternight an' tha've gorra get summat inside yer. I'll get Mrs Welsh ter do tha' some frummenty. 'Ow's that? It'll stick ter tha' belly an' it's not what tha'd call real food. An' if 'e asks me I'll lie in me teeth an'—'

'No, Kizzie, no. Lord, I can manage a day without food. What you'd call proper food. Bring me a couple of slices of Mrs Welsh's freshly made bread and a jug of water.' She smiled conspiratorially. 'You can put butter on the bread and ice in the water and when he asks, if he asks, you can say truthfully I've had nothing but bread and water.'

Within ten minutes Kizzie was back with a tray spread with a beautifully laundered cloth. On it sat a platter of bread thickly plastered with creamy butter, the bread straight from the oven, the butter from the dairy, and a fluted glass jug with a lid, filled with water liberally speared with ice. There was also a vase filled with hothouse roses, tiny pink buds decorated with baby's breath.

Charlie felt a lump come to her throat and when Kizzie had placed the tray on the table beneath the window she put her arms about her and hugged her.

'Food fit for a king, Kizzie. Thank you.'

'Mrs Welsh sent them flowers, lass. Tha' knows they're all wi' thi' an' them lads. Mind, 'e said nowt about them 'avin' bread an' water so tha've no need ter worry about them starvin'. I'll tekk 'em up a good dinner. Mekk 'em feel better. Now tha' get tha' teeth inter that there bread an' butter an tha'll not go far wrong.' She hesitated. 'Tha' knows keys in't lock. He ses tha've ter stay 'ere but I reckon tha'll need the wotsit so tha' just ring tha' bell an' I'll be up directly. Eeh . . .' She shook her head sadly. 'What's ter become of us all, tell me that?' just as though the whole household were in grave danger.

Charlie ate the lovely fresh bread, still warm from the oven, with lashings of the good butter Sally Harper made in the dairy. The iced water was refreshing and she wondered idly why it was that water with ice in it tasted so much better than without it. She wasn't really hungry. Her mind was too active with the problem of what she would do next. Her brothers, Robbie so vulnerable and James not much stronger; how could they stand up to the life their father imposed on them? It wasn't as if they went to the local grammar school where at least they would be out of the house for a good part of the day. The older boys, Henry and William and John, could withstand their father's indifference, his . . . she was going to say cruelty which she supposed it was, though apart from the beatings, which seemed to give him some perverse pleasure, he barely infringed on their lives. They were well fed, clothed and slept in warm beds. The servants were fond of them and did their best to bring some warmth into their lives but they were growing up afraid of their own shadows, always looking over their shoulders to see if Father was watching them, even in the most innocent of pastimes such as the game of football in which the ball had landed on the conservatory roof. An accident.

She sighed and after ringing the bell to be let out of her room to visit the bathroom, this time by Nancy, the parlour-maid,

Kizzie being busy with the boys, she changed into her night-dress and allowed Nancy to make up the fire and put her to bed.

'Sleep well, Miss Charlie,' the maid said sympathetically, wondering, as they all did, what was to happen to this courageous young girl. It was the first time she had stood up to her father, cruel bugger that he was, though she wouldn't dare say that in the presence of Mrs Banks or Mr Watson. But the way he treated these children of his was a crying shame, the servants all agreed. She sadly turned the key in the lock before returning to the kitchen.

It was exactly ten thirty the next morning when Arthur Drummond summoned his daughter to his study. He was in a good mood, for he had enjoyed his day's hunting and his meeting with Miss Elizabeth Parker who, though twenty-five years old and a mystery to her family and friends as to why she was not yet married, had made a big impression on him.

But it made no difference to Arthur Drummond. His daughter must be taught a lesson. She had defied him and it was up to him as a parent to make sure she was made to realise that he ruled the house and his family. Spare the rod and spoil the child had been his father's motto and he felt the same.

'You will take your punishment now, Charlotte, or would you like Henry, or perhaps even Robert to take it for you? It is up to you.' He smiled as he smacked the palm of his hand with the switch. He knew her answer, of course.

She wept, not only with the welts that criss-crossed her buttocks but with humiliation as she ran up the stairs, every step an agony, to her room where Kizzie waited for her.

# 2

Brooke Armstrong handed his last guest into her carriage on the smoothly brushed turning circle at the front of his home then stood back, the courteous smile clamped to his face.

'It's been a lovely weekend. We have so enjoyed it, haven't we, Clive,' gushed Lady Parker while her husband nodded pleasantly and her daughter fluttered her long eyelashes at Brooke before casting them down modestly, which he thought ludicrous in view of her age. She had been doing her best to draw him into her net all weekend, for she was ruthless in her search for a husband she considered suitable. He supposed he must fit into that category. Thankfully, she had turned her charms on Drummond when she realised she was wasting them on himself! She was very pretty with dark hair and green eyes, had an impeccable pedigree and was the only child of Sir Clive and Lady Parker who were wealthy and desperate to get her married. Twenty-five was really an old maid. She had had her chances, many of them, but had been too choosy and somehow they had passed her by.

Brooke Armstrong was, he supposed, one of the most sought-after bachelors in Yorkshire and meant to remain that way until he had met the woman with whom he might find it possible to live for the rest of his days. That woman was definitely not the spoiled Elizabeth Parker. She had been outrageous in her pursuit of him and he had found himself in some tight corners where it had taken all his tact and diplomacy, even downright rudeness, to extricate himself.

He was ready for marriage, or so he was told, and his vast wealth and social position attracted every marriageable female for miles around which could become extremely tedious. Matchmaking mamas had thrown their simpering sixteen-year-old daughters in his path ever since he had returned home but he had adroitly managed to avoid them and the matrimony they had in mind.

The last ten years had been good ones, for when he was twenty his father had bought him a commission in the King's Own Yorkshire Light Infantry where he had served with distinction and had even won a medal or two. He had fought in many battles: on the North-West Frontier; Khartoum in the Sudan and the small mountain state of Chitral, were he was wounded. His father died that year so Major Brooke Armstrong was forced to resign his commission and return to Yorkshire to look after the family estate of King's Meadow. He found, to his surprise, that he enjoyed it!

He watched the smart carriage drive round the circle then disappear along the avenue of stately lime trees that led to the wrought-iron entrance gates half a mile away. The lime trees were still bare since they did not open their leaves until April, the denuded branches delicate against the frosty winter sky. In the summer they provided a cool, sweet-smelling walk and he believed his cook, Mrs Groves, dried the flowers and made them into a refreshing lime tea. They had been planted by the first of the Armstrongs generations ago, said to have done service to George IV – of what sort was something of a mystery – who had granted them the land, and given the name of King's Meadow to the thousand or so acres that made up the estate. There were several farms, cattle and arable, a grouse moor, woodland, wild moorland over which Brooke and his weekend guests had hunted, a lake, a stream where good fishing might be had and he was pleasantly occupied in the management of it all. His mother had also left him a woollen mill in Dewsbury which brought him more wealth but he had a manager and efficient overseers to run that.

He turned and entered the front door of the house, calling to one of the maids to tell Percy to saddle up, bending to the sudden swirl of dogs who escaped through the kitchen door into the wide hallway.

'Get down, you fool, and leave Nellie alone: you'll have her over. Come along, don't get left out . . . yes, yes, you can come with me. I know you don't like being shut up all weekend but I can't have you leaping about over fine ladies like—' He stopped speaking abruptly, aware that the housemaid was all ears and it was not polite to criticise his guests, but, God strewth, he was glad they were gone. He'd done his duty to all those who had entertained him in the past and now he could get down to something he enjoyed, which was riding round the estate and having a word with – and casting a sharp eye on – his tenants. After the weekend he had just spent playing the dutiful host to some rather boring guests, though he had enjoyed the hunting, he felt like an amble on old Max to see what was coming into growth in his woods and fields and perhaps have a beer with Jack Emmerson, one of his tenants whose wife brewed the best ale on the estate. Jack had just purchased a bullock which was said to be extremely hard to handle. He was the largest of King's Meadow tenants, leasing one hundred and ten acres. He was a good farmer, hard-working and punctual with his rent. Fuller's Farm, as it was called, again the origins of its name lost in the mists of time, had a pretty farmhouse with a small orchard between it and the lane that ambled through the woodland to the main road to Overton.

'Come up, Max,' he said to the horse, nodding at Arch, the stable lad who opened the gate for him, setting the animal to a canter while the dogs, a black Labrador, a Jack Russell and a retriever who was the wrong colour, raced ahead of him, delirious to be out of the stable yard and away from the sedate walks Percy and Arch allowed them when Mr Armstrong had guests.

Mrs Emmerson's kitchen was old, as was the farmhouse, with a floor of buff and pink and primrose coloured tiles. It had an old-fashioned wide hearth with the spits and the oven to the side and a big black dresser set with bits of brassware and pewter plates and mugs. The farmhouse had been in the Emmerson family for as long as the Armstrongs had been at King's Meadow and each housewife had seen no reason to change it. He was offered a glass of Mrs Emmerson's cowslip wine and a piece of her best plum cake, or would he prefer some home-brewed ale. He chose the ale!

The two men drank their ale hanging over the stout fence that stood between them and the enclosure where the new bullock eyed them suspiciously. He was certainly a fine-looking beast. He was docile enough now, Jack said, but the bugger'd have to be watched for he had a nasty mean streak and that's why he'd got him cheap.

'Tekks two on us ter move 'im, that's why theer's a ring through 'is nose, like. A couple o' poles fastened to it an' us'll 'ave 'im. Yon's a right good beast, Major, an' already I've chaps waitin' wi' their cows. Tha've only ter say't word an' that lad'll serve thine an' all.'

'I shall bear that in mind, Jack. Now, I must get on. Those dogs of mine are bristling up to yours so if we don't want a fight . . .'

'Nay, mine'll do as tha're told.'

'Well, good luck with him, Jack,' his landlord said as he mounted the patient grey on which he always did his rounds. Stand without tethering, would Max, and could be led on a thread but he did like a good gallop, one that accorded with his age. They set off along the edge of Seven Cows Wood, the bare trees to his right, going at full speed through the knee-high grass which in spring and summer would be carpeted with poppy, clover, meadowsweet. Going flat out, or at least what Max could manage at his age, Brooke's nose almost on the grey's neck, he was on the girl who ran out of the belt of woodland before he had time to shout a warning and when she went down his heart came to a shuddering stop before re-starting and beating so fast he could hardly breathe. Max whinnied in distress, rearing up on to his hind legs as he did his best to avoid the prone figure so that Brooke almost slid from the saddle but scarcely had the horse's forelegs touched the ground again than he was off his back and bending over the figure of the girl. She lay flat on her belly, her arms stretched out, her face pressed into last year's rotting leaf mould. She rolled over as he reached out a trembling hand to her, for she had frightened the bloody life out of him, and though he could see she was dazed she seemed to be uninjured. At once he was furious, like a mother whose naughty child has just run into danger and survived; he wanted to lash out at her but her expression cleared and he found himself looking into the most amazing eyes he had ever seen. They were a vivid aquamarine blue surrounded by thick lashes the same shade as her hair and eyebrows. She was not exactly beautiful for none of her features was perfect. Her mouth was wide, a bright poppy red, her cheekbones high and flushed with a delicate wild rose, her jaw square with an obstinate set to it and her hair was what he could only call tawny-coloured. Neither brown, nor ginger, nor chestnut but perhaps a mixture of them all.

'You bloody fool,' he snarled, reaching down a hand to help her up but she ignored it, getting to her feet unaided. 'What the hell were you doing, dashing from the tree-line like that without even stopping to see if—'

'This is not a high street, sir, where one can expect traffic. I was running . . .'

'I could see that, woman, but surely you must have heard my horse's approach. Or are you deaf as well as half-witted? Besides which you are trespassing. This is private land.'

'I am not here to poach your game or snare your rabbits. I was merely walking.'

'*Walking!* You were doing no such thing and you can count yourself lucky that Max here is old and has the sense that a younger animal might not have.'

'You are extremely rude and your language is quite offensive. It is not the language of a gentleman and I would be obliged if you would get out of my way and allow me to continue my . . . my walk. I was not aware that I was trespassing, and for that I apologise. Your land must run beside my father's. I shall make sure in future that I stay where . . .'

The three dogs ran back and began to nose at the hand of the girl and at once she turned to them, smiling, then squatted down to pet them in turn. She seemed to wince a little as she knelt and Brooke's expression of indignation turned to one of concern. 'You're hurt,' he said, but she shook her head and as she did so a glorious mass of hair became unpinned, falling about her shoulders and down her back in a bright, gleaming cloak. At the sight of it, and combined with her incredible eyes, something in his chest moved painfully. He studied her, wondering where on earth she had come from though she had spoken of his estate running beside that of her father's. She had the well-bred voice of the gentry so he deduced she was not a farm girl, nor a maidservant out for a walk, if maidservants had time for such exercise, and her outfit seemed to prove that. She wore a well-made tweed skirt that reached her ankle bone in shades of coffee and chocolate-brown fleck with a short fitted jacket to match, brown lace-up boots, sturdy for walking. On her head, clinging for dear life by a hatpin, was a woollen beret with a pom-pom on top, her hands were encased in brown leather gloves and a long, woollen scarf was wrapped around her neck.

Suddenly, some likeness, he didn't know how, perhaps the colour of her hair or the thrust of her little chin, reminded him of someone in whose company he had recently been.

'You're Drummond's girl,' he gasped, amazed at the way he had reacted to her and also to whose daughter she was. She was only a child really, though she was well developed, eyeing her full, well-rounded breasts. Fifteen . . . sixteen perhaps but why should it make any difference to him? The way she had darted out from the woodland, heedless and unthinking, not even hearing the hoof beats of his horse, could have caused a nasty accident, to her, to him and to old Max. He didn't know why he should be so furious, after all nothing had happened to any of them, but for some reason he was incensed.

'Do you normally dash about like some wild thing, uncaring of whom you may hurt?' he heard himself saying. 'Max did well to avoid—'

'I'm sorry,' she gulped, all defiance leaking away. She bent her head to that of Ginger who was licking her face kindly as though she knew the girl was troubled. 'I . . . I wasn't thinking . . .'

'Well,' he said, his own anger ebbing, 'perhaps you will be more careful next time.' He felt a bit of a fool actually, for no harm had been done but she had given him a fright. Max was calmly nibbling the grass where the meadow edged the wood and for a minute or two nothing further was said. Charlotte buried her face into the dog's silky fur, wrapping her arms about her and the animal wriggled in ecstasy; when eventually she rose to her feet all trace of the tears she had shed had vanished into the animal's coat. She looked at the man in front of her, knowing who he was but since they had not met before and she was a well-brought-up young lady, she offered him her hand.

'Charlotte Drummond,' she told him abruptly.

'Brooke Armstrong,' he answered, taking her gloved hand.

She saw a tall, lean man with well-muscled shoulders dressed for riding in a tweed jacket of similar colours to her own, buff-coloured breeches and knee-high well-polished riding boots. Under the jacket he wore a buff-coloured jumper, warm and hand-knitted, and he also had a woollen scarf wrapped about his neck. He was quite old, she decided, but not unattractive, dark-complexioned, his face slashed with dark eyebrows, his chin thrusting arrogantly and his mouth firm though it curled up at the corners as if laughter were not far away. He had a dark, vigorous head of hair which the breeze had whipped about his head and which was tumbling over his eyebrows. His eyes were compelling as though they had searched far horizons, with fine lines fanning out from the corners, and almost colourless, a pale, silvery grey with very black pupils, as startling in a way as were hers and they looked at her in a way she found quite disconcerting.

'Well, I suppose I'd better get back,' she murmured. 'They will wonder where I am.'

'They?' He was intrigued, he didn't know why.

'My brothers.'

'Ah, yes, your father told me he had sons though he didn't mention you.'

'He wouldn't!'

She had turned away, ready to walk back the way she had come but suddenly he wanted her to stay, again he didn't know why.

'Won't you sit down for a moment and get your breath?' indicating a fallen tree trunk on the edge of the woodland. He was startled when she began to laugh, in a manner that might have been described as hysterical though he could not think what he had said to evoke it.

'Thank you,' she said through the laughter, 'I don't think I can.'

'Why not, Miss Drummond, are you . . .?'

'Please, don't ask. It would be too difficult to explain.'

'Very well.' His voice was cold. 'I will detain you no longer.' But somehow he found himself unable to move away. She looked so unutterably *sad* – was that the word? – as though she had a troubled mind and he knew that Ginger, who was older than Dottie and Floss, sensed it by the way she leaned against the girl's leg. He glanced away to collect his thoughts, his very strange thoughts, and noticed, almost absently, great flocks of rooks and starlings down on the fields of Holly Farm and a pair of beautiful bullfinches in a hawthorn bush. Spring was coming, he thought absently. The gorse on the moorland just beyond the fields had been in blossom but the sharp frosts of the past week had nipped off the bloom. It had been a mild winter up to then and the hazel catkins were out. He saw this with the part of his mind that was not occupied with the drooping figure of the girl who had hurtled so precipitously across his path and who was beginning to make her slow way back towards the wood that led to the Mount.

'Miss Drummond,' he called out and she turned back to him.

'Yes?'

'Do you ride?' he asked, astonishing himself.

'No.' She was astonished too. 'My father won't . . . we have no . . . No, Mr Drummond, none of us has been allowed to ride. My father does not believe in it. At least not for his children!'

'You just walk, you and your brothers . . . in these woods, perhaps, or . . .'

'I really must go, sir. I am pleased to have met you.'

Her young dignity touched him in the way the tumble of her hair and the compelling colour of her eyes had done.

'Then good-day, Miss Drummond.'

He caught Max by the rein and gracefully mounted him then, without a backward glance, put him to the gallop back the way he had come. The last Charlotte heard of him was his voice.

'Come, Ginger, come, Dottie . . . Floss.'

Ginger glanced back at her then raced to catch up with the others and her master.

She didn't know why but she often found her thoughts returning to that day when she had met Mr Drummond at the edge of Seven Cows Wood. During the next few months she sometimes thought she heard his voice coming from downstairs when her father gave a dinner party, wondering why it should remain in her memory and still be so clear that she should recognise it. She and Robert, and sometimes James, would hang over the banister to watch Father's guests arriving, noticing particularly one very pretty woman who seemed to appear frequently. She wore the most gorgeous evening gowns in pinks, blues, reds, a rich ruby which was a particular favourite in honour of the coming coronation. They were 'two-piece', with a skirt and bodice, the bodice neckline square-cut or round and low to show the tops of her splendid white breasts. They had transparent sleeves or what was known as an angel sleeve, a long square panel floating from the armhole and reaching almost to the ground. The bodice was decorated with beads, or spangles or artificial flowers, another gown with silvery lace and ribbons of silver tissue, all from Poiret in Paris, though Charlotte was not aware of it. Very expensive, she was sure and absolutely up to the minute. She had a tinkling laugh which was often heard above the polite conversation around the dinner table and once coming from a dark corridor that led to the back of the house and was seldom used since it gave access only to the gun room. It mingled, strangely, with that of their father. She was, so Kizzie told them, the daughter of a baronet.

It was in April that she saw him again. She was walking with Robert in the little spinney that lay on the edge of Father's property and through which ran a tiny stream, a particular favourite with the boys. There was a graceful willow covered all over with great golden catkins around which bees were humming busy gathering pollen, and stretching as far as the eye could see was a vast carpet of wild daffodils.

'Look, Charlie,' Robert called to her as she sat herself on a fallen tree trunk, dreaming of nothing in particular, 'look at the tadpoles. They're going mad in the water wagging their dear little black tails. Come and see. What a shame the others aren't here. You know how John loves tadpoles.'

The four older boys were having lessons with Miss Price who had released Charlotte and Robert, saying that Robert was too young for algebra and Charlotte too old. She had, of course, asked permission from the children's father and had found him surprisingly acquiescent, quite amiable in fact which was not often the case. They had all, meaning the servants and the children, noticed that the head of the house had been in an unusually good mood these last few weeks, Charlie more so than the others, for though they had all been beaten several times for minor misdemeanours, it had not been on their bare buttocks. She and her brothers had been particularly careful not to anger their father, as best they could, since many times in the past they had been unaware that they were sinning. He had been out with the hunt until the season ended and away from home visiting friends, house parties, Kizzie explained, though they were not awfully sure what that meant. Sometimes he had people to stay at the weekends, most of them, including the lovely lady whose name was Elizabeth Parker, Kizzie told them, spending a 'Friday to Monday'. Kizzie seemed to find out a lot about Father's guests and kept Charlotte, James and Robert, at least, entertained with her descriptions of the activities, charades and fancy dress affairs

and such, though Henry, William and John considered themselves too old to listen to such gossip!

She was startled when a voice that was not Robert's interrupted her reverie.

'Miss Drummond, it seems it is my turn to trespass. I do beg
your pardon and please forgive the little beggar who is trying
to eat your skirt. I'm trying to discipline him without the others
exciting him but it seems . . . Taddy . . . Taddy, come here at
once, sir. Oh, damn it . . . will you . . . I'm sorry . . .'

The puppy, a mixture of black Labrador and another
unknown breed, was leaping all over Charlotte, licking her
face and nipping at her hands, yipping with delight, and at his
onslaught Charlotte fell in a most unladylike way over the back
of the log and landed in a clump of daffodils flat on her back
with her skirts up, showing a great deal of black stocking and
frilly white petticoat. Her laughter rang out, bringing Robert
hurrying from the stream to join in the fun and for several
minutes, until Brooke swept the pup into his arms, there was
joyful chaos.

Brooke Armstrong was curiously silent though his lips
twitched in what wanted to be a smile. The reason was Charlotte
herself. He was enchanted, he could think of no other word. She
enchanted him with her unaffected laughter, her unconcern
with the amount of leg and petticoat she had revealed, her
childlike delight with the small animal which was struggling to
get back to her. Her hair, which he realised had a life and
direction of its own, was once again tumbling about her neck
and down her back, the April sunshine painting it with the glow
of autumn leaves. The boy, her brother he supposed, was
fiddling with the puppy in Brooke's arms which now turned
his attention to the boy and he happily handed the animal over to
him. The boy put him down and began to run and in the way of
small animals the pup ran after him and with a sigh of relief
Brooke sat down next to Charlotte on the fallen log.

'I do apologise for the bad manners, mine and the pup's. Give me a month and I'll have him obedient.'

'Oh, no, don't break his spirit, please. I have seen what—' She stopped speaking abruptly.

Wisely Brooke did not question her on what she had been about to say. He had seen the cruel twist to Arthur Drummond's mouth and the sudden coldness surge in his eyes and he had heard rumours concerning his strictness – to say the least – with his family. He had learned that the girl who sat beside him was sixteen, probably almost seventeen and not the child he had first thought her, and each time he had dined at the Mount he had hoped that she would perhaps be present for she was old enough. This was the first time he had seen her since he had almost run her down on Max.

They talked politely for ten minutes; about the coming coronation of their new King which was to take place in June; the death of his own father and Brooke's part at Chitral; the ending of his career as a soldier and taking up the running of his family estate.

'And you, Miss Drummond, what do you intend to do with . . .' He was about to say 'the rest of your life' when he knew quite definitely what he hoped that would be!

'Me? Mr Armstrong, what can I do? I am a woman and the only career open to me is to stay at home until some offer for me is made to my father. That or become a governess.'

Brooke wanted to smile, since if he had anything to do with it, and he meant to, she would never be the latter!

# 3

They were in the schoolroom when Father and Miss Parker entered. Miss Price was supervising their reading, all six of them with a book suitable, in Miss Price's opinion, to their age. Charlotte was deep in *Jane Eyre* which she had read before but the charismatic Mr Rochester had her mesmerised and she could understand exactly how Jane felt in loving him. *King Solomon's Mines* was Henry's choice, William's was *The War of the Worlds*, John was bent over *Kidnapped* and James was reading the new book by Rudyard Kipling called *Kim*. Robert did not read very well; Charlotte privately believed it was the influence of his father that made him slow, and he was stumbling through a book of nursery rhymes following Miss Price's finger. When the interruption occurred he was murmuring hesitantly:

> Blow, wind, blow! And go, mill, go!
> That the miller may grind his corn;
> That the baker may take it,
> And into rolls make it . . .

They all looked up as the door opened and at once the boys, on seeing the lady at Father's side, got to their feet. Charlotte rose more slowly and for some reason her heart missed a beat. Miss Price was twittering and simpering, as it was not often her charges' father deigned to visit the schoolroom, but with a regal lift of his hand, Arthur Drummond silenced her.

'Good morning, children.' He smiled. 'And what a pleasant morning it is to be sure.'

It was all they could do not to exchange startled glances but the lady let go of Father's arm and sauntered over to the round table, glancing down at the books that were spread out on the red plush cloth.

'*Jane Eyre*! Mmm, I used to love *Jane Eyre*, did you know that, Arthur, when I was a girl, which was not so very long ago,' she lied.

The children exchanged furtive glances, for they had never heard anyone call their father by his Christian name. He was smiling in the strangest way, standing by the open door and watching the lady as she moved round the table studying the books the boys had been reading. Miss Price jumped hurriedly to one side or she would have been swept away since the lady seemed not to see her or even acknowledge her existence and Charlotte was immediately aware that the lady was accustomed to ignoring those she believed to be beneath her.

'Miss Price, you may leave us, if you please,' her employer told her. 'I have something to discuss with the children.'

'Of course, sir.' Miss Price scuttled from the room like a little mouse getting out of the way of a prowling cat.

'Now then, children,' when Miss Price had closed the door quietly behind her. 'This lady is Miss Elizabeth Parker and she is to be your new mother.' He walked across the room and lifting Miss Parker's hand put it possessively in the crook of his arm. 'Yes, I'm sure you will be pleased to hear that she and I are to be married quite soon. Next month, in fact, and you, Charlotte, are to be a bridesmaid.' He smiled thinly, then was astonished when the lady on his arm shook it gently, interrupting him.

'Now, Arthur, don't go so quickly, if you please. You must not take things for granted. You know I have many female friends who will all want to be part of my wedding day. And I have cousins too. I am not sure whether it will be possible for – Charlotte, is it? – for Charlotte to be a bridesmaid.' Particularly as she is so pretty and might take the limelight from me, though this, of course, was not spoken. Like a great many pretty women Elizabeth Parker only had plain friends! 'And you have not yet introduced me to your family. This is Charlotte, that has been established, but will you not tell me the names of your sons.'

Charlotte saw the expression that flitted across her father's face and knew exactly what it meant. This lady who was to be, or so it seemed, his new wife, had the upper hand at the moment but just let the marriage take place and she would quickly learn who was the master in this household. She would be mistress but only on the domestic side and for the rest, *like the rest*, she would do and be exactly what Father told her to do and be. She wondered if she would be beaten with her drawers round her ankles, then flushed a bright, rosy pink at the terrible picture this evoked.

The introductions were performed, the boys making their polite bows, their faces absolutely expressionless as they had learned, showing no emotion, though she guessed at what they were feeling. Would this lovely young woman make any impact on *their* lives? Would Father treat them any differently? Perhaps the softening effect of a new wife would lessen the absolute power, the strict discipline their father cast over them. Would he be kinder, leaving them to their own devices as he became involved with the domesticity a new wife would bring? Would the beatings become more moderate? Only this week they had all been summoned to his study to take their punishment for not acting as the children of a gentleman should. The lake was a draw to the boys and had been ever since Nanny had taken them down to feed the ducks. On this occasion they had made paper boats which Thomas, the coachman, who had grandchildren of his own, had shown them how to do and unfortunately James had got his feet wet doing his best to retrieve the one Robbie had made. Charlotte often wondered how Father knew when some small disaster overtook them but he did and they had been 'chastised' as he called it for the misdemeanour! Perhaps the lady, Miss Parker, who was to be Mrs Drummond would divert Father and bring a new, relaxed routine to the schoolroom.

'Well, this is all very pleasant, Arthur,' the lady in question said, looking round the schoolroom. It was what one could only call functional, no more than that. Those who had lived through Victoria's reign did not believe that children needed comfort or brightness. A hideous black stove, which threw out a modicum of warmth, was not lit today since it was May and fires were discontinued at the end of April. The room was furnished with the large, round table where the children did their lessons, six ladder-back chairs, shelves around the drab green walls on which the children's book were lined, a scrap of carpet on the floor, well worn, and some thin cotton curtains at the window, put there by Arthur Drummond's grandmother.

It was clear that Miss Parker was eager to leave and as soon as their father and his bride-to-be were out of earshot and before Miss Price returned there was a babble of voices, all speaking at once and all speculating, Robbie with some excitement, on what this would mean to them. It would not alter their lives, they realised that, since they shared nothing, not even a meal, with Father but perhaps he would let them get on with their lives which were pretty miserable, they all agreed, without looking perpetually over their shoulders. If he was absorbed with his new bride perhaps they would—

Their speculations were interrupted by the sudden reappearance of their father and they sprang apart as though they had been up to something wicked.

'Oh, Charlotte, you are to dine with us this evening. Miss Parker and I are having a small dinner party to celebrate our engagement and you are to be included. You may have nothing suitable to wear so you and your maid will be taken into Wakefield at once where, I believe, there is a dressmaker who can fit you out with a ready-to-wear gown. While you are there she will measure you for some outfits that you will need if you are to . . . well, back to your lessons.' And he closed the door crisply behind him.

They stared at one another in amazement. *Her maid.* Did Father mean . . . surely not Kizzie who was a maid of all work in the household with no particular function, but who else could it be? Kizzie had been with them since their mother died and had helped Nanny with the younger children but now they were all in the charge of Miss Price. Certainly Kizzie had been friend and support of Charlotte in her adversity, always there when needed. She had helped her with her hair, seen to her clothes as a maid did, sewing torn hemlines and . . . well, Charlotte could not really put a name to Kizzie's duties but she and Kizzie were to be off to Wakefield to choose a gown for this evening with absolutely no supervision except that of Thomas.

The excitement was intense and had Arthur Drummond known of it he would have been annoyed. The whole household was in a state of animation, for they were all very fond of Miss Charlotte and were all of the opinion that their master treated her, and her brothers, very harshly. To be going into Wakefield with no one but Kizzie was unbelievable and then to be included in the master's dinner party, well, it was hardly to be credited.

'Will you look out for some marbles for me, Charlie,' begged James.

'And I'd love a set of toy soldiers, the ones from the cavalry, you know . . .'

'And a fort to put them in; oh, Charlie, I wish we could all go . . .'

'P'raps this lady's gonner mekk a difference ter them bairns, Mrs Banks,' Mrs Welsh said to the housekeeper, and they all prayed so as they waved Miss Charlotte and Kizzie off from the stable yard where Thomas had hitched up the carriage.

She and Kizzie were in a state of such exhilaration as they viewed the wonderful display of lovely gowns that Miss Hunter, who had been warned by Miss Parker to expect her, had ready for her that had it not been for Miss Hunter's competent expertise in what suited whom, only the good Lord knew what she would have brought home. She had no experience although perhaps her natural good taste would have led her to the right choice, but with Miss Hunter's advice she purchased a simple cream-coloured two-piece gown of a material unknown to her called soie-de-chine. It had an accordian-pleated top skirt over a plain skirt of the same material. The neckline of the bodice fell off her shoulders and had 'angel' sleeves. The skirt was pointed at the front and the back, the points just touching her instep. Miss Hunter had evening shoes of cream satin and stockings of fine ribbed silk to match. There was even a satin cape to cover her shoulders as she travelled to or from an evening entertainment. In her hair Miss Hunter advised a tiny cap of cream sequins to sit on the crown of her head nestling in her hair which would be dressed full and loose. She and Kizzie were quite speechless at her changed appearance. She stood in a daze of enchantment as one of Miss Hunter's assistants measured her for day dresses, another evening gown in a pale duck-egg blue, a walking outfit, a riding outfit, for it seemed Miss Hunter had been informed she was to ride, and for another dress whose purpose was not revealed to her. In the fantasy that had come upon her so suddenly she had not even thought to ask!

'Where is the nearest toy shop, Miss Hunter?' she asked when all the measuring and choosing of fabrics was finished and when it turned out it was within walking distance she and Kizzie walked up there followed by the carriage. She bought a big net of marbles, a set of lead soldiers, a very realistic fort, a mimic gun said to be a copy of what the cowboys in America used, a mechanical railway engine and a copy of *The Last of the Mohicans* for Henry. She and Kizzie linked arms, their heads close together, two young girls carried away with the fun they had had that day. The bill for all the lovely outfits would be sent to Mr Drummond, Miss Hunter had told Miss Drummond and her maid, but the things bought at the toy shop came out of the money that Kizzie had saved from her wages and which Charlie had promised to pay back as soon as she could. She wasn't quite sure how since she and her brothers received no pocket money but in the excitement of the day she was simply carried away.

They gasped with admiration as she entered the schoolroom to show them her gown, even Miss Price who was still dwelling on how Mr Drummond would react to the toys Miss Charlotte had bought for her brothers. They had been enthralled and Henry, who had his nose deep in the adventures of the Indian tribes, was open-mouthed at the loveliness of his sister.

She entered the drawing room shyly, knowing that some of her father's guests had already arrived, stepping like a young fawn into an unknown glade of a forest and was immediately conscious of the hush that fell over the gathering. Oh, Lord, what had she done? Was she overdressed, or perhaps not smart enough for a celebration such as this? Was she showing some part of her undergarments that should not be seen? But surely Kizzie, who had helped her dress, would not have let her come downstairs in a state of disarray. They had watched her, as many of the servants as could manage it, come down the stairs and their faces had been rapt and admiring. She was aware of Miss Parker standing by her father's side, her arm linked in his, an unreadable expression on her face. Had she been a woman of the world she would have recognised jealousy.

And there he was, walking towards her with his hand outstretched to take hers, a pleasant smile on his face, a smile of approval and something else she could not identify. He took her hand and drew it through his arm and then turned to the company who began to smile and nod for they did not often see this lovely girl of Drummond's. In fact they were hard pressed to remember if they had *ever* seen her. She did not hunt as her father did, or join the shooting parties he gave but it seemed she was to be a part of this evening's celebration which was only right since Elizabeth Parker was to be her stepmother.

'Ah, here is my daughter,' Arthur Drummond said, a false smile on his face. 'A little late but she can be forgiven since it is her first entry into society. Now let me introduce you to my guests, Charlotte.'

Having put her on the wrong foot, so to speak, he took her from Brooke Armstrong though she seemed inclined to cling to him which was no bad thing, he supposed, watching out of the corner of his eye as Elizabeth at once made for Armstrong and began to flirt with him. He'd soon knock that out of her once they were married; in the meanwhile let her have her head.

At the dinner table Charlotte was placed next to Mr Armstrong which pleased her. She could not say why because she hardly knew him but the others she knew not at all. Miss Parker's parents, another elderly lady and gentleman whose names she could not remember who were relatives of Miss Parker and a score of friends and acquaintances who were younger but who all seemed to be on the best of terms with the bride-to-be.

'And when is the great day, Elizabeth?' one of them asked, lifting his glass of wine to his lips and smiling at her over its rim. Charlie noticed that her father did not seem to like the gentleman though she thought only she would be aware of it. But then she of them all knew her father best.

'The last Saturday in June, Roly, but never fear you will receive your invitation in good time, will he not, Arthur?' She smiled roguishly at her fiancé.

'Indeed, my dear. The guest list is already drawn up. Sir Clive and Lady Parker have been given the names of those I would like included so all is going forward as it should. I'm afraid my side of the family will not be well represented since I am the only son of an only son but I'm sure Elizabeth will more than make up the numbers, won't you, my love. My children will attend the service but not the reception. My youngest son is only six years old, you see, but Charlotte, of course, will be there.'

'And will you be a bridesmaid, Miss Drummond?' the elderly lady, whose name Charlotte could not remember, asked her.

Charlotte clutched about her for an answer since she had not really been told by . . . by Elizabeth whether she would or not. She had so many friends and relatives who were all longing to play the role, Elizabeth had implied, but when she looked desperately to her father for help he merely sipped his wine and smiled.

'I'm not absolutely . . .' she began.

'The roses will be at their peak then and surely a June bride will want roses in her bouquet,' a quiet voice beside her said and at once the ladies all began to twitter on what kind of flowers they had had at their wedding or what they hoped to have *when* they married and the subject of Charlotte's part in the wedding ceremony was forgotten.

She turned to Brooke Armstrong and gave him a grateful smile of such brilliance he had to turn away lest he be seen with the expression on his face of the deep, welling, growing emotion she aroused in him. Deep, yes, ever since he had first seen her playing with his dogs at the edge of the wood, deep and hidden in the unfathomable complexity of his nature which even he could not understand. Growing with the dawn of each day when he woke up with her in his mind as she had been in his night dreams. He had seen her only twice, both in the lovely environment of nature's bounty when she had been herself with nothing to hide from him, again responding to the appeal of an animal. The puppy he meant to give her at the first opportunity. The pup he had saved from Dottie's litter not even knowing at the time why he had done so. He loved her as a man, a mature man who has known women from the age of fifteen but had never loved until now. He had known in that secret part of him that no one had ever reached that one day she would come, that woman who had been created just for him, which sounded as foolish as a schoolboy with his first love, and now she was here, still a child in many ways, but when she was ready he would claim her and he had told Arthur Drummond that, well, not all of it, but that he wished to – what was the word? – *court* his daughter and the man had given his permission and had promised not to speak of it to her. He did not wish her to be frightened by his sudden declaration of love and he had said so to the cynical, worldly wise man who was her father.

As he turned away from her he found Arthur Drummond's eyes upon him and was infuriated when the man gave him a small nod as though of approval. Surely the man wasn't going to reveal what they had discussed earlier in the week.

The meal was splendid for Mrs Welsh was a superb cook. Asparagus soup followed by lobster pudding, boiled capon with white sauce, lobster salad and to finish charlotte russe, vanilla cream, gooseberry tartlets, custards, cheesecake, cabinet pudding and iced pudding, and a selection of ices. There were wines to match each course and, to celebrate the occasion, champagne.

'No wine for Miss Charlotte,' her father told the butler, Watson, in a loud voice, drawing all eyes to her and the fact that despite her inclusion in this evening's celebration she was, in his opinion, still a child. 'Though I believe a glass of champagne would be in order as this is a celebration to introduce her new mother into the family.' He smiled ironically and Elizabeth smirked.

Brooke restrained himself from taking Charlotte's hand which was clenched in her lap beneath the table. She flushed, more, she realised, in temper than embarrassment. Although she had been included in this *special day*, her father seemed determined to show her up, to mortify her and she did not know why. He had always been harsh in his treatment of his children but she could see that the guests were somewhat puzzled by his behaviour.

'Will you be walking tomorrow, Miss Drummond?' the man beside her asked quietly, watching Drummond in an attempt to work out what he was up to. He was deliberately slighting his daughter for some reason, smiling as he sipped his champagne, and it suddenly occurred to him that the man was jealous. *Jealous.* He knew he had to let his lovely daughter go, give her to some man in marriage. And Brooke had asked for her. She would belong to another man and no longer be Arthur Drummond's to do with as he pleased as daughters were in their society. She had been brought up to the realisation that she would marry, have children, run some gentleman's home and though he accepted that, he didn't like it! *He didn't like it!* He was not in love with Elizabeth Parker. Lusted after her, true, but Charlotte meant something more to him than merely a daughter. Brooke felt his skin crawl wondering what went on in this house and at that moment made up his mind that he would marry this young woman at the earliest opportunity. Get her away from the curious relationship that he sensed lay in the father. He had never cared for Drummond though he knew their friends and acquaintances thought him a hell of a good fellow. A good shot, a superb horseman, a wonderful host, amusing always, but there was something strange in the way he kept his eyes on his daughter. He saw that Elizabeth had noticed it and he watched as her eyes grew cold and her mouth thinned, then she laughed at something the man beside her said to her and the moment was gone. He would seek out Charlotte, woo her, he supposed, and marry her the first bloody moment he could.

'Pardon?' her flushed face turned to him.

'I wondered if you would be in the wood tomorrow. I would suggest a gallop but I know you don't ride.' And I intend to rectify that as soon as you are mine.

'Well, I hadn't planned to, but if . . .'

'I have something for you . . . and your brothers, of course,' he added hastily, for her face had clouded over as he spoke. Young ladies did not receive gifts from young single gentlemen unless it might be a posy or something equally innocuous.

'Really!' She smiled that wide and brilliant smile he was becoming familiar with.

'Really. I shall be taking my dogs out about eleven. They like to have a good run and I usually manage an hour. I wish you had a horse, Miss Drummond. I should like to show you – and your brothers, of course – some of my land. I'm sure my tenants would—' He stopped speaking in horror, for he had been about to say he was sure his tenants would love to meet her, knowing they would at once realise that this young woman was special to their landlord and what he would have in mind for someone special in his life.

'Yes, Mr Armstrong? Would what?' Charlotte was aware that her father was watching her and a dreadful fear dribbled through her veins. Dear God . . . oh, dear God, if only she could; but if she left where would she go and what would become of Henry, of William, John, James and Robbie?

'Mrs Emmerson at Fuller's Farm makes the best cowslip wine in the county and the best plum cake and she would be made up, as they say in the north, if you would sample them.'

'Does she live far from Seven Cows Wood, Mr Armstrong?' She took a spoonful of strawberry ice cream and placed it delicately in her mouth, licking the spoon like a child, savouring it for a moment and Brooke's fascination spread through him and revealed itself on his rather sombre face. There was not a guest round the table who did not know what it meant. The only one who did not was Charlotte herself.

'No.' His voice was harsh and she looked at him in surprise. She rather liked this middle-aged gentleman who had been so polite and kind with her on each of the occasions they had met. He had berated her when she ran out in front of his horse that first time but since then he had been pleasant. Had she said something to offend him? But he sipped his champagne with composure, his grey eyes steady and uncompromising on her face.

'Then perhaps we could walk there. Mrs Emmerson sounds nice and I love plum cake. So does Robbie.'

'Of course, bring Robbie and any of your brothers who might care to come. We could . . . have a picnic. Mrs Emmerson would oblige, I'm sure.'

For a moment she looked delighted, then her gaze turned to her father who, though he could not hear what was being said, never took his eyes from them.

'Well, we'll see.'

Brooke Armstrong resolved to speak to Arthur Drummond before the week was out. Perhaps there might be another wedding in June!

# 4

They stood in a line in front of his desk in order of age, their young hearts pounding, their faces pale, for what had they done wrong now? They had spent a lovely morning with Mr Armstrong who had the most wonderful surprise for them in the shape of a puppy who he said they were to call Taddy, short for Tadpole since he was so small. That's if they agreed, he had added hastily. He was a glossy shade with some of his mother's ebony and a sprinkling of white which Brooke thought Jack Emmerson's collie might have had something to do with. The children loved him. Taddy was now in the stable with the grooms and Charlotte was convinced that Father had got wind of him and that was what this was about.

She was wrong.

'I have had Brooke Armstrong here just now and after discussing the matter with Elizabeth we have decided upon a course of action concerning not just Charlotte and her future but you boys as well.'

Uncomprehendingly they waited, their faces disclosing their bewilderment. What had kind Mr Armstrong got to do with *their* future? Charlotte had dined last night with Father and his friends in celebration of Father's engagement to Miss Parker and Mr Armstrong had been there. Apparently he had visited Father this morning, either before or after they had met him and discussed something that was to affect them all but their young faces revealed their total lack of understanding.

'Can you not guess, Charlotte?' Father asked and when Charlie shook her head he smiled strangely. 'Well, my dear, it seems you have made an impression on Brooke Armstrong which I suppose is no surprise since you are . . . quite pretty. He informed me this morning that he wishes to marry you and has asked my permission to speak to you. Of course, I said yes since it is a good match. He is keen for the wedding to take place as soon as possible so a date has been set for the weekend before Elizabeth and I pledge our vows.' His voice was ironic, almost derisive and they were not to know of the conversation that had taken place between him and his bride-to-be when he had told her, laughingly, of Armstrong's offer.

'Let him have her,' Elizabeth had declared forcefully, then smiled flirtatiously to soften her words. Arthur Drummond did not love Elizabeth Parker and had she not been the only child of a wealthy and influential man it is doubtful he would even have glanced at her despite her attractiveness. He himself was often short of 'brass' as they said in Yorkshire, and it did no harm to add to it. He was keen to purchase a pack of hounds and hunters did not come cheaply. He hunted during the winter, took to salmon fishing in the spring and the grouse season in August kept him busy here on his own estate or on those of his many acquaintances, some up in Scotland. Elizabeth was no youngster and if she did not bear him a son he did not care since he already had five but he had noticed how she eyed Charlotte, nine years younger than herself, and to get rid of his daughter and ally himself to another prosperous county gentleman might be useful.

'And the boys?' Elizabeth had prompted, for Elizabeth Parker, who did not really know her fiancé at all, fancied having him all to herself without a ready-made family to interfere in her new life. Like Arthur, she was not in love but having reached the age of twenty-five without finding a husband to suit her she thought she had him in Arthur Drummond.

'What about the boys?' he asked lazily, not really caring, smiling inwardly at this woman who thought she could get the better of him.

'Are . . . would they not be better at school? Surely one of the good public schools would prepare them for the future life of a gentleman. A governess is suitable for young boys but the older ones . . . er, Henry, is it and William would do far better among boys of their own age.'

'And Robert, who is only six?'

'Young boys from good families go away to school at the age of eight. It toughens them for what lies ahead. My father is governor at Woodlands in Northumberland and I'm sure that if he approached the board . . . after all the boy will soon be seven, you told me.'

'True. What a minx you are, Elizabeth, or should I say a spider spinning away your fancy web.'

'I prefer minx, my darling.'

'Well, why don't you come upstairs and prove it to me.'

The children stood before him, their faces expressionless as he explained to them that the boys were to go to school the day after he and Miss Parker were married. Both Charlotte and Mr Armstrong and he and Miss Parker would be away on their respective honeymoons and so Thomas and Miss Price would accompany them to their new school and then, probably at Christmas, they would come home to spend the holidays with him and their new mother.

His cold smile played over them but none of them spoke. It was doubtful that Robert even understood. He was aware that something stupendous was happening that concerned his brothers and sister, and himself, of course, but he could not quite get his mind round it. His hand crept into Charlie's but his father saw it.

'Let go of your sister's hand, sir,' he barked. 'You are not a baby,' and as though his words had unfrozen her heart and allowed the blood to race once more along her veins, Charlotte sprang into life.

'I suppose this is her doing, is it? Our new mother. She doesn't want us under her feet and so I am to be married off to the first man to ask for me and my brothers whisked off to school as far away as possible. Robert is too young and so is James and if you imagine I agree with all this you are mistaken. I will not marry Mr Armstrong and I will not allow my brothers to be sent away as though they had done something wrong. Mr Armstrong cannot be serious, Father. We barely know each other.' She was beginning to breathe heavily now in her distress and fury. She leaned forward and placed both her hands on her father's desk, thrusting her face into his so that for a second he reared back, but a snarl was beginning to shape about his mouth and his eyes were the icy colour of the lake frozen in winter. A dark, murky brown with what looked like glints of silver in them, a sign of his own rage.

'That is enough, girl. You are to be married on the 23rd of June and Miss Parker and I will follow on the 30th. Your brothers will travel, by train of course, up to Newcastle upon Tyne on the Sunday following and then on to the coast at Whitburn where Woodlands is situated. They will be ready for a new term when it begins. That is my last word on the matter so if you will be good enough—'

'Oh, no, it might be your last word but it is not mine,' Charlotte shrieked and in the kitchen the servants stood rigidly to attention as though it were one of them who was receiving the lashing of the master's tongue, even Watson. She was incensed and the boys, especially the older two, longed to take hold of her and restrain her, for surely she knew it would do no good. When had Father ever changed his mind, about any-thing, relented, given in, allowed any one of them to voice their point of view? They had always been afraid of him even when their mother had been alive and had done her best to interpose herself between his cold anger and the cowering children. But Charlie would not have it and Arthur Drummond found himself wishing just one of his sons had her spirit.

'Go to your room, Charlotte. We will discuss this when you are—'

'No! I will discuss this now. I will not marry Mr Drummond and the boys will not go to school and you can tell your fiancée—'

With a swift movement her father stood up, stepped round the desk and before he had time to think, so great was his fury, he struck her across her cheek with the back of his hand. She fell across the small table on which the drinks tray stood and the whole lot crashed to the floor, including Charlotte. Robert and James were crying noisily and in the kitchen Kizzie had to be forcibly restrained by Mrs Banks and Mrs Welsh from bursting through the green baize door and down the hallway to the master's study.

'It will do no good, girl,' Mrs Banks hissed in her ear. 'Leave it be.'

'Help your sister to her feet, Henry,' his father told him coldly, 'and then you will all go to your rooms and stay there until I send for you. As for you, Charlotte, you might as well know that at this moment Brooke Armstrong is at the rectory talking to the minister and Miss Hunter is in the process of making your wedding dress and garments for your wedding journey. You will believe me when I say you are to marry Brooke Armstrong or there will be dire consequences for you and your brothers. It is a good marriage, a suitable marriage for my daughter and I'm sure you will come to recognise it.'

And it will do me no harm, either. A liaison with a man of his consequence could be very useful to me. My marriage to the only child of a powerful man, a titled gentleman, and this girl, who is inclined to be defiant, wedded to one of the richest, *landed* men in the county, what could be more advantageous?

'You will come to see I am right, my dear,' he said silkily. 'Now, go to your room and rest and you boys, go to your rooms. I will inform you of all the arrangements later.'

If Brooke had known what was happening at the Mount he would have been horrified. His intention had been to befriend Charlotte, to move slowly, to gain her trust, if not her love, not yet at any rate, and he had said so to Drummond, though not in so many words. And to do that he must see her, meet with her in the summer countryside, just the two of them, or with her brothers if she preferred, take the dogs, wander through the woods, talk, laugh, share opinions, get to know her and have her get to know him. Move at *her* pace, even if it meant postponing their wedding for months. He would not have her bullied, he had told Arthur Drummond. He did not add that he loved her and Drummond had not mentioned *love*, since it seemed to Brooke he would not even know the meaning of the word. He was *not* speaking to the minister as her father had told Charlotte. It was too soon for that. Charlotte would pick her own wedding date but in the meantime he began to make plans to invite her, with her maid, of course, since everything must be correct, above board, to visit what would be her new home. King's Meadow. She must be allowed to choose and design her own bedroom – the bedroom he would share with her – smiling inwardly and with a shiver of anticipation, like any schoolboy in love for the first time, he thought ruefully. What an absurd situation to be in at his age, ready to moon over a girl fourteen years younger than he was, but did it matter?

After lunch he had Max saddled up and calling to Dottie and Floss and Ginger he galloped across his land, skirting fields rippling with growing corn, hay, wheat, waving to men working in the warm sunshine, parting small herds of grazing cattle, cows that rocked away in alarm at his approach, entering Seven Cows Wood where he had first met her. Flinging himself off Max's back he threw himself down in the shade of a massive oak tree, leaving Max untethered. The dogs flopped down beside him, their tongues hanging out, breathing hard.

Should he have a dinner party to which he would invite her, with her father and his fiancée, naturally, and one or two couples who he knew would be kind with her? Without mentioning marriage he would let her see how he lived. He lay back drowsily looking up into the foliage of the tree, watching a caterpillar hatched from the eggs of the mottled umber moth as it devoured a leaf. His mind was at peace and his heart was full and he sighed with great contentment. He had started his courtship of Charlotte Drummond!

She was brought down to his study later in the afternoon and he was startled at the state of her face. His temper had got the better of him but he had not realised he had hit her so hard. She had best be kept to her room for a while until she was fit to be seen. She had the beginnings of a black eye and her cheek was red and swollen but she stood proudly before him, meeting his eyes with her own which revealed her defiance. He had discussed it with Elizabeth and she had been adamant that the girl must be made to see how advantageous this marriage would be and that if she proved difficult there must be some pressure that could be brought to bear to *persuade* her. It was not that Elizabeth Parker wished Charlotte to marry Brooke Drummond for any particular reason. She had wanted him for herself. Arthur was second best but she did want the girl out of the house. The house that would be hers. Charlotte was far too pretty to have at Elizabeth's dinner table, and far too young, which might not show Elizabeth up in a good light. Elizabeth did not like competition. She was twenty-five and at the height of her beauty but that would not last for ever, and as for those great boys, the sooner they were sent away to school the better. She might – she hoped not – but she might have a child herself and she wanted no rivalry between her child and these others. She did not say this to Arthur, of course, but she congratulated herself that she had persuaded him to see matters in the way she wanted him to see them. She was handed into her carriage for her return journey to her home, smiling with satisfaction, not knowing that she had had not the slightest influence on her future husband, for he knew exactly how to handle his children and needed no advice from her, though at the moment it pleased him to let her think that she had some hand in the running of her future home.

'So, Charlotte, now that you have had time to think about it may I assume that you are willing to consider Brooke Armstrong's proposal of marriage? I would like to think you will make no objections for, believe me, whatever they may be I shall overcome them. You should know that. He is a very suitable match and—'

'No, Father, I do not wish to marry Mr Armstrong. He is an old man and I do not love him.'

'It seems he *loves* you,' her father sneered.

'I'm sorry for that but there is absolutely no chance—'

'Really!' Her father, who had been lounging in the chair behind his desk, stood up and walked to the window, noting with some satisfaction that she flinched as he moved past her. He looked out into the garden, studying with complacency his lawns, his flowerbeds, the placid smoothness of his lake on which ducks glided, finding them all in perfect order just as his life was. His gardeners were busy in a shady border giving the soil a good dressing of something or other ready for planting stocks and asters, all very pleasing to the eye, but suddenly a small shape flew across his perfect lawn and began to frolic about Malachy's legs. The man dropped his spade and looked about him furtively then picked up the puppy, for that was what it was and with a word to Denny, the second gardener, hurried across the lawn and disappeared round the corner of the house towards the stable yard.

He could feel the explosive rage well up in him. He hated dogs, he didn't know why, particularly puppies, nasty little yapping things and this one, presumably belonging to one of the outdoor servants, had been introduced into his household without his permission. He opened the window and shouted to the remaining gardener who had resumed his work, unaware that his master was watching him.

'Hey, you there,' Arthur Drummond called out, 'come here at once.'

Denny, looking thoroughly intimidated, ran across the lawn and stood at the window. 'Yes, sir?' he quavered.

'That bloody dog. To whom does it belong? I want the person to come—'

A voice from behind him made him swing round in amazement and at the sight of the battered face of the master's daughter, the gardener's heart missed a beat in sympathy. He had heard, in great detail and with considerable fury from Kizzie, about the state of Miss Charlotte's face and who had caused it.

'It is my dog, Father,' Denny heard her say calmly.

'Your dog?' her father asked her menacingly. 'And may I ask how you acquired it?'

'It was given to me by Mr Armstrong, Father. The man you wish me to marry. He meant it for us all, Henry, William, John—'

'Yes, Charlotte, I know the names of my sons. What I would like to know is when this . . . this creature came into your possession?'

Denny stood indecisively by the open window, wondering what he was supposed to do but the master had moved away. Malachy was just rounding the corner after taking the escaped puppy back to the stable so with a wave of his hand and a mouthed word or two, Denny and the head gardener beat a hasty retreat.

'We met Mr Armstrong while we were walking in the wood and he had his dogs with him. We . . . the boys and I were . . . well, the next time we saw him he brought one of the puppies for us. I saw no harm.'

'You take a great deal upon yourself, Charlotte. You did not think to ask me?'

'You would have said no, Father.' Charlotte sighed for she knew whatever she said, or did, in any matter, it would be wrong.

'Yes, I would and I think it is time you realised who is the master in this house in which there is no mistress, yet. So, let me say this to you. I will have my way on this marriage of yours, Charlotte. You will marry Brooke Armstrong at St Luke's Church as soon as it can be arranged and that is an end to the matter.'

'I don't think so, Father. When the parson asks me if I do, or whatever the words are I shall just say "I don't" and then—'

'Madam, you cannot possibly imagine you can get the better of me. If you do not obey me in this it is not you who will suffer but your brothers. They are to go to a boarding school in Northumberland which you will appreciate is a great distance from here. I believe there is a sort of preparatory school that will take Robert.'

'Oh please, Father, not Robbie . . . not Robbie . . . He is so young and will fret.' She almost fell to her knees in entreaty.

'He will be with his brothers. At least at the same school but in a different part, of course, and I'm sure—'

'No, I beg of you. Can you not send him – them – somewhere nearer?'

'They all need discipline, my dear, which it seems I am unable to give them, but, of course . . . well, there is another school I am considering somewhat nearer . . .'

'Please, please . . .' Charlotte's face twisted in her agony for her brothers but particularly for her little brother who was still a baby in many ways. Without her he would not survive the rigours of a public school; away from home, even one such as this, he would not . . .

'The answer is in your hands, Charlotte. There is a school, a decent school near York where the older boys could go and which, of course, is within easy travelling distance. You and your Mr Armstrong could get over there in a day, or have the boys to stay with you at King's Meadow. I doubt they would wish to stay here with myself and my wife but they would be quite welcome if they did. I also wondered if Mr Armstrong would be willing to have Robert to live with you at his home, after you are married I mean, since you seem to think he would not be able to cope with boarding school. There is a very good grammar school in Dewsbury, I believe. He seems very eager to have you for his wife so I'm sure he would be agreeable to this plan. If not, or if you feel you cannot bring yourself to marry this very rich, very pleasant gentleman then you must make your own arrangements for your future. I believe there is always a need for governesses. Of course, the boys will still be sent to boarding school, all of them.'

There was a long silence, a silence heavy with the threat of a strong man who would have his way whatever the consequences to others. At one fell stroke he was to rid himself of his family, at least the housing of them. He was willing to pay for an expensive education for them; after all he was, or would be, well able to afford it and besides, his friends would not comment on it adversely since it was entirely proper to send older boys to public school. Most families of his class did. And it was quite understandable that a newly married man would want to have his bride to himself. Further, what could be more natural than to have his daughter, who was of marriageable age, wed to a man of means and property, a man with a good name?

He sat down behind his desk, reached out and took a cigar
from the box, put it to his lips and lit it, blowing smoke up to
the ceiling. He smiled. Charlotte watched him and her eyes
glittered with such contempt, such hatred, such loathing even,
that another man might have looked away in shame. But
Arthur Drummond was no ordinary man as his behaviour
towards his children, especially his daughter, in the past had
shown. He was a dark, perverted man and for a strange
moment Charlotte felt sorry for the woman who was to be
his wife. She had no idea what kind of man she was to marry
but then what was that to her, *now*!

Charlotte turned on her heel and walked towards the door,
her head held high, her shoulders squared, her back straight.
She opened the door and without another word walked
through and up the passage to the hallway. Kizzie was standing at the top of the stairs waiting for her. Kizzie had bathed
her face earlier, her own wet with tears, no word spoken, at
least not between them though Kizzie had had enough to say
in the kitchen.

'Lass?' she questioned, putting out a hand then with-
drawing it as Charlotte walked past her. Later Charlotte
would break down and cry in her arms but at that moment
she was caught in an icy world from which she could not
escape.

'I'm all right, Kizzie. I'll have a cup of tea.'

'Let me bring tha' summat ter eat. Tha've 'ad nowt
since—'

'No, please, just a cup of tea and then I must go and see the
boys. Is Miss Price with them?'

'Aye.'

'Well, I shall send her away for I must talk to them. I believe
I shall have the power to do that now, Kizzie, at least for a
while. It really is quite amazing . . .'

'What is, chuck? 'Asta got summat—'

'It seems I am to be married, Kizzie, and very soon.'

'Lovey . . .' Kizzie's voice was no more than a whisper.

'So you see I must go and talk with my brothers. I'd be obliged if you would tell the others. In the kitchen, I mean, then . . .'

'Oh, my lass . . .'

# 5

Their new King, to be called Edward VII, was to be crowned on 26 June so Brooke asked his bride-to-be if she would like to spend a few days in London after the wedding and watch the procession. They were to go on to Paris and perhaps she would care to travel to Italy; Florence was lovely at this time of the year but it was up to her, he added, struggling to fetch the girl who was to be his wife on 23 June out of the polite passivity that seemed to have come over her since he had presented her with the puppy. She was not the same warm, lively person who had been so rapturous about his gift.

He had not seen her for ten days after the conversation he had had with her father, the explanation given that she was unwell, a slight summer cold, which surprised him since she had not struck him as the sort of young woman who would take to her bed on such a slight indisposition. Arthur Drummond had been most hearty when he had called at King's Meadow to tell Brooke that his daughter was agreeable to being his wife and had wanted, naturally, to come with him to tell Armstrong herself. As soon as she was recovered she would drive over with her maid to discuss the arrangements for the big day. He could not stay long, he said, since he was off to York with his older boys to see them safely installed at Barton Meade, a public school with a good reputation, but he had just wanted to inform Brooke that all was well. He went on to explain.

'My sons have had a good grounding with Miss Price but I feel they need the rough and tumble of living with other boys to finish off their education. Yes, thank you, a quick whisky, if you don't mind, and the preparations for my own marriage are taking up some of my time but as soon as she is improved my daughter will be in touch with you. I beg your pardon? . . . My youngest son? He is to go to the grammar school in Dewsbury until he is eight when he will join his brothers at Barton Meade. I believe my daughter has a request of you, Brooke – I may call you Brooke, mayn't I, since we are to be related? Thank you – but Charlotte will speak to you very soon, I'm sure.'

She drove over with her maid a few days later, ostensibly to be shown her new home and to tell him how honoured she was by his proposal but it seemed to Brooke she was distant, cool, as though she had been well rehearsed in the pretty speech. She was very correct, gracious even, but she appeared to be totally disinterested until he was forced to ask her outright, as was his way she was to find out later, if she was certain that this was what she wanted.

'When I spoke to your father it was with the intention of . . . in the future, asking you to be my wife. He was somewhat precipitate in speaking to you since we barely know one another and you are very young. I want you to know that if this . . . if I'm not to your . . . well, no one is forcing you, Miss . . . no, I shall call you Charlotte and you must call me Brooke. We can become friends, if you are willing but I will not . . . not . . .' He ran his hands through his dark curling hair which was already dishevelled, and Charlotte felt her frozen heart move a little, for this man was not an enemy and was doing his best. 'I do not wish you to be *made* . . . your father is . . .'

He was leading her across the gravel from the carriage. There was a circle of grass in front of the house with a statue of some sort in the middle and the carriage had driven round it, coming to a stop by the front door. Kizzie followed them, decently dressed in a plain outfit as befitted a maidservant. She liked him. This was the first time she had met him and when

Miss Charlotte had said vaguely that 'this is my maid' he had turned and smiled and asked her *her* name. She liked him and thought that Miss Charlotte would be all right with him.

'Dost tha' want ter marry this chap, Miss Charlotte?' she had asked anxiously as she bathed her swollen eye. 'Only it's bin that sudden we're all of a flummox in't kitchen since none of us knew it were in't wind, like. Oh, we know 'e's bin 'ere a time or two but tha've never sed owt.'

'There was nothing to tell, Kizzie. I've met him twice in the wood with his dogs and then he brought Taddy but I had no idea he was interested in me – that way, I mean, and then my father told me he . . . Mr Armstrong wished to marry me. The boys were to go to school and I was to marry Mr Armstrong. They arranged it there and then, so I was told, and it seemed I had no choice.'

'But wharrabout you? What dost tha' think o' this arrangement?' Kizzie's face hardened. 'It'll be 'er,' she said. ''Er what's ter marry't master. Wants rid, she does. I never liked 'er from't start. But just wait while she's wed 'im, she'll be sorry. I tell thi' I'd not like ter be wife to 'im.'

They were in Charlotte's bedroom to where she had been banished when her father blacked her eye and where she was to remain until she was fit to be seen. They all knew, naturally, in the kitchen, for such an incident could not be hidden. They had been shocked to the core by what had happened to Miss Charlotte. They had known the master was . . . well, *strict* with his children when he got his dander up for they had heard the little boys crying after a beating and Kizzie had had her doubts about what he did to Miss Charlotte, but she was a servant and what could she do about it? But the smack across the face was the last straw. Kizzie ranted and raved and Mary and Nancy, the parlour-maids, talked of giving in their notice as they were fond of Miss Charlotte who was always nice to them, but then they might not be given a decent reference by the new mistress.

'I have no choice, Kizzie, and Mr Armstrong is a very nice man. He seems kind and . . .' She sat listlessly on the window seat staring sightlessly out at the lush green of the lawn and the bold colours of the flowerbeds. Kizzie had brought her up a bowl of Mrs Welsh's delicious and nourishing soup with some of her fresh bread straight out of the oven. Kizzie had reported that their little mistress was not eating so Mrs Welsh had set to with her special skills to make up some dish to tempt her. She prepared a syllabub made with white wine, nutmeg, sugar and milk with whipped cream on top, an egg custard and a tall glass of her own orange wine.

'If that don't put a lining on her stomach at least it'll make her feel better!' she told them all, referring to the wine as she set out a dainty tray with a small vase of rosebuds from the garden.

Now Charlotte allowed him to lead her across the gravel towards the house and a smallish door under a verandah. She had to admit it was a lovely house built of the honey-coloured stone of the district. It had eight windows across the top storey and a large bay window to the left of the terrace and several more further to the right. Wicker chairs and a small round table stood on the verandah. To the left was a high stone wall in which was set an arched wrought-iron gate leading to another garden and a smaller adjoining house. Beyond that, though she could see little, seemed to be several buildings, presumably stabling and what appeared to be a dovecote.

'I thought we could have coffee or chocolate out here since it is such a lovely day,' he told her, 'after you have seen the house and perhaps you could tell me what you would like in the way of . . . of . . . well, if there is anything you would like changed.

Your . . . your bedroom perhaps. I don't know your taste . . . in furniture, I mean, or colours but whatever . . .'

He was aware he was babbling but she was so composed, so silent, so . . . so *dignified* he felt the need to fill that silence with words, any words that might make her relax, but she merely answered politely.

'Oh, no, Mr Armstrong, I wouldn't dream of altering anything in your home.'

'It is to be your home too, Charlotte,' he answered roughly.

'No. Oh, yes, I see what you mean but everything seems to be lovely so . . .' Her voice trailed away as though she were in a dream, a hazy unreality that had nothing to do with Charlotte Drummond. That's how she felt, as though she were watching some other girl drifting through this beautifully furnished, lavishly carpeted house, looking at pictures hung on plain walls, pictures of the sea and tiny boats and vague outlines of buildings, a galleon on fire reflected in water, the sun rising, or perhaps setting over water, all delicately framed.

'I'm fond of Turner,' he told her quietly.

'Really, they're lovely.'

'And that's Constable, all of them only prints, of course,' pointing to a picture that seemed to be nothing but clouds with blue and grey and greens and she bent forward to peer at it, the first time she had shown an interest since she had stepped from the carriage.

'Do you like it?' he asked her.

'I know nothing of art, I'm afraid.'

It was the same wherever he took her. One lovely room after another, all furnished not in the Victorian style which was heavy and overpowering but in an earlier period she did not recognise but which was light and airy and uncluttered. She followed politely in his wake as though he were a guide in a museum and behind her Kizzie did the same but she was fascinated and thrilled with what she saw and believed that when Miss Charlotte was this man's wife and herself again she would like it too.

'Have you any preference for a colour scheme or a particular piece of furniture in this room? It will be your bedroom . . .' and mine too, though he did not say so. 'It looks out over the garden at the front of the house and has its own bathroom through here . . .' opening a door that led into a magnificent room which even Charlotte found amazing despite her stupefied state. It was large, square, with two decorative windows set with panes of coloured glass. Beneath one of them was a large white bath on fluted legs, adorned with gleaming brass taps from which water spouted as he demonstrated. There was a holder across it containing scented soap, a loofah, snowy white face-cloths and next to it a white-painted towel rail covered with thick white towels. On another wall stood a white hand-basin, again with soap, this time in the shape of a shell, with brass taps and supported by fluted, decorative sides. Over it hung a large plate-glass mirror with an etched border. The floor and the walls were all done in glossy white tiles painted here and there with blue flowers. The water closet had a plain wooden lid but was itself decorated with the same pale blue flowers and the high-level cistern above it had a china chain-pull.

The luxury of it took Charlotte's breath away and she had a fraction of a second of pleasure, for though she did not want to marry this man and be parted from her brothers it seemed there would be some compensation for doing so! During the school holidays her brothers would be able to stay with her, and perhaps, since she was to have a rich husband, they could have horses. She would be able to do so much for them, give them a life they had not had with their father.

'Is it to your liking?' Mr Armstrong asked her diffidently and she was not to know that he was the least diffident man in the world and that he had the strongest desire to take her by the shoulders and shake her until her glorious hair fell about her. She was tearing his heart from his chest with her neutral acceptance of her surroundings, which he was offering to her with more love than he could ever have imagined himself feeling. It was not that she was inattentive. Her eyes moved from one object to another but never looked at him. She glanced behind her every now and again and he realised she was making sure her maid was still with them. What did she think he might do? Throw her on one of the beds and ravish her? Her one remark, or rather question, was about her maid.

'And where is Kizzie to sleep?' she asked. 'I wish her to have her own room.'

'Kizzie?' He was bewildered.

'My maid,' turning again to indicate the quiet woman at their backs.

'She is to come with you? I thought you might care for one of—'

'Oh, no! Kizzie will come with me, and then there is . . .' She hesitated, her gaze going off somewhere over his shoulder so that he was tempted to turn round to see what she was looking at.

'Yes, what is it?'

She moved to the window of the room that was to be hers, the room that she had not yet realised she was to share with him, he was sure. He followed her and stood beside her looking out over the gravel drive and the circle of grass.

'There is my brother, Robbie. I suppose Father told you he is to go to the grammar school in Dewsbury. He is too young for the school in York where his brothers are going and until he is I wish him to remain with me.'

There was a long silence while he digested this request. His face was totally without expression and she might have just asked him if it would be all right for her to have her dog with her. She did not turn to look at him. It was not really a request she had made but a demand. *I wish my brother to remain with me!* To live with them. To be there at every meal. To sit with them in the evening when he had hoped to spend time alone with her. At all times except when he was at school there would be a six-year-old boy forever hanging about her skirts. It was intolerable.

'You do not agree,' she said sadly as the silence lengthened, and when he still did not answer she sighed and turned away. 'You see I cannot leave him on his own with Father and . . . and that woman, so if you do not wish it I cannot marry you. I must have him with me. Father tells me that I must find a post as a governess or . . . or perhaps in a school. I think I could teach young children and he and I could find lodgings some-where. But . . . Oh, dear God . . .' Her hand went to her mouth. 'I had forgotten, Father swears that . . . well, I suppose I will have to . . .' She turned to him passionately, her eyes pleading.

'Yes?'

'Please say you will take Robbie. I will keep him out of your way as much as possible but if I don't become your wife as Father says I must he will send the boys, all of them, including Robbie, to a school up in Northumberland and I will . . .'

Again his heart wrenched in agony, *her* agony, but this time he gave way to his feelings and with a small sound in the back of his throat he put his arms about her, drawing her to him gently, calming her, just holding her as friend holds friend and it began then. Kizzie felt a lump come to her throat and without a sound drifted from the room and left them alone.

'Don't, Charlotte, don't worry so. You may have your Robbie to live with us as long as you promise that you and I can spend time together *on our own*.'

'When he is at school, Mr Armstrong.' Her face was radiant.

'And providing you call me Brooke.'

'I will. Oh, how can I thank you, you are the kindest, best man.'

'No, no, do not make me into a saint.' He was laughing now and so was she and when they left the room Kizzie saw that they were holding hands.

She really was the most beautiful bride any of the congregation had ever seen. Her eyes shone with the blue-green depths of aquamarine like the waters of the sea off the Cornish coast, one guest remarked, and her cheeks were flushed with rose. Her tawny hair had been brushed and brushed to the gloss of copper by Kizzie, and was in a full roll about her head like a small crown. Her gown was of white satin with a separate back-fastening bodice with small puff sleeves and the skirt was padded at the hem and gathered into a small train. Her full veil was fastened to a small Juliet cap that nestled in the crown of her hair and was made entirely of white rosebuds and she carried a small posy of the same flowers in her white, elbow-length-gloved hands. She was smiling at her handsome groom who was immaculate in a dark grey frock-coat with a light grey waistcoat and grey gloves. Her five brothers stood in a row behind her, as she had insisted they be present to see her married and for the moment she held the upper hand with her father. He gave her away then turned to the woman who would be his bride the following week.

They both made their vows with great clarity, and at the back of the church where the servants stood, Kizzie wept, with happiness this time, for she was certain her young mistress could not have been in better hands.

This, her own, was the first wedding Charlotte had attended so she had never heard the wedding service before. She promised to obey her husband though she was not exactly sure what to *honour* him meant. She did not love him and since he had not asked for her love or offered his it seemed easy enough.

The reception at the Mount was crowded with Arthur Drummond's friends and acquaintances, all of them telling one another that old Arthur was a lucky dog, not only in his daughter's choice of husband but in his own choice of wife. Wealth would pour into his coffers, and Armstrong's family and that of Arthur's bride-to-be wielded great influence.

They drank champagne and ate the colourful, light confections at which Mrs Welsh was a genius and after changing into what was known as a 'going-away' outfit designed for her by Miss Hunter she and the stony-faced groom drove away to a buzz of congratulations and good wishes. The guests were considerably startled when, as the newly married couple stepped into their carriage, they were accompanied by the bride's youngest brother, a lad of six, who apparently was to live with Mr and Mrs Armstrong. No wonder Brooke Armstrong was poker-faced! Seated beside the lad was a plump young woman with a good-natured face who was, it seemed, the new Mrs Armstrong's personal maid. The boy was to be in her care and had been enrolled at the grammar school in Dewsbury and why he was not to live at the Mount with his father and his new wife was certainly a matter for a great deal of speculation. Of course the lady Arthur Drummond was to marry on the following Saturday was known to like her own way, spoiled by her doting parents and no doubt expecting to be treated the same by her new husband.

The newlyweds were to spend the night at King's Meadow then travel to London to see their King go triumphantly to his coronation and spend a few days sightseeing and visiting the theatre, but before that Charlotte must settle her bewildered young brother into his new quarters with Kizzie close by. She had done her best to reassure Robbie that she would be gone for no longer than a few weeks; that Kizzie, whom he loved and who loved him, would always be here for him. He was to be allowed to have Taddy to sleep in his bedroom with him and Charlotte told him that if he were to go down to the paddock Mr Armstrong had a lovely surprise for him.

The boy was radiant with delight as, with the struggling puppy clasped in his arms and Kizzie beside them, he was introduced to Merry, a small brown pony who was to be his very own. Percy, the groom, would teach him to ride and when she and Mr Armstrong – who Robbie had understood was Charlie's husband – returned from holiday she expected to see him riding the animal round the paddock.

All the while this was happening her husband stood, his face quite expressionless, at her side and waited patiently as the day drew in, dusk fell, then darkness – as she tucked Robbie into his new bed with Taddy wriggling beside him – and she was faced with the harsh reality of getting into bed with her new husband.

Kizzie, though she was herself unmarried, had tried to open the subject of what lay ahead of her but they were both so embarrassed it came to nothing other than an earnest belief on Kizzie's part that Mr Armstrong would be kind to her.

' 'E'll not be brutal, lass. 'E'll do 'is best not ter 'urt tha' . . . well, tha'll know wharra mean?' A question more than a statement. Kizzie was a country girl and had been brought up with a knowledge of breeding animals and since she was from a big family she had even helped in one or two of her mam's deliveries. But Miss Charlotte was gently bred. Her own mother had died when Miss Charlotte was ten years old so there had been nobody for the lass to . . . well, to discuss these things with. Then again, girls from her young mistress's class were kept in woeful ignorance of anything to do with the marriage bed.

She was horribly shy as she sat waiting in the big bed where Kizzie had put her. Her hair fell down her back in a shimmer of golden copper and her eyes were huge in her pale face. Brooke had given her plenty of time to change from her going-away

outfit into the pretty, lace-trimmed nightgown Miss Hunter
had supplied. He entered the room without hesitation, for he
had decided it must be done at once or it might not be done at
all. She was innocent, looking no more than thirteen until the
lamp beside the bed revealed the swell of her lovely breast
peeping above the bedclothes. He removed his richly pat-
terned dressing gown and to her horror was totally naked
beneath it.

'Shall you remove your nightgown, Charlotte?' he asked
politely, standing beside the bed with what on her brothers had
been a somewhat inoffensive little piece of their anatomy,
growing huge and distended from a thatch of dark hair
between his thighs.

She pulled the coverlet up to her chin. 'I think not,' she
quavered.

'Then I shall do it for you. We are husband and wife and I
wish to see you as you see me.'

'No, absolutely not.'

'If we are to get on, Charlotte, and I believe we will, we must
have some understanding between us. I have done my best to
accommodate you in the question of your brother and your
maid. Now I ask something of you. Do you refuse?'

Her strength came from somewhere; her defiance, the
toughness that was hidden beneath her delicately lovely ex-
terior came from a deep well inside her. It had withstood the
violence of her father's perversion and his cruelty to her and
her brothers and she had emerged with a stamina that would
never be beaten. She threw back the cover, stood up and
pulled her nightgown over her head, flinging it to the corner of
the room. Her breasts were high and proud, her back was
straight and her face bore a look that said that though she was
afraid she would not weaken.

She was so resolute in her determination not to allow this
man to see her fear she did not hear the quick indrawn breath,

nor notice his expression of awe which were both quickly withdrawn.

'God, but you're beautiful,' he whispered, then he put his arms about her and drew her into what she did not recognise as a loving embrace. He put his mouth to her throat, then her breast, taking a nipple into his mouth and making her gasp. Her arms hung flaccidly at her side and when he raised his mouth to hers for their first kiss she was bemused more than frightened to feel his tongue, his teeth biting gently. He laid her down and she was so amazed at it all that the final pain of penetration was over and done with almost before she realised it had happened. He shuddered and groaned and fell across her, his face to her breast and when, five minutes later, she raised her head to study him he was fast asleep.

So that was what all this fuss was about, she thought, as she gently disengaged herself, unaware that women could share the pleasure of it. He turned away, muttering, still asleep and within minutes she was asleep herself. In the night she was awoken by his body pressed passionately to hers but this time, knowing what to expect, she submitted sleepily and then was astounded when morning broke to find herself held fast in his sleeping arms.

# 6

There was a great deal of coming and going as she and her husband readied themselves for their journey to London with constant interruptions from Robbie who could see no reason why he should not come with them. He was not to start at the grammar school until the new term in September which was *weeks* away and he would love to see their new King crowned . . . pardon, they were not to see the crowning, very well, but at least he would see the procession and then they could go to the Tower of London and—

'Darling,' she interrupted him gently. 'Mr Armstrong and I are married now and we are going on our honeymoon. Do you know what that is?'

Robbie frowned. 'No.'

'It is something that happens to people who are just married. A holiday so that they can get to know one another. And they go alone, just the two of them.'

'That means you won't want me then.' Despite the strictness of his upbringing Robbie Drummond was not a surly child, inclined to be cheerful, in fact, due to his beloved Charlotte. Now he was surly because he was bewildered. His whole life had been turned upside down and Charlotte now belonged not to him and his brothers but to this man who was to take her to places he had hardly heard of. He had Kizzie, of course, who was a constant in his life and she had told him that Mr Armstrong was a kind man but how was he to manage without Charlotte?

They were seated on the elegant sofa in the elegant drawing room, Charlotte dressed in her fetching new outfit which Miss Hunter, under instruction from Mr Drummond who had told her his daughter was to be married, weeks ago, had designed and made for her. She had taken all her measurements when Miss Drummond had been fitted with an evening gown. Further evening gowns, day dresses, costumes, called now skirts and jackets, or a suit. Suits for walking and travelling, riding outfits and tennis outfits, a Chesterfield tweed coat, capes with fur linings, footwear, stockings, even parasols, gloves and the finest, prettiest underwear and night attire that money could buy, and the bills, Mr Drummond had instructed her, were to be sent to Mr Brooke Armstrong at King's Meadow. Her future husband. Miss Hunter was to spare no expense! Today Charlotte Armstrong was dressed for travelling in what was known as an Eton jacket with swallow tails and oval revers under which she wore a long waistcoat with a high-necked collar band and a velvet stock. A mermaid costume skirt completed the outfit and all in a pale shade of dove grey with boots and gloves to match. Her hat was a cartwheel, large-brimmed and covered with tiny white daisies. She looked quite superb! Except for the hat. Brooke didn't like the hat. She was not that sort of a girl, or woman, he supposed he should call her after last night, to wear a hat. She was a creature of woods and fields, the outdoor, walking, running, laughing, harum-scarum, as he had seen her in the garden, not a fashion plate, but she was still superb. She filled his heart so that it felt it might burst and he wanted nothing more than to kneel at her feet and bury his face in her lap and tell her so. Hold her tight, cling to her as the boy was doing and with shame he realised he was jealous. Of her brother!

At the door he waited impatiently. The carriage was at the front ready to take them to the station at Wakefield and by train from there to London. Their luggage was stored in the carriage and the servants were hanging about as best they could waiting to see the master and their new mistress set off on their wedding journey. Kizzie was in the hall doing her utmost to get hold of young Master Robbie who was clinging frantically to his sister and they all were aware, for they knew him best, that the master was not pleased. And could you blame him? Just married and to be held up from beginning his wedding journey by a six-year-old who was not even related to him, except by marriage!

'Darling, you must understand that Mr Armstrong and I really have to leave now or we will miss our train.'

'I'd like to go on a train, Charlie.'

Brooke tapped the step with his foot then got out his pocket watch and glanced at it. *Darling!* Would she ever call him 'darling' as she did the boy? He could see her love and concern for her brother and tried to understand it. He knew with a sinking heart that moved heavily, coldly in his breast, that it was the fate of her brothers that had made her marry him and the thought nearly crucified him but he had been so desperate to have her he had not cared at the time. He loved her and surely his love would generate the same in her. He had been gentle with her last night and she had politely given in to him and that was what it was. Her sense of fairness since she had made a bargain and meant to keep to it, and politeness! She would submit to him whenever he cared to reach for her, he knew that, but it was not what he longed for. Give her time, he told himself, ready to curse out loud, but it was hard to be patient. The dogs were swirling about, including the puppy who kept jumping up at anyone who stood still for a moment and the maid was hovering in the doorway doing her best to prise the damn boy away from Charlotte.

'Charlotte, I must insist that we leave now or we will miss our train.' But as he spoke the telephone shrilled in the hallway and, as they always did since it frightened the lot of them to death, the servants jumped uneasily, each one hoping another would answer the thing. It was relatively new, at least to them, though Mr Johnson had told them that all the best people had them these days. Mr Johnson was the butler and knew about such things. Theirs was kept on a small shelf under the grand staircase and this alone was enough to put even the bravest of them off, for it was dark and poky though the master had promised to put in one of the new electric lights which he had installed in the rest of the house. The telephone was called a Candlestick model, very smart and very modern.

Mr Johnson walked with that ponderous, majestic walk that seems to be the requirement for all butlers and vanished into the little 'cubby-hole' as the rest of them called it; for several moments all was silent until Mr Johnson reappeared.

'It's for you, sir,' he told his master, then herded the servants in the general direction of the kitchens which were situated at the back of the house.

Robbie was still clinging like a vine to Charlotte when he returned and Brooke felt the irritation rise in him again despite the news he was just about to impart.

'The King is very ill,' he stated, then turned and walked to the window that overlooked the drive, where Todd, the coach-man, stood patiently waiting beside the horses who were growing restive. He was soothing them and looking towards the house as though wondering when the master and mistress would appear. They'd have to get a fair lick on to reach the station to catch their train for London.

Both Charlotte and Robbie stared at Brooke in surprise. The King couldn't possibly be ill. He was to be crowned in a few days, 26th June to be precise and today was the 24th!

'Did it say what was the matter with him?' Charlotte asked at last as though it were the telephone itself that was in the know.

'That was a friend of mine who works as a journalist in London. It's just been announced that the coronation is to be postponed but as yet it seems there is no news as to the cause of His Majesty's indisposition.'

Why does he talk like that? Charlotte wondered. So formal as though he were informing a meeting what was taking place in the capital city. I am his wife and Robbie is a small boy and yet there is a stiffness in our relationship that was not there the couple of times we met in the woodland and the garden and even at the dinner party Father gave that I was allowed to attend. He had been relaxed, ready to smile, she thought. Now he barely looked at her and spoke as though she were a stranger. Which she was, she thought sadly. They had been married a scarce twenty-four hours. They had spent the night together, slept, she remembered, in one another's arms and now he was different.

Charlotte was too inexperienced to realise that her husband was stiff and awkward because of the boy who was nearly sitting in her lap. He hadn't wanted him, though she didn't know it, visualising how it would be with a child forever demanding her attention and his worst imaginings had come true. Her brother was looking at him with suspicion, a competitor in his demand for his sister's attention and unless Brooke took a firm hand and laid down a set of rules so that he and his new wife could spend time together, alone, which Charlotte would take exception to, it would always be the same. Of course the boy would join his brothers at the boarding school at Barton Meade when he was old enough, but when would that be? Not for a couple of years! Dear God, he had made a rod for his own back here and how was he to make certain that he didn't get beaten down with it?

He turned abruptly, walked to the fireplace and rang the bell and when Connie, the parlour-maid appeared, bobbing a curtsey, he asked her to send in Kizzie.

Kizzie entered the drawing room but did not, as the parlour-maid had done, bob a curtsey.

'Yes, sir?'

'Kizzie, I wish you to take the boy away and amuse him. Take him to see the horses or something. I wish to talk to my wife alone.'

Kizzie looked at Charlotte for confirmation but Brooke saw it and his face hardened.

'I have given you an order which I expect to be obeyed. My wife, I'm sure, will agree with me that he cannot expect to . . . well, just take him away and—'

'I don't want to be taken away, Charlotte,' Robbie told her, wrapping his arms about her neck in the obvious belief that she would tell Mr Armstrong that though he couldn't go to London with them, when she was here she wanted him with her. She had always, as far as she could with Father, protected him, cherished him, been not only his big sister but his mother.

'Brooke, I really . . .' she faltered and Robbie glared at his brother-in-law.

'Charlotte, I wish this young man to go with your maid and leave me to talk with my wife. I'd be obliged if you did not argue with me.'

'Brooke, please, he is only a baby and has been uprooted—'

'At your request, Charlotte. I promised he could live here with us but that does not mean he is to be present in our lives every hour of the day.'

'Don't be ridiculous.'

He nodded at Kizzie to step forward which she did, unwinding the boy from his sister, for she knew, if Charlotte didn't, that though the master was a fair man, patient, kind, thoughtful, generous and would be loving if given half a chance, he was the master in this house and would have his own way. He was a man. He had been a soldier who had commanded other men. He wanted his bride to himself and Master Robbie must learn to accept it, besides which he and

Miss Charlotte were off to London to see the King's procession and to their own wedding journey.

'Come on, lad, come wi' Kizzie. Shall us ask Mrs Groves fer some apples? Horses like apples an' then tha can get used to 'em.'

Casting a reproachful look at Charlotte, since he had been sure she would tell Mr Armstrong . . . well, he wasn't sure what but she should have stuck up for him. Reluctantly he left the room clinging to Kizzie's hand.

'Now then, Charlotte,' her husband said briskly. 'We've missed the ten thirty-five but there is another at two fifteen which will get us into London in time for dinner. We'll still have our trip to London, see the sights but until we know how the King is . . .'

'Could we not stay here, Mr . . . er, Brooke? At least until we know of the King's condition. Then if—'

'No, Charlotte, we can not. We will go to London, await the news of the King and if he does not recover soon, travel to Paris and then on to Italy as planned.'

And that is what they did. Robbie was in tears as he waved goodbye to the carriage but she knew she must not weaken. She waved to him until the house disappeared and then leaned back shoulder to shoulder with the man who was her husband, her own heart leaden, for how was she to make a life with this man who was an unknown quantity to her, a man who could do as he pleased with her, take her where she did not want to go, which was away from her little brother who was lost without her. True, Robbie was to have a pony of his own and perhaps he would take comfort from that and from the presence of Kizzie.

To her quiet delight she found that she enjoyed the company of Brooke, as she called him with increasing ease as the days passed. They were in Florence when the King was finally crowned on 9 August. Apparently he had been struck down with an illness diagnosed as acute appendicitis and an emergency operation had been performed at Buckingham Palace. It had been entirely successful and so the coronation was held.

'Good old King Teddy,' her husband drawled, a cigar between his lips, a glass of champagne in his hand. They were dining on the terrace of the luxurious hotel, like all the other luxurious hotels they had stayed in where they ate off fine bone china and drank from cut-crystal glasses. First Paris with its delightful round of gaieties, a drive in the Bois de Boulogne, theatres and intimate little suppers afterwards, for there was no doubt Brooke was an amusing companion. They drank a great deal of champagne, bought dozens of chic outfits including a long cape of pale grey fur. He bought her jewellery, a strand of pearls and another of gold, diamonds to set in her hair and drape round her wrist, a negligee with an ermine trim. They made love, or Brooke made love to her every night, often in the early morning and now and again in the afternoon too. She found it quite agreeable once she had became used to his demands which, as the weeks passed, became more insistent. In full lamplight he explored her body from the crown of her head to the soles of her feet, returning to the most intimate parts of her that she scarcely knew existed, dwelling there with his hands and his mouth, bringing himself, if not her, to a shuddering climax which she now took for granted. They ate romantic dinners, went to race-meetings and elegant little concert halls and fascinating, pavement cafés, shopping, always shopping, not just for herself but for anyone she cared to spend his money on. He indulged her, amused her, entertained her and had it not been for the nagging little worries she had about Robbie and her older brothers at their new school she would have loved every minute of it. They moved on in easy comfortable stages to Marseille, Milan, Venice, Florence, Rome and then, at the end of September, they travelled home.

They were all waiting, the servants in a row in the wide hallway, smiling and bobbing and bowing to greet their new mistress who was not the frightened young girl who had left them three months ago but a beautifully, expensively dressed young woman of some sophistication. Kizzie was there at the end of the line, for as the mistress's personal maid it was she who would climb the stairs to the lovely bedroom where their mistress's many, many trunks were waiting to be unpacked.

'Where's Robbie?' was the first thing she said and the master frowned, for he had had her exclusively to himself all these weeks and did not relish the boy hanging about her neck the minute she got home.

'He's at school, madam,' Mr Johnson told her, nodding to them all to return to the kitchen.

'An' if he weren't at school 'e'd be down at paddock,' Kizzie added blithely. Kizzie had settled in to this comfortable, cheerful household where she found they were all prepared to accept her with great equanimity. Of course, she herself was only too happy, until her young mistress returned home, to help out anyone who asked her. She didn't mind scrubbing the scullery floor if Rosie was busy scouring pans, she was heard to say, endearing herself to the scullery-maid. Would Jane Porter like a hand in the dairy or Katie Abbott in the laundry? She'd be glad to 'peg out' in the garden beyond the stables or even do a bit of ironing with the flat irons. Four of them were kept on the hot plate at a time and used in order. As one cooled, another could be quickly taken up while the others reheated. There was always a great deal of washing and ironing, for there were seven indoor servants including Kizzie and then the family, Mr and Mrs Armstrong and young Robbie. She had fitted in a treat, she was to tell Miss Charlotte once they were alone, and so had Robbie. She studied her young mistress with a careful eye since she was pretty certain the master would be a real man in the 'bed' department but there seemed to be no sign of a baby yet, not even in Miss Charlotte's eyes where, to an expert like Kizzie, the first indication of pregnancy lay.

Robbie was allowed to dine with them that first night, as a treat, Charlotte told him carefully, since she had got the measure of her new husband by now and he would not take kindly to having a chattering schoolboy at the dinner table each night. Besides which, Robbie was only six years old and would go to bed early. Normally he would eat with Kizzie in his own rooms, a playroom cum study with a bedroom adjoining it.

He seemed to have settled, like Kizzie, into his new home and routine and his conversation never stopped, causing Brooke to frown slightly, the main reason being his passionate devotion to his new pony, which he could ride without being on a leading rein now, he said proudly, and the dogs, particularly Taddy, who slept in his room. His pony, Merry, was a 'corker'; or so Percy said, and on Saturday, his new chum from school, a boy called Webb was going to ride over and Percy would take them to Round Hill Wood. They were to *gallop* across the fields and did Charlotte think it would be all right if Webb stayed the night?

'Webb, that's a strange name for a boy, darling.' There it was again, she called her brother darling, an endearment she had never yet bestowed on him! Any endearment, come to that!

'Oh, that's his surname, Charlie. He calls me Drummond. Christian names aren't used at our school.'

'And do you like it, dearest? Your school, I mean, and don't slurp your soup, sweetheart. It's not manners to eat so quickly.'

'Sorry, Charlie,' he said, continuing to consume his soup hungrily. Johnson moved silently and deftly about the dining room, helped to serve by Nellie, the head parlour-maid.

Following the soup came lamb and roast potatoes, a simple dish to suit the boy, Mrs Groves had obviously thought, and then apple pie with lashings of fresh cream. There was cheese afterwards, a platter of Stilton, Cheshire, Cheddar and Gloucestershire with which Brooke drank port.

'Did you know there's a tennis court at the back of the house, Mr Armstrong?' the boy asked smilingly. Robbie was enjoying himself immensely. He had no competition from his brothers which, as the youngest, had held him back. He had Charlie's undivided attention and the man, Charlie's new husband, seemed disinclined to talk at all which suited young Robbie down to the ground. He was, on the whole, perfectly happy here at King's Meadow though he had not expected to be, especially since Charlie had a husband now, an unknown quantity to Robbie. The servants made a fuss of him which he had never experienced before. Kizzie was there to mother him while Charlie was away and the future looked sunny. And if he, Robbie, was allowed to eat with them and talk as he had done this evening, it seemed everything was to turn out as he liked it. School was not bad and Webb was a bonus, his pony another and the discovery of the tennis court had excited him no end. He could see him and Charlie having a lovely time here with no father to subdue them, for it appeared the chestnut mare in the paddock, named Magic, was to be hers. There were lovely walks and rides and now, a tennis court.

'Yes, I know,' Brooke said tonelessly, in answer to his question.

'Do you play then, sir?' Robbie smiled artlessly at the man who seemed unlikely to stand in his way.

'In the past, I have.' Brooke was looking at his wife who was also smiling, but not at him. She looked so beautiful, her face flushed and happy as she watched and listened to her brother prattle on. She wore one of her new Doucet gowns, bought in London. It was simple, made of lace the exact colour of the coffee and cream they were drinking and about her neck was the gold and diamond choker he had placed there on their first night as man and wife. Her hair had been brushed to a tawny gloss by Kizzie and then piled carelessly in a tumble of curls on her head and a coffee-coloured satin ribbon threaded through it. She had her elbow on the table and leaned her chin in the palm of her hand as she gazed indulgently at her little brother. Brooke could stand no more but was at the same time ashamed of himself, for this was a child of whom he was jealous. Her small brother who surely was no obstacle to him.

He stood up abruptly, slapping his hand on the table Mr Johnson, who was standing with his back to the sideboard waiting to clear, jumped a little and almost dropped a tray of crockery.

'Right, young man, time for bed, I think,' Brooke told him sharply. 'Your sister and I have—'

'Oh, no, please, Charlie. I have lots to tell you and I want to—'

'That is enough, if you please. And do not interrupt me, or any adult, when I or they are speaking. It is very—'

Robbie stood up and turned imploringly to his sister. He was enjoying himself so much and after all Charlie was *his* sister and this man must be made to realise it.

'Charlie, tell him, please. I haven't seen you for ages and ages and I wanted you to ask John or Ned – they're gardeners by the way – to do something with the tennis court so that you and I can play as—'

'Johnson, ring the bell if you please, or better yet, Nellie, go and fetch Kizzie. It's time for Master Robbie to be in bed and tomorrow I will speak—'

'Charlie, Charlie, please tell your . . .'

Charlotte stood up slowly and moved round the table to

take Robbie's hand in hers. She started towards the door but Robbie made the mistake of glancing back triumphantly at Brooke.

'May I ask where you are going, Charlotte?' Mr Johnson stood rigidly to attention and Nellie, who was making her own way to the door in order to fetch Kizzie, froze on the spot. Neither of them had ever seen this side of their master before.

'I intend putting Robbie to bed, Brooke. That is what you want, is it not?'

'You are not his nursemaid, Charlotte. You are my wife. Now then, Nellie. Tell Kizzie that Master Robert is ready for bed and to come here and fetch him. You and I will move to the drawing room, Charlotte. I shall light a cigar and since it is a warm, clear night I think a walk in the garden would be pleasant.'

# 7

The first months of their marriage were awkward but polite, the biggest problem in their uneasy relationship the presence of Robbie, who could not seem to accept that she was not wholly his as she had been all his young life.

Brooke rode out twice a week, leaving their bed – where he had made vigorous love to her the night before and often again before he left – to ride round his estate since he was an assiduous landlord. He had been a soldier all his adult life and had learned discipline and known hardship, but although he knew little about farming, he was determined to learn. He inspected Cec Eveleigh's excellent Fresian herd at Holly Farm, his pigs and his sheep, moving through the autumn sunshine on to Jack Emmerson's golden fields of corn and wheat and barley, drinking, as he always did, a glass of Mrs Emmerson's home-brewed ale or her cowslip wine. He was invited to inspect pigs, geese, laying hens and arrogant cock- erels. Even the dairies were not overlooked and he observed that it was no wonder there was such a plentiful supply of fresh eggs, milk, butter and cheese readily available at his table. He had no need really to oversee any of the farms for they were all good tenants, paying their rents on time, keeping their stock in good condition and the farm buildings in repair. Stables were spotlessly clean, hedges trimmed and yard and enclosures pleasant and well kept. He rode through great belts of old timber rising from a jungle of undergrowth, two miles across and about a mile deep with a shallow mere at its centre on which water lilies floated. He made estimates of the value of the timber. He spent many evenings poring over accounts, assessing profits from his land but at the same time wondering what made him so concerned with it all since he could well afford to hire an agent and perhaps spend more time with his young wife.

As soon as he and Charlotte returned from their honeymoon he took out his guns and joined his neighbours in the shooting season which had begun on 12 August with grouse, continuing with partridge on 1 September and pheasant on 1 October. Many ladies were included, for in the past he and his neighbours held shooting parties where wives were present. When Charlotte was more settled he meant to invite friends from all over Yorkshire to shoot his birds which had been hand-reared by his gamekeeper. In November the foxhunting season would begin and as autumn drew on he and Arthur Drummond, also back from his wedding journey, the Ackroyds, the Dentons and others of the Danby Hunt took the young hounds out 'cub hunting', teaching the puppies to hunt. Foxhounds may hunt mammals other than foxes by natural instinct and have to be trained and encouraged to make the fox their only prey. Cub hunting consists of training the young hounds – which were owned by Arthur Drummond who could now afford a pack thanks to his rich young wife – by first surrounding a covert with riders and foot followers to drive back any foxes attempting to escape and then 'drawing' it with the puppies, allowing them to find, attack and kill young foxes.

Charlotte was horrified when Brooke explained it to her and asked her, since she was learning to ride, to come with him one day.

'You will meet and make the acquaintance of many of my friends, which will be a good thing, for we must soon go out into society and return hospitality so it would be an advantage to you if you—'

'How absolutely appalling. Deliberately to train young puppies to attack and kill.'

'But how else are we to train our hounds, Charlotte? The season starts in November and goes on until March or April and I shall be spending a good deal of my time with the hunt. As you are under eighteen you will wear a tweed jacket but I and other members wear scarlet. You must have seen us out—'

'I shall be wearing neither scarlet nor tweed since I shall not be joining you. Oh, I enjoy riding, the little I have learned so far but I shall not be out killing innocent animals. It is barbaric.'

'Charlotte, as my wife you must conform to the ways of our society. I don't expect you to shoot but ladies are expected to join shooting parties. Charlie Denton of Park Mansion puts up a magnificent luncheon. His servants bring everything out into the woods that surround his house and—'

'Stop right there, Brooke. I shall not shoot nor hunt nor take part in any of the horrendous activities which your friends . . .'

Brooke's face became hard and there was visible menace in the set of his mouth. 'The fox is considered to be vermin by the farmers who fear losing their valuable livestock. Your own father is to be Master of Foxhounds now he has his own kennels, and with the death of old Willy Jenkins the position has become vacant. His wife is keen on hunting and I'm sure she will take you under her wing. I will take you out myself if you prefer.' His voice was clipped and she knew she had angered him but could be no other way.

They were seated in the splendid dining room, its walls papered in pale green watered silk with chairs in the same colour, at the enormous oblong table of English oak. The rich burgundy carpet softened the footfalls of Mr Johnson and Nellie as they served them. The table was set with the heavy silver cutlery, the delicate bone china and cut-glass crystal to which Charlotte was growing accustomed. This evening she had been dressed by Kizzie in what Kizzie thought correct, since Charlotte was not normally overly concerned with her clothes. She wore a crimson silk gown with a low décolletage, pencil slim with a tiny train, while Brooke was dressed in the proper evening wear of black and white even though they were alone.

The argument, if you could call it an argument, continued since the master was getting more and more enraged. Mr Johnson had worked for him and his father before him and knew that Mr Brooke was a man who contained his feelings and very rarely lost control but his wife's flat refusal to have anything to do with the activities he enjoyed, and not only him but his friends, was something he had not expected. She, like her brother, had had a birthday recently and was now seventeen but she was extremely young to be the wife of so prominent a landowner. He and Nellie stood like statues by the serving sideboard, waiting to take the master and mistress's soup plates away and serve the second course but Mr Johnson made a small gesture to Nellie to slip out to the kitchen and inform Mrs Groves to hold the salmon since the master and mistress might be a while yet. Brooke and Charlotte did not notice her go but she could not wait to tell the others of the row going on in the dining room.

'She've said she'll 'ave nowt ter do wi' 'untin' nor shootin',' she told them dramatically.

'What!' Mrs Dickinson was amazed, for that was what the gentry did all winter and how was the young mistress to pass her time if she did not mix with them.

The cloth with which Kizzie was wiping a bowl slowed and she sat down suddenly. She had seen this coming though she was not quite certain what she meant by that thought. There would be trouble if Miss Charlie did not conform to the rules of the class into which she had married. She had done nothing in her life but be with her brothers while her father gadded about, going nowhere, having no friends, just staying in the schoolroom but now she was the wife of a gentleman who had friends who were gentlemen and she had to fit in. She must see if she could talk to Miss Charlotte and explain to her that if she did not conform her marriage could be rocky. It had not had a good start, for they all knew of the difficulties with Master Robert and his possessiveness of the master's new wife, beside the sad fact that Miss Charlotte did not love her husband and had only married him because of her father and his threats.

They were not surprised when the master left the house, calling for his bay and galloping like a madman down the drive, presumably to his club, where gentlemen went to get away from recalcitrant wives!

Brooke had thought he was content, or would have been had it not been for the minor irritant of young Robbie Drummond. And the fact that Charlotte was not yet pregnant, though he supposed four months was not very long and God knows he tried hard enough! He would dearly love children of his own and if he had, perhaps the presence of Robbie Drummond would not be quite so aggravating. Also, with Charlotte pregnant or with a new baby, her obstinacy over her brother would cease. The boy should be spending more time with that friend of his and not, as now, with his sister. He had believed his wife was beginning to feel at ease in her new home and the life she led, though he often wondered what she did all day. She was learning to ride and to play tennis – the latter from a book that she had found in the library – on the newly refurbished tennis court where she and her brother played what seemed to be hilarious games. He would often hear her voice over the roof of the house begging Robbie to be fair . . . no, that was out and he was cheating and the ball must be inside the line.

This afternoon he had left Bruno, his tall bay, in the care of Arch who was in the stable yard grooming Samson, hissing softly with each stroke of the curry brush, calming the animal who was inclined to be restive. Walking through the yard and letting himself out of the gate, Brooke had wandered round to the tennis court where Robbie was triumphantly calling out that it was 'love thirty' and Charlotte better watch out for he meant to win this game. Charlotte was at the other end dressed in the latest tennis outfit, considered to be quite daring. The dress was of white linen with a short skirt above the ankles and her straw boater had been abandoned and lay on the grass at the back of the court. Her energetic exercise had loosened her hair which drifted round her head and down her back to her buttocks in a thick, curling mass. Of course he saw it like that every night when he joined her in the bedroom but somehow, seeing her like this, impatiently pushing it back from her face, gave him a hollow feeling at the pit of his belly and an uncomfortable bulge in his crotch. If she had been alone he might have drawn her behind the high privet hedge that surrounded the court and in the privacy of the summerhouse beyond, drawn her skirts up and her drawers down and made vigorous love to her. But the damned boy was there.

Irritably he called out, 'Who's winning?' not caring but wanting her to look at him. Instead his words put the boy off and when he drew back his racquet to serve he hit the ball out of court.

'Oh, dammit,' he said, 'you made me lose my swing. I'd have got that point if—'

'Robbie, don't be rude and you must not swear.'

'But—'

Brooke had had enough. 'Go to your room, boy,' he barked. 'I've had all I can take of your impudence. Your sister makes excuses for you—'

'No, I don't,' Charlotte challenged.

'No, she doesn't. You're the one who spoils it all,' her brother added.

'Go to your room at once and stay there until sent for.' There was a pain in Brooke's chest and throat as he did his best to stop himself, for no matter what he did it seemed the pair of them teamed up against him which was bloody ridiculous. A six-year-old boy . . . no, the little sod was seven now having had a birthday a couple of weeks back. He was white-lipped with sudden anger and something else that was very familiar. 'I swear to God, if you aren't out of my sight in two minutes I'll . . .'

'Yes, *what* will you do, Brooke? Beat him as my father once did? That would—'

Before she could say another word he turned on his heel and strode back the way he had come, conscious as he did so that the boy was smiling at his retreating back, having won yet another round. He did not see his wife's expression, which was one of sadness. She did not want this constant antagonism between her and Brooke over Robbie and she was often cross with her little brother for causing it, yet the boy had known nothing but misery from the man in his life before she married and she did so want to make it up to him. Her brothers would be home at Christmas, four of them to confront her husband. In fact bedrooms had already been designated for them, two to a room at the back of the house and how would things be then? She loved them all and wanted to make up to them what they had missed since Mother had died but if Brooke continued to resent Robbie, which she knew he did but tried desperately to avoid, her life would be wretched. He was her husband and she should put him first, for had he not rescued them all from misery and downright cruelty, besides being owed her loyalty. And she must be honest with herself, she had begun . . . no, she had *always* liked him. He was a good man . . . oh dear . . . oh dear!

She watched him turn the corner from her sight. 'Charlie . . . come on, Charlie, let me serve again. That man spoiled the last one forever interrupting like—'

With a flash of temper she had not known she possessed she turned on him, flying across the court and even leaping the net though she almost tripped on her long skirt. She grabbed him by the ear and began to draw him towards the house.

'Ow . . . ow, you're hurting me,' he yelled, more amazed than hurt, for Charlie never chastised him except in a very *soft* way.

'I'll hurt you even more if you don't apologise to Brooke at once. He is my husband and deserves your respect so we will go at once to his study.'

'Charlie, don't . . .' He began to cry and for a moment she almost relented but she had seen and for a split second had understood what was in her husband. Her little brother whom she loved dearly was taking advantage of that love and was doing his best – in his childish way – to separate them. And if she wasn't sterner he might succeed. She had married Brooke though she had not wanted to but she had seen a secret side of him . . . well, caught a glimpse of it and she found, amazingly, she did not want it to disappear again.

And now she had further antagonised him by a downright refusal to hunt the fox or shoot the damned birds which seemed to be the only activity he and his friends enjoyed!

That night, for the first time, he did not come to her. He had a dressing room off their bedroom furnished with a bed with a black bearskin thrown across it, a luxurious crimson carpet and a dressing table, mirrors and wardrobes filled with his expensive clothes, all beautifully crafted in dark wood. His favourite prints hung on the walls and the heavy curtains were crimson. He had not, since they were married, spent one night there. The room they shared was in peach silk and white lace, the bed curtains of the finest, lightest silk drawn up into a gleaming crown and tied back with lace ribbons, the carpet decorated with peach blossom and pastel-tinted clouds. As feminine as his was masculine.

She lay on her back, her head turned to the wide windows, the curtains of which she had drawn back. There was a full moon and it was almost as light as day. Kizzie had brushed her hair until it snapped round the brush, waiting for Mr Armstrong to appear as he did every night but when he had not come after five minutes of brushing she laid down the brush, sighed and left the room. She had heard, as who had not, of the quarrel – if it could be called that – and the tears and lamentations that had come from Master Robbie; and not only about the tennis court and whatever had gone on there, but the hot and angry argument over Miss Charlotte's refusal to hunt and shoot and she was sorry, for Kizzie was of the opinion that given a little time to shake down together, husband and wife would do very well. Miss Charlotte, in her attempt to make Master Robbie happy and assuage her guilt at what he had suffered in the first seven years of his life, was causing and widening the rift between husband and wife and now, after only four months of sharing his wife's bed, he had gone galloping off in a tearing rage and was sleeping in his dressing room. Kizzie's mam, in the belief that one day her daughter would marry, had said to her that she and her husband must never go to bed on a quarrel. Quarrels, of course, were made up in bed and that was one of the advantages of a small, two-bedroomed cottage filled with children. There was nowhere else for her pa to sleep so he and Mam had, with a cuddle, become friends again. If only the master and Miss Charlotte could do the same.

He was not at breakfast the next morning and when Kizzie enquired casually of Mr Johnson where the master might be she was told that he had breakfasted early and ridden off but no one had been told to where or when he would be back.

Robbie was at school where he was taken each morning in the gig by one of the outdoor servants. After idling about in her bedroom for half an hour, picking up a book and putting it down again, Charlotte opened her wardrobe and without calling for Kizzie – after all she had dressed herself for most of her life – threw on clean underclothes and her riding habit, tied her hair back with a silver satin ribbon, pulled on her boots and the kid trousers she wore under her skirt and flew downstairs, her hair swinging down her back in a most unladylike way.

The servants watched her open-mouthed as she flew past them in the kitchen, Kizzie ready to stop her. She had thought her young mistress was ensconced by her bedroom fire with a book and here she was like a mad thing dashing into the yard and calling for her horse.

'I shall go out alone, Percy,' as the groom moved to help her into the saddle, the side saddle he expected her to use. 'Oh, and I would be glad if you would put me astride. Now you know we have practised it several times so don't pull that face at me.'

'But, Mrs Armstrong, ma'am, master'd 'ave me 'ide if I was ter let yer go out—'

'The master will never know unless you tell him, Percy, for I shan't.'

'Oh, please, ma'am . . .' The groom was almost crying but he took off the side saddle and fetched another from the tack room while she tapped her foot impatiently.

'You must teach me how to saddle my own horse, Percy,' she said, 'then I will have no need to bother you.'

''Tis no bother, ma'am, but will yer not—'

'No, I will not.'

'I must come wi' yer. Yer might come off in a ditch an' then where'd us be,' he mumbled as he cupped his hands to help her into the saddle but before he could say another word she was through the open gateway and across Old Lady Brook Meadow towards Clough Wood several miles away.

She managed to stay on though she found it strange to ride astride after so many lessons in the side saddle but she drew Magic, who was a placid, good-natured mare, chosen for these qualities by Brooke, to a trot and then a walk and when she reached the wood she scrambled off, wondering idly how she was to get back on, tied the reins to a branch so that Magic could graze and sat down in the roots of a great oak, leaning her back against its trunk and her arms on the roots as though she were in an armchair.

She was startled when the four dogs suddenly and joyously scrambled all over her. The yard gate which had been left open for her return had enabled the dogs, when let out of the stable where they spent the night, to race after her. They licked her face energetically in greeting then settled down companionably beside her, Ginger, the retriever, resting her muzzle on Charlotte's lap. She stroked the silky head and stared up into the branches of the tree. Drifts of leaves were falling and settling on the ground and in this mixed woodland the hawthorns and beeches were beginning to close down for the winter. It was rather sad and though she and Brooke had so far rubbed along pleasantly enough she could see storms coming. There was the constant friction with Robbie and she made up her mind to encourage him to bring home a school friend other than the faithful Webb. The trouble was that none of Brooke's acquaintances seemed to be young. The Emmersons, the Eveleighs, the Nicholsons, the Killens, who were all tenant farmers on Brooke's land, had children, for she had seen them playing about the farms when she rode out with Percy but they attended the little local school in the village of Overton. She wondered idly if it might be possible to send Robbie there until he went to Barton Meade with his brothers. She might wander down there one day and have a word with the teacher, find out her views on education and assess what benefit it might be to Robbie. *And to Brooke and herself!*

The dogs dozed in a patch of sunlight and she allowed herself to dream a little, though what about she was not sure for her thoughts circled languorously in her head. A sudden movement on the far side of the small grove caught her attention and to her amazement a fox cub wandered out of the undergrowth and began to follow the movement of a leaf that floated past its beautiful little face. The dogs, who she would have supposed might have caught the cub's scent, dozed on in oblivion and she scarcely dared breathe lest she wake them. From behind the cub, hidden in a clump of fern, another face appeared, or rather just a pair of gleaming eyes above a pointed nose. The vixen, surely mother to the cub, stared at her with those yellow eyes as though assessing the danger before she made the tiniest sound and at once the cub stopped its frolicking and as if at some maternal command slipped back into the undergrowth which barely moved with its passage. Then there was nothing and Charlotte knew they were gone.

And these were the lovely animals that Brooke and others would kill! These shy creatures whose babies played like young children, unafraid but obedient to their mother's call.

Slowly she rose and at once the dogs rose with her, lazily wagging their tails, ready to go with her wherever she wanted them to go and for a moment the thought crossed her mind that the dogs, the horses like the one who carried her safely about the estate, even the cat which curled round her legs in the kitchen, purring ecstatically, were so trusting and eager to be her friends. Brooke was casually kind to his animals and would not deliberately be cruel but there was such unfairness in this world and she did nothing but accept it. She lived a life of luxury and ease. She had a cook to make her any dish she required, maidservants to clean her home, a laundry-maid to wash her garments the moment she took them off, men and women to wait on her, enabling her to sit by her fire all day and do absolutely nothing.

So what was she to do with the remainder of her life? She had been married since June and every night – apart from last night – her husband made love to her and yet in all these months he had not impregnated her. Was she not to be a mother? If not, what was her purpose in this world that Brooke had created for her?

Finding a fallen tree trunk she managed to steady herself and Magic and gain the saddle, find the stirrups and with a sound that Percy had taught her, urged the mare forward. The dogs swirled about her then raced ahead and slowly, reluctantly, she moved across the fields until she reached the stable gate where Percy was waiting for her.

'Oh, ma'am, thanks be yer 'ome,' he babbled as though she had been to London and back. He helped her to dismount and as he led the mare towards the stable a young girl moved dejectedly away from the closing kitchen door. Her head was bowed and when she lifted it there was such a look of despair on her face that Charlotte hesitated and put out a hand.

'What is it?' she asked, but the girl merely shook her head.

'Come inside,' Charlotte said gently, 'and tell me.'

# 8

They all stopped what they were doing and stared in amazement as their mistress entered the kitchen with an arm round the strumpet who had just been sent on her way by Mrs Dickinson. Even Kizzie who was usually big-hearted and not at all judgemental, frowned at the sight and Mrs Groves seemed unable to restrain her mouth.

'Well,' she snorted, 'it didn't take you long to find a fool to sympathise with you. The mistress has a soft heart and God knows she is—'

'That will do, Cook, if you don't mind,' Charlotte snapped. 'Fetch a chair for this poor girl and put a cup of tea in her hand, and be quick about it,' since they all appeared to be frozen with shock and unable to move.

'But, Mrs Armstrong, ma'am, we've just sent this . . . this woman off with a flea in her ear. Can you not see what she is? I'll not have such trash in my kitchen among decent girls.'

'*Be quiet*, Mrs Groves. This is my kitchen, not yours as it happens to be in my house. My husband's house and I will have in it whom I please. Now then,' turning with a smile to the girl who hung her head so that her hair, which was uncombed and knotted, hid her face. Reluctantly she sat down on the chair Charlotte pulled out for her and when the cup of tea was flung down on the table before her she grabbed it eagerly and sipped the contents until the cup was empty.

Ignoring the servants who still watched with fascinated stares, Charlotte knelt down at the girl's feet and took her hands in hers.

'Now tell me what troubles you,' she began.

'Hmmph,' Mrs Groves spluttered, ' 'tis plain as the nose on your face what troubles her. Got herself in a—'

'That's enough, Mrs Groves. I'm surprised at you, really I am. Have you no compassion for someone who—'

'I'll not have my girls corrupted by a—'

Charlotte stood up and rounded on her cook. 'Mrs Groves, I thought you were a Christian. You go to church on a Sunday, for I've seen you set off. Now then,' turning back to the girl who sat dejectedly in her chair, totally unaware, it seemed, of the currents of disapproval that eddied about her. These women who worked in the kitchen, good women who had never been in trouble and probably had never even had the chance to *get* into trouble, looked down on her, despised her and she knew it. But still, the lady had been kind and she had had a reviving cup of tea.

She stood up shakily, for it was a while since she had eaten. 'I'll be on me way, ma'am,' she said quietly and was amazed when the lady turned on her indignantly.

'You will do no such thing. I wish to hear your story and see if there is something can be done to help you. Mrs Groves shall cook you something nourishing and then we will see.'

'No, I will not, ma'am, beggin' your pardon. Let her take her . . . her belly elsewhere.'

'You will do as I say, Mrs Groves, or you can find other employment. I will not have a servant speak thus in my own kitchen. Now then, what have you bubbling on the stove? It smells good. I'd be obliged if you would put a bowl of whatever it is . . . pea and ham soup, thank you, Rosie,' to the little scullery-maid. 'Pea and ham soup it is.'

Watched by them all, including Kizzie who, though she did not approve, was elated that her young mistress had not

backed down before the imperious Mrs Groves, the girl tucked
in hungrily to the soup and as though by magic a faint colour
crept into her cheeks. She ate daintily, and when she had
finished she murmured a faint thank you to Mrs Groves.

'Now, tell us your name,' the mistress of the house, and the
situation, asked the girl.

'Jenny, ma'am. Jenny Wainwright.' She looked humbly
down at her empty bowl.

'And where are you from, Jenny?'

But Jenny just shook her head.

Charlotte understood. The servants, all of them, even Kizzie,
were standing round in an intrigued circle, eager to hear the
story of this young girl, who, it was obvious, was in the middle
stages of pregnancy. Her skirt was hitched over a plainly visible
swelling, pulled up slightly at the front. She wore an old shawl,
much patched, which had fallen back as she ate.

'Come with me, Jenny,' Charlotte told her, ignoring the
gasp of horror that came from the maidservants. Surely the
mistress was not going to take this bad girl into the house, the
*front* of the house where she and the master lived, perhaps into
the drawing room, but she turned and smiled at them all and
for some reason that smile smoothed their ruffled feathers
somewhat. They did not approve, of course, for women who
got themselves with child without a wedding ring on their
finger were, once upon a time, driven from a village on a rail to
the sound of rough music, as the saying went. This girl had
already been turned away when she had asked for work, any
work, casual work, at the back door and had the mistress, who
was known to be kind-hearted, not come in at that moment,
would have been halfway to wherever she was going.

'I shall put Jenny in my bath and see if I have something for
her to wear. She shall rest and have a nourishing meal and then
we will discuss what is to be done with her. What is to be done
*for* her,' and with that she led the stunned girl from the kitchen.

'Well, what d'yer mekk o' that, Mrs Dickinson?' Mrs Groves asked, reverting to her native dialect in her astonishment.

'Nay, don't ask me, lass,' Mrs Dickinson replied, reverting to hers.

The girl, five months pregnant, she whispered to Charlotte, as she cowered in the bathroom, had been bathed, her hair washed and put in one of Charlotte's nightgowns. With the grime removed she proved to be very pretty! After eating a hot meal of lamb cutlets, roast potatoes, fresh cabbage and gravy followed by syrup sponge and custard, part of the meal Cook had meant for the servants' dinner, she was asleep in a spare room.

They were just sitting down to it before they prepared luncheon – for one – for their young mistress, when they were again thunderstruck as the mistress burst into the kitchen. They stood up as one and she stopped in her tracks.

'Oh, Lord, I'm sorry, I did not think but really, please go on with your meal. I just wanted to ask for the keys to the building on the other side of the gateway at the front of the house. I've never been through there and I'm sure you must have them, Mrs Dickinson.' Mrs Dickinson had a great bunch on a chatelaine fastened to her belt and Charlotte was certain the ones she wanted must be there.

'The building next door?' the housekeeper said faintly, obviously wondering what the dickens her mistress was up to now. They were all aware that she had put the trollop, as they all called her, into one of the spare beds after feeding her, so what did she want with those particular keys?

'Have you the keys, Mrs Dickinson?' Charlotte asked patiently.

'To the Dower House? Well, yes, I have but—'

'The Dower House? I see. Is that what it is? Well, may I have them?'

'But . . .'

'Please, Mrs Dickinson, I haven't got all day.'

They had all sat down again at the table but could not bring themselves to resume eating with their mistress present. Hesitantly Mrs Dickinson took several keys from the chatelaine and handed them over to her mistress.

'This one's for the front door and the—'

'Yes, yes, I'll sort them out. Now, when you have eaten would you come to the drawing room, Kizzie.' Charlotte nodded to them all and left the room.

Within five minutes Kizzie joined her.

'That was quick. Did you finish your dinner?'

'As much as I wanted. Now then, my lass, what's all this about? 'Ave tha' lost tha' senses, fetchin' that girl inter't th'ouse? Tha' knows she's ter 'ave a bairn an' 'er not wed by't look of 'er.'

'No, she's not married and yes, she is pregnant but her tale is one that disgusts me and if I can help her I will. She was turned out of her job the minute they found out about the child and do you know how she came by that child? No, well, it was the son of the house who persuaded her . . . seduced her and do you know whose house it was? Park Mansion, the home of Sir Charles and Lady Rosemary Denton with whom my father and my husband are acquainted. They hunt with them, shoot with them, and this – I will not say *gentleman* – this man with whom she thought she was in love, took her to his bed and got her with child. She was turned out a week ago and since then she has been living rough because her own family have disowned her. All she wants is work and a safe place until her child is born. She does not ask for charity and what would have happened to her when the child came I don't know but I intend to see that—'

'Lass, lass, listen ter tha'self, will tha'? What'll master say when 'e 'ears yer've took in this stray an' where's she ter stay fer none o' them in't kitchen'll work wi' 'er. They're not bad, Miss Charlotte, but that's 'ow they was brung up. There's standards, tha' see, an' this lass, well, what did she think was ter 'appen? That young master'd marry 'er? Tha've ter be sharp in some 'ouse'olds where there's young gentlemen an' she should've known better an'—'

'Yes, yes, Kizzie,' Charlotte interrupted impatiently, 'but there is no use going over what can't be remedied. She is to have her child in four months' time and in the meanwhile I intend to keep her here and put her to some task within her capabilities. And that building, the Dower House, will do nicely. I don't wish to outrage the sensibilities of the maidservants so you and I will go to that house and see what can be done. If it is suitable she can stay there until her child is born and . . . well, we will put our heads together.'

'Nay, Miss Charlotte, the master'll not like it.'

'I don't suppose he will. Men seem to be singularly heartless when it comes to females who are – what is the expression? – *done down* by other men. Well, I intend to have my way on this.' She stood up purposefully, jingling the keys Mrs Dickinson had reluctantly given her.

They went out by the front door and crossed the gravel drive to the arch let into the high wall that separated the Dower House from the main one. The wrought-iron gate was well oiled and made no noise as they opened it. Beyond the wall was a paved courtyard. To the left-hand side of the courtyard was a building whose purpose was not clear, with a clock on top of it, all built in the same lovely honey-coloured stone as the main house. On the right-hand side was the Dower House, built on to the main house but standing back so that it did not obtrude. It had a porch with four flat windows on the top storey and two on either side of the porch. A pretty little house, which was unlived in.

'Well,' Charlotte mused, 'this looks promising.'

'What d'yer mean, lass?' Kizzie asked. She stared dubiously at the little house then watched her young mistress unlock the front door and step inside. She followed her, entering a pleasant hallway with doors off it and that led to a staircase. To the side of the staircase was another door and when they ventured down the passage found it opened into a large, sunny kitchen. It was all spotlessly clean and it was obvious that the servants had at some time been told to keep it that way. There was a parlour and a dining room, handsomely furnished with pretty curtains and pictures of landscapes on the walls, a laundry and a scullery off the kitchen, all three rooms stocked with the requirements for the work that was done there. Outside the back door they stepped into an enclosed garden where flowers were well tended and beyond that vegetables grew neatly in rows, again all well cared for. Upstairs were four bedrooms furnished comfortably with every requirement a woman of taste might have arranged and there was even a bathroom with running water and a flush lavatory.

'Well,' Charlotte said again, moving from room to room with Kizzie so close behind her she almost stood on the hem of her skirt. 'Who would have thought . . . I wonder who lived here?'

'Nay, don't ask me, Miss Charlotte, and what I want ter know is what's in tha' mind. 'As it owt ter do wi't pregnant lass 'cos if tha's thinkin' of puttin' 'er in 'ere which I know tha' mean to, then—'

'I do, Kizzie, and I mean to find her some employment that she can manage and that won't offend the servants since they seem to be easily offended. She cannot remain in the house. She's in trouble and—'

'She'll not be t'first nor will she be t'last. I've lost count of 'ow many 'ave bin turned away from not just King's Meadow but tha' pa's place. They come from all over lookin' fer 'andouts an' finish up in't work'ouse, I've no doubt.'

'Do they, Kizzie?' Charlotte put her hand on Kizzie's arm and spun her round to face her.

'Aye, they do that, lass.'

'It's a crying shame, Kizzie, it really is. These girls are not wholly to blame for their condition but the *gentlemen* involved get off scot-free.'

'Nay, not all of 'em. Some of these lasses 'ave . . . 'ave bin wi' chaps 'oo 'ave decency ter marry 'em.'

'But not those who are taken advantage of by so-called gentlemen who take their pleasure of ignorant young girls.'

'No.'

'So what happens to them, Kizzie?'

'Their bairns're dumped inter orphanages and they – their mams – tekk ter't streets or . . . or . . .'

'When you say the streets you mean . . .?'

'Aye, lass,' Kizzie said sadly. It would never happen to her, for she was a decent, respectable young woman, besides which she was plain and would attract the attention of no man. 'Prostitution.'

Charlotte was appalled. She had been gently reared and in ignorance of what went on in the wider world beyond her home, like all girls of her class, but she knew what the word meant. She moved to the window of the bedroom in which they stood and looked out on to the pleasant courtyard. There was a white-painted wrought-iron bench against the far wall, placed in the sun. The courtyard was bordered by beds in which late summer flowers grew and chrysanthemums were coming into their own, yellow and bronze and white. Across the cobbled courtyard was the second building which had a wide double door and large windows along the ground floor. All peacefully dozing in the sunshine. Pigeons called to each other and the dogs began to bark at the back of the main house. She could hear someone singing, a man's voice, and a woman laughed. It was lovely and she felt the rightness of it flood through her, for surely here was something she could do that was not concerned with entertaining – though she supposed she would be obliged, as Brooke's wife, to occupy herself with the task. She had been married since June. She had servants to comply with her every wish so that she might, as the wife of a gentleman, be free to pass her days in idle pleasure and she admitted to herself that she was bored. She liked to ride and play tennis but they were hardly worthwhile occupations. She wanted to do something that stretched her mind, an occupation – but what? There was a quality about this girl who slept in her home that had stirred a sense that lay dormant within herself and she felt it might lead to something important. She had, at that particular moment, no idea what it might be but she could feel the excitement rise within her. That, and something else. Compassion, she supposed. The sight of the girl, Jenny, moving hopelessly across the stable yard had touched her and without thought she had instinctively gone to help her.

She stood for several minutes at the window and Kizzie watched her and waited. At last she spoke.

'If I was to put her in here would you move in with her? I sometimes have the feeling you are not quite settled at King's Meadow. That there is not a *proper* . . . that you have not found a place that suits you. You would be in charge, of course, for my husband would not allow me to . . . to be a part of . . . an *active* part of . . . I don't even know what I mean to do . . .' Her voice tapered off.

'I should think not, lass. Tha' place is wi' thi' 'usband and tha' family. I don't know what 'e'll say about all this. 'Appen 'e'll put a stop to it but yes, I'll move over t't Dower 'Ouse if 'e agrees. I want ter be near you, my lass, but I've no proper job 'ere except pretend ter be tha' maid so it'd suit me grand ter 'ave runnin' o't place ower t'way.'

'He surely wouldn't turn Jenny out in her condition, Kizzie. He's got a good heart, I know. Oh, I also know he is part of the class that causes many an illegitimate child to be brought into the world. Dear God, I've seen those children from the orphanage on their way to church on a Sunday. All dressed alike in drab grey and their hair cut short so that you can't tell the boys from the girls. Subdued and obedient to their cold-hearted supervisors. No, if I can help girls like Jenny I shall. It relieves me to know you'll stay with her until . . . well, first I must speak to Brooke.' She remembered his coldness towards her and his decision to sleep in another bed the previous night. Would he return home this evening to dine with her? Would he stay at home and spend the night in her bed? Well, she would soon find out.

Lifting her head in that defiant way Kizzie knew so well from the days when the master used to beat her and her brothers, Charlotte strode towards the stairs and the open front door. She had done her best not to be defeated by her father's treatment of her and perhaps it was this that drove her now to try to alleviate the future of Jenny and her child which, when it was born, Jenny would have no choice but to assign helplessly to the orphanage. And if there was this one there would be bound to be others she would drag under her protective wing. Kizzie knew her young mistress and was well aware that her kind heart, if not guided, would lead her into what could only be disaster. The master would not allow it and if Miss Charlotte dug her heels in what chance had they of making their marriage work? Kizzie wanted nothing more than to see her lass happy with perhaps a child of her own. There were already ructions over Master Robbie and his tantrums, so this would put further strain on their relationship.

The girl was awake when Charlotte quietly opened the door and popped her head round it. She lay in the bed, her face peeping over the covers, anxious but at the same time refreshed after the good meal she had eaten and the sleep into which she had fallen.

'Ah, you're awake, Jenny,' Charlotte said, smiling, moving towards the bed. 'Do you feel better?'

Jenny tried to sit up but Charlotte gently pushed her back and sat on the edge of the bed. 'No, stay there. I'll ring the bell and have one of the maids bring you up something to eat and drink and then you—'

Jenny freed herself from the bed covers and sat up, appalled. 'Eeh, no, ma'am, yer musn't do that. I'm grand an' if I can 'ave me clothes I'll be off. Them lasses in the kitchen think nowt a pound ter me an' yer can't blame 'em so I'll not bother yer no more.'

She began to push the covers back with the intention of climbing from the bed and the thin nightdress Charlotte had dressed her in revealed the swell of her belly. Jenny put her hand protectively to it and the gesture moved Charlotte immensely. This young girl, in so much trouble, life and death really, still felt the need to safeguard the child that was the cause of her predicament.

'Your clothes have been taken away. Katie, the laundry-maid, will wash them and return them to you. In the meantime I'll find you something to wear and—'

'Eeh, no, ma'am,' she said again, clearly distressed that this lovely, kind-hearted lady, no older than herself, it seemed, should be taking so much trouble with Jenny Wainwright who had been foolish enough to fall in love with and give in to young Joel Denton's demands. 'I'll be all right,' she continued bravely. 'Me sister lives in Leeds an' 'appen she'll tekk me in if she can persuade 'er 'usband. She's bairns of 'er own an' . . .' She faltered, for none knew better than she what her sister's husband would say.

'Nonsense, Jenny. There is room for you here until—'

'They wouldn't stand it, ma'am,' Jenny said simply.

'Who?'

'Them lasses in't kitchen. They'd not work alongside me. I'm best lookin' fer work . . . well, in Leeds. I'm good for a few months yet and—'

'And then what, Jenny? Even if you could work until your child is born how will you find work and, more to the point, if you find it, how will you manage it with a child? Now, get yourself out of bed and sit by the fire while I go and find something for you to wear.'

Jenny looked about her at the pleasant room. She had, of course, as a housemaid, been in a room such as this before but only to clean it. Now she noticed the good fire in the grate which Kizzie had replenished while she slept, the comfortable rocking-chair before it, the plain but good furniture, the clean white nets at the window and the soft carpet on the floor. There was even a bowl of roses on the dressing table.

Jenny began to cry. A soft sobbing that spoke of her utter hopelessness in the face of her desperate situation. Charlotte longed to put her arms about her, comfort her, for she was such a fragile little thing and how was she to cope with what lay ahead of her? She had soft silver curls that fell to her shoulders, shining after her bath. She was small, ethereal with delicate features and pale blue-grey eyes. Her neck was long and slender, her shoulders narrow; she had thin wrists and long-fingered hands and Charlotte could see why a man, any man, would find her attractive. She also wondered how such a fragile little creature had managed to do the hard work expected of a housemaid!

She stood up briskly. 'Now, before you go chasing off to this job you are so certain is yours, you will have a decent meal and an outfit to put on. Unless you mean to traipse across Yorkshire in that nightgown. My friend, who is also a servant in this house and so is not grand or inclined to despise you or she would not be my friend, will show you where you are to stay.

Yes, stay, for until your child is born you are going nowhere. I will brook no arguments, Jenny. Can you sew?' she asked suddenly.

'Yes, ma'am. I was to become Miss Marian's maid until they discovered . . .'

'Good, then you can earn your keep by sewing, looking after my clothes and . . . and Robbie is always tearing something or other.'

'Robbie, ma'am?' Jenny's eyes had begun to shine through her tears.

'My little brother. Now I'll go and find you something to wear.'

As she walked briskly towards the bedroom she shared with her husband her heart quailed, because in the challenge of caring for this poor deserted creature who had stumbled into her life she had forgotten she still had the problem of how she was to break it to Brooke.

# 9

He came tearing into the house seeming to be in much the same rage as he had left it. She was still upstairs with Jenny but the sound of his horse's hoof-beats scattering the gravel on the drive alerted her to his arrival. Percy, realising his master's mood, came running in a lather round the corner of the house to grab Bruno's reins, then the sound of the front door banging violently to brought Charlotte to the top of the stairs. She held a bundle of clothing in her arms, dresses she had foraged from her wardrobe hoping to find something for Jenny, something simple, suitable for a maidservant.

She didn't know how to address him. Where have you been all evening? Why did you not come home? The memory of last night – was it only last night? – and the expression on his face when she had taken Robbie's hand and moved towards the door with the intention of putting him to bed, was still fresh in her memory and she was sorry, for she knew she had been in the wrong. Robbie could easily have gone with Kizzie and she, Charlotte, should have remained with her husband then none of this would have happened.

She smiled hopefully, not knowing how the smile tore at his heart. He had spent the night at his club in Wakefield, drinking and brooding and declining the offers of other members to engage him in the sort of games they played there. A game of poker perhaps, Jack Ackroyd suggested, wondering why Brooke Armstrong, with a young and pretty wife at home, was lounging in the smoke room with a glass of brandy in his hand. Billiards was discussed but Armstrong politely declined, burying his nose in his brandy glass.

'Brooke, you're home,' she said, shifting the garments from one arm to the other.

'As you see. I think a change of clothing is in order.' He moved up to the top of the staircase and she stood to one side to allow him to pass.

'I was just . . .' she began.

'Yes?'

'Sorting through some of my things. I have so many dresses and this girl . . .'

'Girl?' He moved towards the open door of their bedroom, clearly not interested.

She followed him hesitantly. 'She came to the kitchen door this morning. Very young and in . . . in trouble; so I said . . . well, I told her she . . . Mrs Groves was furious but it wasn't altogether the girl's fault and I felt so sorry for her. Mrs Groves isn't speaking to me and the others . . . Oh, I hope you won't tell me to turn her out because really, I would have to . . . to disobey.'

At the door to their room he stopped and slowly turned to face her. His face was totally without expression and she, who had been right behind him, clutching her armful of dresses, almost bumped into him. Her spirits sank, for though she knew he was a good man, generous and kind-hearted – look at the way he had put up with Robbie's tantrums all these weeks – he was her husband and the master of this house. If he said no how would she manage to help poor Jenny, poor pretty Jenny whose silvery curls and slender figure had attracted the attention of young Master Joel Denton?

'Would you like to explain what the hell you are talking about?' he asked her coldly.

'Oh, Brooke, I'm sorry about last night, really I am and you were right to be angry.' She said it placatingly and again his heart hurt him. His love for her, the protective tenderness in which he longed to wrap her burned within him and he thought he didn't give a damn what she was after, since it was clear it was *something*; he would gladly let her have it if only she would go on looking at him as she was doing now. But instead he continued in the same cool vein.

'What do you want, Charlotte?' he asked abruptly.

'Well, it's not for me but for this poor girl who came to the kitchen door today,' she continued eagerly. 'The other servants despise her and I know they won't work with her so I thought that if you would let me I would put her in the . . . well, they said it was called the Dower House and she could sew for me. She was to be a lady's maid, she said, before Lady Denton found out about her condition and when Jenny, that's her name, told them it was Joel who had seduced her Lady Denton went wild and turned her out. That was a week ago—'

'The Dower House,' he interrupted and the way he said it made her heart sink. 'My grandmother lived in the Dower House when my grandfather died and my father brought my mother as a bride to King's Meadow. That is what it is for. To house the mistress of King's Meadow when a new bride comes. It is not for housing pregnant maidservants, which you seem to be telling me, maidservants who are no better than they should be, so I would be glad if you would give the girl some money and send her on her way. That is the end of it, Charlotte, and now I shall have a bath and some lunch and ride out to see Jack Emmerson's bull which is to service my . . . well, that is hardly a subject for young ladies so—'

'I can't believe you said that, Brooke. No, not about the bull but about Jenny. Are you so pitiless that you would—'

'Please do as I say, Charlotte. I presume you have fed this . . . this girl and are to put her in one of your dresses so if you would get on with it we will forget it.'

'Oh, no,' she hissed, 'we will not forget it.' Her fury exploded so quickly she herself was surprised. Brooke took a hasty step back as she advanced on him. 'You will have to throw me out with her, for I will not have this child – she is but seventeen – turned out to fend for herself while that . . . that bastard who got her in the family way gets off scot-free. I am amazed by your attitude, for I mistakenly thought you were different from the *gentlemen* with whom you mix. I imagined that if you had done the same as Joel Denton you would at least have made some provision for . . . for the mother of your child but it seems you are the same as the rest. I shall put Jenny in the Dower House and there she will stay until her child is born and then she shall choose what she wants to do. The child can be adopted if Jenny wishes or she shall keep it and I will help her in whatever she chooses to do. She is in a room upstairs and when she is dressed she will go to the Dower House and Kizzie will go with her.'

She was panting with fury and Brooke felt the hot rage and the even hotter passion rise in him. He wanted to tear the dresses from her arms, drag her to the bed and take her like a common whore. Throw her down, fling her skirts about her head, tear down her drawers and subjugate her to his will. *His will.* God, she was quite glorious in her madness, that magnificent, recalcitrant mass of her hair flowing about her head and shoulders like a banner, but he had had years in the army where discipline and self-control had been instilled into him.

He turned away as though in complete indifference. He had spoken. His word was law and he expected it to be obeyed. She glared at his back for several moments then whirled away and ran from the room. He heard her footsteps run along the hallway and up the stairs to the next floor. A door banged and then there was silence. His whole body sagged and his chin sank to his chest. Dear sweet Jesus. First that blasted boy, her brother, and now this. What was he to do? He could not bear the thought that she might do as she threatened and run off with this girl. He didn't think she would but she had been so white-hot with anger, with him and his absolute refusal to see this her way that she had said the first thing that came into her head. Hadn't she?

Well, bugger it, give her time to come to her senses and realise that it just would not do and everything would get back to normal. Whatever normal was. They were neither of them happy, he admitted to himself. She had not wanted him as a husband and he, in his eagerness to have her for his wife, had mistakenly believed that once she was his, in his bed as she was in his heart, he could make her love him as he loved her. Her brother would settle down, find his own life, his own friends at school and would barely impinge on the life he and Charlotte would have together. Not only had that *not* taken place but now she had dragged in some creature from the streets and proposed to give her a home until the slut's child was born. Sweet Jesus, what was he to do?

He wandered to the window, pushing his hand through his hair, staring sightlessly across the deepening autumn land-scape, his mind busy and yet at the same time not really focusing on the problem, since it seemed insoluble, when a movement caught his attention. Two women walking slowly across the gravel towards the wrought-iron gate in the wall that divided the main house from the Dower House. A third woman followed carrying a great bundle of what looked like clothing. The three had evidently just come from the front door, which stood directly below the windows of the bedroom he shared with Charlotte.

Charlotte had her arm about the figure of a girl who was so thin the bulge of her belly seemed enormous and following them was Kizzie, like a shepherd guarding two of her flock and making sure they reached the safety of the fold. They passed through the gate and vanished from his sight. He pressed his forehead against the glass of the window and groaned. Then he turned violently and headed for the bathroom. He ran the bath, stripped off his clothes and plunged into the water, lathered himself, washed his unruly hair, leaped from the bath, towelled himself dry, flung on his breeches, a warm jumper, his riding boots and ran from the room as though devils were after him, which he felt they were.

He badly startled the servants in the kitchen as he raced through, then did the same to poor Percy who had only just finished settling Bruno and was grumbling to Arch about the master, who was definitely not himself lately.

'Fetch Bruno,' he shouted.

'But, sir, he've only just . . .' the bewildered groom gabbled.

'Never mind, Max will do and be quick about it.'

The four dogs, including Taddy, excited by the unexpected outing, followed him, barking madly. He galloped across the park, which was studded with enormous oak trees, until he reached the woodland and it was here that he finally felt the madness slowly ebb from him as he began to notice the onset of autumn and the hint of winter to come. He loved this place and the peace and emptiness of it reached into him, steadying the wild thoughts of his lovely wife and her seeming inability to return any of the feelings he had for her. She was friendly, polite and accepted his attentions in their bed with equanimity. But that was all!

He sat on a fallen tree trunk and looked about him, the dogs sprawled at his feet with the exception of Taddy who was too young to lie down calmly with the others. They watched him tolerantly. The sun was low in the sky and drifts of leaves littered the ground and Taddy snuffled and dug vigorously in them. Brooke noticed there was some fine timber in the park itself: a group of birch trees looked quite glorious, the tiny leaves on the pendant branches resembling showers of gold. Taddy barked frantically and chased a rabbit foolish enough to pop its nose over a clump of grass. There was a flock of thrushes and finches busy with hawthorn berries and a wood-pecker laughed somewhere. The dogs cocked their ears and with a sigh, one now of peace, Brooke rose, called to Taddy and unhurriedly mounted Max, directing him towards the edge of the wood and home.

A fire was brightly burning in the kitchen range and a basket of logs stood beside it. The kitchen was old, almost what might be called a cottage kitchen with a floor tiled in pinks and browns and creams, well scrubbed. The previous occupants, Brooke's grandmother and those before her, had been ladies and had never entered this part of the house but those who had, the kitchen-maid, the cook, the housemaid who had looked after them, had never been asked if it suited them. They had, after all, come from cottages with kitchens similar to this. An enormous dresser was crammed on every shelf with good, hard-wearing English stoneware in pleasing patterns of trailing willow, enough, Charlotte thought, to cater to a staff of a dozen. Dinner plates, side plates, cups, saucers, soup tureens, gravy boats, sugar bowls and milk jugs, all obviously meant to be used by the servants. The range was blackleaded, its brass handles were polished to shining magnificence, and it was set in a sort of chimney space. Above it a wide shelf held meat platters, candlesticks, big jugs and a colourful vase in which someone had placed a few humble wild flowers. From the shelf hung bunches of herbs, which filled the room with their fragrance. There were three rocking-chairs with padded cushions in a cheerful scarlet and four rush-seated chairs surrounded a big, well-scoured, oblong table.

'I must remember to praise Mrs Dickinson when I return, Kizzie. I must say she has kept this place spotless. Now, you sit there, Jenny,' placing the speechless girl in one of the rockers before the fire, 'while Kizzie and I look at the rest of the house to see which bedrooms you are to use. Now don't start that again,' as Jenny began to cry. 'There's no need for it.' Charlotte knelt at Jenny's feet and took her hands in hers. 'You shall make yourself useful in many ways, won't she, Kizzie? You shall have good food and when your baby comes . . . oh, please, Jenny, don't . . .' for the girl cried as though her heart would break and even Kizzie, who thought her young mistress was out of her mind, felt the compassion well in her. What with one thing and another, the master being furious at the whole event, which he was sure to be, and then the problem of young Master Robbie, Miss Charlotte was storing up a lot of trouble for herself.

Charlotte was wise enough to send Robbie over to the Dower House to 'see if you can help Kizzie and the new girl Jenny who badly need the services of someone like yourself. And have your dinner with them, if you like,' which flattered him enormously. She dressed carefully in one of her new evening gowns, a pale duck-egg blue, low-cut to reveal the slope of her white breasts and inclined to slip off one shoulder. In her hair she had threaded a duck-egg-blue satin ribbon, leaving curls to tumble beguilingly about her neck and shoulders. She felt sly in a way, for she was aware she was dressing to please Brooke but when she entered the drawing room where he was standing by the fireplace, one arm along the mantelshelf, a glass of brandy in his hand, she could see he was charmed. She was ashamed really, something of a fraud, artful, she supposed she would have called it in another woman, lulling Brooke into a false sense of . . . well, she didn't even know what she meant. She only knew she wanted him to be in a better frame of mind than he had been this morning. 'There are more ways of killing a cat than choking it to death with cream.' Now who had said that to her? It seemed a bit foolish but she knew what she meant and if she was to get her own way in this – *in what?* – she must have Brooke's approval, even if it was reluctantly given.

'You look very nice, Charlotte, very nice indeed. That colour suits you. Now, would you like a drink: sherry, perhaps, or . . .?'

'Sherry would be lovely.' Then before she had time to think or even wonder at her own daring, she moved across the carpet to stand before him. Reaching up she placed her mouth on his and kissed him lingeringly. She felt him respond at once and for a moment she knew only brilliant happiness. His mouth was smiling beneath hers. His arms came round her, his hands clasped one another in the small of her back and he strained her to him. Their lips folded and caressed, for Charlotte had learned many things about the human body and what pleases it from her husband in their bed since that first awkward night and though she had never reached that strange rousing that Brooke did, she knew she had the power to stir it in him. His mouth wandered down her chin and the lovely arch of her neck. Her head went back and she made a small sound in her throat which he answered helplessly. This was the first time since their marriage that she had begun what seemed to be the preliminaries to making love and she could sense he was delighted. His hand fell to her naked shoulder, pushing down the neck of her gown and exposing the lovely, rosy-peaked globe of her breast. His lips took the nipple and bit gently and for some reason Charlotte began to moan and a delicate filament in the pit of her stomach unfurled and shivered. For a moment Brooke lifted his head, turning it as though looking round for somewhere to lay her, but at that moment the door burst open and in flew a small figure, babbling and laughing excitedly at the same time. Hastily Brooke covered his wife's nakedness and thrust her behind him protectively to give her time to put herself together. She had begun to laugh quietly and for some reason the sound infuriated him.

'. . . she's ever so nice, Charlie, and said that any time I wanted to I could go over to see her. The Dower House, it's called . . . no, get down, Taddy, for goodness sake,' as the young dog had come in with the boy and the pair of them seemed to make up a whirlwind that threatened the safety of the many pretty ornaments that stood on low tables about the room. 'Have you been over there, Charlie? It's lovely and she – she's called Jenny – is going to stay there with Kizzie. D'you suppose I could live there, too?'

'What a bloody good idea,' Brooke roared, startling both Charlotte and the boy, but Robbie was in no way dismayed. He had found a new friend who seemed to like him and he liked her and he could not wait to tell Charlie all about it.

'Anyway,' he went on, 'get *down*, Taddy . . . what do you think?'

'Well, for a start you will get that animal off the drawing room sofa and remove him to the stable where he belongs with the other dogs. Dear God, you don't find *them* leaping about in the house.'

'Well, you don't let them,' Robbie began, ready for a fight since he had expected to be greeted with his sister's usual loving interest in his concerns.

'Isn't it time you were in bed, boy?' Brooke asked from between clenched teeth. He had the most painful swelling in the crotch of his breeches and his breath was not yet steady from the delightful and totally unexpected advances of his wife. She had been lovely in his arms, for some reason not at all the acquiescent young woman he had known in the past months. Exciting, *excited*, eager, whimpering in her throat as though begging him to take her but now this little sod had, as usual, spoiled it all and she was ready to laugh, *to laugh* at his exploits and even, he thought, to make excuses for him.

'Oh, Brooke, let him tell us what he has been doing. I haven't seen him all day. Now then, darling,' turning to her young brother who ran into her arms followed by the puppy.

'Tell me all about your new friend. Brooke and I are about to have dinner and—'

Brooke strode across the carpet and rang the bell with such force it nearly came away from the ceiling. Both Charlotte and Robbie watched him in amazement and when a breathless Nellie knocked on the door and entered bobbing a curtsey her master snarled at her.

'Where is that woman who has the boy in her care? What's-her-name?'

'Kizzie, sir?' Nellie bobbed another curtsey just to be on the safe side.

'Fetch her here at once.' He glared round the room and Robbie huddled next to Charlotte which further incensed her husband.

'She's over at Dower 'Ouse, sir, wi'—'

'Yes, yes, well, send for her immediately. It is time Master Robert was in his bed and—'

''E 'asn't 'ad 'is supper yet, sir,' Nellie was unwise enough to say.

'I believe he has had something and if he hasn't Kizzie can give him what he needs. Now look sharp, woman. My wife and I are waiting to dine.'

Again Nellie curtseyed then scuttled from the room.

'He's in a tearing temper,' she told the others, managing to speak without dropping her aitch.

'He were in one this mornin' an' all. What's he want?'

'Someone's ter fetch Kizzie an' get Master Robbie ter bed. Not that lad's happy about that, I can tell yer, an' that dog's enough ter give yer the screaming ab-dabs, yappin' an' . . . oh, fer the Lord's sake, Rosie, run over ter't Dower House an' fetch Kizzie or there'll be murder done in't drawin' room.'

They ate the delicious meal Mrs Groves had prepared for them, barely speaking. Brooke Armstrong was not a man to make small talk and every attempt on Charlotte's part to start a conversation was brusquely parried.

'We'll take coffee in the drawing room, Johnson,' he told the butler. He stood up and politely held his wife's chair, took her hand and led her, somewhat bemused, in to the drawing room where, when they were settled with their coffee and the servants had left, he addressed her coldly.

'Why should you feel the need to dress tonight, Charlotte? Usually you run in to the dining room in whatever you happen to have on. More often than not in your riding clothes but tonight, for some reason, you are beautifully dressed, correctly dressed and I wonder why.'

He had lit a cigar and as he waited for her answer he blew a perfect smoke ring up to the ceiling.

She smiled defiantly. 'Well, and why shouldn't I put on one of the lovely gowns you bought me in Paris. I particularly like this one—'

'The truth if you please,' he interrupted her, dragging on his cigar.

'That is the truth.'

'You wanted to impress me, did you not? To please me. To – what is the expression? – soften me up, so that you could persuade me to let you have your way on this new scheme you have devised.'

'It is not some scheme, Brooke, or if it is then I think it is a charitable one. That girl out there has been wronged.'

'It takes two, my dear Charlotte, unless she is claiming young master Denton raped her.'

'No, she is not but he lied to her. He is to go to university and told her she was to go with him. He would put her in a cottage where she would have their child but when his mother questioned him he said that Jenny had made it all up. It is disgraceful . . .'

'It is disgraceful, if it is true.'

'Brooke, how can you say that. She is—'

'Clever, I would say. She has deceived you and thinks herself to be lying in a bed of roses but that is not my problem. What I don't like, Charlotte, are your efforts to deceive me.'

She was shocked. 'I have not deceived you, Brooke. You were not here and—'

'Is it not a deception to dress up like a—' he almost said whore but stopped himself in time. The bitterness and disappointment of an hour ago when he had been triumphant in his belief that the gown and the embrace, the kisses, were from her heart, that she truly felt what he did, were like ashes in his mouth. 'It has all been done to slither me quietly into something I might be sorry for. A woman in my grandmother's house, a woman bearing an illegitimate child, perhaps more than one, for when it gets abroad that young Mrs Armstrong is offering a comfortable bed under a dry roof and food galore, all the prostitutes in Wakefield, Leeds and Huddersfield will come flocking.'

'No, no, that will not happen and besides, if they are as badly done to as Jenny, then let them come.'

'If you want something, Charlotte, ask me for it, honestly. I cannot bear you to come up on the sly . . .'

'*Sly*, I am not sly.' She was incensed. She stood up, trembling with rage and dishonour. 'I don't know how I got the idea but I always thought you were a generous man, with a good heart, but it seems I was wrong. But hear this. I will not put Jenny out nor will I turn away from my door any woman in need.'

He was consumed with a black snarling anger as he reached for her. Sweeping her from her feet he lifted her into his arms and slammed through the drawing room doorway, knocking Nellie, who had come to see if more coffee was needed, to one side as he raced up the stairs. He shouldered his way into their bedroom and with an inarticulate cry threw her on the bed, stripped first himself then her and for the first time since their wedding night made her cry out in a voice that could be heard in the silent kitchen. Well, if mistress wasn't with child by morning it wasn't for want of trying on master's part!

# IO

The servants were to be disappointed, as was their master when, during the following months it was made clear that the mistress was not with child. When she was not over at the Dower House, which the servants quickly got used to, she rode out most days on Magic, *astride*, which Mrs Dickinson and Mrs Groves grieved over, for how was she to give the master a son – which was everyone's hope – if she was forever galloping about the park. It was well known that riding jiggled a woman's inside about allowing nothing to settle, meaning the heir to King's Meadow. Mind you, it certainly kept young Master Robbie happy to ride with his sister at the weekend and Percy was heard to say the boy was becoming a grand little horseman. He was allowed to ride out on his own now and was a different lad from the mardy kid who had come with his sister to King's Meadow on her marriage last June. The tenant farmers kept an eye on him when he played with their children round the farmyard and the fields and his one wish was to join the hunt with his brother-in-law and his own father who was Master of Foxhounds. When he was a year or two older, the master told him, he might consider it and in the meanwhile stop sulking!

That was another thing the master and mistress had argued about. His schooling! It was not the thing for a boy of his social standing to go to the village school although it certainly made life easier for every one of the staff since the boy had started to attend the school where the children of the tenants went. Well, as the mistress said to the master, and Nellie overheard it, her brother was no scholar and he would be off to join his brothers in a year or two where he would learn to be a little gentleman. At the grammar school he made no friends other than Webb but Webb lived some distance away and could not be expected to come over to King's Meadow to play with Robbie except infrequently. In the meanwhile, if she was to make life easier between herself and her husband the boy must have friends of his own age closer to King's Meadow and the grammar school in Dewsbury was too far away.

Before she made her final decision Charlotte drove the little gig into the village of Overton with the idea of investigating the standard of education at the school which the children of their tenants and the village children attended. It stood on the main road with a bare playground to the front and on the ground hopscotch squares were painted and skipping ropes were available, plus whips and tops which suggested that some enterprising person had made an effort not only to teach children but to make their play more varied. She was pleasantly surprised. She had expected a sort of mix between Dame and Sunday school but the Education Act some thirty years ago had led to the first state schools and this was one of them.

'May I help you?' a pleasant voice asked her as she stood hesitantly in the doorway. A young woman in her mid-twenties wearing a dark, serviceable dress with a white apron over it stood in the doorway of a classroom. She could hear childish voices chanting what she was later to learn were verses from the *Child's Easy Reading Book* dating back to mid-Victorian times but found to be very effective.

> *Higgledy, Piggledy, my black hen,*
> *She lays eggs for gentlemen,*
> *Sometimes nine and sometimes ten.*
> *Higgledy, Piggledy, my black hen,*

*One, two, three, four, five,*
*Once I caught a fish alive,*
*Six, seven, eight, nine, ten,*
*Then I let it go again.*
*Why did you let it go?*
*Because it bit my finger so.*
*Which finger did it bite?*
*This little finger on the right.*

The book was a mixture of pictures, of the hen, the eggs, the fish and the finger, with the numbers in figures and letters and was surprisingly effective in teaching the children, she was to learn from the young woman who had accosted her. Miss Seddon had been born in Overton and had attended the school in which she was now the headmistress. At the age of twelve, ambitious, bright and clever, she had become a monitor which meant a teaching assistant. When she was thirteen she had become a pupil teacher. At great sacrifice from her family she had entered the Queen's Scholarship Examination and as a successful candidate she had won a place on a real teaching training course and with a first-class qualification she had returned to the school where she had begun her education.

There was an infant class up to the age of six. A dozen or so well-scrubbed but ragged children were crammed on benches in varying degrees of boredom with, here and there, a bright child eager to learn, all in charge of a pupil teacher. Another larger classroom housed the older children. Both rooms had narrow windows, purposely high so that the children could not see out of them and be distracted and here, thanks to the improvements fought for by Miss Seddon, two children shared a dual convertible desk. The walls were painted a plain white but were covered with paintings by the children. The only defect in this otherwise well-set-up school was the heating. It was December and the cast-iron stove provided the only warmth in the main classroom. The children all wore their outdoor clothing, as did Miss Seddon.

Charlotte was impressed with Miss Seddon and with the girl who taught the infants and while Miss Seddon's monitor took over her class, she and Miss Seddon, who thought she could see a benefactor in the wife of the wealthiest landowner in the parish, discussed young Robbie Drummond's future schooling and it was decided that he would begin lessons at the Overton village school after Christmas.

Robbie was delighted. He could ride his pony to school, as did the friends he had made with Jack Emmerson's lad, and the offspring of Cec Eveleigh, Davy Nicholson from Primrose Farm and the sons of Jeff Killen of Foxworth. He was settling in and with his new routine and the attachment he had formed with Jenny Wainwright who was getting close to her time and needed, she told him, someone to fetch and carry things for her and generally be her friend since she had no other, they saw less and less of him in the big house. Whenever Brooke was out of the place, hunting, shooting with friends, riding his acres, fishing his trout stream and inspecting his farms, Charlotte spent time with Jenny and, with a sigh of relief, the servants relaxed in the general atmosphere of calm that now pervaded King's Meadow.

It was in January that Charlotte, walking round to the Dower House on a bright, frosty morning, first got what she called her revelation. She had been made love to by her husband every night since the terrible day of Jenny's arrival and Brooke's explosion of rage over Robbie. She realised that he desperately wanted a son, wondering at the same time why gentlemen were so obsessive about it but supposed it was only natural that an heir was needed to continue the line. She also realised that every night he was unconsciously stamping his own possession of her. She obliged him willingly, remembering that wild night when he had carried her upstairs and, she decided, he had almost raped her but at the same time knew that was not so. He had brought her to a height of what she could only call exhilaration. She knew no word to describe how she felt but for that one time only she had matched Brooke in his explosive and, to her, unaccountable frenzy. He had kissed her cheeks, her mouth, the outline of her ears and throat, the length of her breastbone and thighbone, turning her this way and that, totally absorbed until her body was ready to dissolve into his, to flow over him and through him. She was lost, bemused and when he entered her in a turbulence of male joy she had shouted out her own. She had been mindlessly content but it had never happened again and she thought that perhaps she was trying too hard to achieve it.

The ground was hard with frost and the sun was a hazed pink disc in the sky. Smoke drifted from the Dower House chimneys and the grass on which she walked was stiff and crisp beneath her feet. There were pink flushes on the frozen soil and each twig and blade sparkled separately as the sun caught them in its brightening pink glow. The world was so crisp you could almost hear it crackle, she thought as she knocked on the door and entered the house. There was a blazing fire in the grate and Jenny sat before it, sewing serenely, her face placid and plump, for the months she had spent at King's Meadow had produced in her not just the normal weight of a pregnant woman but the bonny bloom that was naturally hers and which hard work and worry had denied her.

Kizzie sat opposite her but rose immediately to 'mash' the tea or would Miss Charlotte like a cup of chocolate? she asked.

They sipped contentedly, the three women, for when Master Robbie was at school this was a solely female establishment.

'What are you making, Jenny? I should have thought you had enough baby garments to clothe the whole village by now.'

Jenny smiled. She did all Miss Charlotte's sewing, mending torn hems, darning Master Robbie's socks, repairing the rips in his breeches and even embroidering motifs on Charlotte's nightgowns but this was not one of those. She did exquisite sewing. She had a small pile of torn-up rags in a basket by her side and in her lap lay a piece of what looked like hessian; she pushed through the hessian with some sort of a hook, then drew a thin strip of material selected from the pile in the basket through the hessian and out to the front.

'Nay, don't tell us tha've never sin a rag rug, Miss Charlotte,' Kizzie asked. 'We allus 'ad one in front of fire at 'ome. That way tha' use up all yer old bits o' material from clothes what are no use ter wear. Mind, this 'un is what Jenny calls a "wall 'anging". She's gonner purrit on t'wall on a sorta frame. Isn't that right, chuck?' Kizzie had become rather fond of Jenny in the months she had lived with her.

Jenny nodded and held up her work for Charlotte to see.

'Why, Jenny, that's quite lovely. Where did you get the design?'

'She medd it up 'erself. Drew it on t' hessian and then follers the outline with that there 'ook.' Kizzie was as proud as punch of her clever protégée just as though the whole thing was her idea and it was then, with Kizzie obviously made up with her relatively new position, confident and doing all the talking, for Jenny was still a shy little thing, that Charlotte began to form her idea. That was all it was. Not even an idea really, just a little light shining in the darkness of her mind. What Jenny was to do when her baby was born had not yet been discussed. She would not give up her child, she had said stoutly, but somehow she must earn a living. No matter what Charlotte said or did or how she pleaded in the kitchen with the maidservants, it was very evident that Jenny and her illegitimate child would never be accepted by them, not even as a lowly scullery-maid.

★     ★     ★

Charlotte had taken an instant liking to the young teacher at the school in Overton and trusted her to put as much learning into Robbie as he was capable of imbibing. He was happy and no longer clung to her as the only stable thing in his rocky world, or the world he had once known. He had become more confident and since he was not in his, or Charlotte's company as much, was less inclined to annoy his brother-in-law. Sometimes Charlotte rode over with him to school, not to intrude but to discuss his progress with Miss Seddon.

On this particular day Miss Seddon was occupied for a moment, but her assistant, who popped her head out of her own classroom, told her she would not be long and would Mrs Armstrong be good enough to wait in the hallway.

Miss Seddon could be seen talking earnestly to a girl who sat blubbering on the other side of her desk then, with a speed that bemused Charlotte, the girl sprang up, raced from the room and darted back down the passage to where Charlotte imagined the kitchen, if such existed, would be.

Miss Seddon stood up and came to the door, somewhat discomposed, and ushered her into her office. 'I am so sorry to keep you waiting since I know you wish to discuss your brother's progress. Do sit down. Now, Robert has become quite an asset to his class, Mrs Armstrong. He is a lively, imaginative boy and invents many games for the others to play. In this cold weather especially' – she shivered inside her rather thin grey coat – 'they have to keep on the move at playtime and I believe they are playing King Solomon's Mines of which they have never heard and Robbie, in the part of the hero, is fighting the natives. It is the children's admiration for him that has given him confidence and I believe when he moves on to public school he will cope very well. Now, if you don't mind, perhaps a cup of tea. I have a certain matter I must attend to and then I will return to continue our discussion.'

Charlotte was quite taken aback, for Miss Seddon did not appear to be quite herself, watching as she vanished up the passageway following the distraught girl.

It took only ten minutes for the matter Miss Seddon spoke of to be completed then she returned and sat down by the tiny flickering flame of her fire, drawing her coat about her. 'Very sad, very sad,' she was murmuring. 'These girls have a chance to make something more of themselves than their mothers did but they . . .' She shook her head and sighed.

'What is it, Miss Seddon?' Charlotte leaned forward and placed the lukewarm and very weak cup of tea on the desk.

'This particular girl could finish her education and then move on to her first job as a scullery-maid in a wool merchant's home on the outskirts of Halifax. Not much, but a decent start in life,' Miss Seddon told her, then watched with consternation, as did Charlotte, when the girl, a tall girl but plumper than would be expected, came from the back of the school and hurried along the passage towards the front door and out into the village street. She was weeping. Charlotte stood up and watched her go, wondering what Miss Seddon had said to upset her so.

Miss Seddon, looking even more distraught, invited Charlotte to re-seat herself. It was cold, for the only heat in the building was in the big schoolroom and the poor excuse for a fire in the fireplace of Miss Seddon's office. Their breath could clearly be seen about their mouths and Charlotte made up her mind then and there to do something about it.

'Anyway, to return to Robert,' Miss Seddon said. 'As I say I'm happy to tell you he is doing well and next term I am going to try him in the big class. He seems to have settled down and though he was behind the others of his age when he came he has caught up. He is happy, you see, and I believe that a happy child will flourish. I think that his . . . background' – she was trying to be diplomatic, for Arthur Drummond's reputation as a hard man was well known in Overton – 'has held him back. His friends here at the school are all . . . all from stable homes, from families where they know they are . . . well, I will say no more except he is doing well. I know he is to join his brothers at public school when he is old enough but he will be ready then to leave the . . . the safety of your love and support. He tells me they were all at King's Meadow at Christmas, his older brothers, I mean, and that you had a wizard time.' She smiled. 'His words. He is becoming a—'

'Yes, thank you, Miss Seddon,' Charlotte said somewhat impatiently, for she could not get the picture of the anguished young girl she had seen running from the school out of her mind and she was eager to know who she was and what the trouble was, though anyone with eyes in her head could see the girl was with child.

Miss Seddon blinked, since Mrs Armstrong was usually very keen to talk about her brother and after all that was why she was here, interrupting Miss Seddon's class which had been left in the charge of her monitor.

'Yes, Mrs Armstrong?'

'That young girl who ran from your office as I came in. Is she to have a baby? She seems very young and I was wondering . . .'

'Yes, very sad. She is a pupil, or was. She has been a naughty girl and I was forced to ask her to leave. The parents of my pupils are . . . well, you know the sort of problems this causes.'

'What sort of thing, Miss Seddon? Surely but for the grace of God go you and me.'

Miss Seddon looked vastly offended. 'Mrs Armstrong, I cannot believe you said that. Ruth Hardacre comes from a decent family but they are horrified at what has befallen her and have turned her out. She came to me for help.'

'Which you refused her.'

'I have no way to help her, Mrs Armstrong. This is a school not a home for fallen girls. I must think of my pupils. There is nowhere . . . nothing to be done here. I must think of the good of—'

'Where has she gone?' Charlotte rose to her feet imperiously and Miss Seddon, though she had a good heart and would help if she could, knew that Mrs Armstrong was not pleased with her.

'I told her there was a home for girls in her situation in Wakefield. There is a lying-in place for when she is brought to bed or they would take her in at the workhouse.'

'Where has she gone now, Miss Seddon, if you please? When she ran out of here where was she headed?'

'The river, she said, but of course she did not mean it.'

'How old is she?'

'Fourteen.'

'There is no river, Miss Seddon.'

'I'm sorry, Mrs Armstrong but I have a school here which is my responsibility and I can assure you if I could have helped the girl I would but . . .' Miss Seddon was genuinely sorry and very flustered, for at heart she was a kind woman. 'There is the reservoir off Moss Lane but I'm sure she did not really mean it.'

'Would you care to risk it, Miss Seddon, because I wouldn't,' and before Miss Seddon, almost weeping by now, could answer Charlotte whirled round and flew from the office and out to her gig. The patient little pony, which often drew the mower but was now elevated to pulling the gig, turned his head and whickered in welcome and when she flung herself in the gig, set off at a spanking speed along Moss Lane, having enjoyed the mouthfuls of grass he had managed to garner from the strip of vegetation in front of the school. The reservoir was on the right of the lane and even from the gig Charlotte could see that there was a thin film of ice on it. She jumped from the still moving vehicle and ran across the strip of field that divided it from the lane and was just in time to see the figure of the girl step out on to the ice and vanish beneath it.

Without thought she jumped in and grasped the girl's hair which appeared on the surface and with a great heave and a lot of rude words she had heard in her father's stables, pulled viciously until the girl, who had begun instinctively to help herself, for the mindless clinging to life was in us all, clambered on to the bank.

'You great gormless beggar. There is no reason for you to drown yourself and if we don't get you, and me, back home we'll both catch our deaths.'

'Yer shoulda left me,' the girl mumbled.

They were both shivering and Charlotte knew that they must get home as soon as possible. With her arm round the girl she dragged her, stumbling, to the gig where the pony waited for instructions. She shoved the girl, dripping and shivering, into the gig and with a quivering 'Get up, Misty,' she set off in the direction of King's Meadow.

Kizzie did not bother asking questions! This was another of Miss Charlotte's lame ducks, pregnant like the other and she wondered how many more they would have before the master put his foot down. Ruth sat in front of the roaring fire, wearing one of Jenny's capacious nightgowns, spooning broth into her mouth. She had been put in the bath, which had filled her with awe and had been struck speechless by the splendour of it all and by her luck in landing up here. She was not pretty like Jenny who was hovering round her like a mother hen, urging her to eat up but she was plump and good-natured and simple. She had obviously attracted the attention of some man several months ago but when asked who it was she could not remember.

'There were a couple who give me a bob or two, worked at colliery wi' me pa. Nice chaps,' she told them equably, causing Kizzie and Jenny to exchange glances, for at least Jenny had been in love with the gentleman who had seduced her. Ruth was evidently not a full shilling, in Kizzie's opinion, and when Miss Charlotte came over, after having a hot bath and dressed in a warm woollen gown and her good winter cloak, they sat and looked at this girl who had somehow fallen into their care.

The kitchen was in an uproar, Charlotte said, and when she had spoken sharply to them they had turned sullen.

'Mrs Armstrong, ma'am,' Mrs Dickinson had begun, clearly on her high horse. 'We're all that sorry for these girls what get themselves into trouble, though I must say an' t'others agree with me that they've only theirselves ter blame. None of my girls'd dream of allowin' any man ter interfere wi' them . . .' Mrs Dickinson was losing her grasp on the rather high-toned way of speaking on which she prided herself.

'Your girls have a steady job and a safe place of work, Mrs Dickinson. They know that their lives are sheltered and that people care about them. You care about them. Mrs Groves cares about them. This is a good place to work and I should think you would be ashamed of yourself for the unchristian way you treat Jenny and Ruth.'

'Ruth, is it?' Mrs Dickinson tossed her head but Charlotte walked out of the kitchen with her own head held imperiously high and what Mrs Dickinson had to say on the subject of Ruth was lost.

Ruth was not as personable as Jenny, in fact she was rather coarse. She had kicked up a fuss and caused a great deal of trouble by flinging herself dramatically in the reservoir, but that was not all. She was heard to say in Kizzie's hearing, though she didn't know Kizzie was listening at the time, that she was made up with her position at the Dower House and it was obvious she was not in the least interested in learning the art of rug-making which Jenny promised to teach her.

'Wha' for?' she asked. 'I like it 'ere wi' nowt ter do an' that lad in't stable's not 'alf bad. I could earn meself a bob or two if—'

She was astonished to find her ear caught in the sharp pincers of Kizzie's fingers.

'D'yer know 'ow lucky you are 'avin' a good 'ome like this wi' you in the state yer in, lady? Mrs Armstrong shoulda left yer in bloody reservoir in my opinion an' if I 'ear yer've bin seen 'angin' about stable lads I'll 'ave yer outer 'ere afore yer can say "knife". Is that clear?'

The next day Ruth had gone and Nellie, in Wakefield on her day off, reported triumphantly she had seen her on the arm of some burly chap, drunk as a lord!

# I I

It had snowed in the night, a light fall which had frozen the moment it touched the ground and the gardens were a silvery delight, sparkling in the winter sunshine, but it was not a morning to linger.

Charlotte, Kizzie and Jenny were sitting with their knees up to the kitchen fire, the three of them sipping a cup of hot chocolate. Charlotte was complaining that even on the short journey from the big house to the Dower House her nose had gone dead and it hurt her to breathe the air was so cold. Everywhere had been silent on her walk from the back kitchen door − accompanied by the disapproving glances of the servants − through the stable yard, across the vegetable garden to the kitchen door of the Dower House, a strange hard silence as though even the trees, the wintry plants and the animal life that usually rustled about the garden were struck dumb by the iciness of the day.

The kitchen was full of steam, billowing from kettles and pans, for hot water was needed or would be very soon as Jenny was near her time. She sat in the rocking-chair, full and fecund and rosy, her silvery hair brushed and shining, a very different Jenny to the one who had begged at the back door in the autumn. The fire crackled and leaped up the chimney and Kizzie rose to check the supply of coal in the brass coal scuttle. She was the eldest in her family and was well used to the drama of birth − and death − and she knew quite positively that the girl who sat so placidly opposite her would shortly go into labour. It was an instinct brought about by the occasion of her mother's yearly confinements. Jenny had been well cared for over the last four months and was strong, sturdy, young and would stand the hard task ahead of her. She was patiently working on one of her rag rugs, in a lovely design, a perfect flower spreading in its centre. She was blending various shades of pink for the petals, two shades of yellow for the centre, worked on a large piece of hessian dyed an attractive blue for the background. The edges of the petals were outlined in black. It was quite exquisite, resembling a pink lotus, each petal shading to a darker pink at its point.

They were startled when there was a rapid tattoo on the kitchen door and without waiting for one of them to admit her and the door being unlocked, Rosie the scullery-maid burst into the kitchen, her nose like a beacon, her cheeks blazing with the cold, the shawl she had evidently thrown hastily about herself hardly enough for the frozen world through which she had obviously hurried.

'Rosie, what on earth . . .?' Charlotte began, for it was not often that the servants from the big house came here where the 'scarlet woman', meaning poor Jenny, resided.

'Oh, mum, yer ter come at once, if yer please. Mrs Groves's in a right takin' an' ses after all this time an' on a day like this 'un yer'd think she'd've kept to 'er own fireside but 'ere she is, large as life an'—'

'Rosie, what on earth are you talking about? What does Mrs Groves want with me, for goodness sake? Can you not—'

'Oh, please, mum, I've not ter stop, Mrs Groves ses, 'cos the kitchen table's only 'alf scrubbed an'—'

'What . . .'

But Rosie had turned on her heel and scampered for the door to the passage and was out and dashing across the back yard as though the hounds of hell were at her heels, which to her was what Mrs Groves, who owned her to all intents and purposes, was in the kitchen.

'I'd better go, I suppose,' Charlotte said doubtfully. 'To be summoned like this . . . it must be important.' She reached for her ankle-length fur-lined cape and threw it about herself, then, with a light touch on Jenny's shoulder, she moved towards the door. 'I won't be long,' she told them because she knew that Kizzie was expecting Jenny's labour to begin today and needed her help.

She entered the house by the kitchen door and found the place in an uproar. Mrs Dickinson and Mrs Groves had still not recovered from the sudden, though not unexpected, arrival of the mistress's three brothers from their school near York at Christmas. Big rowdy lads with appetites to match who had kept them busy from morning until evening, cooking and baking, quite apart from the normal Christmas meals. Mrs Groves said she had never made so many mince pies in her entire life and the Christmas cake, an absolute masterpiece and expected to last until Twelfth Night at least, had been demolished by the end of Boxing Day! And the muck they brought in! Despite the time of the year they had enthusiastically played *tennis*, would you believe, putting up the net and rattling round on the court until they were scarlet-faced with their exertions. The stumps and bats had been rooted out and they had had a go at cricket on the front lawn and then, with Mr Brooke's permission, had taken turns on Magic, Max, Misty and Merry and though they had never ridden in their lives owing to their father's lack of interest in them, they had put up a good performance, or so said Arch who had watched anxiously in case one of his beloved animals should be distressed. The eldest lad, who was apparently called Henry and who was sixteen, had spent the Christmas holidays with a friend in York, but the other three, William, fourteen, John, twelve and James who was eight had descended on King's

Meadow like a horde of locusts, eating them out of house and home before they had gone back to school. Robbie, excited by the presence of his brothers, had been a real handful and the master, it was plain to see, had been hard pressed to keep his temper.

Charlotte had been amazed at the difference six months away from their father had achieved. Her brothers had been confident, articulate when round the dinner table and despite their loud and bumptious ways, had become favourites with the servants. They were good boys, polite and obedient, thanks to their father's upbringing but it was a relief when they returned to school.

They did not visit their father and he did not invite them!

'It's Mrs Ackroyd, ma'am,' hissed Mrs Dickinson now.

'What is?' Charlotte asked, bewildered.

'She's come ter call. I've put her in the drawin' room. Well, with you not here I didn't know what else ter do. Her carriage is on the drive and that coachman of hers must be frozen so I—'

'Oh, bring him in, Mrs Dickinson and give him a hot drink and then I suppose you had better serve something; what do ladies drink?'

'She asked if you were "at home" and really, Mr Johnson didn't know what to say. We knew you were over there' – with a contemptuous nod of her head towards the Dower House – 'so he said you were but were . . . well, he didn't know what ter say. Yer first caller, you see, and so she—'

'Yes, very well, bring in some . . .' She was at a loss as to what was the accepted drink at this time of the day.

'Hot chocolate, ma'am?' Mrs Dickinson ventured.

'Yes, that will be warming on such a cold day. Now, I'd better go in.'

Mrs Dickinson looked quite horrified and the others exchanged glances, eyebrows raised, for what else could you expect of their decidedly unorthodox young mistress.

'Not in that gown, ma'am, I beg of you.' Mrs Dickinson and Mrs Groves were clearly appalled.

Charlotte looked down at the plain grey drill, the fabric like a stout twilled linen, that she had donned this morning. Eminently suitable for delivering babies, which she had expected to help with today, but certainly not for greeting a caller of Mrs Ackroyd's apparent standing. But surely Mrs Ackroyd would not stay long. Charlotte was eager to return to Kizzie and Jenny to whom, though she knew nothing of childbirth, she might be of invaluable help.

'What's wrong with it, for goodness sake? I am tidy and—'

'But Mrs Armstrong, Mrs Ackroyd is the wife of an influential gentleman, an acquaintance of Mr Armstrong and will expect to find you in morning attire, as she is. Very smart, if I might say so. I had occasion ter speak to her, explaining yer wouldn't be long. A lovely colour of coffee au lait, a separate bodice an' skirt with a three-quarter-length jacket of what I am sure was sable an' her hat was the very latest. Nellie gets this magazine, yer see, an' it's the thing to have bird's wings and ribbons and . . . well, she's very – what's the word, Nellie? What? Yes, that's it, "chick" but listen ter me going on. Please, ma'am, run upstairs and put on—'

'Oh, fiddle-de-dee, I haven't time to be bothered with callers today. And what I want to know is why she has taken so long to come. I have been here for nearly six months and not one lady has . . . well, I don't know what the correct procedure is since we never had callers at the Mount but I suppose . . .' She made her way towards the door that led into the hallway and was watched by them all, for was this their young mistress's introduction into society which, so far, had completely ignored her? Mrs Dickinson held her hand to her mouth since in her opinion the manners of the mistress of the house reflected on her servants and what was their caller to make of theirs?

Charlotte was seriously put out as she did not want to miss the birth of Jenny's baby and if this woman, whoever she was, detained her long it might be over by the time Charlotte returned.

Her caller was standing in front of one of the wall hangings that Jenny had done and which Charlotte, liking it so much, had hung on a wall opposite the window so that the full light fell on it. If one had not known better it might have been mistaken for a painting. It was of a carpet of bluebells under a canopy of sycamore and ash trees in the woodland at the edge of Brooke's land. It must have been spring, for the leaves of the trees were young and tender and mixed in with the bluebells were toothwort, yellow star of Bethlehem and yellow arch-angel. Jenny, of course, had never seen such a magical place but had copied something similar from a picture she had seen in a book Charlotte had retrieved from Brooke's library and the colours were glorious. The sun shone on the trunks of the trees and where it touched they were a pale reddish brown and on the other side the colour of dark chocolate. Even Brooke had admired it and made no objection to it being hung in his drawing room.

Mrs Ackroyd swung round as Charlotte entered the room. She was already sipping a cup of chocolate and was indeed as *chic* as Mrs Dickinson had described her. She was also young, pretty and smiling.

'There you are, Mrs Armstrong. I do apologise for disturbing you at what was obviously a very important task but I said to Jack I couldn't let another day go by without calling on you. I have been most remiss, I admit, but the season has kept me busy and Jack insists I accompany him, you see.'

'The season?' Charlotte faltered, quite bowled over by the friendliness of her visitor. The season was quite unknown to her though, of course, her father had barely been at home as he went about what was obviously a traditional English activity among the upper classes. Just as she knew nothing about callers and calling since her mother had died when she was so young.

'Yes, you know. You were still away when the grouse began and hunting keeps one so busy. The fox, you see, and my husband is devoted to his hounds and again insists I take an interest. This ends in March as you probably know.'

'No.'

'Then there are the point-to-points, the country race-meetings, the organised shoots and I said to Milly – Milly Pickford, you know – we really must do something for Brooke's new bride. She must surely have settled in by now, so here I am. Brooke is most remiss in allowing you to moulder away here with no sort of fun at all. Have you been presented, Mrs Armstrong? No! Really, what a rogue your father was not to . . . well, never mind. It's too late now, I suppose. Now I intend to give a dinner dance next month and I am here to extend an invitation to both you and your husband.' She smiled triumphantly and to her utter amazement Charlotte found herself liking her. For the past five months she had been involved in her own concerns, the Dower House, Jenny, her efforts to become a good horsewoman, her brothers at Christmas and the idea that was still fermenting in her mind but which she had discussed with no one nor done anything about. Now she cast her mind back to how she had managed to pass the time with no consideration for what she secretly knew were her duties to Brooke. She realised that a lady in her position should have been socialising as was the custom in her class but she had ignored her obligations, indeed had given them little thought and Brooke had not seemed to mind.

'Well, that is very kind . . .' she began but Mrs Ackroyd had turned back to Jenny's hanging.

'I was admiring this lovely thing on the wall. It took me several minutes to realise that it was not an actual oil painting.

Did Mr Armstrong's mother leave it, or perhaps do the work herself? It really is exquisite.'

Charlotte felt herself warm even more to this cheerful young woman who, she dimly remembered, had been at that dinner her father had given last year when he had announced his engagement to Miss Parker.

'No, it has been worked by a . . . a friend of mine. She is to have a . . . well, she has time on her hands and . . . but please, may I offer you another cup of chocolate?' indicating that Mrs Ackroyd might like to sit down, but her caller shook her head. She knew the rules of polite society even if her hostess didn't, rules going back into the dim and distant time of the young Queen Victoria and to which her contemporaries still adhered. A quarter of an hour's conversation only and then the hostess accompanied her visitor to the door to take leave of her. Mrs Ackroyd had left her husband's card and her own as was proper.

'Now don't forget the date, Mrs Armstrong. I'll send you a formal invitation.' And with a last smiling wave Mrs Ackroyd climbed into her carriage where her coachman held the door for her and after tucking a fur rug round her, climbed on to his seat and set off at a fast pace towards the gates.

Charlotte, her thoughts immediately winging back to Jenny, hurried down the hallway, grabbed her cape, raced past the open-mouthed servants and out of the kitchen door. She sped across the vegetable gardens and burst into the kitchen of the Dower House. Kizzie and Jenny were seated exactly where she had left them, sewing placidly. She breathed a sigh of relief.

'It was Mrs Ackroyd, Kizzie. Daft thing wants me to go to a damned ball or something but I shan't go. Brooke doesn't seem to—'

'Tha'll go, Miss Charlotte, if I'ave ter tie yer up an' tekk yer in't carriage meself.' Kizzie barely looked up from her sewing and for a moment Charlotte was speechless.

'What?'

'Tha' 'eard.'

'And what, may I ask, has it to do with you, Kizzie Aspin? If I do not care to go to some silly ball when I would much rather stay at home and—'

'An' wharrabout tha' 'usband? 'Oo, I might say, 'as been mighty patient wi' yer for the last five months. 'E's a gentleman wi' gentleman friends an' their wives an' is used ter movin' in society but out o' consideration for *you* knowin' tha' weren't used to it 'e give you all winter ter settle inter yer new position in life but now yer gotta consider 'im. It's no good pullin' tha' face at me, Miss Charlotte. You was married to 'im against yer will, I know that, but you agreed to it an' now yer've gotta play your part. Tha's a lady, married to a gentleman and that's that. Tha'll go ter this dance or whatever it is and then, when th' invitations come in yer'll accept them an' send out yer own. Lass, tha' owe it to 'im. Think on warr 'e's done fer them lads. Right!'

Charlotte sat down slowly in one of the chairs at the table and considered what Kizzie had said and knew it to be true. She had done exactly what she had wanted to do ever since she had married and had been content. She enjoyed riding and walking the dogs, her time with Robbie and her visits to the village school in which she was taking an increasing interest. Her brothers were settled. She got on quite well with the man who was her husband. In fact she rather liked him. Apart from the bed thing which she put up with since she had no choice, she was even happy at times. She had Kizzie and Jenny and when Jenny's baby was born she meant to disclose her plans for the future and they did not include gadding about frivolously from party to party. Nor giving parties and such as Kizzie was implying. She would be too busy for that. Besides, Brooke didn't seem to mind what she did and she really had no idea how *he* spent his time. She had not even seen her own father and his new bride. Brooke had not suggested she should invite them to King's Meadow, nor visit them. Really, what had anyone to complain of, particularly Kizzie?

She sighed deeply and both the young women looked up at her sympathetically.

'Well, you could be right, I suppose. I'll speak to Brooke tonight and see . . .'

'Good lass, now I'll—'

Whatever it was Kizzie was about to say, or do, was interrupted by a sudden gasp from Jenny who leaned forward in her chair and clasped her hands to the small of her back then just as quickly sat up again as the other two sprang to their feet.

'No, no, it's all right; just a twinge,' then threw herself forward again with clenched hands, pressing on the seat of the chair each side of her thighs.

'Right, that's it, lass. Up the jolly old dancers wi' yer an let's get yer inter bed.' Taking both of Jenny's hands, Kizzie drew her gently from the chair and began to lead her towards the narrow hallway and the stairs, accompanied by a hovering Charlotte. Before you could say knife, Kizzie had Jenny undressed and in her bed lying on her side.

'Now, Miss Charlotte, tha'd best get tha'senn back 'ome an' leave this ter me an' Jenny,' Kizzie began but Charlotte continued to weave about the pretty bedroom, longing to help but having not the faintest idea how to go about it.

'Oh, 'ere it comes again,' Jenny moaned.

'What?' from Charlotte.

'Another pain, my lass?' asked Kizzie in a matter-of-fact voice.

'Aye.'

'See, let me rub tha' back an' you, Miss Charlotte, if tha' must stay, let Jenny 'ave a 'old of yer 'ands.'

They struggled for what seemed hours to Charlotte, both women who had never borne a child pausing reverently for the pains that Jenny received with a gasp at their peak which gave Charlotte a chance to rub her crushed fingers.

Some time later Charlotte ran downstairs to inform a worried Tess, who was under-housemaid and was knocking at the back door, sent by Mrs Groves, that she was busy and would be home when she could.

'Only master's asking after yer, ma'am,' apologised Tess. 'It bein' dark, like.'

Charlotte looked around her and was surprised to find it was so. 'Tell my husband I will be home as soon as the baby is born. I am wanted here, you see.'

Tess bobbed a respectful curtsey and scurried away into the blackness of the garden but it seemed to Charlotte that she had hardly got herself up the stairs again when another commotion in the kitchen drew her to the landing.

'What is it, for God's sake? Can you not see I'm busy?' and was amazed when Brooke's voice floated up to her and was even more amazed at his words.

'Will I send for a doctor, Charlotte? Is . . . is your friend in trouble?'

She looked down the stairs and standing at the bottom holding a lamp was her husband, still dressed in his breeches and the warm tweed jacket he wore for riding. Underneath was a long-sleeved jersey with a roll collar. His hair, which always seemed to be in need of cutting, curled about his head and over his eyebrows in a most attractive manner.

He looked up at her anxiously. 'Can I help in any way?'

Afterwards, a long time afterwards, she realised it was then that she had begun to love him.

'Ask 'ooever it is ter see ter that 'ot water, Miss Charlotte. Us'll not be long now,' just as though she and Jenny were in labour together.

Charlotte looked down the stairs into her husband's eyes. He held the lamp high and she could see an expression in them that told her, she didn't know how, or even wonder at it, that he was on her side and always would be no matter what was taking place. He had never told her of his feelings except those he felt in their bed and they were more or less unintelligible murmurings that told her of his own pleasure. There was a wariness in his face that seemed to speak of something though the words could not be spoken and she felt a stirring in her breast, a strange stirring she had never known before, but before she could drift down the stairs towards him, as she found she had a great need to do, an irritable voice from above made them both jump and the moment had gone.

'Wheer the devil's that water, our Charlotte? Will tha' get a move on. An' fetch them towels that're airin' by't fire.'

Brooke smiled. 'The voice of our leader, it seems. We had better obey, don't you think, or we might both get a smacked bottom.'

She tried to brush past him and was not surprised when he made no move to let her. As their bodies touched she was surprised by the frisson that passed between them but this was no time to be dwelling on such things. Above, a thin cry wafted down to them and they could hear Kizzie's reassuring voice murmur something. Charlotte grabbed the towels and Brooke lifted the big pan and the kettle of water which were bubbling away on the fire. Together they climbed the stairs and entered the bedroom where Kizzie was telling Jenny, 'Push, girl, that's it, my lass. Soon be over . . .' Jenny bore down on the pain and both Charlotte and Brooke froze to the spot in awe. Jenny lay with her legs asprawl and as they watched a dark crown appeared, then an ancient face screwed up in what seemed to be annoyance. The child gave a great yell as it almost bounded on to the bed, trailing the cord and Charlotte began to cry in wonderment. She reached for Brooke's hand and found it waiting for her.

'How beautiful . . . how beautiful,' she wept, then turned her face into her husband's shoulder, glad of his arms about her.

Kizzie, whom nothing seemed to faze, ordered them about as though she were the mistress and they her servants and it was not until Jenny was sitting up, rosy and placid and lovely with her daughter in her arms that she turned in her astonishment to view her master and mistress, both dishevelled but awed by what they had seen here this night.

'Well, tha' did right well, both on yer, an' thank the Lord fer a ·lass.'

They walked back through the dark, hand in hand. They used the back kitchen door and as they closed it to behind them they were just too far away to hear the arrival of Ruth at the Dower House. She had her newborn child in her arms, the cord still trailing from its navel!

# 12

They had barely reached their bedroom, both of them charged with some sort of energy brought about by the birth of Jenny's child and which both were aware heralded a new momentum in their relationship when, closing the door hurriedly behind them, Brooke put his arms around her and drew her fiercely against him. He was murmuring something, she couldn't make it out, but with a breathless gasp she burrowed herself deeper and deeper into him, her head thrown back as his lips travelled along her jaw line and down her throat.

She did not wait for him to help her but began to unbutton the bodice of her dress, at the same time doing her best to keep as close to him as this allowed. He was fumbling with the fastenings of her skirt, pushing it down to her hips from where it fell to the floor, then it was her underwear until she was totally naked except for her shoes. He lifted her up and she draped her legs about his waist, her arms tight about his neck, the singing pleasure of it coursing through her, quite overcome by the sensation which she had known only once before.

'Darling . . . darling . . .' he was moaning. 'I must . . . let me put you down for a minute . . .' his voice harsh in his throat. She helped him, tearing at his shirt collar, his breeches, his underclothes, kneeling at his feet to struggle with the confusion of underdrawers and boots, both of them laughing as she did her best to get the former over the latter. When he was as naked as she was they stood for a moment to gaze wonderingly at one another. She thought he was quite, quite beautiful, with the virile, masculine beauty of the male. Long, graceful legs, muscles that were flat and flowing smoothly from the curve of his chest and shoulder to the slight concavity of his belly and thigh. He was tall, powerful, dark, his body shaped by the life he had led as a soldier and the outdoor pursuits he now enjoyed. His back was broad and his muscular forearms structured like the rest of him by the hours he spent in the saddle. His strong, handsome face, flushed with passion, had broad cheekbones and a solid jaw and his mouth was firm, even hard, but it had a sensual lift at the corner which spoke of humour. His silvery grey eyes, had, at this moment, darkened with his lusty need of her but what spoke more tellingly was the lordly lift and thrust of his loins.

He dragged her into his arms and she began to make a soft mewing sound in her throat as she pressed even closer to that wondrous, unexpected moment that both of them longed for. He almost threw her on to the bed and she gloried in his roughness. His face strained triumphantly above hers and she reached up with her teeth to worry his lips and at that moment there was a light tap at the door. They were so engrossed in the magic, the suddenness, the whipping up of their greed for one another they did not hear it, but when it came again, louder this time, it percolated through the passion, the heat, the ardour and Brooke lifted his head from her rosy nipple and roared his frustration.

'What the bloody hell . . .' He had been about to take this changed wife of his, plunge himself into her, ravage her, though how can a woman be ravaged willingly? He only knew that he could have knocked senseless whoever was intruding on this most important moment of his life with Charlotte. 'Can we not get a bit of peace in our own room, for God's sake?' he raved.

'Brooke . . .'

'Go away,' he snarled at the closed door. 'Can't whatever it is wait until tomorrow?'

'No, sir, I'm that sorry but I must speak ter Miss Charlotte.'

It was Kizzie's voice on the other side of the door. They both slowly came from that sensual world which they had entered so astonishingly, looking in a dazed sort of way at one another, for had they not just left her with Jenny and her newborn, all of them, including Kizzie, secure in the knowledge that the birth had been achieved successfully with no complications. The child had been healthy and they had left the Dower House happy that all was well. Now here, thirty minutes later, was Kizzie asking for her mistress.

'I must see what . . .' Charlotte began but Brooke, his desire roused beyond his control, held her back. She had never refused him in the past, nor seemed unwilling, but it had been a dutiful acknowledgement to his needs, not hers. But tonight had been different and he was not about to give it up without a fight. Particularly with a servant.

'No, Charlotte. We know that mother and child are well, for we saw them no more than thirty minutes ago so there is no need—'

'Please, Miss Charlotte, ah can't manage on me own. Tha' needs ter come an' . . . well, I think tha'll need ter call doctor.'

Charlotte slipped from the bed, somewhat unsteady on her feet, and moved towards the door, conscious that her husband who had been so kind and helpful tonight had flung himself away from her with a groan.

'Dear God, am I always to come second . . .'

For a moment Charlotte hesitated, since she had also been roused, ready for what had seemed to be a new start in their marriage, a shared experience that would be agreeable to them both, but Kizzie would not have come knocking on their bedroom door for some trifling thing. Something must have happened: perhaps Jenny had begun to bleed or . . . or the baby had . . . well, she was not awfully sure what could have happened to the baby since she had had no experience with infants. She had been ten years old when Robbie was born and her mother had died and there had been servants, nurses, a doctor in attendance.

She turned for a moment to the rigid figure of her husband who lay on his back with his arm across his eyes. 'Brooke, I'm sorry, I must just see what Kizzie wants, what has happened since . . .' but he continued to lie where she had left him. If she was to go, then go she must but she was not to expect him to approve. In fact he would never forgive her! This was the first time since their marriage that she had been as mad for him as he was for her and now . . . his aching member throbbed with need and he would never forgive her if she went.

She threw on her negligee and opened the door to Kizzie who was in a state of disarray that told of something quite out of the ordinary, for Kizzie was a calm, organised young woman who let nothing much faze her. Now her hair was coming down about her face, the apron she wore had blood-stains on it and though it was as cold outside as the Arctic, she wore no coat nor even a shawl.

'What is it? Has Jenny . . .?'

'Nay, lass.' Kizzie seized her hand and began to draw her towards the head of the stairs leading down to the hallway. 'Jenny's alreet. 'Tis t'other 'un.'

'T'other 'un?'

'Aye, Ruth. 'Er what left a while back. She's 'ad 'er bairn but she's in a bad way an' theer's nowt I can do. She needs a doctor. Bairn's in a bad way an' all. Miss Charlotte, I can't manage two on 'em an' a poorly baby. Will yer telephone yer doctor?'

'I don't know a doctor, Kizzie. I've never had cause to need one.'

They both hurried down the stairs and when they reached the telephone stared at it as though it might have some answer for them but Kizzie knew they could not afford to dither because the girl, Ruth, fourteen years old and said to have taken to prostitution in the last few weeks, would bleed to death if nothing was done. Kizzie had cut the cord, separating her from her child but it, another little girl, was lying, unwashed and unattended, while Kizzie fought to save the mother's life.

Charlotte stood, gnawing on her knuckles as she struggled with this dilemma that Kizzie was expecting her to solve but really there was only one person who could point them in the right direction and he was upstairs, hating her in his frustrated anger.

There had been no mistress at King's Meadow since Brooke's mother had died, but Mrs Dickinson, that most careful of housekeepers, had left a notebook on the telephone stand, in which she had written the telephone numbers she considered might be needed in an emergency and one of them was a Doctor Chapman.

'There's a Doctor Chapman here,' she mumbled as she rifled through the pages.

'Telephone 'im, lass. Theer's no time ter waste.'

Yes, the doctor was at home, a cool voice at the other end of the line told her, but he had just got into bed and could it not wait until morning? . . . Oh, Mrs Armstrong, King's Meadow, of course, just a moment, the voice changing noticeably when it was discovered to be the wife of one of the wealthy land-owners in the district on the other end of the line.

The doctor was on his way, the voice eventually told her, coming over in the gig and would be with her in ten minutes. Could she perhaps say what . . . no, of course not, she quite understood, but by this time Charlotte had hung up and was hurrying upstairs to put on some warm clothing and Kizzie had left to return to the Dower House.

Brooke was not in their room and when she knocked timidly on the door of his dressing room his voice told her coldly that unless she was prepared to get back into her own bed with him beside her she could bugger off!

She waited at the front door of the house, conscious of Mr Johnson, the butler, hovering at the top of the staircase wondering if he could help her in any way, for the noise she and Kizzie had made had apparently awakened the rest of the servants.

'No, Johnson,' she told him absently. 'Go back to bed. I am waiting for the doctor.'

'The doctor, ma'am? Is the master taken ill?' He began to descend the stairs but she waved him away in a peremptory fashion. 'No, no, the master is well,' but is in a foul mood, she wanted to add.

'Shall I . . .?' the stately gentleman asked but Charlotte told him to go back to bed, leaving him wondering if it was not the master who was ill, and obviously not the mistress, what was wanted from a doctor.

The doctor arrived, his little gig skidding on the ice-coated gravel drive. He flung himself at the door, but Charlotte was out and had hold of his arm before he could reach it.

'This way, Doctor; Doctor Chapman, isn't it? We have not met before but I am Mrs Armstrong.' She still had hold of his arm as though afraid he would escape, dragging him hurriedly towards the gate that led to the Dower House. He looked bewildered and indeed began to struggle somewhat, since his wife had informed him as he was about to sink into a much needed sleep that Mrs Armstrong of King's Meadow was ill and here she was in the best of health, seemingly, and taking him away from the main house.

'It's one of my servants, Doctor; well, not actually that but she is a woman who needs medical attention and your name was in the book.'

*Book!* What was the woman talking about and where the devil was she taking him?

'She has just . . . well, you will see when you examine her. She is apparently losing blood.'

'Please, I beg you, Mrs Armstrong, let me get my breath. Losing blood? Has she had an accident?'

'No, a baby.' Charlotte opened the door of the Dower House and pulled him through and there was Kizzie leaning over the bedraggled figure of young Ruth who was sprawled in a chair by the fire. She had her legs wide open and Kizzie was doing her best to staunch the blood that was pumping from her, holding a great bloody mass of towels to the base of her belly. Ruth was whiter than the white, ice-coated world outside, her hair hanging about her in bloodstained draggles as though she had pushed her hands, which had been at her belly, through it.

'Dear God!' the doctor ejaculated, for a moment totally appalled, then his medical mind took over and pushing Kizzie out of the way he knelt down and proceeded to work between Ruth's legs while Kizzie and Charlotte watched in wonder.

'More towels and hot water,' he ordered. He took instruments out of his bag and seemed to thread a needle and slowly, slowly, the blood was reduced to a trickle then it stopped. There was blood everywhere, on the doctor, on the chair, on the rug and Ruth was soaked in it from her waist down but miraculously she was still alive. The doctor gave his orders in a crisp voice, saying nothing about the unusual circumstances in which he found himself, for if Charlotte had searched all the parishes around King's Meadow she could not have engaged a more competent or modern-thinking doctor than Wallace Chapman. He had concerned himself with obstetrics and gynaecology at the infirmary in Wakefield and travelled to Huddersfield and Halifax in his research. He had spent some time in Africa and had been involved with the women and children dispossessed by the war and living in the terrible places built by the British. But that was behind him, though he still was concerned with the tribulations of poor women in childbirth. He was in his forties, Charlotte thought, tall and thin and hollow about the chest, raw-boned, pale-complex-ioned, untidy, wearing shabby tweeds with leather patches at the elbow.

He gave them instructions that he expected to be obeyed and within an hour Ruth was bathed and asleep in a clean bed, drugged with something Doctor Chapman produced from his bag. The baby was attended to, cleaned up properly, and having examined – with no sign of astonishment – the other mother and child, probably wondering what the devil the young Mrs Armstrong was up to, he promptly put Ruth's baby to Jenny's breast, which was overflowing with milk and not one of them, not even Jenny, was allowed to argue.

Only when he was seated at the kitchen table with a cup of Kizzie's scalding, almost black tea in his hand did he revert to the man who had stumbled across the yard after Charlotte. He became diffident, shy almost, as though aware that he was in the company of the wife of one of Yorkshire's wealthiest and most influential gentlemen. One who rubbed shoulders with others of the gentry and one who could do a great deal to help the women and children whom Wallace Chapman tended.

'May I ask how you came to telephone me, Mrs Armstrong? I don't usually . . .'

'Your name was in my housekeeper's telephone book, Doctor. I assumed you were the Armstrong family doctor and so—'

'My uncle was a doctor in these parts and I took over his practice when I returned from Africa. I live in the family home, since I am the only member left, but I have never been called to King's Meadow before.'

'We're all healthy and, of course, I myself have only been here for five months so I had no knowledge of . . . but I thank God that you were there, Doctor, or Ruth would have died.'

As though that was explanation enough she and Kizzie calmly sipped their tea, smiling at the doctor but Doctor Chapman was intrigued. What was the lovely, very young, well-bred wife of Brooke Armstrong doing with a woman who was so obviously of the lower classes and one who had had, if his experience of such matters was correct, a great deal to do with men in the last few months and had, probably because of it, delivered a premature baby. A baby who had not much chance of surviving. The mother was very damaged, in fact he was pretty certain she had been raped, despite her condition, and here was Brooke Armstrong's wife acting as a nurse and God knows what else to these two young women who were not of her class or anything like it. Was her husband aware of it? There were not many men, at least of Brooke Armstrong's station in life, who would allow their wives to involve themselves in such matters. He and his wife had a room at the back of their large, three-storey house to which often in the night a woman or even a child might be seen creeping perhaps beaten by a drunken husband or father, raped, bleeding and bruised. He and Emily would tend them without comment, in a kind but unemotional way, and there they would stay until they were well enough to move on, probably back to the same situation from which they had escaped. They relied on the charity of the town's wealthy and here, perhaps, was a woman, the wife of one such, who might be applied to for the wherewithal to keep up his small clinic, as he liked to call it.

'I wonder, Mrs Armstrong, if I might ask how you have two such young women in your household. Both delivering a child on the same night and only you and your . . .'

'Friend. Kizzie is my friend and has been for many years. This small house, the Dower House, was standing empty so I had the idea . . . Well, to start at the beginning, Jenny, she's the first one, came knocking on the kitchen door looking for work. My servants – well, you will be aware of the attitude towards unmarried mothers – they were turning her away, you see. She had been seduced . . . Lord, it's the usual story, Doctor, a maidservant interfered with by the son of the house and given notice when it was found she was with child. I took Jenny in, against the wishes of my husband and my servants, I might add, and I intend to help her in any way I can. She does the most beautiful wall hangings. She makes rag rugs and I think something might come of her talent, but aside from that she has been treated abominably. I'm sorry, this is a simple but well-known story but . . . Really, Doctor, I find my life . . . it has no particular focus to it so I thought if I could help girls like this . . . Yes, you might look surprised, Kizzie' – turning to smile at the startled servant – 'I know I have said nothing to you but I am not cut out to be the sort of wife . . . so many of them do absolutely nothing except indulge themselves and though I am not against pleasure I would like to . . . Dear Lord, I sound like some "do-gooder" who interferes in the lives of others but I'm not, really. I came up with an idea for these girls to earn a living without—'

'Recourse to the streets,' he finished for her.

Her face lit up and he thought idly how lovely she was. Her face glowed with good health and her incredible blue eyes, the colour of the aquamarine in the ring he had put on his wife's finger when they married, inherited from his grandmother, were pierced with the brilliance born of her enthusiasm. He loved his wife dearly, they were well suited, both being of a practical, no-nonsense sort of nature. She was bonny, with a good figure like this young woman but she had given him no children, or perhaps *he* had given her none, so the work they did with the underprivileged gave them both a great deal of satisfaction. He had a feeling this night's events were to be of great importance to him and to Emily.

He stood up and placed his empty cup on the table. Both the women stood with him, waiting to hear what he had to say. He was satisfied with both his patients though the second girl's baby was very frail.

'I'll come tomorrow if I may, Mrs Armstrong. I think . . . how many rooms do you have?' he asked abruptly, surprising both Charlotte and Kizzie.

'There are four bedrooms here but across the courtyard is a building with a second storey in which . . . why, Doctor? What have you in mind?' Charlotte asked eagerly while Kizzie shook her head dubiously, for she knew Charlotte's generous impetuosity and where it might lead.

'Some of the women I treat – put together again really – are not fit to leave but we have not the room to accommodate them all and some are in a pretty bad way. They come off the streets and have a rest then are forced to go back because they must earn money. Their babies are put in the orphanage and it's very distressing. But if . . . may I talk this over with my wife and—'

'What have you in mind?' she asked again.

'Mrs Armstrong, I am very tired and my wife will be waiting up for me. I have patients to see tomorrow, the infirmary at Wakefield, the Clayton Hospital and girls in our care.'

He drifted towards the door in an absent-minded way. Charlotte followed him, walking with him to his gig and when he had gone returned thoughtfully to the Dower House. She scarcely noticed the bone-biting cold as she let herself in to find Kizzie still sitting by the fire. She sat down opposite her, putting her hands to the blaze and for several minutes neither of them spoke. The first one was Kizzie.

'What d'ost mean ter do, my lass? What's on tha' mind? Summat is an' it's ter do wi' these girls an' Jenny's rug-makin'. But whatever it is I can tell thi' this, the master won't like it.'

'No, I realise that, Kizzie, but it can't be helped. I shall try to make him see that it will make no difference to our marriage,' hesitating as she thought back to that bewildering moment in their bed only hours ago. She had been carried on a wave of longing, of passion, of a need for Brooke's body to merge with hers but, with one exception, not in the way it had done up to now. All the nights she had submitted to his love-making, though they had not been unpleasant for he had never been rough with her or, after that first time of penetration, hurt her, none of them had exploded in her as strongly as this night had done. She had wanted to roll her hips and buttocks until she rode him as she might her mare, to explore him as she had never done before, from head to toe, to pore over him, to stun him with her own naked body, to glow and purr like a cat and make him do the same. God in heaven, where had such thoughts come from and why, on this particular night? What had she felt for him? Was it . . . could it be love? Or was it just the simple climax of two healthy bodies coming together – at last . . . at last – both feeling the same incredible sensations? She didn't know; she only knew that it would take something special to regain it. She could see that cold anger on his face and then . . . nothing, for he had a trick of wiping all expression from his face and she was saddened. But she could not turn from this road she had chosen, chosen months ago when Jenny had fallen at her doorstep and Brooke had been no more than a shadow in her life as he went his own way. Only in their bed had he shown any emotion and that had been his body crying out, not his heart or his clever mind. His body had wanted hers and so he had taken it. She had become used to his cool, appraising stares but now she was confused and lost and—

Kizzie's voice interrupted her thoughts again.

'If yer ter keep these lasses *an'* their bairns an' if what Doctor Chapman ses, others from 'is place, I'll need some 'elp. I can't manage 'em on me own. Oh, I know when Jenny's on 'er feet again she'll do 'er share but I'm none so sure of t'other 'un. I don't trust that Ruth, I'll tell yer that fer nowt.

Anyroad, what d'yer say ter fetchin' over one o' me sisters? Our Megan's lookin' fer work. She's fourteen an' a good lass an' does as she's told. She could sleep wi' me an' then when—'

'I'm going to open a sort of factory, Kizzie. With Jenny to show us how to do it, and you too, for you say you are familiar with rug-making, we can set up that building on the other side of the courtyard and set the girls to work. There's plenty of room for . . . for whatever Jenny thinks necessary and with . . . well, I shall have to find out where to get the materials needed and—'

''Old on, lass, 'old on. 'Ave yer thought what the others'll say?'

'What others?'

'Your 'usband fer one. Them over at big 'ouse fer another.'

Charlotte lifted her head and set her shoulders in that defiant way she had and which had got her into trouble with her father in the past.

'Oh, you leave all that to me, Kizzie. I'll convince them – all of them!'

## 13

Robbie would be delighted to ride over to the cottage where Kizzie's mother lived, he told them, and should he bring back the sister Kizzie asked for on the back of his pony? Merry was not very big but she was strong and he was sure she could manage a double load. And where on earth had these babies come from and what were they doing in the Dower House?

It was Saturday and since he was not at school he had eaten a good breakfast at the table in the kitchen where Mrs Groves indulged him with bacon, eggs, mushrooms, tomatoes, sausages and fried bread, followed by several rounds of toast and butter, with marmalade, of course. Well, the master had gone off with himself at first light, the mistress was over at the Dower House so there seemed no point in setting the breakfast room table for one small boy. He was just about to run out to the stables when the mistress had come in from the stable yard that adjoined the back garden of the Dower House and had asked Master Robbie to accompany her as she had a job for him.

'What sort of a job?' he asked suspiciously and all movement about the kitchen stopped as the maids waited for the answer. They were all aware that the mistress had been at the Dower House; that the doctor had been called and, by way of the grapevine that existed in all households, that a young woman had arrived with a baby and that . . . that loose woman who had been living there for months had given birth. Mrs Armstrong looked tired, still dressed in the same outfit she had worn yesterday, so what new disaster had come to plague their poor master?

'Come with me and I'll tell you,' Charlotte told Robbie but then she sighed, for the servants would have to know some time what had happened so what was the use of being secretive now?

She turned and addressed the room. 'Jenny's baby was born last night, a girl, and another . . . young woman has also had her child, a girl as well, and came to our door for help. We need a maid to give Kizzie a hand and as I know none of you is willing to help these unfortunate girls . . .'

There was a loud sniff and eloquent 'hmmph' from Nellie, and Mrs Groves turned away in disgust, not at Nellie but at the way the mistress was going on about these wicked girls. No wonder the master had stormed out this morning, his face like thunder and her, his cook, only just out of bed and pulling herself together with scarce a cup of tea in her hand. Connie and Tess, who were always up first, had stared in amazement as he banged the door to, then exchanged knowing glances. There was a storm brewing, no doubt about it.

'So, Robbie, if you have had your breakfast will you come over to the Dower House and . . . darling, it's only a message I want you to deliver.' And the message had been for Kizzie's mother who would be doing them all a big favour if she could send her daughter, Megan, Kizzie had said, to help her sister.

Robbie, who was capable of saddling Merry himself by now, did so and then led her through the gate that divided the big house stable yard from the one at the back of the Dower House. He tied her to the ring in the wall, and entered the kitchen door from where he could see Kizzie in the scullery, vigorously pounding what looked like towels in the sink, her arms going ten to the dozen. There seemed to be a big pile of laundry in a bucket waiting to have the same treatment.

'Miss Charlotte's in't kitchen, lad, but be quiet. She's just got them bairns ter sleep.'

'Bairns?' he faltered.

'Aye, my lad. Bairns. Babies. Two on 'em an' if tha' don't get over ter me mam's an' fetch our Megan both me an' Miss Charlotte'll be dead on us feet.'

'Kizzie.' He was astonished. Though he had heard the talk of babies in the kitchen at the big house he had not known who Charlie was talking about. Jenny lived there, that he knew, but now there seemed to be not only Jenny but babies as well. 'Where did the babies come from, Kizzie?' he asked, but Kizzie was cudgelling the towels as though her life depended on it and had no time for idle chatter, her attitude said.

'Tha'll find out soon enough, Master Robbie. Now, 'op on that pony o' thine and ride ter me mam's. She lives in Green Lane. Go through Birks Wood and on ter Wood Lane until tha' comes ter Rose Cottage. Tell 'er there's a job goin' fer our Megan an' for 'er ter get over 'ere quick smart. 'Ave tha' got that, lad?'

Megan Aspin, called by all and sundry by the diminutive Meggie, was on the kitchen doorstep at the big house within the hour and was astonished when she was greeted by an irritable maidservant who told her she was not required here and to get back to where she came from.

'But our Kizzie sent fer me,' she stammered.

'Well, yer'd best get round there then. Through that gate,' Nellie said shortly, nodding at the gate in the stable yard and shutting the door in Meggie's flabbergasted face.

'Am I glad ter see *you*,' Kizzie greeted her as she pulled her into the kitchen, which she eventually found. There had been a man in the yard, just about to lead a horse from the stable, who had directed her, for it seemed the male servants of the household were not so censorious as the female.

'See, sling tha' shawl on that there 'ook an' then 'ang that washin' on't line, will tha' chuck, though it'll probably freeze in this weather. Kettle's on an' when tha've done that we'll 'ave a nice cup o' tea. Miss Charlotte's seein' ter't bairns but she an' Jenny'd be glad of a sup. Ruth's still asleep. Now don't stand there wi' tha' gob 'anging open. Do as tha's told an' then I'll tell thi' all about it.'

Meggie was the double of her older sister though not quite so tall. A big-boned lass with strong arms and an even stronger back, her mam had been reluctant to part with her but she was fourteen and needed a job. Their Kizzie had gone to the Mount at the same age and then on to King's Meadow when Miss Charlotte had married. She had done well and regularly sent money home and there were good prospects for a hard worker like their Meggie. She would not have been so sanguine if she had known that her innocent lass was to work among 'fallen girls' which was how Jenny and Ruth would be described.

Robbie was in the fire-glowed kitchen, having got there before Meggie. It had proved impossible for his pony to carry the two of them so Meggie had walked over. He was gazing into the cradle that Charlotte had brought over from the big house and in which the prettiest little baby was asleep. Rosy rounded cheeks, long dark lashes, a rosebud of a mouth which sucked hopefully as though on her mother's nipple and a wisp of a curl were all he could see but he was quite enchanted. The other infant, cradled in his sister's arms, was not so endearing but then, in Charlotte and Kizzie's opinion, *her* mother was not half so pretty as Jenny and since the father was unknown who could say where she got her looks. And she was thin, pallid, her head seeming too big for her body. Robbie was not enchanted with this one!

'Charlie, where did they come from and where's Jenny?' he urged her to tell him.

'This one' – pointing to the baby in the cradle – 'is Jenny's daughter. She is to call her Rose, and this one . . . do you remember Ruth? She didn't stay long, but this is hers.'

'But—'

'Look, sweetheart, Kizzie and I are very busy with all this going on and really have no time to explain but we will soon. You have been an enormous help fetching Megan but I think it might be a good idea if you went over to Fuller's Farm and your friends there and . . . well, played with Mr Emmerson's children.'

Robbie wasn't exactly sure he wanted to ride out again on this frosty morning but he was satisfied that Charlotte and Kizzie were pleased with him.

'Can I come again? I'd like to see Rose though the other one's not as pretty, is she?'

'Well, we can't all be—'

'Mmm, I know what you mean. There isn't anyone as pretty as you, Charlie.'

Charlotte smiled. 'Come and give me a kiss then.'

He permitted himself to be kissed then, with a shouted goodbye to the two women in the scullery, dashed through the back door and attempted a flying leap on to the back of his pony. He managed it, trotting off with the feeling that so far it had been a darn good morning.

She was in bed when Brooke returned, so deeply asleep she didn't even feel him climb into bed next to her. He had struggled with himself, still deeply angered by her behaviour of the night before, on whether to sleep alone in his dressing room. He had spent the day inspecting his tenanted farms and had actually had a meal with Jeff Killen and his family at Foxworth which was why his servants had not seen him until late afternoon. He knew something had happened at the Dower House, of course, since it was his wife's sudden exit at Kizzie's behest that had enraged him. For a startling but exquisite moment in time he and Charlotte had been equal in their desire, lifted to heights he had never before known, with her or indeed any woman, and he had been triumphant that at last she was responding as he had dreamed she one day would. Nevertheless she had gone, left him in that stunned state a man reaches when he is at the peak of his desire and ready to climax. He had said he would never forgive her but as he studied her sleeping face in the dim glow of the fire he knew he would always love her, always, always forgive her, do his best to accept whatever she did. Or so he believed at this moment. Her good heart, her generous nature would not allow her to turn away from whoever needed her and he must let her see that he was one of them. One of those who needed her. He was naked and she was in one of the flimsy nightdresses they had bought together when they were in Paris.

He bent his head to kiss her shoulder, sliding his lips along the curve and up to her throat and in her sleep she smiled and murmured something. Encouraged, he slipped his hand inside the nightdress and cupped her breast, gently rolling her nipple which rose at once into a peak.

'Darling . . . darling,' he whispered, turning her towards him and when she opened her eyes he bent and kissed her lips.

'Brooke . . . there you are,' she murmured, not at all surprised to find him beside her.

'Yes, here I am. Who did you expect to find in your bed?'

'My husband . . . darling . . . where have you been?'

'Here, always here, my love . . . my love . . .' He did not know what he was saying, nor care in the sweet tenderness of the moment. He ran his hand down her body, his lips still busy with her lips, her throat, her breast, then lifted her nightdress and in one practised movement, lowered himself on to her and slowly entered her. She was moist and ready for him. Her arms wound round his neck and she arched her body to meet his and together for only the second time in their marriage they moved to a peak of ecstasy which made them both cry out.

'Charlotte . . . Charlie . . . my love . . . my sweet . . .'

'Brooke . . . Brooke . . . that was . . . wonderful . . .' she sighed then at once fell asleep, curving her body close to his. He smiled in the firelight then, with her entwined in his arms, he too fell asleep.

When he awoke she was gone!

And so was Ruth when Charlotte burst into the kitchen of the Dower House. Meggie was on her knees scrubbing the floor, Kizzie was at the range stirring something in a pan that smelled delicious and Ruth's baby was grizzling piteously in the drawer that Kizzie had filled with soft little blankets and made into a makeshift cradle. There was no sign of Jenny or her child.

'She's gone,' Kizzie said.

'Who?' though of course she knew.

'Can tha' not guess?'

'Dear God!'

'Aye, dear God indeed, fer that lass'll kill herself the way she's goin'. 'Course she left bairn which'll not last the day.'

'Jenny . . .?'

'Oh, she's all right. Loves 'er bairn and is feedin' it right now but she 'asn't enough milk fer two. Or . . . or . . . she don't want ter feed the child an' tha' can't blame 'er. 'Er own comes first. When that there doctor comes 'appen 'e'll know 'ow ter get 'old o' summat ter feed poor kid. Our Meggie might 'ave ter run ter't chemist fer some o' that baby feed.'

Charlotte sat down wearily, watching as Meggie's arm swept back and forth on the already clean floor, moving her bucket with her. The girl was going to be an asset, there was no doubt about it. She had been here last night to allow herself and Kizzie to get some much needed rest but, sleeping beside her sister in the big bed Kizzie occupied, she had not heard Ruth creep out.

She sighed deeply and stood up. She was just about to go up the stairs to have a word with Jenny when the door burst open and her husband, whom she had left peacefully sleeping, burst into the house and then into the kitchen.

'I thought I might find you here and it won't bloody well do, Charlotte. I wish you to come home at once and sit down, as my wife, to breakfast with me. Mrs Groves is cooking right now and I'm hungry. She informs me that you have not eaten so you must be, too. Come along. Your place is with me not . . . not with . . .' He swept an arm in an arc to indicate Kizzie and Meggie who were both pressing themselves up against the side of the range.

He was incensed, maddened, not only by his sense of betrayal after the wonder of last night but also by a desperate anguish, for he had thought that at last they had come to an understanding. She was his wife, his beloved wife who last night had seemed to love him, or at least to be on the edge of it, and now, here she was again turning from him and he couldn't stand it. There was a terrible blankness in his eyes. A dangerous, almost murderous expression clamped on his face born of his frustrated disappointment. Charlotte backed away from him but he had not yet done with her.

'Are you to come then?' he asked almost pleasantly.

'Presently . . .' she faltered.

'Oh no! You will come now or I will close this place down. Dismiss Kizzie and this other woman, turn out these women you have brought to my home, and their brats, and . . . and . . .'

He had run out of words.

'Brooke, please, you can't mean it.' Her face was deathly white and her expression haunted. She too remembered last night and the loveliness of it. She did not want it to end like this, which it would if she did not do as he asked. In fact, if she did as he asked it would end, for she would never forgive him.

'And by the way,' he continued, having got himself under control. 'We have a card in the post this morning from Patsy Ackroyd confirming her invitation to her party and about which I knew nothing. When were you going to tell me, Charlotte? Well, never mind, get your cloak and let us go home. Good morning, Kizzie and . . .'

'Meggie, sir, my sister.'

'I see, then good morning to you both. I trust you can manage without my wife, for you will not see her over here again. If you do it will be in direct opposition to my will and this place will immediately be shut down. Charlotte?'

She moved like an automaton towards him, allowing him to take her arm and lead her from the room and from the house. And from the vision she had had of a life for herself. She was not a socialite like Patsy Ackroyd and others of her sort. She was not cut out to live the life of the wife of a gentleman who expected her to receive callers, make calls in return, entertain his guests, be smart and amusing as Patsy was. To ride to hounds, to attend shooting parties, house parties, balls and dances which he enjoyed, to travel here, there and everywhere to what were called 'Fridays to Mondays'. So what was she to do with herself if she was denied a natural outlet for her ambition to be herself, to use her brain? She was not prepared to be treated like a child or some woman Brooke employed to run his home.

She didn't know. Not yet. But by God, she'd fight. When she had recovered somewhat from the shock of his declaration she'd fight like a tigress to be what she wanted to be, whatever that was, to do what she wanted to do, whatever that might be. She would . . . she would compromise, give in on things that didn't matter like this damn party on Saturday but she'd have her way, choose how, as Kizzie often said.

So, each day, when he left the house on his estate business she slipped out of the side door and visited the Dower House.

She would see the doctor's gig by the side gate, well away from the servants' gaze, meet him in the kitchen of the Dower House where he was desperately trying to save the scrap of humanity that was Ruth's baby, confer with him on the best course to take – he had suggested trying baby food – and generally help Kizzie and Meggie for the short time she allowed herself. She was pretty certain the servants knew and she felt slightly guilty because she knew Brooke trusted her. But she could not just sit in her drawing room and twiddle her thumbs waiting for God knows what. She couldn't even embroider for heaven's sake!

''E told tha' not ter come, lass,' Kizzie had said to her. 'Tha' knows 'e's a man of 'is word an' if 'e closes this place down an' dismisses me an' Meggie what'll Jenny an' 'er baby do? Where'll they go? Doctor ses another few days then she can get up but she's not strong enough ter . . . well, I dunno.'

'Kizzie, dearest, I will let nothing happen to you, Meggie or Jenny. Let me worry about the master. I shall have to do as he wishes but I'm bloody well not going to give up this place. I discovered another little gate to the side of this house leading on to a lane and up to the back door, quite hidden from the big house. It means the doctor can come without being seen. Trust me, I'll find an answer. I shall fight and scream in front of the servants and anyone else before I'll let anyone turn you three out nor the babies. He'll . . .' She gulped, remembering that perfect moment a few nights ago, saddened that it had not returned. Would it ever?

'Eh, lovey . . .' Kizzie shook her head sadly.

She caused a minor sensation when she entered Jack and Patsy Ackroyd's ballroom on her husband's arm and those already dancing made her smile for they were so busy staring at her and Brooke they kept bumping into one another, the women tripping over the small trains of their evening gowns before they regained their equilibrium.

Brooke had made love to her every night since the day he had laid down the law about the Dower House but it had not been the same. She had submitted, as she had done in the past, but she had viciously damped down the small flare of desire that had done its best to burst into life when he caressed her. They were back to the first days of their marriage when they had both been scrupulously polite with one another.

Now she was doing what he had asked by socialising with these people who were the elite of the district. Jack Ackroyd, though he was in wool as were many of the company, did not actually *work* in his mills and factories but had inherited what he had from men, millmasters, who had started the woollen industry a century or more ago. The Ackroyds lived in an impressive house just south of Wakefield, Calder Field, which had vast gardens, woodland, tennis courts and stables containing Jack's dozen or so horses, since both he and Patsy were keen members of the Danby Hunt.

'Well, I can see you're going to give me a lot of pleasure, Charlotte. I may call you Charlotte, mayn't I?' Patsy chortled as she hurried to take them from the butler who was announcing them. Her husband, who was a good deal older than her, was not quite sure how to deal with this radiant creature nor his young wife's reaction to her arrival.

'There are a lot of stuffy people here,' she had said in an aside to him, 'so I invited them to make up a few younger ones,' then turned brightly back to Brooke and Charlotte. 'And what a gorgeous gown; it must be Worth or Doucet, not bought in Wakefield, I'm sure. Now tell the truth, Brooke, where did you take your wife to acquire such a garment? You put us all to shame, indeed you do.' Charlotte wore a silver sheath, shimmering in the soft wall lights Patsy preferred, a slim line that showed off her perfect figure, flaring at the knees like a mermaid's tail, the bodice slipping carelessly off one shoulder to reveal the whiteness of her skin. In her hair she wore a silver ribbon which was meant to hold it in place but in fact allowed it to escape in an enchanting tumble of curls.

'Paris,' Brooke admitted coolly, for he had disapproved of the defiant way Charlotte wore it, 'on our honeymoon,' glancing down at Charlotte who so far had said not one word.

It was the same all evening and the guests, men and women, all whispered to one another that though Brooke Armstrong's wife was quite startling in her loveliness, she was very dull! She was seen to chat with several of the ladies when she was not dancing, as she was never short of a partner, the men clustering round her to take her on the floor, but she merely smiled and allowed them to hold her in their eager arms to dip and sway about the room.

'She asked me if I had ever visited the West Riding Industrial Home for Females,' Milly Pickford told Maddy Hill, shocked to the core, for what lady would do such a thing.

'Well, she's decidedly odd, I must say: she asked me if I knew of any young women taken into the Wakefield Union Workhouse. What would I know of such a thing, I ask you?'

'She questioned me on Charles's shoddy mill, for heaven's sake, as if I would know the slightest thing about it,' Rosemary Denton cried. 'Really, I don't think she will fit in at all!'

She danced several times with her husband but it was noticed by several of the ladies who sat out, some of them with marriageable daughters who must, of course, be chaperoned, that though he spoke to her she barely answered him, her face averted.

She got through it. She had done as he asked and in the carriage ride home, though he said not a word, she knew he was only barely holding in the temper she had not known he had until a few days ago. She reached the safety of their bedroom without a word being spoken, for there were servants still about, but with the door closed behind them he grabbed her from behind as she walked towards her dressing table and whirled her to face him.

'So is this how it is to be?' he hissed, his breath hot on her face, breath that reeked of brandy.

'I don't know what you mean.'

'I think you do, madam. If I will not allow this mad idea you have of taking prostitutes off the streets and housing them and their offspring you will treat me and my friends to the contempt you think we deserve. You behaved abominably tonight.'

'I was as good as gold.'

'Really. Well, tell me this. For what purpose did you ask Milly Pickford if she had ever visited—'

'So, she told you, did she?'

'Her husband did and—'

'I know. You won't have it—'

He hit her then, twice across the face, viciously and accurately so that her neck muscles wrenched in agony and her head, reeling backwards, struck hard against the wall. Then he tore her lovely silver gown from her, stripped her naked and threw her on the bed.

He made her pregnant that night and though she fought him, bit him, snapping at his face with her teeth, she gloried in it, and so did he!

# 14

She drove the gig herself with Kizzie beside her and nobody tried to stop them, for the yard men had had no instructions from the master. It was March and the month had come in like the proverbial lamb with a warm breeze which was welcome after the bitter cold of February. The sun shone from a pale blue sky and though Charlotte felt the sighing sadness of the last few days weigh heavily upon her the sunshine lifted her spirits a little. The country lanes along which Misty stepped out smartly were just coming into the glory that would be spring: primroses in the midst of their crown of green leaves, celandine buds, coltsfoot and field speedwell scattered in the waist-high banks and the buds of daffodils standing up above the grass, straight, like little lance-heads among their spears of green.

Jenny and the babies were well enough to be left in Meggie's capable hands and surprisingly, since she was not what Kizzie would call a *taking* baby, Meggie was quite smitten with Ruth's little thing, giving most of her time to her since Jenny doted on Rose and now that she was out of bed would let no one else go near her! Meggie had asked tentatively if Kizzie would mind if Ruth's infant could be called Pearl.

'Eeh, 'tis not up ter me, lass, an' why Pearl?' Kizzie had asked her.

'Well, she looks like one, our Kizzie,' though to Kizzie's certain knowledge their Meggie had never clapped eyes on such a thing. 'Sorta plain, pale, but wi' summat smooth about 'er.'

'Tha' can be a bit daft at times, our Meggie.' Kizzie had been amazed but she didn't care what the infant was called.

Charlotte came to the outskirts of Batley, guiding Misty along cobbled highways lined on either side with small terraced houses, the actual road busy with horse-drawn vehicles, farm carts, small gigs such as the one she drove, men on horseback, men dragging handcarts, and all moving steadily towards the centre of the town. It was Thursday, market day, and the market-place was a sea of covered stalls where anything might be bought from a reel of cotton, new and second-hand clothing, boots, farm eggs, butter, jars of honey, farm implements, lidded baskets filled with cackling hens, and as they moved nearer to the square, the busier it became. There were tramlines running beside the market and a tramcar rattled by pulled by horses. When it stopped a dozen people alighted, mostly working women come to spy out a bargain on the stalls.

Charlotte had been given instructions by a helpful passer-by as to how she might get to the nearest shoddy mill. The passer-by, a respectable working man in his decent go-to-market suit and bright blue neckerchief, looked somewhat surprised that this well-bred and well-spoken lady in her gig should ask for such a thing. No, she didn't know the name of the mill, she told him, but as she had learned there were many such in the town of Batley, perhaps he could direct her to the closest.

The name of the mill turned out to be Victoria Mill owned by Edward Ramsbottom and it was off Commercial Street. Aye, just go straight on . . . pointing his finger along the road.

Commercial Street was cobbled, like most of the streets in the town and the gig bounced in the ruts. It was, like the market-place, busy with men in caps, women in shawls, a donkey pulling a small cart, a boy pushing a trolley on wheels in the centre of the road so that they were forced to swerve to avoid him, women in aprons and boys in knee-length trousers.

Lining the road were dozens of shops: Smith's the watch-maker, Salter's Boot Store, Clayton's Garment Store, the front of each shop shrouded with a canopy as though the sun were cracking the flagstones, Kizzie murmured.

They turned at the corner of Rutland Road as instructed by the helpful working man, drove along it for a hundred yards and there it was. Their destination. Victoria Shoddy Mill. Edward Ramsbottom, prop.

Charlotte drew in her breath. 'Well, here it is, Kizzie. Our future and theirs.'

'If I knew what tha' were up to 'appen I might understand.' Kizzie looked at the wide gates that opened into a yard that was a hive of activity: a positive whirlwind of men and wagons, great bales that looked to be made up of filthy tatters lying about the yard. More loaded wagons edged past them as they stared in horrified fascination, disgorging more bales to those already piled there while others took away bales that seemed no different to those that had just arrived.

Shoddy was the result of mixing old rags with some virgin wool, a process developed almost a hundred years previously. The rags came from old clothes which were collected by ragmen for a price, the rags being then sold to the rag merchant. Another source was new rags bought by the rag merchant as scrap from clothing manufacturers and tailors. It was these rags that Charlotte was after.

'Rug-making, Kizzie,' Charlotte said absently. 'I told you about it earlier.'

'What?' Kizzie turned to stare at her.

'Rug-making. With Jenny to show them how, I mean to employ girls—'

'Prostitutes?'

'No, not particularly. Girls who are in trouble and can't get work. Like Jenny. But not just to make sturdy rag rugs to be sold on the market and laid on the kitchen floor, but wall hangings, like the ones Jenny makes. When Patsy Ackroyd sat in the drawing room she spotted Jenny's work and was greatly interested. She thought it was a painting. So there we have two outlets for the girls' work.'

'Two. Good God, lass, dost know what tha're talking about? Dost 'onestly think Mr Brooke'll let thi' go in that there mill an' deal wi' men?'

'He won't know, Kizzie.'

'It'll get back to 'im, lass. There's nowt 'appens 'ereabouts that don't get back to 'im.'

'I'll just have to take the chance then, won't I?'

Avoiding the wagons and the men who stopped work to stare at her and Kizzie, she drove in through the gates and pulled up in front of steps leading to what might be offices. Climbing down from the gig, she beckoned to one man who seemed to have a knowing air about him and, when he had hurried across, asked him politely if he could see to her horse and gig and if he could direct her to Mr Ramsbottom's office.

He would have willingly helped her, for she was a good-looking young woman but his mouth dropped open and he seemed to be speechless.

'Is there something wrong?' she asked him, aware that the yard which had been so noisy a minute or two ago was now as quiet as a churchyard.

'Mr Ramsbottom,' she prompted him, glad when Kizzie sidled up to her, standing close.

'Nay, lass,' the man croaked. 'Mr Ramsbottom don't come 'ere. 'Is manager's in't th'office though. Reckon tha' could talk to 'im.'

She was dressed in one of her fashionable outfits bought in Paris. A skirt, flared and reaching her ankle bone and a three-quarter coat in a shade of dove grey with gloves and kid boots to match. Her hat was plain by the standards of the day, for knowing she would be entering a factory she had put on a dove-grey boater with a ribbon round it in yellow. She looked glorious, the sunshine putting golden streaks in her tawny hair which was tied up with a yellow ribbon into a bun just beneath the brim of her boater. She was excited and there was a flush of rose in her cheeks, though one of them looked suspiciously – to them who knew about such things – as though she had been thumped and her poppy lips were parted, ready to smile.

'Bloody Nora!' one brawny fellow whispered. 'What's goin' on?' But none of them could answer since they were as amazed as he.

As she and Kizzie approached the doorway indicated by the fellow holding Misty's reins, a man in a suit, totally different to the men in the yard, stepped down from the bottom step, quite speechless with astonishment for a moment since women, *ladies*, like her did not enter places like this.

'May I help you?' he enquired when he had regained his speech, looking her up and down with great interest, his eyes appreciating what he saw.

'I am here to speak to . . . to the manager so if you would direct me to him I would be obliged.'

'Well, *madam*, I'm not sure whether Mr Scales can see anyone just at the moment. He is a busy—'

'And you are?' cutting through his somewhat affected speech, which sounded as if he hadn't always spoken thus.

'I am his . . . his . . .'

'Yes?' She lifted her head imperiously.

'I work in the office.'

'Then will you be kind enough to announce me to Mr Scales.'

The man shifted uncomfortably and at her back an interested crowd of men and boys nudged one another and waited to see what would happen next, the interruption to their work most pleasing to them. It was not often – in fact never – that a lady such as this one brightened up their day.

She followed the clerk up the steps with Kizzie at her back.

As Misty trotted up the drive they could see the doctor's gig standing by the gate of the Dower House.

'Now what's 'appened?' Kizzie asked anxiously. They had left Jenny quite recovered from the birth of her baby, and both babies doing well. At least Rose was doing well and Pearl . . . *Pearl* . . . was beginning to pull round with the attention Meggie gave her. There was no need for him to call again, he had told them only last week and now he was here, so what catastrophe had befallen their little household while they had been away?

They pulled up, leaving their gig next to the doctor's, jumping down on to the gravel and hurrying through the front door into the kitchen. Doctor Chapman was sitting by the fire opposite Jenny who was nursing her baby. He was calmly sipping a cup of tea while Meggie hovered by the kitchen range, a grizzling Pearl in her arms. In a chair pulled up next to the doctor's was a young girl, probably about fifteen, and even as the two women hesitated in the doorway it was evident she was one of Doctor Chapman's waifs, those who came to his home in the dead of night asking for help. She was pregnant, sported a black eye and a badly split lip which seemed to have been sewn up, as a small thread hung from the wound.

Doctor Chapman stood up politely and smiled.

'Ah, there you are. I was just saying to Megan I really must go for I have visits to make at the Clayton. The Clayton Hospital in Victoria Square, you know?'

They didn't, not really, but they both nodded, eyeing the young girl in the chair.

'This is Violet,' deepening his smile as he turned to the girl. 'As you can see, she is to have a child and last night her father gave her . . . well, you can see what he did to her so I have brought her here to you.' He hesitated, looking from one to the other. 'That is all right, isn't it? You did say you were to take in girls who were in trouble and would have employment for them?'

Charlotte took a deep breath, remembering the snarling fury on her husband's face as he burst into this very room and ordered her to come home; his stated intention to close the place if she did not obey him; to turn out these vulnerable children, for that was what they were. The evening spent at the Ackroyds and what had happened when they returned. Her face was bruised on one cheek though Kizzie, the most diplomatic of friends, had said nothing and then he had . . . he had . . . she almost said *raped her*, in her own mind of course, though she knew it had not been rape. If it had she had been a most willing victim. What was he to say when he learned of what she had done today? When the wagon arrived carrying the shoddy she had bought? When she showed him quite blatantly that she meant to go her own way and be damned to the Ackroyds and the rest of them. Mr Scales had proved to be a very pleasant young man who obviously was enthusiastic about his work. He gave them quite a wordy explanation on the source of the goods he worked with, explaining that the 'tatters' they saw in the yard had come from Poland, from the gypsies of Hungary, from the beggars and scarecrows of Germany, from the frowsy peasants of Muscovy, along with snips and shreds from monks' cassocks and noblemen's cloaks, lawyers' robes, waxing lyrical on what was apparently of great import to him. They would be shredded by 'devils', the machines that turned them into what was called mungo fibre, after they had been sorted and put into baskets by quality and colour. She and Kizzie had picked over what was on sale, queried the price and even, on Mr Scales's recommendation, inspected the canvas and hessian to be had at a stall on Batley Market.

Now she placed a comforting hand on Violet's arm, noticing that the girl flinched as though used to human touch only in the form of blows. Doctor Chapman watched her, then, satisfied, moved towards the door.

'I can see she is welcome here so I'll get along. Let me know' – glancing in the direction of the telephone – 'if you should need anything. He hesitated for a moment. 'What you are doing is very worthwhile, Mrs Armstrong, but are you sure your husband approves?' There were not many gentlemen of Brooke Armstrong's standing who would agree to his wife taking in these girls and giving them a place to have their babies with a decent roof over their heads and, not only that, but providing them with decent work in what was practically his own home. Most females of Brooke Armstrong's class were little better than possessions, pampered, true, well cared for and protected as one might care for a decent horse. They were bred to be, if possible, decorative in the drawing room, fertile in the bedroom, useful in the running of the home and were given little freedom to pursue their own interests. There were exceptions, of course, women of wealth and strength of character, mainly unmarried, who forged their own lives. Many of them were raising their heads above the parapet, ready, if asked, to fight for their rights, as they saw it, in the new movement of suffragettes, the Women's Social and Political Union, in which his own wife was interested. And why not? He himself was a keen advocate of women's suffrage; after all, had not Emily been beside him, fought beside him, in everything he believed in and surely had the right to be his equal in everything.

But the young, lovely Mrs Armstrong who could be no more than seventeen or eighteen was not made of the stuff of his Emily!

Charlotte exchanged a glance with Kizzie, for none knew better than she what Brooke would say and perhaps do. *Try to do!*

'My husband is not . . . not in total agreement, no, but he is a kind man, generous, fair and will come round when I explain what I am doing and why. I am not the sort of woman to spend my days calling and leaving cards—'

Realising she was saying too much, she clamped her rosy lips together and moved towards the door, indicating that she was to show the doctor out. She opened the door, watched by Kizzie though Meggie and Jenny were absorbed by the infants they were cradling and Violet seemed to be senseless and in a private hellish world of her own.

Wallace Chapman turned in the doorway.

'Have you had a fall, Mrs Armstrong?' he asked pleasantly.

'A fall?'

'I notice your cheek is bruised.'

Involuntarily she put her hand to her face where Brooke's hard hand had struck her, then she forced a smile.

'Ah, yes. I walked into a . . . a . . . door, Doctor.'

'I see. It's surprising how many females do that. I may have something in my bag for that if you would care to—'

'No, no, thank you, Doctor.'

'Very well, as you like.' Then he was gone, striding towards the gate where his gig waited.

When she turned back into the kitchen Kizzie was already ushering the stunned figure of Violet towards the staircase murmuring about a bath and a rest.

She dressed carefully that evening in a gown of pale, duck-egg-blue silk helped by Kizzie who had left her charges in Meggie's increasingly capable care. The bodice was low-cut with transparent sleeves of the same colour. It had a wide, boned waistband, the skirt flared and very full at the scalloped hem. Kizzie had brushed her hair, but instead of dressing it neatly in a coil at the back of her head, fastened it to the top of her skull in a curly knot. It fell from the blue ribbon that exactly matched her gown, the curls reaching to the middle of her shoulder blades. She made no attempt to hide her bruised cheek!

'Will tha' not . . . powder tha' cheek, love?' Kizzie asked her tentatively.

'No, leave it. Perhaps he will be more amenable to what I have to put to him if I look vulnerable. He will feel guilty. It is not his nature to be violent, especially towards a woman and it might make my own position a bit stronger. He will be sorry and will feel the need to make it up to me.' She sighed. 'At least I hope so.'

Kizzie shook her head sadly. 'Aye, tha' knows best.'

She was already in the drawing room sipping sherry when he strode in, still in his riding things. He was brisk and yet at the same time awkward if such a thing was possible, ready to smile if she did, watching her carefully. She did her best to appear calm, but not too calm as if the blow had not mattered. She turned her head to stare into the fire so did not see the look in his eyes, a look of contrition, of deep sadness, a mixture of concern and desperation as he did his best to hide his true feelings. She looked exquisite in her lovely gown, her brave smile flickering across her face. He was a man of deep silences, a man of calmness, a man who retreated into a distant part of himself when faced with the love he felt for this woman, the passion that astounded him. And yet the mark of his hand flamed on her cheek and he could have wept. Sweet Christ, he had done this to her. The one person he loved more than any other who walked this earth, who he would gladly die for and in his madness and bitter disappointment he had blindly struck out at her, then . . . then had he raped her, taken her against her will? It hadn't seemed so at the time, for she had met him in a thunderous explosion that had carried them up in a soaring wave of pleasure before depositing them into the drifting shallows of peace. They had slept, but before she awoke he had crept into the dressing room and climbed into the bed.

He had not seen her since.

'I'll go and change,' he told her now. 'I won't be long.'

Robbie had been in to say goodnight, kissing her with sly tenderness, for he had been hoping to stay up and chat about his day but she had bundled him off with Nellie, smiling as he cast reproachful looks over his shoulder.

When they were seated at the dining table eating the excellent asparagus soup Mr Johnson put before them there was silence for a while, neither of them knowing how to begin a conversation. Was she to set about him for what he had done to her? But surely not in front of the servants. Was he to apologise for what he had done to her? But surely not in front of the servants. Were they simply to ignore it and what had caused it and, hopefully, continue as a country gentleman, his wife and their life together? Their lives were mapped out for them by the station into which they had been born. He was a gentleman, she was the daughter of a gentleman. They mixed – or should do, *would* do – with others of their class and the mad idea she had conceived had been nipped in the bud. He was not an ogre and would find places for the women she had housed in the Dower House and for the children they had borne but he would close the place down and she would agree. That was the end of it.

Mr Johnson moved in his silent and dignified way about the room, helped by Connie, taking away their plates, putting the second and then third course before them, offering wine, nodding to Connie, who had taken over from Nellie, to do this and that, then standing motionless before the sideboard in case something might be asked for. The dining room was soft and warm and elegant, the surfaces of the woodwork gleaming in the light from the candelabra in the centre of the table and the logs burning brightly in the fireplace. The silver, which Mr Johnson had polished in his butler's pantry and which had been in the family for generations, was complemented by the pristine napkins, each one folded by the parlour-maid into wings in the way Mrs Dickinson had taught her. Hothouse roses from one of John Dudley's many greenhouses decorated the length of the table and the setting for romance could not have been more propitious, or so Brooke thought as he surreptitiously watched his wife.

He was to be sadly disappointed. They had finished their meal, chatting equably of this and that, nothing of consequence, a gentleman and his wife, he telling her of a scheme he had spoken of with his tenants whereby they could participate in farming tasks, a sharing of seeds for crops, of animals and any profits that would be made. He had ridden long and hard, for he felt he needed to get away from the scene last night and was pleasantly tired, wondering in his mind if they would sleep in the same bed tonight and was he to make love to her. Gently, tenderly, something to make the last time fade away and yet, did he want it to fade? She had been magnificent. He had spoken with Joel Denton who he had met cantering through Overton and Joel had been filled with admiration for Brooke's wife. Charlotte, of course, had not engaged Charles and Rosemary Denton's son in problems of wayward females and their illegitimate children or the Wakefield Union Workhouse and so he had thought her delightful and very, very lovely. In a most respectful way, naturally, for she was the wife of Brooke Armstrong but his approval had been balm to Brooke's sore heart.

'There is to be a ball at Park Mansion, or so Joel Denton tells me, to which we are to be invited. A hunt ball to mark the end of the hunting season. A great affair with all the county there. Rosemary Denton is a wonderful hostess,' he began.

'I'm sure she is but it's not certain I shall be able to attend.'

The bombshell of her words dropped into the drawing room, exploding in his smiling face. 'Not . . .' he spluttered.

'No, I shall be busy with my girls and the employment they are to be given. Rugs! Rag rugs.' Her voice was crisp but if he had cared to look, which he didn't, he would have seen the pulse in her neck beating wildly. 'Kizzie and I have been to Victoria Mill in Batley today and ordered the shoddy to make them. It will arrive tomorrow so you see I am to be very busy.'

With that she stood up and walked gracefully from the room.

# 15

They did not speak to one another for a week. He ate alone from a tray in his study to the bewilderment of the servants who wondered in private if the goings-on in the Dower House had anything to do with it. He slept in the dressing room and each day after a solitary breakfast leaped on to the back of Max or Bruno and galloped off, hardly giving Percy or Arch time to open the yard gate.

'Bugger if I know what's up wi' 'im,' Percy grumbled to Arch. 'Tha'd think old Scrat 'imself were after 'im, way 'e tekks off.'

''Appen it's not old Scrat but young mistress,' Arch replied knowingly.

'What's that serpposed ter mean?'

'Jane in't dairy, 'oo 'ad it from Rosie, tell'd me master an' mistress're not best friends at moment.'

'Oh aye, an' what's that serpposed ter mean?' Percy asked again.

Arch lowered his voice. 'They're sleepin' in separate beds.'

Percy looked shocked. Him and his missis had never slept apart in all their married life. Mind, with six young 'uns and only two bedrooms, they had no choice, but it ensured that many an argument was resolved in the most satisfactory way!

The end of the fox hunting season approached and the promised written invitation to the hunt ball arrived from Sir Charles and Lady Rosemary Denton. The ball had been held at Park Mansion as far back as any of them could remember, since Park Mansion had the most magnificent ballroom in the county of Yorkshire.

She was about to bite into a slice of hot, buttered toast, her feet to the fire in her bedroom, still in her filmy, oyster-coloured negligee when he knocked politely on the door and entered at her invitation to 'come in'. His heart was pounding, and so was hers at the sight of him, but they both hid it from one another, pretending an indifference neither of them felt.

'Good morning,' he said coolly. 'I apologise for interrupting your breakfast but I have just received Charlie and Rosemary Denton's invitation to their ball. I wish you to accompany me.'

It was a crossroads in their marriage and both were aware of it. There had been a week of cooling off, giving them both time to consider their future together. The matter was, of course, in his hands. She was his wife. The wife of a gentleman and his word was law. King's Meadow was his home and it was he who decided what occurred in it. He had threatened to turn out the two young girls, one of whom was expecting a child, the other with a young baby, and, so he was told, an infant abandoned by its mother. He could shut the Dower House, lock it up and put a stop to the mad scheme his wife seemed intent on introducing. The opening of what was, in essence, a factory, or a mill, or whatever name you cared to give it. And not only that but she had told him she was not to perform the social duties of the wife of a man in his position. Something inside him had broken when she had sat in the drawing room and calmly told him she did not think she could attend the Dentons' ball, intimating that she would be far too busy for such an inconsequential affair, but naturally, he would not allow that! He was not a man who particularly cared for such occasions himself. The dinner parties, the balls, the social get-togethers his friends and neighbours thought so important. But he was a man of his time. A conventional man. A punctilious man, a man of breeding who conformed to the dictates of his class. The luncheon parties, the dances, the house parties attended by people from many parts of the country and even abroad, titled people, some of vast wealth. Tea parties, tennis parties, bridge parties, all meant to pass the time of the idle rich. He enjoyed the sporting events. Shooting pheasant and grouse in season. Deer hunting in Scotland to which he was often invited, again in season, and where he had a notion to build a small cottage in order to avoid – to him – the tedious company of the ladies and gentlemen who were his fellow guests, the supposedly pleasant company, polite and punctual, the conversations, witty and knowledgeable, the adultery committed under the roof of his host. Tea for the ladies served at little tables round the fire, the gentlemen playing their interminable games of cards. All very sophisticated and he had been brought up to accept it as the life of men like himself and, when he had one, his wife.

Fox hunting was his particular favourite and in his heart, where his wife, his young, lovely and much loved wife was treasured, he had dared to hope that she would be his companion in all these pastimes.

Then he had his estate to care for. His tenants to oversee, his gamekeeper to confer with, problems to be solved, farm buildings and cottages to be inspected, repairs put in hand, stock to be checked, wood and moorland to be given attention, hedges, dry-stone walls, streams, ponds on which an eye must be kept, vermin exterminated, all under his careful management.

But still the unwritten rules and conventions of his class must be complied with and this exquisite but wary creature who eyed him defiantly must learn her place in it, and obey.

She lifted her head imperiously, the gesture somewhat ruined by the slice of toast in her hand and the smear of butter around her mouth. It took all his control not to smile.

'I don't wish to attend the ball, Brooke. I don't hunt and apart from Patsy – I forget her surname – I did not enjoy the company of the women at her party. I found them shallow and with very high opinions of themselves for no reason I could see. I shall be busy from now on. I'm busy today arranging my girls' training in hooking rugs and at the end of the day I am too tired to gad about—'

'Is that so?' he interrupted. 'Well, we can soon solve that problem by closing the Dower House, returning the shoddy stored in the stable block opposite and finding alternative accommodation for the waifs and strays you have gathered about you.'

'And how do you intend to do that?'

'What?'

'Find alternative accommodation for these girls?'

'They are maidservants, aren't they? Good maidservants can always find employment.'

'With a child in their arms?'

He was momentarily nonplussed. It seemed such a simple thing. He had many acquaintances with enormous house-holds, big houses that needed staff to run them and maids were the silent and efficient young women who kept such places clean and running smoothly.

'Their children must go into care,' he said at last.

'They do not want to be parted from their children.' She glared at him, her face rosy, her startling blue-green eyes brilliant with outrage. 'That is the whole purpose of my scheme. To allow them to keep their babies but at the same time have decent work in a safe, comfortable home.'

'They should have thought of that before they allowed a man to interfere with them.' Then he could have bitten his tongue for uttering such an unfeeling remark.

She became still then, on her face such a look of contempt he wanted to throw himself at her feet in abject apology. How could he be so crass? But it was too late. He had said it, not really meaning it, for it was not in his nature to be callous. The expression on her face tormented him but if he was to have mastery over her – when all he wanted was her love, not her submission – he must stand fast.

'You are vile,' she hissed. 'I had no idea you could be so brutal.'

Her words cut him to the bone, sliced into his heart but still he did not show it though she pinned him to the wall with an arrow through him. His face remained impassive. 'You are at liberty to think so and I can see . . .'

'Yes?'

'Perhaps we might come to some understanding. A compromise.'

'Compromise? In what way?'

'The servants – the kitchen staff, the housemaids – do not care to associate with these young women whom they see as . . . as . . .'

'Whores?'

He winced. The word on her lips seemed to besmirch her. To sully her own purity, and she *was* pure. No longer a virgin, of course, remembering the hours they had known in their marriage bed, but her body had been given to one man, himself, her husband.

'You said the word, not me, but these girls you have taken in have been disgraced in the eyes of decent women and they do not wish to work with them.' He hesitated, uncertain how to go on and she waited expectantly, a small bud of hope blossoming in her heart. He smiled, a smile that did not reach his eyes. He longed to go to her, take her in his arms, tell her of his deep, yearning love, that she was his world, his reason for living and if it meant letting her have her way in this mad idea, to have her love him in the same way, then she was to go ahead. That they would let polite society go to the devil no matter what they thought of her, no matter what they might say of her, but he couldn't. This was his sphere in life, his inheritance, how he had been brought up and she must conform, as he did, as his friends and neighbours did.

'You wish to . . . to house these women and children?'

'Yes,' she said eagerly, leaning forward so that her lovely breasts almost escaped the flimsy lace of her nightgown. For a moment he was totally bewitched and his breeches became uncomfortably tight at the crotch.

'Is Kizzie to help you?' His voice almost cracked with emotion but he remained cool, disinterested, as though her answer meant very little to him.

'Oh yes, she will remain in the Dower House to supervise their living arrangements, the children and their needs. She has her sister, Meggie, to help her.'

'And the . . . the rug-making?'

'Jenny is the expert there. She will—'

'Jenny is . . .?'

'One of the girls. She has a baby, Rose, who is several weeks old now, and then there—'

'So there is really no need for you to be involved as far as I can see.'

'Of course there is. I will supervise the—' She broke off in mid-sentence since it seemed he had tripped her up. At the moment she was not needed, that was true, for with only two girls, Jenny and Violet, to produce the rugs, with Kizzie and Meggie to run the house they could manage without her but this was not what she had planned. She intended to make the empty building across the yard into a rug-making factory, to employ at least half a dozen girls under the tutelage of Jenny, and Charlotte would be in charge of it all: buying the shoddy, arranging for its delivery, the book-keeping and finding an outlet for the finished product. But he had said *compromise* so what had he in mind?

He was leaning against the door frame, his hands thrust deep into the pockets of his riding jacket to hide their trembling, his lean, tanned face expressionless, his silvery grey eyes watchful. A thought flitted through her mind, a vague thought that surprised her, of how attractive he was.

'Charlotte, I am not in favour of this scheme but I must admit that I cannot bring myself to turn out women and their children with nowhere for them to go. No, don't get excited,' as she leaped to her feet with the evident intention of throwing her arms about him in gratitude. Much as he desired it, he knew she would not care for what he had to say next.

'I am prepared to let them stay for a month or until the second young woman has had her child. You have already bought the raw materials so it would be logical to use them. The side gate that lets into the lane and is not overlooked by the rest of the house can be used since I will not have wagons and carts or whatever else is involved trundling up and down my drive, perhaps blocking the carriage turn-round. This is a trial only and providing it does not interfere with or disturb the running of our home let us see what they make of it. But – and this is not for discussion – there are to be no more. Girls, I mean.'

'But Doctor Chapman has some terrible cases of ill-treatment—'

'Then he must deal with them at the hospital.'

'And afterwards, when their babies are—'

'I said I would not argue with you. There are two of them there now, you say, and when the second one bears her child, three infants. Kizzie and her sister can look after them quite comfortably I should have thought so in that case there is no need for my wife to be involved. Do you understand? You will not go near the Dower House. If there is a problem Kizzie will attend you here. I think that is all I have to say.'

She jumped to her feet so violently he recoiled, her face flaming with indignation.

'Well, that might be all you have to say but this is what I have to say. I am trying to help young women who were unfortunate enough, or perhaps foolish enough, to allow themselves to be seduced, or even raped by a man and then abandoned. There is the workhouse, of course, but here they can—'

'Yes, yes, so you have said but my decision is the same. They may work for a month, then if they have been discreet and are a nuisance to no one, by which I mean the other servants, I will consider your continuing your experiment. But I repeat, you will have absolutely nothing to do with it. It will not concern you. You are the wife of a gentleman and will act as such. You will supervise the running of this house, entertain when I ask you, call and be called upon by our friends—'

'Your friends,' she spat at him.

'Accept invitations from these friends, mix in polite society, *conform* to society and carry out your social duties as the wives of other gentlemen do.'

Before she could speak again he turned abruptly, opened the door and left the room.

Within half an hour she was bursting through the door of the Dower House into the kitchen, considerably startling Jenny who was peaceably nursing her child by the fireside.

'Nay, what's ter do?' she quavered, starting up so violently that the baby was torn from her bursting nipple and let out a roar of outrage.

'Where's Kizzie?' Charlotte's gaze swept round the cosy kitchen as though expecting Kizzie to pop up from behind the rocking-chair.

'She's upstairs wi' Violet, Miss Charlotte. Violet's poorly an' Kizzie's sent fer't doctor.'

'Poorly? What does that mean?'

'She's startin' wi't babby.' Jenny sank back and urged little Rose's pursed mouth back to her breast. 'She took badly in't night an' that bairn o' Ruth's yellin' 'er 'ead off fer want o' summat ter eat. Real bedlam it be,' though she herself seemed unconcerned by it all.

'Who has telephoned the doctor?' Charlotte asked anxiously as she reached for an apron that hung on the hook behind the door.

'Master Robbie were 'ere an' offered to fetch 'im 'cos Kizzie were that busy.' Jenny bent her head over her child who stared up at her with total absorption, her starfish hand lying contentedly on Jenny's bounteous breast.

'When did this happen?' Charlotte was halfway up the stairs marvelling at the undivided attention a mother gives her child to the exclusion of all else. Was it common among all women or was Jenny, having no one else on whom to lavish her love, unique in her manner? She seemed not to care about anyone or anything other than Rose, refusing even to share her milk, of which she had plenty, with Ruth's abandoned and somewhat sickly child.

Violet was lying in her bed in the room she shared with Jenny, her body still for the moment, but even as Charlotte entered she began to writhe and moan. Meggie was on the far side of the bed, her hand clutched painfully by the woman giving birth. Both she and Kizzie were in a state of disarray, with stained and crumpled aprons, hair hanging from their caps and anxious expressions on their flushed faces. From the next-door bedroom came the sound of Pearl wailing.

Kizzie turned. 'Oh, thank the good God, lass. Will tha' see ter't bairn? There's milk ready on't range in a saucepan an' only needs warmin' up.'

'But what—'

'Nay, lass, tha' can see we're up to us eyes in it 'ere.'

'Yes, I can see that, but I thought Violet's baby wasn't due for another two months so . . .'

'Well, it's on its way now an' bugger's arse first so . . .'

'Arse first?'

'Look, Miss Charlotte, us've no time ter be chattin' ter thi'. Doctor'll be 'ere soon, I 'ope, but until then will tha' see ter't bairn what's skrikin' its 'ead off. That there Jenny might've 'elped but no, she 'ad ter feed 'er own as if that couldn't wait. I dunno, tha'd think—'

She was interrupted by a shout from downstairs as the doctor arrived, accompanied by a beaming Robbie full of his own importance at being what he considered the saviour in the drama.

'Now then, Violet, what's this then?' Wallace Chapman said cheerfully as he entered the room, very loud and competent and at once all four women, even the one labouring on the bed, felt better. 'Let's have a look at you. We'll soon have you to rights. A bit soon or have you mixed up your date? It's happened before and it will happen again, I'm sure.'

He proceeded to inspect Violet, prodding and poking and peering, but gently, speaking in a soothing voice so that all was calm.

'The child is the wrong way round and the mother is exhausted,' he said in an aside to Kizzie, 'so we must help her.' Pearl continued to wail piteously.

'Feed the baby, Mrs Armstrong, if you please,' he went on, so, loth to leave the room, Charlotte ran next door, plucked the crying infant from her crib, scurried down the stairs and placed her unceremoniously in Robbie's arms, where the baby looked up at him with unfocused interest and he looked down at her in horror.

'Charlie . . .' he cried.

'Feed her, Robbie. There's the milk in the pan and there's the bottle. Jenny will tell you what to do. See, Rose has gone to sleep, so please, Jenny, give him a hand.'

'Surely there's no need fer all on yer ter—'

Charlotte's voice was stern. 'Jenny, remember who took you in when you were in dire straits. Now, help Robbie, if you please.'

Jenny, who had no idea what 'dire straits' were, nevertheless covered her breast, which had caught Robbie's fascinated attention, put her child in the Armstrong family cradle and, tutting irritably, put the milk on to warm and reached for the bottle.

'I don't know, all this fuss,' she was muttering as Charlotte ran back upstairs.

The breech presentation was dealt with and after a judicial snip to widen the birth canal, Violet's child was born, a girl yelling lustily.

'Well, if she's seven months my name's not Hezekiah Aspin,' Kizzie said tartly as she watched Doctor Chapman cut the cord then place a stitch in the cut he had made. 'An' another lass, an' all. A house full o' women we be.'

'I'll give her something to help her sleep and Meggie can wash the child. A healthy infant and as you say, Miss Kizzie, a full-term child. Now, I think a cup of tea would be welcome then I must be getting back. Put the baby to the breast as soon as Violet awakens. I must say she looks a great deal better than when I brought her here. Which brings me to . . . where is Mrs Armstrong? Ah, there you are,' he said, moving from the narrow staircase into the kitchen. He took the tea offered him and sat down tiredly in the second rocking-chair, sighing.

'I have another young woman at my house. She arrived last night, badly beaten up but no longer with child, thankfully. She hasn't spoken a word yet except what sounds like "be-gorra" so we don't know who did this to her. Irish, I would say, which didn't take much working out! I left my wife tending to her but she is badly in need of somewhere to stay. She can remain with us for a day or two while I keep an eye on her but if she could come to you it would be a godsend. She has a broken arm and, I suspect, broken ribs and is not fit for work so . . .'

'Of course, Doctor. There is room for her here and work when she's recovered. Jenny is to start training these girls as soon as possible. The raw materials are stored in the stable block and as soon as we have set out the working area, the heating and so on, the girls will start working. It will be a while before we can produce anything saleable but with Jenny in charge and with her skill we should be up and running in no time. I think all girls are familiar with hooked rugs but Jenny will show them how to make something rare and beautiful, won't you, Jenny?'

Jenny preened, her composure restored, but their smiling complacency was short-lived when the front door burst open with such a clatter they all, including the doctor who spilled his tea, nearly jumped out of their skins.

It was Brooke Armstrong. He was dressed for riding but his outfit was muddied, his hair tumbling about his forehead, his cheek cut and he was slapping his riding crop dangerously against his leg.

'Mr Armstrong,' the doctor began, 'you seem to have taken a fall. Is there anything—'

'Good morning, sir,' Brooke answered him politely, his voice like ice, his gaze sweeping from the doctor to his wife at whom the ice was directed. 'That is kind of you but I have come to take my wife home where she belongs.'

'Brooke, I really must stay for the moment. Violet has just given birth—'

'Which is nothing to do with you, madam, so if you would—'

'I cannot come just now but—'

'There seem to be enough women to deal with whatever is going on here and therefore no need of your help. So, be so kind as to get your coat and come with me.'

He was dangerous and Doctor Chapman took a step towards him but one look from Brooke stopped him.

'I do not wish to give offence but I would advise you not to interfere, sir. This is between my wife and myself. You will be hearing from her very soon, through me, I might add. Now then, Charlotte, you and I will take our leave.'

Charlotte stood quite still. His words pricked like needles over the surface of her skin making their way reluctantly to her brain. He had been in a hot, violent rage before and had hit her but now his anger was cold and his eyes told her she had best not defy him or she would suffer the consequences, or rather these women and their children would be the ones to suffer. It was in her hands. She had come here this morning with the intention of telling Kizzie what had transpired and then leaving quickly but she had become, without meaning to, embroiled in the drama of the birth of Violet's baby.

'What must I do?' she asked him quietly while the others in the room, including Robbie who had no idea what was happening, stared in apprehension at the cruel face of the man who had shown them nothing but kindness.

'Come home with me, *and stay there!*'

# 16

None of the guests who attended the hunt ball, at least at the beginning of the evening, were aware of the frozen stillness with which Brooke Armstrong and his lovely young wife contained themselves and were not awfully sure of the precise instant when they realised that something, they didn't know what, was seriously awry. Was it when she icily refused his polite invitation to waltz with him and then in the very next moment, as her husband stood beside her, accepted Joel Denton, leaving Brooke stranded at the edge of the floor? She laughed and chatted and, they thought, flirted with young Denton, allowing him to swing her off her feet, the hem of her exquisite gown riding almost up to her knees and showing a great deal of her lacy stockings in a most shocking manner. When the waltz ended, instead of returning to her husband she continued to dance with Joel Denton which was simply not done! She grew flushed and even lovelier, her gleaming, tawny coil of hair, the colour of the fox with which the event was associated, coming loose with curls escaping in tendrils about her ears.

Brooke stood, outwardly unperturbed by his wife's improper behaviour, listening to his wife's father complain about he knew not what, nor cared, for he was focused on the sight of his wife swinging and swaying around the floor, this time in the arms of Jack Ackroyd. She was wearing one of the elegant gowns he had bought her in Paris made of ivory lace moulded tightly round her slender waist and cut low over her splendid

bosom, the bodice slipping from her shoulders in a provoca-
tive way he did not care for. He had bought her jewels,
emeralds and diamonds and rubies, and a necklace of aqua-
marines because, although they were not precious, they were
the exact colour of her eyes. She wore none of them, instead
choosing a simple necklace of seed pearls that had belonged to
her mother and she was magnificent. It was clear every man in
the room thought so, while the women thought her fast.

'. . . and I was saying only the other day to Elizabeth it was
high time we had my daughter and her husband to dine. Now
that Charlotte has settled into her new life as mistress of King's
Meadow and has, presumably, become accustomed to entertaining surely we may expect—'

Arthur Drummond was startled when Brooke turned on
him.

'What?' he snapped and all about them a sudden silence fell.

'I was only saying, my dear fellow, that after – what is it? –
nine, ten months of marriage, you and Charlotte might care to
begin entertaining your neighbours.' He smirked, unshakable
in his arrogant belief that he and his wife were welcome in his
daughter's home, or indeed anyone's home, anyone of note,
that is, and was only surprised that, as yet, no invitation had
been forthcoming. He met Brooke Armstrong on the hunting
field during the season but now that it was ended he was keen
to continue what he saw as an advantageous connection. He
and his new wife were welcome in many houses but none of
their owners was as wealthy or influential as his son-in-law.
Arthur was somewhat strapped for cash at the moment as a
result of one or two schemes into which he had gambled
money and lost, so when he had heard that Charlotte and her
husband were to be guests at the hunt ball he had hoped to
sound out Brooke delicately on the question of a loan. His own
wife was not in attendance this evening, her husband's reason
for her absence given as a slight cold, the black eye and swollen

cheek he had given her hidden from all the servants bar her discreet maid. She was, or had been, in the first months of their marriage, inclined to argue with him, and even to run to her home at Hill Edge and her elderly parents, but her father Sir Clive had soon put a stop to that since he had been glad to get her off his hands at the age of twenty-five and had told her she had made her bed and must lie in it. Arthur's own children, had they been asked, which they weren't, could have told Elizabeth that her husband's complete belief that he should be the absolute ruler in his own home was set in stone and that to argue with him was not only useless but physically dangerous.

'So what do you say, my dear fellow? Can we expect to receive an invitation to your next dinner party at King's Meadow? Charlotte is obviously well able to hold her own when it comes to mixing with polite society,' nodding his head in Charlotte's direction where two gentlemen were almost engaging in fisticuffs over who should take her into supper.

He was astounded and mortally offended when his son-in-law brushed him aside, strode across the shining floor and, taking his wife's wrist in a vicious grip, dragged her, still laughing, towards the doorway that led into the wide hall. They were watched in a silence that was broken only by whispers, though Lady Denton was heard to say 'Well!' in a loud and shocked voice.

Charlotte had already drunk three glasses of champagne, one handed to her as she and Brooke entered the ballroom, another put in her hand by Joel Denton who was enchanted by this hitherto little known wife of Brooke Armstrong, a man he thought to be a dry old stick. Like all the young he considered any man approaching thirty had one foot in the grave. But Armstrong's wife, who could be only a year or two younger than himself, might turn out to be great fun. She laughed and tossed her head in a most tantalising way so he was inordinately put out when Armstrong snatched his wife away and disappeared into the hall.

A buzz of conversation broke out in the ballroom as soon as they left, most thinking they understood now why Armstrong had kept his young wife hidden away for so long.

'Now then, madam,' Brooke hissed to his still merry wife as he propelled her into an ill-lit corner beneath the stairs, 'may I ask what you think you are doing?' His face was rigid with anger.

'Doing?' Charlotte asked, giggling and leaning against him, still clutching her glass of champagne.

'You are making a spectacle of yourself in front of our friends and I demand that you behave as a lady, *as my wife* should.'

'Why, Brooke, I am only doing what you have asked me to do.' She hiccupped, then put her hand to her mouth as a child would. 'I am mixing with *your* friends as ordered. This is a ball and I am dancing. Is that not correct? The young men are particularly complimentary and I am enjoying myself, as you bade me to. You told me—'

'I did not tell you to get drunk and if—'

'Drunk? Am I drunk? Well, if I am it is a very pleasant way to get through this . . . this . . .'

He roughly took the glass of champagne from her hand, in the process spilling some on her gown and a passing footman who carried a tray was startled when a hand shot out from beneath the wide, curving staircase and crashed the glass on to the tray.

'We had a bargain, you and I,' Brooke continued in a deadly voice. 'You were to perform your social duties as my wife and I was to allow those homeless, *pregnant* young women you have taken under your wing to remain in the Dower House. Since we married this is only your second entrée into what is known as polite society, the first where you talked of nothing but fallen women, and you now seem to imagine you can dance and flirt with any man who comes within your range. You are making an exhibition of yourself, and of me. Again! Everyone is talking about you and your behaviour and it is doubtful the Dentons will invite us again.'

'It is you who are making a fool of yourself treating your friends to the spectacle of a—'

'Stop it, stop it, or I swear I will—' Brooke heard his own voice start to rise and with a rush of self-realisation knew that what drove him on was pure jealousy. Sheer, unadulterated jealousy. She was the loveliest and liveliest woman here, drawing the men to her like bees to a flower. She was glorious and his love and need of her was barely under control. He wanted to shake her, hit her, drag her into his arms and kiss her until she, and he, were breathless. Instead he was snarling at her and accusing her of disporting herself in an unseemly manner and turning him into the jealous husband he was.

She stood away from him, no longer under the influence of the champagne, it seemed, and was watching him coolly, then she spoke.

'Are we to return to the ballroom or would you like to take me home? Either way it is of no interest to me. I have agreed to your terms since I will not see these girls turned out on to the streets and their babies put into an orphanage. I cannot believe that that is what you want either. I have mixed this evening with your friends and have even exchanged a word or two with my father – oh yes, while your back was turned he spoke of dining – so I feel I have kept my part of the bargain. I cannot help it if . . . if the young men ask me to dance. I believe that is what we came for.'

'Besides dancing so recklessly I wish you to sit and talk to the ladies with a view to forming acquaintances. There will be tennis parties, visits to Ascot for the race meets, Hendon and . . . and other events this summer, but if you are to do nothing but flirt and prance about the ballroom . . .' He listened to himself with horror.

'Is that what I was doing? Well, I'm sorry if that offends you but I do not see Patsy's husband objecting to—'

'Patsy Ackroyd is not exactly the kind of lady I had in mind—'

'She is lively, which cannot be said of the others.'

'That is not what I meant, Charlotte.' He was being pushed too far and it showed in the way he dragged his hand through his dark, curling hair, ruffling its carefully brushed smoothness. 'Damnation, woman, can you not see what you are doing, making a show of yourself? Even your gown is not quite decent.'

She looked down at herself in genuine bewilderment. 'What is wrong with my gown? You were with me when I bought it.'

'It is . . . you are not . . . look at you: it is slipping from your shoulder and your hair is . . . is wild.' She did indeed look enchanting and his aching heart could understand why the men clustered about her but it would not do. It seemed whatever he decided she would be talked about. Let her have her way with the wild scheme she had conceived, a home for dishonoured young women and their children, a factory – *God in heaven, a factory* – go into business of sorts, or force her into the mould of the wives of his class and have her whispered about because she was beautiful, charming, wildly attractive to men. Whatever he chose he must stand on the sidelines and watch her either disgust them or bewitch them.

Charlotte watched him dispassionately. She had not deliberately set out to draw these tedious young men – and even older ones like Jack Ackroyd – to her side, to invite her to dance and indeed, in one case, to walk with him on Sir Charles's terrace. It seemed they were for some reason enraptured by her. It was a fine, mild evening with a full moon lighting the garden and the young man could see no reason why the exquisite, vivacious wife of the elderly husband, who should by rights be playing cards with other elderly husbands, should object!

But Charlotte, who was young and enjoying the adulation of these rather boring young gentlemen, was wise enough to know that providing she was in full view of Brooke and the other guests she was really breaking no rules.

'I have done no wrong, Brooke. I have done nothing improper and I cannot see what objections—'

'Young Denton swung you off your feet in the polka—'

'Oh really, Brooke.' She was unwise enough to laugh.

With a curse he took her hand and tucked it tightly in the crook of his arm. Almost dragging her, he guided her back to the ballroom, which was almost empty since most of the guests had adjourned to the supper room. The small orchestra was taking a break but there were several couples sitting at the small tables set round the room. They watched, openmouthed as Brook Armstrong towed his somewhat dishevelled wife towards the supper room where he sat her down at a table with Milly Pickford and Maddy Hill who were consuming a dish each of almond soufflé and gossiping about the very young woman who was literally thrust between them.

'I'll fetch you something to eat,' he told her curtly. 'Stay here until I return,' acutely aware that he was making a fool of himself. He bowed courteously to the ladies then shoved his way towards the tables where the excellent buffet provided by Lady Rosemary Denton was set out.

'Well, my dear,' Milly Pickford began, 'you seem to be enjoying yourself,' her spoon halfway to her mouth. 'This is your first hunt ball, is it not?'

'Yes indeed,' Charlotte answered politely, her heart sinking as, looking about her, she saw Joel Denton making his way rapidly towards them.

'Oh, bloody hell,' she exclaimed, words she had heard Brooke utter. Mrs Pickford and Mrs Hill were shocked. 'Brooke will kill me, or him, if that jackanapes does not leave me alone.'

Milly Pickford recovered her composure. 'You should not encourage him, my dear,' she ventured, exchanging a meaningful glance with her companion.

'I do not encourage him, Mrs . . . Mrs . . . I'm sorry, I have forgotten your name. I do not mean to be rude,' for Mrs Pickford, a well-known and important light in her world, had drawn herself up, her, chest thrust out like a pouter pigeon. She stood up, followed by Mrs Hill, and the pair of them, after bowing politely to her for they were ladies if she was not, glided to another table where Lady Denton chatted to Mrs Parker. Soon their heads were together, their glances cast in her direction so that she knew they were discussing her. And worse still, Joel Denton, smiling with satisfaction, sat down beside her.

'There you are, you gorgeous creature,' he said, his eyes devouring her half-exposed breasts, his mouth ready, it seemed, to fasten on hers. 'That husband of yours is an ogre to keep you so imprisoned and when he does let you out watches you like a hawk.'

'Really, Mr Denton—'

'Joel, please, we know one another better than—'

'We do not know one another at all, sir, and I would advise you to take yourself off since that ogre as you call him is descending on us with a face like thunder,' which was true. He held a plate in his hand which he had haphazardly piled with frosted tangerines, tartlets of salmon, caviar, mushroom pâté, truffles, all mixed together in a most unappetising heap.

Joel Denton rose hastily to his feet, backing away from the menacing figure of Brooke Armstrong and was later to say he had feared for his life and what the devil did the man expect when he brought the most delectable creature in their set to a ball. Was she not to speak to another man, never mind dance with him? He himself had distinctly heard her refuse an invitation from her husband to take to the floor so what were they to make of that?

Brooke sat down in the chair just vacated, first by Milly Pickford and then by Joel Denton. He put the plate before Charlotte and though his face was quite without expression there was an ominous air about him that alarmed her.

'What happened to Mrs Pickford and Mrs Hill?' he asked casually.

'I couldn't say. They just got up and walked away.'

'What did you say to them?'

'Nothing.'

'Nothing?'

'I may have sworn . . . cursed . . .'

'You swore in the presence of two ladies?'

'You swear in front of me and besides, Joel was coming over and I—'

'Joel? You encouraged him to—'

'No, I did not. I have encouraged none of this, Brooke.' Her face was pink with indignation and she leaned forward passionately while the room held its collective breath, for it seemed the Armstrongs were to argue in public, and loudly! 'You insisted I come here so I came. These . . . these popinjays mean nothing to me with their endless talk of hunting and the London season and were we to attend Ascot and how ravishing I look. It is not *real*, Brooke, any of it. Were we invited to the Hamiltons whoever they are, who give the most wonderful weekend parties at their country home near Matlock and then there was Cowes . . . Oh, dear Lord! Do you not see? Joel Denton is the man who seduced poor Jenny. A man I despise and yet you expect . . .'

She ran out of steam, sitting back disconsolately in her chair and he had the wild hope that he had not broken her spirit which he honoured, a thought that surprised him, but at the same time she was his wife and . . . and . . . Jesus, Christ Jesus, what was he to do except what he was doing? He had known when he married her that she was an untried girl who had been denied mixing with her own sort but he had hoped . . . God in heaven, he had hoped! What would happen when it was discovered that she was taking girls off the streets, *with their illegitimate children*, and meant to set them up in a business? It would rock the very foundations of the circle into which he, and she, had been born. She would be ostracised and he would be despised for allowing it. Not that he cared for his own sake but . . . oh, bugger it, why could she not see what it would do to her?

She stared down at her own hands which were twisting in her lap, unaware, as Brooke was not, that the company was watching them with disapproving but fascinated eyes. This kind of thing was not done in their society, for good manners and breeding forbade it. Certainly, as in all walks of life, there were undercurrents, marriages of convenience, older gentlemen, having sown their wild oats, wishing to continue their line. They took young wives capable of bearing children then, when a son was assured, both parties went their own way. Very discreetly, of course, offending no one, least of all one another. In public they were a polite couple, perhaps even fond of one another. They would not dream of scandalising their hostess with public displays such as the one just enacted by the Armstrongs. Patsy Ackroyd and other young wives flirted with the younger sons of good family and even took lovers but it was all done so circumspectly that no one was any the wiser and if they were, had the good manners to keep it to themselves. They were self-indulgent, monied, pleasure-seeking, but never guilty of ill-breeding.

Now this new wife of Brooke Armstrong, who himself came from an old family, had caused this scene. To be truthful it was

Armstrong himself who had worsened the situation by snatching her from young Joel Denton's arms, who was known for a naughty boy, and dragging her from the ballroom, disappearing for ten minutes, and then dragging her back again where he thrust her between Milly Pickford and Maddy Hill, with ice-cold instructions to remain where he had put her. But, according to the two ladies, she had insulted them by swearing like a stable boy!

'This is not a success, is it, Brooke?' she said sadly at last. 'It seems I am not a lady in the eyes of—'

'You come of a good family and should be conversant in the ways of society,' he said through clenched teeth.

'I was not trained, as other girls are trained by their mamas, Brooke. I had five brothers and was, as far as my father was concerned, no different from them . . .' remembering the beatings. 'Until he decided to marry me to you' – not realising how she crucified him with those few words – 'I was treated as they were. I know nothing of running a great house or the conventions of polite society, as you call it, and furthermore have no interest in them. I want to do something worthwhile. I have nothing in common with—'

'Then you will have to learn,' he interrupted harshly, his heart bleeding for her. 'But for now I think it best if we go home. We are an embarrassment to the Dentons so fetch your wrap and we will make our polite farewells. Let us hope—'

'That they will forgive me,' she said wryly.

'Yes.' His voice was soft now, but not with understanding. 'It seems you are determined to despise the conventions of the society in which we move. You are determined that ordinary social duties are beyond you and you will not conform to them but, my dear, I'm afraid you must.'

Brooke knew in his wounded soul that he sounded like some pompous, stiff-necked and arrogant fool but it seemed this was how he must be if he was to bring his young and foolish wife to heel. If he did not nip this thing in the bud right now he would never have the life he had envisaged when he married Charlotte Drummond.

He was vastly annoyed when, as they bade their coolly polite host and hostess goodnight and thanked them for their hospitality, Charlotte turned and waved to Patsy Ackroyd who stood in the doorway of the ballroom, a wide grin on her face. Patsy was arm-in-arm with Joel Denton!

They did not speak in the carriage on the journey to King's Meadow, both gazing out into the moon-lit night, both busy with their own fragmented thoughts. Johnson was waiting in the hall, surprised, they could tell, that they were home so early.

'I trust the evening was a success, sir, madam,' he said, as they made their way towards the stairs.

'Thank you, Johnson,' the master answered.

'Will I send Nellie to help the mistress, sir?' he asked, since Nellie, who was parlour-maid and with Kizzie over at the Dower House, had hopes of becoming Mrs Armstrong's lady's maid.

'No, thank you, Johnson,' the master said and instead of entering the adjoining bedroom in which he had slept for several weeks he followed the mistress into the bedroom they had once shared, closing the door firmly behind him.

Johnson was not one for gossip. After all he was the butler, the head of the household staff, but he could not help himself when he found Mrs Dickinson and Mrs Groves still sitting with their feet up before the kitchen fire.

'He's gone into her bedroom,' he whispered to them, though the rest of the servants were all in their beds. They knew at once what that meant.

'Well, it's about time an' all,' from Mrs Groves with a satisfied expression on her face.

★    ★    ★

He made savage love to her in their bed that night as though putting his mark of possession on what was his and when he was replete, lying exhausted on her breast, both of them slicked with the sweat of their exertions she told him that she thought she might be pregnant with their child, wanting to add that for all his exhortations to conform to the conventions of their class, it was nature and not his words that were to force her to do just that!

# 17

Lucy Jean Armstrong was born on the night of 23 December and was the most beautiful child anyone had ever clapped eyes on. The servants who had crowded round her when she was brought down to the kitchen in the arms of her proud father – along with a bottle of the finest champagne to celebrate her birth – even her four uncles who were at King's Meadow for the Christmas holidays agreed. In fact Lucy's father quite had his nose put out of joint by their admiration and exuberant presence in the bedroom he shared with his wife and who had all wanted a 'hold' of their new niece.

'Aye up,' he said smilingly the next day, in a fair imitation of the Yorkshire dialect that was all around him in his own servants. 'Would you chaps bugger off and let me have a few minutes alone with my wife and daughter? That means you as well, Robbie,' who would have curled up on the bed beside his sister. Robbie had just begun to realise that with the arrival of Lucy Jean – Lucy for Brooke's mother, Jean for Charlie's, and his own, of course – he would have two rivals for his sister's attention and was doing his best to stake a claim while the 'kid', as he called her, was bundled in her father's arms. For the past three or four months, as Charlie became more cumbersome – apparently, astonishingly, the baby was growing inside her! – he had, when he was not at school or playing with Jed or Tad Emmerson, or Davy Nicholson, accompanied Charlie on ambles through the fields and wood-land of King's Meadow. He had just turned eight now and could be trusted to watch over her, a trust he was proud of and he did not care for the idea that this new kid might spoil things. It was Jed who had told him where the baby was to come from, Jed being a farm lad and knowledgeable about such things. He had not believed him at first but as his sister grew fatter and fatter he was forced to admit it must be true.

Reluctantly he climbed from the bed and followed his four brothers from the room. They all donned warm coats and after teasing the maidservants who were all in a swoon over the new baby as they went through the kitchen and persuading Mrs Groves to give each of them a huge piece of her second Christmas cake, the first being saved for Christmas Day, they dashed out into the drifts of freshly fallen snow to play. Even Henry, who was a great boy of seventeen, threw snowballs with enthusiasm, all the brothers falling about in hysterical laughter as the four dogs chased the snowballs and looked so funny and bewildered when they failed to catch them. They would have galloped off on the horses that their brother-in-law kept in his stables but the snow was too deep, drifting several feet high against walls and hedges. Their high-spirited shouts could be heard even in their sister's bedroom.

'Thank God for that,' Brooke pronounced with a heartfelt sigh, 'a bit of peace at last,' moving to the bed where his wife lay. He held his precious child possessively in his arms, unaware, as all of them seemed to be, that the infant was quite ordinary as all other newborns are, red-faced with indignation, with no more than a blob for a nose, an open mouth revealing shining gums and a tongue aquiver ready to give voice. She had not yet revealed the colour of her eyes but her hair was what could only be called ginger, a throwback to Charlie's side of the family who had all been what had been called 'carrot-tops'. 'And where the devil did she get the ginger hair?' Brooke asked plaintively, accusingly, but grinning just the same, since in his eyes the baby was perfect. 'And we'll have to watch those lads and the servants, for the child is in a fair way to being spoiled with all this adoration.'

'And who is the worst culprit?' Charlotte asked him indulgently. 'You would have taken her into your own bed last night if I'd let you, though that nurse you insist should remain would have had something to say. That's another thing, Brooke. As soon as I'm allowed to put a foot out of this bed she's out of the door. I swear if she calls me "mother" once more I'll throw something at her.'

He looked at his wife in her nest of pillows, her hair still lank from the sweat of her labour, her eyes deep and tired in her pale face and his own softened with love. He was distracted for a moment from his doting contemplation of his child and began again the argument which had been going on for the past six weeks when Doctor Chapman had told her and Brooke he had engaged a nurse to be installed a week before the baby was expected.

'Thank you, Doctor,' Brooke had said. 'I know we can trust you to find some sensible, experienced woman to care for Charlotte and the child. My wife will—'

'Your wife is quite capable of caring for her own child, thank you, Brooke Armstrong, and will be up and about—'

'We'll see about that, lady,' Brooke had snapped. 'If Doctor Chapman thinks a nurse is necessary, and I agree with him, then that is all there is to say about it.' He turned to the doctor who sat awkwardly balancing a cup of coffee on his knee. 'You will attend to it, won't you, Doctor?'

'No, he won't! Now, Doctor Chapman, you know I am a young, strong and healthy woman, don't you? Not one of those faint-hearted ladies who insist upon remaining in their beds for weeks on end after giving birth.'

'Well, yes, Mrs Armstrong, but if your husband wishes you to—'

'I do, Doctor. I am of the opinion that Charlotte should stay where she is for at least a fortnight then keep to her room and rest. A wet nurse will be needed . . .'

Brooke had explained the matter delicately to Milly Pickford – for it was not quite the thing a lady and gentleman should discuss – in a quiet moment when he was dining with Chris and Maddy Hill. Milly had given birth four times and all her children had lived, so he chose her to explain why his wife could no longer move about in society. Not that Milly Pickford was eager to resume her acquaintance with Brooke's wife after the fiasco at the hunt ball but it was the custom for ladies in their society to retire from the social scene when they were with child and to stay hidden for at least four weeks after giving birth and she had told him so.

'Well, I'm not sure I agree, Mr Armstrong,' the doctor told him now, for Wallace Chapman treated women who, a day after being delivered, were back at their looms or scrubbing buckets, leaving the new infant in the care of the half a dozen children they already had. It was, of course, not necessary for Mrs Armstrong, who had a dozen servants and a doting husband to care for her, but a month seemed overlong to him.

Since Charlotte had disclosed her condition to him Brooke had known a time of great peace and contentment. He had been ready to weep with joy in the most unmanly way when, with a cool expression, she had told him she was to have his child. He was jubilant. Not only was she pregnant but her condition would surely put a stop to the nonsensical scheme she had devised in the Dower House. He meant to find homes for all the girls who were housed there. Somewhere they could keep their children, so surely that would please her and the one without a mother could be adopted by a worthy childless couple. She would be too busy caring for her own child, which was one reason he was willing to allow his wife her way on the subject of the nurse. He'd said nothing to her of his plans, naturally, for a pregnant woman must not be upset, especially if the pregnant woman was his wife. He would let her play her role at the Dower House if it kept her happy for the period of her pregnancy but when the child came and they were both safe, he would clear it all up. He had influence and power in the town and no one would suffer. Besides, she would need Kizzie to help her with his new daughter and the other children he meant to give her as soon as she was recovered from the birth of Lucy. He had gathered the servants together and instructed them that they were in no way to interfere with their mistress's philanthropic arrangement at the Dower House. Let her have her way. The only activity she was forbidden, which was only right and proper, was that she was not to ride! Percy and Arch would make sure of that. They would not be entertaining until the baby was born since no undue exertion must trouble her.

They were all intoxicated with the birth of the child and needed no instructions from the master to watch over her, to coddle her, to give in to her smallest whim. A baby in the house! At last! And what a pet she was, they told one another, though where that ginger hair came from was a bit of a facer. Still, perhaps it would darken to the same colour as the mistress's. And the master was made up. Coddle her! The mistress and her new daughter would have more coddling than she knew what to do with, for they would be fighting with one another to share in the joy a baby in the house would bring. They all had their own jobs to do, true, but if there was any task they could perform, preferably to get one in the eye of that stuck-up nurse, they would be there ready to do it!

Charlotte watched her husband as he strolled around the room, the baby in his arms, crooning some tuneless noise and wished he would go away. Put the baby in her arms and leave her to study the tiny creature with no one studying *her*. The tiny fascinating human being who was her daughter and who was not yet a day old. A scrap with a red little face and Charlotte had not the faintest idea what to do with her but whatever it was she meant to be alone to get on with it. She was amazed by her own helplessness, for after all she had nursed, winded, dressed, even bathed babies over at the Dower House but then they had not been her own and there had been a mother to hand them to. But this newborn infant who could not even hold up her head defeated her, filled her whole mind with anxiety and she longed for the door to close on the pair of them and leave her to puzzle it out.

'Shall I take her to her wet nurse, Charlotte?' Brooke was asking her. 'She's waiting in the nursery and if I don't get her back there within the next few minutes the dragon will be down to claim her.' He rocked his child with an expression on his face Charlotte had never before seen. She had sometimes noticed the tail end of it when she had caught him looking at herself but she really could not identify it. He was gazing down at his new daughter, his face transformed with tenderness, a love, a possessive bewitchment that was unmistakable. 'I'll have to go,' he added, bending his head to kiss the rounded cheek nestling against his chest. 'Boyle' – who was the cowman in charge of Brooke's small herd – 'is taking Clover up to Fuller's Farm to his bull and I said I'd give him a hand. It's a bit unmanageable – the bull I mean – and will take some handling.'

He moved towards the bell to summon the nurse but Charlotte held out her arms. 'No, give her to me. What with first you and the boys and then every servant in the house making some excuse to sidle in and see her I've hardly had a chance to get a good look at her myself.'

Reluctantly he placed the baby in Charlotte's arms as though not quite trusting his precious child with anyone but himself, even the child's mother, then after a brief kiss on his wife's forehead he left the room.

Lucy stirred then, taking Charlotte by surprise, turned her rosy mouth to Charlotte's breast and, though it was covered by the plain nightgown the nurse had thought suitable for her to wear, nuzzled against her nipple. Quite without thinking, for had she not seen the girls at the Dower House do the same, she uncovered her breast and allowed the eager mouth to latch on.

It was as if a bolt of lightning went through her. It didn't hurt, in fact it was quite glorious and inside her something glowed, melted, ran like honey in her veins and a great, peaceful love came. A love that she had never known before, not even for Robbie. So this was motherhood! This tiny human being had been a stranger to her, just a heaving burden she had carried inside her but she was that no longer. She was her child and she would defend her to the death if called for.

While her child slept at her breast she let her mind drift back over the past six or seven months and all that had taken place during that time. It had allowed her, while Brooke was jubilant with her long-awaited condition, in fact he was euphoric, believing it would finally curtail her activities, to carry on without restraint the scheme she had long planned but which he had balked at ever since it had been brought to his notice. She was aware that her pregnancy gave her power to do as she pleased, within reason, and she was sharp enough to know the boundaries – for it was believed that gravid animals, and that included human beings, must not be upset, must not be denied, however lunatic their desires. Nobody interfered with the growing number of young women at the Dower House nor the comings and goings of wagons containing labourers, painters, bricklayers, carpenters and their materials. Others brought furniture, stoves, bedding and all the necessities for decent living and the doctor was a frequent visitor since there were so many babies and young mothers who needed attention. They followed Moss Lane, turning into what was simply called the Lane. It was on the very boundary of Brooke's land with Birks Wood on the right, with no houses or cottages so that no one was disturbed or even saw them reaching the gate that led into the back yard of the Dower House. It had once been used to deliver coal directly from Caphouse Pit, groceries and such, to whoever was in residence at the Dower House and could not be seen from any window in the main house.

There were six young women there now and six babies. Jenny's Rose was almost a year old, an exquisite toddler on whom Jenny doted. Indeed she was so grateful to Mrs Armstrong not only for taking her in but also allowing her to keep her precious daughter, that she was willing to do any job asked of her. She worked on her special rugs which Mrs Armstrong called 'wall hangings', whenever she had a moment because she now helped Kizzie and Meggie with the running of the house. She and Rose – the only mother and child to do so – shared a bedroom in the house, and she was even allowed, providing she kept away from the main house, to take her child walking in the lovely gardens. John and Ned were considerably startled one day when they came face to face with her, for not only was she a stranger but she was very pretty, as was the baby whose hand she held. One of Mrs Armstrong's waifs, they were aware, and John, who was a family man himself with two grandchildren, immediately hunkered down and held out his hand to her but, never having seen a man except the doctor, Rose hid behind her mother's skirts. When Charlotte was told of the incident by Kizzie she felt a great sadness for the Dower House children.

Pearl, Ruth's abandoned child, had been more or less adopted by Meggie since no one else wanted her. She was the same age as Rose but was wilful, stubborn, plain, naughty, causing many an argument between Kizzie and Meggie, for Kizzie thought a smart smack on the bottom was the answer and refused to listen to her sister who said Pearl was 'high-spirited'. A child of barely twelve months! Violet named her little girl Pansy, and Aisling, who had almost been killed she was so badly beaten and had miscarried her child, recovered and begged to stay, pleading with her almost indecipherable Irish accent, even though, without a baby in her arms, Doctor Chapman could have found her employment elsewhere. This was the first home Aisling had ever known, for her savage and drunken father and indifferent mother had a dozen other children – those who had lived – and had neither the inclination nor the brass to make one. She was a quiet girl, bonny now that her bruises had healed with that look of her Irish ancestry, green eyes, freckled complexion and lustrous dark hair.

Cassie, Edna and Maudie were the last three to be brought in by the doctor, for he could see the place had reached its capacity. All three were bashed about and pregnant, Edna and Maudie bearing sons. Cassie named her child Anne, Edna's boy was Arthur and Maudie gave birth to Jack. Charlotte and Kizzie often pondered on why these poor, mistreated girls chose the names they did for their children. Was it some memory of a loved family member, or in the case of Edna and Maudie the names of the men who had got them into this sad condition?

The ground floor of the building opposite the Dower House had gradually been turned into a sizeable workplace where the shoddy was stored and rugs of every size and colour began to pile up in readiness for the day when Charlotte would seek out a market. Jenny did all the designs and taught the girls to work them, for these were not to be any of the haphazard floor mats flung down before kitchen ranges as seen in cottages up and down the country. They were in themselves works of art and Charlotte had secret hopes that the high-class carpet shop in the Bull Ring in Wakefield might be interested. If not, there were always the market stalls in the weekly market at the back of the cathedral.

On the upper floor a large dormitory and a bathroom were built, the bathroom a marvel to its occupants since none of them had ever used anything but a tin bath – occasionally – and an outside privy. There was a comfortable, warm bed and a chest of drawers for each girl, with cots or cradles for the babies and though it was impressed upon them that they were free to leave whenever they wanted, to take their chance in the unforgiving world, none of them, with the exception of Ruth, did so.

But Jenny's work was special. Charlotte had brought her a book from the library at King's Meadow, a book of paintings by famous artists, such as Gainsborough, Romney, Turner, Constable, Landseer, Millais, Whistler, plus the French who were scarcely known, Monet, Cézanne, Matisse but not Picasso since he would not be understood! From these Jenny chose the simple, countrified, pretty pictures that a family might enjoy. Each one took her a long time to accomplish but it was accepted among the other girls that she was the 'top' girl. She was in charge of the workroom, the supervisor, the designer.

Charlotte had also been busy, as Miss Seddon hoped she would, at the school at Overton. New stoves had been put in both classrooms and a constant supply of coal was readily available. New books, the latest in child education, were delivered, separate desks, one for each child, bright pictures for the walls, milk, a nourishing meal at dinnertime, and already those children were showing the benefit. They had all the amenities Charlotte meant for her own nursery and schoolroom though it crept into her mind that Lucy could do no better than Miss Seddon but what Brooke might say to his precious child going to the village school was a bit daunting. Anyway there was plenty of time for that. Five years!

And that was one of the problems she would have to overcome, for no child, or children, of hers was to be taught by a third-rate governess as she and her brothers had been. Robbie was to go to the grammar school in Wakefield in the autumn, which had been in existence since 1590 and had a wonderful reputation, and there was a girls high school where, when she was old enough, Charlotte meant to send Lucy.

She was interrupted in her musing by the abrupt and irritated arrival of the nurse who barely knocked on the door since she considered herself of such importance. She was horrified to find 'mother' snuggled down in bed with the baby, nurse's baby, in her arms!

'Mrs Armstrong, I really must protest. Baby should have been brought to the nursery half an hour ago and I was given to understand Mr Armstrong was to bring her. I'm surprised she isn't crying for a feed right now. The wet nurse is waiting and I'd be obliged if you would—'

'And I'd be obliged if you would not treat me as an imbecile, Nurse. My child is—'

'My responsibility, madam,' Nurse interrupted unwisely. 'I was engaged, as was the wet nurse, to see to baby's needs. Mothers must rest and—'

'Poppycock!'

'I beg your pardon. Mother and baby are—'

'As you can see *baby* is asleep quite peacefully. I fed her myself, you see, from my breast which was full of milk and what a relief it was to both of us, I can tell you, so you can send the wet nurse packing and yourself as well. My husband will pay you for—'

'I cannot go against the doctor's orders, Mrs Armstrong,' though the nurse was not at all sure she approved of Doctor Chapman, who was filled with new-fangled ideas which Nurse abhorred, but work was work and a wage was a wage. 'Besides, it is not quite the thing for mothers such as yourself to feed their own children. You are a lady.' Nurse, however, was not certain she agreed with that description despite the fact that

Mrs Armstrong was the daughter of one gentleman and the wife of another.

'Thank you, that will be all, Nurse. No, you shall not take the child. In fact I wish the cradle to be brought down here and placed by my bed. Please send someone over to the Dower House and ask Kizzie, Miss Aspin, to come at once.'

Nurse tried to argue. She was in command when a child was born and not only baby, but 'mother' was in her charge. The servants were expected to run and pander to her every wish and here was this . . . this *child*, for Mrs Armstrong could have been no more than seventeen or eighteen and with her hair hanging about her head in the most unladylike way looked about twelve!

'Madam . . .'

But madam had had enough. 'Please do as I say at once or must I ring the bell and get two of the men to escort you from the house?'

'Well!' Nurse flounced to the door and as she opened it a commotion could be heard coming from downstairs, the noise of many voices all speaking or crying at once.

'What is it? What is that noise?' Charlotte asked anxiously, clutching her baby to her as though whatever it was might harm her. 'Will you go down and—'

'I no longer work here, madam, so I will leave you.'

'But it sounds as though—'

'Nothing to do with me.' And with another flounce Nurse disappeared, apparently on her way to the nursery to pack her bag.

For a moment Charlotte lay rigidly in her bed then what sounded like a groan of agony floated up the stairs and before she knew it she was out of bed. Lucy was placed safely in the centre of the bed, tucked up so that she could not possibly fall and without donning her dressing gown Charlotte ran along the landing and skimmed downstairs so quickly she almost fell.

She burst through the kitchen door where the dreadful sounds were coming from and for a moment her heart literally stopped beating. They were all there, Mrs Dickinson, Mrs Groves, the maids, wringing their hands, and strangely several of the outdoor men and, even stranger still, Jack Emmerson, Cec Eveleigh and Jeff Killen from Foxworth Farm. Robbie stood pressed up against the kitchen wall, his face like paper, his eyes wide with shock, staring at the kitchen table where Brooke Armstrong lay, his head thrown back, his hands clutching his thigh from which blood was seeping.

Jack Emmerson, who was bending over Brooke, looked up and saw her, making nothing of her lawn nightdress and bare feet.

'I did me best, ma'am, but that bugger got 'im cornered and . . . well, I'ad ter shoot 'im.'

'He's been shot,' she managed to whisper, looking at Brooke who surely should not be screaming on the kitchen table.

'Not Mr Armstrong, ma'am. The bloody bull, but not before it gored Mr Armstrong.' Jack's face was anguished.

'The . . . the doctor?'

'On his way, ma'am, but . . . well . . .' He seemed to be telling her something dreadful and Charlotte contemplated her life without Brooke in it. It was unimaginable, unbearable, for she loved him so.

# 18

Jack Emmerson was nearly in tears and he was not, as his wife could confirm, a man who showed his feelings.

'Bloody bugger just went mad. Well, us knew 'e were a bad sod, didn't us, Dicky?' Dick Boyle nodded his head. 'But 'e could smell t'cow, tha' see. Us, me an' Mr Armstrong, 'ad a pole each, fastened to a ring in 'is nose.' He turned as though he must explain the procedure to the silent, white-faced, horrified group of servants. 'A bull, specially a bad-tempered beast like this 'un needed two men ter 'old him. Some'ow . . .' He bent his head and Dick Boyle put a comforting hand on his shoulder. 'Some'ow Mr Armstrong lost 'is end so there were only me ter 'old 'im. Sweet Jesus, 'e were strong. I 'adn't a bloody chance . . . 'e 'ad 'im down – master – an' I thought 'e's a gonner . . .'

Charlotte whimpered deep down in her throat.

'Oh, missis, I'm that sorry, but master weren't used ter . . . anyroad, my chap – I shoulda let 'im – well, 'e got shotgun off byre wall; us allus keeps it there in case. Good Christ, 'e moved fast, did Francie, an' bloody thing went down like a ton o' bricks; not on top o' Mr Armstrong, thank the good Lord but not afore 'e 'ad 'is 'orn in 'is thigh. My missis put a sheet – one of 'er best just off th'airer in't kitchen – ter try an' . . . but blood, it won't stop.'

'Where the dickens is everybody?' a voice shouted from the yard. 'Stop that, William, larking about like a schoolboy.'

'I *am* a schoolboy.'

'Pity about the snow though. I thought the lanes would be clear but Magic couldn't cope and even Max wasn't up to it.'

'I say, where the hell are Percy and Arch? Do we have to unsaddle the horses ourselves? I don't know if I can remember what Percy told me. Let's leave them for a minute, chaps, and go and beg a hot drink and something to eat from Mrs Groves . . .'

They burst into the kitchen, four big, handsome, rowdy boys, cheeks glowing, eyes sparkling, full of themselves in the confidence they had acquired since they had left their father's house. John was first through the door, stopping in mid-sentence so that those behind him all crashed into his back.

'Watch out, you fool,' Henry protested, but the scene that met their eyes appalled them and they fell silent. But their entrance had broken the nightmare spell those in the kitchen were under. Mrs Dickinson and Mrs Groves, Nellie, Connie, Tess, even Rosie blubbering as usual until a look from Mrs Groves silenced her. Mr Johnson, who knew he should be directing his staff since he was butler and they were in his charge but the truth was, never having been in this position before, he simply didn't know what to do.

'Jesus . . .' whispered Henry, then, as he spoke, the servants all began to bustle about doing they knew not what, just anything that might help the poor master in his agony. The gate they had brought him home on was still on the kitchen table and him on it. Blood from the gaping wound in his thigh was beginning to drip on the floor and Jack Emmerson turned his face to the wall in despair, evidently blaming himself for what he believed would be his landlord's death. Mr Armstrong wasn't used to farming methods, to bulls enclosed in small yards because of their meanness. He should have insisted on Dicky or one of his own cowmen to hold the sod. He would never forgive himself.

Again the back door was flung open. This time it was Doctor Chapman who took one look round then bellowed, 'Everybody out except you two' – pointing to Mrs Groves and Mrs Dickinson – 'and what the hell are you doing out of bed, Mrs Armstrong?' Kizzie was behind him and within seconds the kitchen had emptied, the outside men to the yard – not too far – and the women to the housekeeper's parlour so as to be handy if needed.

'Where's the baby?' was all Kizzie said.

'In my bed,' Charlotte croaked, edging closer to Brooke despite the doctor's words and at once Kizzie called for Nellie and despatched her to check on the infant. It seemed no one trusted the nurse! She and the doctor then bent over the now – thankfully – unconscious man on the table. They had watched in fascinated wonder as Doctor Chapman had inserted a needle into the master's arm and at once he was quiet. What a marvel this doctor was, for he seemed to know all there was to know about the latest medical techniques.

'Fetch back four men,' the doctor ordered and there was a scuffle on the doorstep on who they were to be. Percy, Arch, Henry, since he was a big strong lad, and Adam, the handyman, inched over to the doctor.

'Now then, lads. You must lift Mr Armstrong off the gate which the ladies and I will remove then hold him steady *and flat* while one of the women, you' – addressing Mrs Dickinson who had not been spoken to like that since she was a 'tweenie' forty years ago – 'I want a large clean sheet on the table and you men must place Mr Armstrong back on to it. Pass me my bag, Kizzie, thank you, and get Mrs Armstrong a chair or put her to bed.'

'I'm not leaving here until my husband has been . . . has been . . .' She didn't know how to finish the sentence but her face was set in rigid lines of determination and so was her jaw, which told them they would have to carry her out kicking and screaming if needs be. She was glad of the kitchen chair though, which she hitched to the head of the table while the four men lifted their master as gently as though he were made of porcelain on to the snowy sheet Mrs Dickinson had spread.

Without a word they left reluctantly.

'Now I must cut Mr Armstrong's clothing from him. Hold him, Kizzie, while I administer the anaesthetic.'

'But he's already unconscious, Doctor.'

'I know, but he might come to. Thank God for the doctors who helped to bring anaesthesia to the human race. It makes our work so much easier and God bless Joseph Lister,' he told those in the kitchen who wondered who the dickens he was talking about. Mr Johnson, feeling inadequate, stood by the back door ready to shout for help should it be needed.

'Very well. Scissors please, Kizzie.' And to the horror of the two women, who despite the 'Mrs' had never married nor even seen a naked man before, the doctor cut every bit of clothing from their master's body.

'Burn them,' he told them and to tell the truth they didn't want to touch them for they were so dirty, much of the 'dirt' appearing to be animal dung but you could not argue with a doctor who was attending to what appeared to be a dying man, could you? The doctor had anaesthetised the master, then, satisfied, he began his work.

'A warm blanket, if you please, madam,' he growled over his shoulder, 'to cover the upper part of the patient's torso which, thank God, appears to be uninjured. Now then, plenty of hot water and then to the wound.'

At the top of Brooke's thigh just below where his manhood nestled – now shrunk to the size of a man's thumb and almost hidden in the thicket of his pubic hair – there was a gaping, bloody hole through which a splinter of bone pointed to the ceiling. Charlotte moaned and stood up, longing to do something to help this man who was, and had been though she had not realised it, the centre of her universe. She had hated him, made love with him, fought with him, borne his child and quite simply would die if he did.

But her senses were reeling. She knew she had been torn during the birth and that Doctor Chapman had sewn her up but something had given way on her mad dash downstairs. The patch of blood on the chair confirmed it so she hurriedly sat down again, for she wanted nothing to distract the doctor from the work he was doing.

'Thank God it missed the femoral artery,' she heard him mutter to himself. With Kizzie's help he took three hours to clean the wound, replace the splinter of bone to its correct position, using first one instrument, then another, repairing torn muscles, sewing this flap of skin to another and though the patient, which was what the doctor was calling him now, would bear a dreadful scar for the rest of his life – which might be short – stopped the flow of blood. He had done the best he could. Infection was what he feared, for a farmyard and the bull's horns were far from clean and then there was the fear that the muck he had found which he – and Joseph Lister – had done their best to clean, might turn the wound gangrenous!

On the opposite side to where the doctor and Kizzie were working Brooke's flaccid hand dropped off the table and Charlotte held it, kissed it, willing him to survive, to come back to her, to open his eyes and smile that whimsical smile that was peculiarly his. To be the strong and gentle man she knew him to be. She brushed back his tumble of hair and was rewarded by a slight lift at the corner of his mouth as though he had heard her thoughts and was doing his best to smile, knowing she was there.

They were all watching the doctor and Kizzie, both wearing what had once been servants' vast, gleaming white aprons covering them from neckline to ankle. They were not so pristine now with blood and other nasty matter adhering to them. The doctor was attempting to protect the stitched wound with a spotlessly clean makeshift bandage torn from a freshly laundered sheet. It was an awkward place to bandage and they were all bending forward, holding their breath as the doctor's clever fingers did their work.

They recoiled when, without a sound, their young mistress slipped from her chair and fell to the kitchen floor. On the chair where she had crouched was a pool of blood!

The doctor's voice was crisp. 'Get someone to carry Mrs Armstrong . . . yes, yes, any of the men, to carry her to her bed. I'll be there directly. You' – pointing at Mrs Dickinson and Mrs Groves, neither was sure but they both jumped forward – 'go with her and pack her tightly between her legs with towels; yes, you're women and should know where I mean . . . the birth canal.'

Charlotte's brother John and Ned were through the door from the yard as a shout went up, exploding into the kitchen which they described later as looking like a charnel house since the doctor was not concerned where his bloody swabs fell. They were both white with shock but under the doctor's instructions they gently lifted the senseless woman and followed by the cook and the housekeeper carried her from the kitchen, up the stairs and into her bedroom. They laid her on the tumbled bed from which she had recently leaped and hurriedly backed out of the room, getting in the way of the two women but glad to be out of it.

'Lift her nightie, Grace,' Mrs Groves murmured, 'there's towels in the drawer . . . aye, that's right, now. Oh, dear God, quick as you like, she's bleeding to death; there, that's it, pack them in, open her legs wider. Oh, sweet Jesus . . . there, that's it.' And as the blood soaked one towel they thrust in another, praying the doctor would not be long, for not only would they lose their master but their mistress as well.

Wallace Chapman looked as though he'd been at work in the slaughter house when, satisfied with both of his patients, he allowed a cup of tea to be pressed into his hand and sat to drink it. Brooke Armstrong still lay unconscious on the kitchen table but his colour was better and the ghastly wound was holding, he thought, since no more blood seeped from him, and the new mother's birth wound, which he had stitched the day before, had been closed again. The servants stood around in postures of white-faced shock, slack-faced with the horror of it all, Rosie weeping, and could you blame her they all said, one or two of the maids doing the same. Hot, strong tea was passed round and little by little they pulled themselves together, the outside men hanging around the back kitchen door waiting for news and up in the nursery Nellie rocked the fractious baby wondering when somebody would come and tell her what to do. She had been an only child and had worked at King's Meadow since she was twelve and so knew absolutely nothing about babies. She was delighted when a timid knock at the door sounded, but the head that cautiously peeped round it was not one she knew.

'I come ter 'elp. Kizzie sent me.' It was one of them trollops from the Dower House but Nellie didn't care if it was old Mother Carey herself if only someone would give her a hand. Tell her to scrub a floor or scour out an oven and though it was not her job she'd do it willingly but she was lost when it came to babies, especially when she didn't know what was happening downstairs.

'Haven't I brung some baby milk so—'

'Thank God . . . er . . . I don't know what tha' name is . . .'

'Aisling. I've not one o' me own but I know what ter do.' Her Irish brogue was so thick Nellie had a job to understand her but she managed to decipher it.

'Thanks, lass. I'll be off then. Is there any news o't master?'

'To be sure, 'e's doin' nicely an' so's missis.'

Nellie stopped at the door, her face dropping. 'Missis?'

'Wasn't she bleedin' something terrible, poor thing, to be sure, but it's seen to an'—'

But Nellie was out of the room and down the stairs like a bullet from a gun while Aisling looked down into the petulant face of the new baby, then, sitting in the comfortable chair by the fire, cradled her expertly before thrusting the teat into the rosy mouth. For a moment Miss Lucy Jean Armstrong wasn't sure whether she liked the teat but in her baby wisdom must have decided it was better than nothing, so began to suck contentedly on it.

'Now aren't you as lovely as the day?' Aisling murmured, not knowing that at last she had found her proper place in this strange household.

Brooke Armstrong slowly came back to consciousness drifting a little, his eyes cloudy and then clearing a bit, seeing nothing much at first but then with a great sigh of relief recognised the canopy of the bed he shared with Charlotte. So he wasn't dead then, or if he was some benign being had kindly placed him in his own room. He was flat on his back and felt so weak he could barely turn his head, wondering what the hell was the matter with him. Why was he trussed up like a mummy from the museum? He did his best to move but then was devoured by a pain so excruciating he screamed, though for some reason no sound emerged from his mouth and surely he would have heard it, wouldn't he? It splayed up from his penis through his belly and chest and was so agonising even his bloody teeth hurt. His leg was on fire and his foot twitched and again he cried out or thought he did and this time someone heard, for a soft hand cupped his cheek and soft lips rested on his and a gentle voice murmured words of comfort. Something pricked his arm and he thought he heard Doctor Chapman's voice, then, sighing thankfully, he fell away into a dark and comforting hole where nothing hurt but he would like to have had another chance of those lips, by God!

The next time he was aware of himself, again in the same bed but with candles glowing about the place, he managed to turn his head, just enough to see her and there she was, sitting right next to his bed with her breast uncovered and in her arms lay a baby whose milky mouth was attached to her nipple. The most beautiful sight he had ever seen! His Charlotte . . . and a baby, his baby . . . what was her name? A lovely child, a little girl, and his . . . his . . . with his dearest . . . dearest . . . his love.

'My love . . .,' he sighed, the first time he had ever called her that out loud and even now barely above a whisper, and at once she rose to her feet and came to him, her smile dazzling, the baby still in her arms and bent over him and nothing was ever the same for them again.

'Oh, my love' she answered, the first time she had ever said those words. She began to weep. 'My darling . . . Oh, Brooke, I thought I had lost you.' Then she leaned over and kissed him and her tears fell on his face. The baby grizzled between them, her mouth searching for the friendly nipple but her mother was absorbed with her father and rather impatiently turned and put her down somewhere then, with the greatest delicacy, lay down next to him.

'I've been waiting for you, darling, and for this.' Her breath was sweet and warm against his neck though she hardly touched him lest she hurt some damaged part of him.

'How long?' he asked hoarsely.

'All my life, I think, but I didn't know it. I needed to love someone; a man, and it turned out to be you.' She sounded surprised and her voice was still choked with those amazing tears.

'My love . . .'

'Yes, I am and you are mine . . .'

'Dear God, I've waited . . . and now I can't damn well touch you. But I meant how . . . how long have I been . . .' He was very weak and his voice was beginning to fade.

She thought he might be drifting off again into that morphine-induced sleep Doctor Chapman had so miraculously achieved. 'A week; the bull at Jack Emmerson's . . .'

'Yes, the bloody bull . . . I remember now . . .' then he slipped away again. Carefully she eased herself from him and turned to the baby who was ready to let her know that it was her turn now. Moving slowly, mopping her eyes, for she was frail herself, she pulled the bell and almost at once Kizzie was there, bending over the master's bed then turning to her and the baby, whose full-throated yell was getting under way.

''Od thi' 'osses, Miss Charlotte, an' give yon baby ter me. Aisling's got some babby milk ter 'elp out so I'll tekk 'er up. Now see, I'm ringin't doctor an' 'e'll be over as soon as that gig can get 'im 'ere. Oh, my lass, my lass, what a worry the pair o' thi' 'ave bin. See, get thi' ter bed; no, I know tha' don't want ter leave 'im but tha' own little bed's right 'ere next to 'is an' when 'e wakes there yer'll be.'

Charlotte allowed herself to be tucked up in the truckle bed that had been brought to lie next to the one Brooke occupied, turning on to her right side so that she could see him but she began to doze and within minutes was asleep so that when Doctor Chapman arrived both his patients were out for the count. Kizzie helped him to pull back the covers on the injured man and gently remove the dressings on his wound. He sniffed at it and apparently seemed satisfied.

'No smell of bad cheese,' he murmured as though talking to himself.

'Bad cheese?'

'Aye, gangrene. Let's hope there's no infection, though this is a strong, healthy man and should recover.'

Looking at the absolutely dreadful injury in Brooke Armstrong's groin, Kizzie found it hard to believe, but if any man could mend her master it was this one.

'Now Mrs Armstrong. I'm afraid we'll have to wake her so that I can examine her stitches, which I might remove.'

Charlotte sat up abruptly when Kizzie gently shook her, then, seeing the doctor smiling down at her, turned at once to Brooke.

'No, Mrs Armstrong, your husband is doing well as far as I can see. It is you I wish to examine.'

'He is . . . Doctor, make him better, please. I cannot bear it if . . . I love him so, you see, and . . .'

Kizzie put her hand to her face, since if anybody knew how Miss Charlotte had felt about her husband it was she. Miss Charlotte had married him for the sake of others, her brothers and at the insistence of her bullying father. Now, it seemed, he had become dear to her and Kizzie felt the emotion well up in her, for did this mean her young mistress was to find the happiness and fulfilment she had previously lacked?

'He will need careful nursing.'

'I will nurse him,' Charlotte said eagerly.

'No, my dear, a professional nurse.'

'That one for the baby was—'

'I know, but I do believe the young woman – Aisling? – is doing a good job which will give you more time to . . . to cosset your husband. Your love is his best medicine, but now let me look at you and see if those stitches can come out; then, when your husband is himself again you and he will be able to . . . to . . . resume . . .'

Kizzie turned away and was ready to weep as she had seen Miss Charlotte do only an hour or so ago because it seemed there was to be a happy household again and with Jenny as her deputy at the Dower House her mistress and master could be the husband and wife, the friends, the lovers Kizzie had always wanted for them.

In an untidy and none too clean bedroom in the home that had once been Charlotte's and her five brothers' a woman bled slowly to death, almost drowning her newborn child before the slovenly midwife in attendance noticed the infant was born.

'Oh bugger,' she groaned, heaving herself from the chair before the good fire she herself had built up. She hastily lifted the baby from between the thighs of what she could see was a dead woman, cut the cord and placed the child, still smeared with the detritus of birth, in the cradle that awaited it. Hastily she rang a bell and when, five minutes later, a young maid appeared, she told her to run for the master.

' 'E ain't in. Gone off on 'is 'orse, Cook ses. There's only me an' Tilly. Cook's restin' her legs, she ses, an' can't get off 'er bum, no, not for nobody. What's up?'

The midwife's voice dropped to a whisper. 'She's gone.'

'Gone where, fer God's sake?' The maid's voice was impatient. How could a woman in labour have gone anywhere?

'Dead, that's where.'

The maid moved slowly across the room and looked at the poor bedraggled figure on the bed. 'Jesus wept. An' babby an' all?'

'No, it's in cradle but—'

'Girl or boy?'

'Nay, I never noticed.'

'Poor little sod. Livin' in this 'ouse wi'out a mam . . .'

'Or a pa, most like!'

'What shall us do?'

'Send fer't doctor.'

'Nay.' The maid reared back. 'I ain't using that there machine.'

'Well, we've got ter do summat. 'Appen send the lad from't stable.'

'Aye,' the maid said eagerly, 'but what about babby?'

''Appen yer'd best ask lad ter fetch master's lass. 'Er what lives at . . . where is it? Married that feller . . .'

The maid looked relieved, speeding from the room as though being chased by the devil, leaving the midwife shaking her head in total disbelief.

# 19

'Mrs Armstrong, you cannot possibly leave your bed, not for a while. You are still not healed completely and I cannot answer for the consequences if—'

'Doctor Chapman, my stepmother has died giving birth to a child and I must go to . . . to my old home to see if there is anything I can do for my father and the baby. There is no one else to . . . we have no family, only myself and my brothers and I feel—'

'Mrs Armstrong, I know it is none of my business but your father . . . people are talking; and there is your husband to consider. He needs you here.'

'I shall leave Nellie to look after him and Aisling can manage Lucy for an hour or so. It's not very far, Doctor. I shall take Kizzie with me; she is reliable and kind and will make sure I come to no harm.'

'But it is only just over a week since you were delivered. I cannot allow—'

'Doctor, please, I must go and I beg you not to tell my husband. He is asleep and need not even know I have gone. Nellie will stay with him and I shall be back before he wakes.'

And so it was that eighteen months after she had left to marry Brooke, Charlotte was driven in the carriage by Todd, the coachman, through the gates of the Mount, her old home, Kizzie beside her, stalwart, sensible and her head filled with instructions from the doctor and dire warnings if she should allow her mistress to become upset. Kizzie was not sure exactly what the doctor meant by that, for Kizzie had no influence over Mr Drummond nor indeed any of the servants at Mr Drummond's home, but as they drew up in front of the house, she took Miss Charlotte's cold hand in hers. They were both wrapped up against the raw winter cold, the mistress in a fur-lined cloak and Kizzie in her own warm winter coat, as was Todd in a huge, many collared cloak and it was clear from the expression on the face of the maidservant who opened the door that she was amazed to see them. She had been kitchen-maid when Miss Charlotte lived there but now, it seemed, she had been elevated to parlour-maid, and where, Charlotte wondered, was Nancy who had once opened the door to visitors.

'Miss Charlotte,' Dolly stuttered, 'us wasn't expectin' visitors.' She wiped her hands down her soiled apron and hastily stood to one side as Charlotte stepped into the hall.

'I can see that. Where is your master, if you please?' From the corner of her eye she could see Kizzie glancing round the hallway which, when Charlotte and Kizzie lived there, shone with cleanliness but now, though not noticeably dirty, was hazed with a general air of dust, of somewhere that was not given a great deal of attention and Charlotte remembered that her father's second wife had not been domesticated.

' 'E's not in, miss . . . ma'am. Gone off on 'is 'orse, if tha' please, ma'am.'

'*His horse!* Do you mean to tell me he is out hunting?'

'Nay, miss, I don't know.'

'Where is Mrs Banks?' who had been housekeeper when Charlotte lived there.

'In't kitchen, if tha' please, ma'am,' and for good measure she bobbed a curtsey.

'Send her to me at once. I will wait in the drawing room. Come, Kizzie.'

The drawing room was as neglected as the hallway and there was no fire. The chill was numbing and their breath hung on the air as though they were in the garden! Charlotte reflected that if this was the general standard here in the main hallway and drawing room what might the conditions in the nursery be?

It took Mrs Banks five minutes to arrive and she had clearly been taking her ease in the kitchen, for her dress was somewhat dishevelled. 'Miss Charlotte . . . Mrs Armstrong, ma'am. We weren't expecting . . . the master said . . . well, visitors weren't expected.'

'Clearly! And visitors is hardly the word I would use. There has been a death in the family and surely . . . surely Mrs Drummond's family are . . . should be . . . here.'

'No, ma'am, at least not yet. Sir Clive has been informed but it is believed he is infirm and . . . well . . . her mam died a few months ago so . . .'

Mrs Banks's expression faltered but it clearly said that this was nothing to do with her. It was up to the master to attend to such things. The body of their mistress had been laid out carefully by some woman the midwife had recommended and was lying in one of the spare bedrooms. The baby was in the nursery and Mrs Banks was awaiting further orders.

'When is the funeral to be?' Charlotte asked her sharply, for she and her brothers must surely attend; this was their father's wife and they owed him some sort of duty, despite his previous cruelty to them.

'I've not been told, ma'am,' Mrs Banks answered primly.

Charlotte stood for a moment while Mrs Banks and Kizzie watched her, then, her mind made up, she walked purposefully towards the drawing room door.

'I will see the child if you please,' for this was, after all, her half-sister or -brother.

Mrs Banks sprang into life, the hands that had been folded across her apron suddenly waving in denial.

'I'll send Dolly up to see if it is—'

'No, you won't. Come with me, Kizzie. What I would like to know is where are Nancy and Mary? You seemed to be ill-served. Dolly, if I remember, was kitchen-maid when I was here last and now she is answering the door. My . . . my stepmother surely . . .'

Mrs Banks could have told a few tales of what had been happening here since the young mistress left to marry. The neglect, the total disorder that had prevailed, since it seemed the new Mrs Drummond had not been brought up to run a household and it was well known that the servants of a house without a competent mistress soon learned to drift through the days at their own pace. That was why Nancy and Mary had left, being decent girls with a proper idea of how a house should be run. Then there were the parties, the drunkenness and . . . and other things that Mrs Banks dared not speak of. At first they had disliked their new mistress with her high-faluting ways but gradually they had begun to feel sorry for her as things had gone from bad to worse. She and the master had had terrible rows but the master was the master after all and would have his own way and now the poor lady was dead.

She trailed after Miss Charlotte and the woman Mrs Banks remembered and who, so far, had not spoken, sighing for what they might find in the nursery; even before they reached the closed nursery door they could hear the weak wailing of the baby. Charlotte opened the door with such force the woman lolling by the fire almost fell into it. She had no idea who Charlotte was, obviously a lady, and at first she tried to brazen out her own neglect of the child in her keeping, babbling that it was weakly and would not take the milk offered. She had risen hastily to her feet, pushing them into well-worn shoes. She bobbed a curtsey and made haste to go to the baby in what Charlotte recognised as the family cradle.

'I were just goin' ter try an' feed poor wee mite,' she declared slyly but Kizzie, with a raised hand, waved her away.

'Leave t' bairn,' she told her peremptorily and the woman fell back, but she had not yet given up hope that this was a temporary interruption and that she could resume her shiftless care of the baby about whom nobody seemed to care.

''Ere, 'oo d'yer think you are, tellin' me what ter do? I were employed ter care fer the babby—'

'Yer doin' nowt o't sort. Now lass,' turning to Charlotte, 'sit down by t' fire and I'll see t't child. Mrs Banks will bring yer a hot drink. We'll wrap bairn up and tekk it 'ome wi' us. Does anyone know t' sex of the baby?'

'Wha'?'

'Boy or girl, fer God's sake?' Charlotte sat down thankfully and pondered briefly on how Kizzie had become so accomplished in the managing of . . . of things. The months she had spent supervising the girls and children and activities at the Dower House had evidently given her an authority she had not had when they lived at the Mount.

'Girl.'

'Where's milk?' Kizzie asked sharply.

'Warmin' in't pan,' the woman answered sullenly.

'An' t' bottle?'

'Ont' dresser.'

'I'll have some 'ot water an' all.' She rang the bell and when a wan-faced maid whom she and Miss Charlotte did not know appeared at the door ordered her to bring up a kettle of hot water and a cup of hot chocolate for the master's daughter.

'Wha'?' The girl looked bewildered.

'Jesus God,' Kizzie blasphemed. 'Are all t' servants in this house 'alf-witted?'

'Wha'?'

Kizzie turned to Charlotte. 'D'ost think tha' could nurse baby fer five minutes while I run down to t' kitchen. This woman 'ere' – indicating the woman who had had care of the child – 'can't be trusted.'

'Now see 'ere. I'll not be spoken ter—'

'Tha'd be wise ter keep tha' mouth shut, lady,' Kizzie snapped.

The baby, her half-sister, was placed carefully on Charlotte's lap while the woman, highly indignant and muttering she had no intention of stopping where she was not wanted, scampered for the door, followed by Kizzie.

Charlotte held her tiny half-sister in her arms, looking down at the wisp of a face and saw there not her father or Elizabeth, but Robbie, Robbie as she remembered him from years ago.

'Sweetheart,' she whispered and put her fingertip on the pale cheek and at once the child stopped whimpering and stared with milky, unfocused eyes into the face that leaned over her.

When Kizzie returned, without a word Charlotte took the bottle from her and guided the teat into the little pursed mouth and at once the baby started to suck. Her little hand clenched round Charlotte's finger and Kizzie watched, knowing exactly what was to happen next.

'As you said we can't leave her here.'

'No. I'll wrap 'er up and we'll tekk 'er 'ome.'

She was put in the nursery, her crib next to that of the baby who was her niece, her half-niece, was it, Charlotte wanted to know. As soon as she was settled, they lay side by side sleeping, warm, fed, bathed, and the question of who was to help Aisling with two babies came up.

'Bring Rosie to me, Kizzie. She has a kind heart and, I believe, a number of younger brothers and sisters. And she'll take orders from Aisling where the others wouldn't.'

And all the while Brooke Armstrong slept peacefully, slowly healing and totally unaware of what was happening in his home. Kizzie thought he wouldn't mind, not with his wife holding him in arms that loved him.

'Tha' father might not like yer taking 'is child, Miss Charlotte,' Kizzie told her as she tucked her, exhausted, into her little bed next to her husband who had not woken once, Nellie informed them proudly as though she were responsible.

Rosie, blinking nervously, stared with wonder at her mistress reclining in the little bed next to the master and wondered, as the rest of the kitchen staff had, what the dickens she had done wrong to be summoned to the mistress's bedside with the master sleeping next to her. She had not seen him since that awful day when he had been brought home on the gate but he certainly looked better now than he had then.

'Ma'am?' She ventured a small bob, wishing she had been told to take off her old pinny before coming up here but they had all been so astounded in the kitchen that it had gone unnoticed.

Missis was very tired, you could see that and Rosie's kind heart softened as she waited to be told she had got the sack or was to be demoted, though what to she had no idea for she was already the lowest of the low. When the mistress told her she nearly fainted.

'We have another baby in the nursery, Rosie, and I believe you are the eldest of seven.'

'Yes, ma'am.' Rosie's voice quavered, wondering if the mistress was out of her wits.

'Good. Then I want you to work in the nursery as nursemaid to . . . to Aisling who is in charge.'

'Very well, ma'am,' Rosie whispered. The mistress, with Kizzie standing protectively beside her, spoke once more. She seemed ready to nod off.

'Kizzie will show you what to wear and what to do. When I feel stronger I will come up and . . . thank you, Rosie. Now go with Kizzie.'

Rosie bobbed and twittered and bobbed again, barely understanding, but Kizzie, who they all knew to be fair and honest with them, led her away, still in a daze.

On the stairs Rosie turned in some agitation. 'Miss Kizzie, wha' about t' kitchen? Cook won't like me leavin' 'er wi'out—'

'That'll be sorted out, Rosie. Another scullery-maid'll be took on. Tha' must be pleased Mrs Armstrong thinks yer capable of lookin' after t' babies. Wi' Aisling in charge, of course,' she added hastily.

There was a buzz in the kitchen which died down as Rosie and Kizzie entered and when they were told coolly by Kizzie, who seemed to be running the house, the nursery, the sick-room and everything in the household at the moment, that another scullery-maid must be found at once they were all stupefied. When it transpired that Rosie, who they had all considered half-witted, was to be the new nursery-maid they were speechless. Not that they minded, for none of the girls wanted to work with the trollop from over the way and after all Rosie had the kindest, softest heart. She'd do well with a baby since she had helped her mam with hers!

Kizzie returned to the sickroom after Rosie was installed in the nursery, 'made up' as she kept saying, in her new simple gown and snow-white apron and cap, to find the master and mistress lying side by side in their big bed, the mistress with her arm over the master's chest, both fast asleep. They were smiling!

Charlotte was young, strong and healthy and soon recovered from the ordeal of childbirth and the harrowing experience she had suffered with Brooke's accident, but Brooke himself seemed unable to find it in himself, despite his own usual good health, to get over his dreadful injuries. The wound refused to heal properly and he was in constant pain which weakened him further. He became irritable. He was an active man and despite the almost constant presence of his wife did not recover as the doctor had hoped.

Doctor Chapman called every day, doing his best to alle-viate what he was beginning to believe was a recurring infection that dragged his patient even further down the slope of pain. Privately to Kizzie he said that he suspected some nasty substance from the bull's horns or Emmerson's farmyard was festering deep in the wound.

'I might have to open him up again, Kizzie, and put a drain in the groin. He is not doing really well at all and I suppose you have noticed how much weight he has lost, and muscle tone too. And you know how he looked forward to his daughter's visits. Now he can scarce be bothered to look at her though I know he tries to . . . well, for Mrs Armstrong's sake he . . . he . . .'

Kizzie put a hand on his arm. 'I know, Doctor. Tha' did talk about a professional nurse at beginnin'. Dost' think . . .'

'No, I don't. There is nothing more healing to him than to have his own wife with him. He watches for her – or did – but now I'm beginning to think he just wants to be left alone.'

'Yes. Dear God, if 'e gives up 'ope . . .'

The doctor shook his head, turning to look back at his patient who lay passively in his bed staring sightlessly at the window. Mrs Armstrong was up in the nursery spending a few minutes with the two babies who at least were thriving and he knew from Kizzie that she had not gone near the Dower House since the accident. He himself often looked in to check on the inmates but Jenny, supervised daily by Kizzie, was coping very well and had even taken over buying the shoddy for the rugs. Given the right leadership it would make a thriving little business. There were five girls there now, nearly all brought in by himself, and six babies, all well looked after and happy in their new environment, although the rugs they made were piling up uselessly, it seemed, in the storeroom at the back of the workroom. He had even bought one for his own wife, a beautiful landscape of primroses spreading beneath the greening ash trees in the bit of woodland at the side of the house.

There had been a double christening at the small local church several weeks ago, that of Lucy Jean Armstrong and Ellen Drummond, the latter name wrung out of her father on the telephone by Charlotte.

'I don't care what she is called, Charlotte,' he had told her after he had reluctantly been brought to the telephone by Mrs Banks soon after Charlotte had fetched the child back to King's Meadow. Neither did he care that she had removed his daughter from his house when she was born. His wife had been buried quickly and none of his children had even been told of the funeral, for which Doctor Chapman had been truly grateful since knowing Charlotte she would have struggled to go.

'But what are we to call her, Father?' Charlotte had asked diffidently.

'Elizabeth had talked of Ellen after her mother but I leave it to you, my dear. I'm far too busy at the moment to consider—'

'She is your daughter, Father,' Charlotte said sharply.

'As you are, Charlotte, and since you are related I leave it to you,' just as though they were discussing naming a new puppy the Armstrong family had acquired. 'Now I really must go. I have guests . . .' and Charlotte could clearly hear the sound of laughter in the background.

'Father, will you not want to see her or . . .' She meant to ask if he wanted his new baby at home.

'I'll let you know, my dear. You can manage for the moment can't you?'

'You have a new granddaughter, Father.'

'So I believe. Now I really must go.'

Charlotte was far too harassed with the care of her husband and the time she spent in the nursery with Lucy and Ellie, as she was now increasingly being called, to argue with her father. The babies were strangely alike, which was not surprising as they were related. Charlotte was driven into Wakefield to the newly opened baby shop where she bought a handsome perambulator big enough for two. It was high with big wheels but very elegant in a lovely shade of maroon lined in grey. Fittings, like the jointed stays that kept the hood up, were made of brass and the grip on the handle was of porcelain. Aisling and Rosie thought they were the last word in fashion as they strolled round the extensive grounds with the babies and even down to the village where everyone stopped to stare. The two little faces, rosy now with rounded cheeks, one with blue eyes, the other with green, lay side by side on their lacy pillows and the gardeners and outdoor men, even from the stable at the back of the house, hung over the perambulator making those strange sounds men and women all over the world make when confronted with babies.

It was the end of February when Doctor Chapman first voiced the idea that he considered it might be better for Mr Armstrong to go into the Clayton Hospital where there was an up-to-date operating theatre where a deeper look at his groin might be attempted.

'I myself will help perform the operation. I'm sorry, Mrs Armstrong, but he is not doing well and it is affecting him. He seems to sink deeper into what I can only call depression as though he believes he will never get out of that bed. Something is holding him back and unless we find what it is he might . . .'

Charlotte felt the painful sinking in her chest that came so frequently now. Every morning when she woke after a restless night it attacked her, for she was beginning to believe, though she did not voice it, let alone allow it to fell her, that her husband, whom she had only just discovered, if that was not too fanciful, was fast slipping away from her. He did his best, she knew that, not to let her see his pain and despair, but she who slept at his side and spent every spare moment with him that she could, knew he was fighting something, not just infection, but the loss of his will to live, to be as he once had been, to ride, to walk, to make love to her, to play with the child he had so longed for.

'Have you discussed it with him, Doctor? He is—'

'He is a sensible man and he knows he is not doing as he should. I think he will take any chance there is to . . . to repair himself. I have done all I can here and quite honestly unless I get him into a properly equipped operating theatre I fear that . . .'

Charlotte felt her heart thudding in her chest and she wanted to scream at him: Do something; do something, *anything*, for this man is my life and I will have none if he dies. But instead she coolly nodded her head.

'Very well. When will you . . .?'

'Now that I have told you I will telephone the hospital and send for a private ambulance. He will be transferred there later today.'

'I will come with him.'

'Mrs Armstrong, there is no need for you to—'

She lifted her head and straightened her back and that stubborn chin of hers, which he was getting to know so well, jutted beneath her firmed lips. 'If you imagine I will allow my husband to fight this . . . this thing on his own you do not know me, Doctor, and by God, you should do by now. I will go to him at once. Kizzie will look after everything until I, until *we* return. Thank God for her, what would I do . . .?'

The servants were all in a terrible state, for the master was much loved and, if they were honest and this time they were, so was the mistress. They had never known anyone go into hospital and it was their belief that those who did never came out again! They watched, unchecked even by Kizzie who knew how they felt, as Mr Armstrong was brought down the stairs on a stretcher, his poor thin face white and rigid with the pain of being moved until, with an oath, Doctor Chapman stopped the men who carried him and stuck a needle in his arm, muttering to himself that he should have thought of it first. At once the master went to sleep and was lifted again on the stretcher and into the waiting ambulance. The mistress went with him and, with tears of sadness, for would they ever see him again, they watched the ambulance doors close and the vehicle drive off.

# 20

Wallace Chapman, since his time in Africa treating Boer women who had been dispossessed of their men and their homes by the war, had become more and more interested in the complexities that often occurred during childbirth, with obstetrics and gynaecology, and though his early training at Guy's Hospital in London had included some surgery, he did not feel able to operate on Brooke Armstrong alone. However he knew a doctor who could. Doctor Preston worked at the Clayton Hospital and was renowned for his success in the most delicate of surgery. A quick telephone call to him from King's Meadow had ensured that Doctor Preston was available, or would be later in the afternoon, and a private room was booked for Mr Armstrong along with the up-to-date operating theatre. Doctor Chapman would assist and Charlotte felt her heart lift a little when she was told. She was sure, if Doctor Chapman recommended him, the surgeon could only be the best and the thought of the doctor, who had done so much for her and her girls, the man who took such care and felt such compassion even for street-walkers, was of great comfort to her.

She rode in the ambulance, holding Brooke's hand, bending over him, stroking his face, trying to make sense of his words, for he was beginning to ramble. His face was skull-like and the gunmetal grey of his eyes, those that had once been like soft velvet, stared at nothing but at the same time seemed now and again to see her, to recognise her.

'Sweetheart . . . my lovely girl . . . don't . . .'

'I'm here, darling. Don't what? Tell me . . . tell me, what do you want?'

His pain was punishing her, crucifying her, his fever rising by the minute and she marvelled at this enormous thing, this love, this enchantment, that had come on her so suddenly that the very thought of this man's death racked her, cut her to the bone with a knife that twisted cruelly and even pierced her heart. There was no doubt in her mind that if he did not live, neither would she. She might still walk about, eat, sleep, be with her baby but she would, nevertheless, be dead. A ghost haunting the earth searching for peace; no, not for peace but for oblivion.

She hovered by the side of the stretcher that carried her love, her life, her heart to the room where he was lifted gently on to a high bed. A nurse in a starched uniform tried physically to remove her when she refused to leave, but she fought her silently until Doctor Chapman shook his head.

'Leave her, Nurse.'

'But, Doctor, I cannot allow her to hang over my patient,' who was muttering and clutching for something which proved, to her amazement, to be his wife's hand, when he calmed somewhat.

Doctor Preston was younger than Doctor Chapman, brisk, quick, wasting no time in having his patient stripped down to a short gown and then removing the dressings that covered Brooke's wound.

'Yes,' was all he said, beckoning to the nurse who pushed past Charlotte, standing no nonsense now and with force but gentleness Doctor Chapman took her by the shoulders.

'Remove this lady, if you please,' Doctor Preston told him.

'She is his wife, Charlie.'

'I don't care if she is Queen Alexandra herself, she must leave and this patient must be taken at once to the operating theatre. 'See to it, Nurse.'

'Yes, Doctor.'

'I'll be there in five minutes, so look sharp.'

'Please . . . please, Doctor, may I not come?' Charlotte began and it was then he turned and really looked at her, his face softening.

'No, madam, I'm afraid you can't.'

'But I love him so and . . .'

'Do you want to hinder me in my effort to save your husband's life, Mrs . . . er?'

'Armstrong,' Doctor Chapman told him.

'Mrs Armstrong, an operating theatre is no place for anyone except those who are working there.' He put out a hand and placed it on her arm. 'I will save him for you, really I will. Now go and wait in the waiting room and when I have finished I will come and tell you exactly what I have done and what *you* are to do to bring him back to health.'

It took two hours to open the wound in Brooke's thigh and to drain the abscess that had formed and would have spread its poison – in fact had already begun – to the rest of his body if not treated. With a drainage tube still protruding from the re-stitched wound he was wheeled back to his room where his wife waited. There were several cold cups of tea standing on the table to the side of his bed and again the nurse had physically to restrain what she saw as his hysterical wife from throwing herself across the patient.

'Charlotte,' a stern voice almost shouted in her ear and a strong hand dragged her quite literally to the far corner of the room.

'Get off me, you fool,' she hissed. Her face was like putty. She was totally, utterly disorientated. She fought him like a demon and it was not until a porter appeared to help Doctor Chapman and the nurse, that she could be dragged from the room. He slapped her across the face, much to the nurse's satisfaction – who had never loved a man nor had a man love her – and slowly she came out of her demented state. Her eyes cleared and the tears that streamed from them slowly stopped.

'I'm sorry. Please, please forgive me,' turning to the nurse. 'I'm so sorry,' she whispered. 'I promise to behave. I'll sit down here' – indicating a row of chairs against the wall – 'and bother no one, but please . . . please, Doctor Chapman, tell me that my husband will recover, that the operation was a success; that you . . . that the doctor who performed it has removed whatever . . .'

Waving away the nurse and the porter who were both inclined to hang about to make sure the patient's wife did not overcome Doctor Chapman and rush back into the patient's bedroom where a nurse could be seen bending over his bed, Wallace Chapman sat beside Charlotte, holding her hand though he was not aware of it. He felt a great wave of sympathy wash over him for this plucky woman who was doing what most women of her class avoided in horror, that is to care for others less fortunate than herself. She had worked hard to house, feed and find work for the six girls who had washed up at the Dower House, fighting her husband all the way. Like all gentlemen of his class he had objected strongly to what she did but she had stood firm and given five young women a fresh start in life, even putting the sixth in the nursery to care for her own child. She had given birth to her own daughter and then seen her husband badly injured. She was still not recovered from the birth of that child and the consequent loss of blood and her dedicated nursing of her terribly injured husband whom she appeared to love to distraction was to be admired, which was a pathetic description of her feelings for him.

'Charlotte – I may call you Charlotte, mayn't I – Brooke is in good hands. There was an abscess which has been drained. Charlie Preston is the best surgeon I have ever known. Like me he was in Africa working with the wounded and . . . well, he has done his very best. Now you must go home and get some rest.'

She leaped to her feet. 'Oh no!' She was horrified. 'I cannot leave him. I shall stay here until he is . . . until he can . . .'

'Sit down, Charlotte. No one is forcing you to go home but remember you have a baby.'

'There are women to look after her. Kizzie will—'

'Kizzie is here.' And from the far end of the corridor Kizzie approached, walking steadfastly towards them. 'She is come to take you home. You have a telephone and I promise that you may—'

That stubborn jut of her jaw and the flame of determined colour in her cheeks told them they were to have trouble with this woman who, it seemed, cared for no one except the man who lay so quietly in his bed.

'I am staying here.'

Kizzie, practical, capable and far-sighted, reached them and her kind face and soft eyes told Charlotte that she knew exactly what she felt though she herself had never known love between man and woman. But she loved Charlotte and she held Brooke Armstrong in a deep affection. She took Charlotte's hands and sat her down, then knelt at her feet.

'Lass, tha'll be no good to tha' 'usband if tha' fall ill thissen. When 'e is able ter come 'ome, 'e will, an' I promise thi' an' me'll nurse 'im with the 'elp of the nurse Doctor Chapman will recommend—'

'That other nurse for the baby was no good,' Charlotte shouted, turning heads along the corridor, doing her best to pull away from Kizzie, but Kizzie wasn't having it.

'That's true but us managed. This 'un will be looked over by thi' an' me an' if we don't like 'er tha' shall say so. Now, get on tha' feet, say goodbye ter't master though 'e still be asleep an' come wi' me.'

'Oh, Kizzie, I can't just leave him. I love him so . . . I only liked him at first but really it was love and I didn't know it and now, when it might be too late, I find I . . .' She was babbling and Wallace Chapman knew she was near to the end and that if she wasn't got home and into bed with Kizzie to watch over her she would collapse.

'I know, chuck, I know,' Kizzie soothed, 'but tha'll tell 'im thassen soon.'

They got her home and put her to bed and she slept for twenty-four hours under the influence of the sedative the doctor had added to her cup of tea. She didn't even wake when her husband was carried in on a stretcher and placed in the bed next to her. She had insisted on sleeping in the truckle bed, saying Brooke would need their bed when he came home. When she woke there was a woman in a nurse's uniform, a properly trained nurse from the hospital who had consented to look after Mr Armstrong and Mrs Armstrong if it was needed, bending over him and he was smiling at her and Charlotte felt a massive wave of jealousy wash over her, since she should have been the first to receive that smile.

'Brooke, darling . . .' She leaped from her bed in the flimsy nightdress Kizzie had put her in, considerably startling Nurse Chambers, herself a spinster lady who wore sensible night-dresses and had never seen such an article in her life. She was ready to throw herself down next to him and bugger the nurse, but Nurse Chambers was in charge and Charlotte was soon to learn it.

'Please don't touch my patient, madam,' she said in an icy voice, 'unless you wish for a relapse. Doctor Preston, who, by the way, will be here soon to examine Mr Armstrong, has been extremely obliging to allow Mr Armstrong to come home but . . . well, I am a thoroughly competent nurse and would have been caring for him in hospital. Doctor Chapman convinced him that Miss Aspin was sensible and so, unless you try to interfere, he may be nursed at home, otherwise he will go straight back to—'

'Now you just listen to me, Nurse, this is my husband who is . . . much loved and he—'

'Charlotte, my love, be a good girl and shut up,' a weak voice said from the bed. 'I am home, with you, and perhaps the nurse will allow us . . . a gentle kiss and if you are very, very good, to hold hands . . .'

'Bloody hell.'

'Now, my darling, you will shock the nurse with your bloodys so go away and allow me to rest.'

'Thank you, Mr Armstrong,' the nurse said, smiling at her patient who winked at her, and Charlotte sat back on her little bed and did as she was told.

She caused another ruction when she learned that the bloody nurse was to sleep in the *truckle bed* next to Brooke, but after her bath and change of clothes and a large bowl of Mrs Groves's hearty vegetable soup and after Doctor Preston had lectured her sternly and threatened to take her husband back to the Clayton she reluctantly gave in and agreed to sleep in Brooke's dressing room, though she was often to be found prowling about outside the bedroom door. Nurse Chambers allowed her to visit, *visit* her own husband once a day when *she* gave her permission.

Charlotte spent time with her baby but her mind was forever wandering back to the sickroom and her frustration that the nurse was in charge and said what was what and when Charlotte could visit her husband. Her tiny sister thrived beside Lucy and the pair of them were the pride and joy of their nursemaids and the rest of the servants. Rosie seemed to have gained in self-importance now that she was no longer scrubbing and scouring and on her knees all day in the scullery, and had proved her worth as a nursemaid under Aisling, though Charlotte often wondered where Aisling got her knowledge.

One morning, when Rosie had been permitted to take the babies round the garden in the double perambulator, it being a fine day, Charlotte found Aisling on her own, scrubbing the table where the babies were changed, so she sat her down and proceeded to question her. She had not known Aisling as well as the first girls, since Aisling spoke with a rich, lilting Irish brogue you had to listen to carefully to decipher and Charlotte had been too busy with her own troubles. But it seemed Kizzie had decided the girl was competent and could be trusted.

'What happened to you, Aisling, that you should finish up at the Dower House, if you don't mind telling me? Why were you . . . er . . .'

'In the family way, so?'

'Yes. I know you lost your baby. I'm sorry.'

'No, thank the Blessed Virgin I did, ma'am. 'T'were me daddy's, yer see. Me mammy was took, God bless her soul' – crossing herself – 'an' there was thirteen of us. Not that they all lived. He was drunk as a fiddler's bitch. I were 'andy an' . . .'

Charlotte put a hand to her mouth in horror, though come to think of it she didn't know why for it seemed to be a common occurrence among the inhabitants of Thornes Lane in the stews of Wakefield where the Irish who had reached there in search of work clung together as exiles will. There was work in the coal fields and though not many of them had seen the green hills of Ireland they still spoke in the broad brogue. Aisling, after several months at the Dower House and with careful attention, was learning to speak so that others could understand her. Not that she mixed much with Jenny and Violet now that she was in the nursery at the big house but she had made a tentative friendship with Nellie who admired her gumption, her obsession with cleanliness, her care and affection for the babies and her loyalty to the mistress. Not that Nellie spoke what was known as the King's English – now that the old Queen was dead – for Nellie was Yorkshire born and bred, but she could read and write and she meant, when they had a day off together, to ask the agreeable young nursemaid to accompany her. Nellie, unusually, liked art galleries, museums, walking in Clarence Park, taking afternoon tea in the smart café there, studying the goods for sale in the best shops in Westgate and the Bull Ring and now that Aisling was as decently dressed as she was and had a few bob in her pocket and could be understood, Nellie had taken quite a fancy to her. They often sat of an evening before the nursery fire when the babies slept and Rosie went down for a crack with the others who now accepted her as equal to themselves. Aisling had never quite got on with the girls at the Dower House, not quarrelling but not mixing with them though she had worked hard, but she was in her natural element now.

'You are happy here, looking after the babies, Aisling?' her mistress asked her now.

'Yes . . .'

'You don't sound too sure, Aisling. Is there something bothering you that I can put right?'

Aisling hesitated as though she were not quite sure whether to speak, then she smiled and shook her head. 'No, ma'am, to be sure I've niver been happier. 'Tis lovely here an' them babies is a joy ter me an' Rosie. And Rosie's a good girl.'

She was an attractive young woman, her green eyes wide and deep-set in a fringe of long eyelashes as dark as her hair. Charlotte knew it was curly and reached as far as her buttocks since she and Kizzie had bathed her when she first came to the Dower House but it was tucked firmly, even grimly beneath her white cap as though she were determined to have it well hidden. Since she had been fed on the good food available to the servants she had put on weight and had a good figure. Charlotte wondered if one of the men had what they called 'tried it on' with her and that was why she was not out in the sunlit garden with Rosie who was plain and thin as a stick.

'Well, I just wanted to make sure you and Rosie were . . . were coping.'

'Oh yes, ma'am, to be sure, an' when I've cleaned up here I'll get into the garden and walk a bit. We like ter go down ter the paddock. Oh, I know the bairns're only a few weeks old but you've seen how they look about them. Sure an' I've never known such clever . . . well, the master'll be wantin' them ter ride an'—'

'Oh, not yet for a while, Aisling.' Charlotte laughed, then rose and Aisling stood up at once.

'An' can I be askin' how the master is, ma'am? To be sure I'd love ter take Lucy ter see him.' For was not Lucy his own child though in Aisling's opinion Ellie was just as lovable but she was no relation to the master.

'Oh, Aisling, I wish I dare but that nurse would probably not allow it. He is recovering slowly but when the drain comes out—'

'The drain?'

'Yes, the badness has to drain out of him, you see, and he has to have dressings changed and the wound irrigated; it is very painful for him but . . .' Her face was so sad that the nursemaid wanted to put her arms about this woman who had been so good to her and who had changed her own tragic life.

'Ma'am, it's not me place ter . . . but wouldn't the sight of his own lovely daughter . . . well, ter be sure, if that nurse ses . . .'

Charlotte brightened immediately and with a lovely gesture leaned over and kissed Aisling on her cheek. 'You're right, of course you're right. I shall go down to the garden and collect Lucy and take her to see her father this very minute. That woman . . . don't get me wrong, she's a wonderful nurse and is devoted to my husband, but I'm going to defy her – disobey her. I want to sleep . . . well, I must go and collect Lucy. Thank you, thank you, Aisling.'

Nurse Chambers had just finished the morning treatment of her patient's wound and he lay in a sweat which she was carefully sponging with gentle hands. She was not a cruel woman, in fact she was sorry that she had to cause such pain with the irrigation of his wound but she could see that Mr Armstrong was slowly improving. His fever was gone and if she could just get some of Cook's good broth, soups, egg custards and all the nourishing dishes she sent up into him he would improve even further. The doctors were very pleased with him and though Doctor Preston only came now and again since the wound was beginning to heal, Doctor Chapman, conscientious man that he was, came every day for a few minutes.

There was a tap at the door and before she could get from the bed to see who was there, it opened and Mrs Armstrong, with her child in her arms, marched in and strode across the room to where Mr Armstrong lay naked apart from the towel that Nurse Chambers had placed across his stomach.

'Darling, you look quite delicious lying there and if Nurse and Lucy weren't here I should climb into your bed and ravish you if you promised not to scream.'

'My love, I would not even struggle so go to it.'

Mrs Armstrong bent over the bed and with their child between them kissed her husband long and lingeringly and the child gurgled with what seemed to be approval.

'*Mrs Armstrong, please,* my patient is not dressed and—'

'Don't worry, Nurse, I've seen him more *undressed* than this in the past. How d'you think I got this baby? See, darling, your daughter thought it was high time to visit her father so here she is and if you will put your arm out flat I will lay her in it; no, leave it, if you please, Nurse, my husband is in need of a cuddle with his daughter. There . . . see . . . she is quite happy and you, my love, is she hurting you?'

'No, by God, and if she were . . .' Brooke slowly put his arm about his child, straining to look down at her where she lay in the circle of his arm. 'I'd like to kiss her, Charlotte, if it could be managed . . .'

'Mrs Armstrong, really. Mr Armstrong must not strain himself or—'

'Don't worry, Nurse, do you think after all the wonderful care he has received at your hands I would allow him to be injured?'

Slightly mollified, Nurse Chambers stepped back, though she kept a careful eye on Mrs Armstrong who she knew to be wilful.

Lifting the placid baby from her father's arms, Charlotte sat carefully on the edge of the bed and held the child under her arms so that her toes almost touched his chest.

'Dear God . . . oh dear, dear Lord, she's beautiful, like her mother,' Brooke breathed and as though she were aware that this was a very special moment, the baby gave a wavering smile. Holding her firmly, Charlotte lowered her until she was face to face with her father and he was able to press his lips against her satin, rosy cheek. Her head wobbled and the nurse gasped but Charlotte held her firmly, cheek to cheek with her father, no other part of her touching him.

When she lifted their daughter and held her in her arms so that Brooke could still see her there were tears in her eyes and his, and truth to tell even Nurse Chambers had a lump in her throat.

'Now, please, Mrs Armstrong, I must ask you to leave and . . . well, I will admit that the sight of his child seems to have done your husband good,' hoping in her medical way that the flush on his cheek was not a return of the fever.

She had no need to worry, for each day Mrs Armstrong brought the child in to see him and he seemed to take no harm from it; in fact the doctors were so pleased with him there was talk of him moving from his bed to a chair by the window from where he could watch the nursemaids with the perambulator, the gardeners who took it upon themselves to wave to him and the dogs racing about. It was March now and the spring flowers were beginning to burgeon in great swathes of daffodils, hyacinths, tulips, scillas and ranunculus, lovingly tended by John and Ned.

And just inside Beggers Wood, which lay at the edge of Brooke Armstrong's land, a man tethered his horse to the branch of a tree and began to make his cautious way to the back of the house.

# 21

Charlotte had not been over to the Dower House since Brooke's accident so on the day the doctor gave him permission to sit in a chair by the window she busied herself in the nursery dressing the two babies and wrapping them up against the cold with the intention of pushing them in the perambulator to see the girls there. Aisling and Rosie fussed around her, clearly convinced that though she was the mother of one baby and the sister, well, half-sister of the other, they should really be in charge. After all, that was what they were employed for. Mrs Armstrong had meant to care for her baby herself with perhaps the help of one nursemaid but since the terrible circumstances of the master's confrontation – though they did not use that word – with Jack Emmerson's bull, she had been totally absorbed with her husband. Which was as it should be. It was a great pity that the shock, or so the doctor explained in their presence, had dried up her milk but then again it meant she had more time for her husband and both the babies had taken to Mellin's baby food. There were Mellin's Food Biscuits for the next stage in their development, all recommended by Doctor Chapman, and the babies were thriving.

They rarely cried but snorted and gurgled as though to each other, waving their hands about as if grabbing at something only they could see. They even turned their heads to stare with great interest into each other's faces. Lucy's eyes were the colour of her mother's, an amazing aquamarine, while Ellie's were green as her own mother's had been. When you bent over them in their shared cot, which was extra large to accommodate them both, their eyes would look straight into yours, their smiles revealing shining gums, their bodies wriggling with joy, then their gaze would shift to a shadow on the wall. And when they were both asleep their nursemaids hung over them anxiously, for surely being so quiet they must be dead! They were adored by every member of the household, even Arthur Drummond's child who was so pretty and sunny-natured; when they were in the garden the perambulator was surrounded by an admiring group of men who poked awkward fingers into their questing little hands.

Today was the first spring-like day, the end of March and the babies were three months old. All the skylarks were up and singing in the high blue sky and the short walk across the stable yard and then to the back of the Dower House was bathed in glorious sunshine. At the base of the fences that bordered the paddock enormous primroses were in bloom and the celandine buds were ready to burst forth. There were blue periwinkle and white violets and the song of the thrushes and blackbirds flirting in the hedges filled the air. She had deliberately brought the babies the back way, for she and Brooke had not yet talked about the enterprise that was beginning to take shape at the Dower House and knowing his previous aversion to the idea she had no wish to upset him as he slowly recovered his strength. Jenny seemed very capable but she was not awfully sure about some of the girls. Though they had been so grateful to find shelter and protection there when their babies were born and they themselves in such dire straits, now that they were recovered showed signs of resenting Jenny's authority. After all, she was only one of them even if she had been put 'up the spout' by the son of the house where she had worked. Kizzie stood no nonsense, of course, and did her best to keep the peace but she was often at the big house helping

Charlotte with Brooke, and Meggie was too busy with a nursery full of babies.

The four girls were over at what was called the workshop, Violet, Cassie, Edna and Maudie, working on a rug each; not one of the special ones that Jenny designed and made but ordinary cottage-type rugs that the wives of working men spread before their grates. They earned five shillings for each rug they made and were free to go to Wakefield on their day off to buy whatever they fancied and on top of that they had free board and lodgings. Violet was willing, and being adept with her fingers and imaginative, was being taught by Jenny to work at what she called the 'high-class' end of the market, producing rugs that were out of the ordinary, meant for those with a bigger income than the cottagers and labourers who in fact could make the rag rugs themselves. She was eager to get on and she and Jenny, their babies both being girls and more or less the same age, had become friendly. They worked hard and were clean, tidy and when they went into town together bought things mainly for their children, now over a year old. Cassie was easy-going, worked diligently on the more mundane rugs and Edna admired her; what Cassie did or said, Edna did or said the same. But Maudie, who was extremely pretty, now that she had got over her initial desperation and terror at finding herself in the family way and was in a safe and comfortable home, could see no reason why she should not be allowed to please herself what she did and when she did it. She made eyes at all the men in the yard and gardens and as Kizzie warned her, if she didn't behave she'd find herself in queer street again and she doubted if Mrs Armstrong would stand for a second fall from grace. Maudie hadn't been knocked about by a bullying father or been attacked in the street by a prospective client but had just been careless with her favours. There had been a lad who had been willing to marry her, believing the child to be his, which she couldn't be sure of, but she had no intention of being stuck in some cottage with a farm labourer for a husband and a baby every year. She loved Jackie, her boy, and unless she left him at the Dower House she could see no prospect of getting away, since she wouldn't desert him, but she missed the free and easy life of prostitution. She was just sixteen and had not yet met the full horrors of her chosen profession and had grand visions of being taken up by some toff and living the life of Riley.

She thought she already had but kept it to herself and when she slipped out after dark to meet him she made sure it was without the knowledge of the other girls. He lived in a big house not too far from the Dower House, taking her there to a fancy room upstairs and she had high hopes he might make her . . . well, she didn't know quite what but it must be better than making bloody rugs! He had some queer ideas though. He liked her to strip naked and then whip her on her bare bum which didn't matter, though he sometimes left bloody marks on her that she had to keep hidden from the other girls!

They were all hard at work when Mrs Armstrong strolled round with her babies and though they had children of their own they made the effort to 'ooh' and 'aah' over them. Neither of them was a patch on Pearl or Pansy or the rest but they knew which side their bread was buttered on and Jenny, whose Rose was already toddling unsteadily about the house, with a sign to her employer, soon had them back at work, reminding them that they were paid by the 'piece'.

The children, six of them, were in the care of Megan, Kizzie's sister, and Kizzie herself when she was not needed at the big house. They were having their morning nap and the two sisters were sitting with their feet to the fire with a cup of tea when Charlotte entered. They both rose respectfully and offered her one but she said she had only come over to check that all was in order. Lucy was awake and at once Megan lifted her from her perambulator and cuddled her, smiling into the dimpled and equally smiling face of the master's daughter. When she tucked her in again she began to wail so Megan reached for her coat – she had moved on from the working woman's shawl now she was in this grand job – and asked permission to walk over with the perambulator to her mam's, which was not far.

When they were alone Kizzie drew Charlotte to the fire.

'Take tha' coat off, lass, and let's thi' an' me 'ave a bit of a crack,' she said airily, and Charlotte knew at once that there was nothing 'airy' about whatever it was Kizzie was to tell her. Kizzie was not one for gossip.

'Master seems better,' she said. ''E'll be out in't garden afore long. Adam was only sayin' 'e 'ad an idea fer a chair on wheels. Mind you, us'll be seein' 'im walkin' as soon as nice weather comes. A bit warmer, like, an' then—'

'What is it you want to tell me, Kizzie?' Charlotte asked her patiently. 'We all know Brooke is improving and that he is absolutely against having a wheelchair. I was . . . well, I was hoping to interest him in . . .'

'What, lass?'

Charlotte's face was alive with excitement and for the moment Kizzie forgot the misgivings she had about one of the girls, leaning forward, her own face alight.

'A motor car!'

'*A motor car!*'

'Well, why not? It will be a while before he can ride but if he had driving lessons and could get out of the grounds it might give him something to interest him until he can climb on Max's back. So far he is so glad to get out of that bloody bed he seems content to be able to look out at the garden. And of course, he spends time with Lucy and Ellie; honestly, you'd think Ellie was his as well as Lucy. He loves them both and sits with them on his knee talking to them as though they could understand a word. Aisling and Rosie get quite cross as though he is taking their jobs from them. Oh, Kizzie, I'm sorry, you wanted to tell me something and here am I babbling on.'

She leaned across the lovely rag rug that Jenny had made, a scene of the evening sun just sinking into a rippling blue sea which she had taken from one of Mrs Armstrong's art books and took Kizzie's hands in hers, peering anxiously into her face. 'What is it?'

Kizzie sighed. 'Well, they've all had a bad time, these girls we have here, and I must say they are on the whole grateful for the chance you are giving them—'

'That's another thing, Kizzie. If we get a motor car I shall learn to drive it as well then I shall be able to get about, looking for buyers for the rugs and . . . Oh, Kizzie, I'm sorry, there I go interrupting you again when you're obviously worried about . . . who? Which one is . . .'

Kizzie shook her head. She had not seen this young woman she loved so animated since her husband had been gored by the bull. That sounded wrong somehow but she had once been filled with plans for 'her' girls and the industry she hoped to start, arguing forcibly with her husband on the rightness of it. Then, miraculously, after his terrible injury she had fallen in love with him and could not bear to leave his side. The girls, the Dower House, the rugs and the business she intended to run had been pushed to the back of her mind. Now, it seemed Mr Armstrong was to recover, though how much would remain of the man he had once been was yet to be ascertained. But her enthusiasm at the idea of a motor car and what it would do, not only for him but for her had brought the Charlotte Armstrong Kizzie had once known back into existence. And now she, Kizzie, was to worry her with another problem.

'There's been a man seen 'angin' around after dark at back o't stables an' Violet, 'oo shares a bedroom wi' Maudie, told me, reluctantly, mind, that she thinks Maudie slips out after t' rest are asleep to meet 'im. An' she 'as money, more than what she earns since she's that slow, or doesn't care, more like. Tha' should see't new bonnet she wears. An' she don't go out wi' any o' t'other girls when she's time off.'

Charlotte leaned back in her chair and stared in horror at Kizzie. Surely Maudie, who had been through so much but had been given a second chance and finished up in a decent home with a decent job which also housed her illegitimate child, would not go down that road again. Had she not learned her lesson? Her baby was about nine months old now, a lovely little boy who any mother would be proud of, but what was to happen if Maudie should get in the family way again? She must be getting money from someone. Some man! But surely none of the men who worked for Brooke would secretively take up with a girl who had once been a prostitute?

'What should we do, Kizzie?' Charlotte turned to the woman who had got her through so many crises ever since Charlotte was ten years old and Kizzie herself only fourteen.

'Nay, lass, nowt fer't minute. Us don't even . . . well, it could be anyone; a man from another . . . tha' knows theer's plenty o' chaps what'd . . .' Kizzie looked uncomfortable and in a blinding flash Charlotte became aware that Kizzie knew who it was.

'Kizzie . . .?'

'Nay, 'ow can I?'

'Kizzie, tell me at once,' she ordered her sternly. 'Brooke will take him to task and have him dismissed or . . . and as for Maudie . . .'

'Lass, lass, don't.'

'Who, who?' thinking foolishly she sounded like an owl.

'It's . . . it's tha' faither.'

Charlotte froze and her mouth fell open, then, 'Don't be ridiculous, don't be so bloody ridiculous. My father has never . . . would never . . . with a servant girl . . .'

'Tha' don't know what tha' pa gets up ter, what 'e got up ter even when 'is wife – first, tha' mam, an' second, while they were alive. Servants talk an' it passes from 'ouse to 'ouse. Violet ses Maudie . . . 'as whip marks on 'er bum, just like what you 'ad. It seems . . .'

Charlotte had lost every vestige of colour from her face. She looked haunted, which she was, by old memories, memories of those scenes in the library with herself bending over the chair, naked from the waist down while her father lashed her with his riding crop or a bamboo cane. It was known that he had not been kind to his second wife, poor Elizabeth who had died, so it was whispered, because she was neglected during her confinement. That he had been riding to hounds as she slowly bled to death and now, with as much concern as if she were a kitten from the stables, he had let his lovely little daughter remain at King's Meadow. Dear God, what was she to do? She could not allow such perverted behaviour to go on under her very nose and say nothing, do nothing. In a way she felt responsible for these girls who had fallen into her care.

'We'd best have Maudie in, I suppose.' Charlotte's voice was weary. She wanted nothing to do with her father who had treated her and her brothers so wickedly but it seemed . . . well, who else could it be since the whole thing had his mark on it, not to mention poor Maudie's behind. Poor, pretty little Maudie.

Maudie stood before them, a defiant expression on her face. She was not daft and knew at once that the mistress was aware of her nightly excursions but she was prepared to bluff it out. It was her concern, wasn't it, and the gentleman was very generous and a smacked bum was nothing to what she had often received at the hands of her own father in the past.

'It has come to our notice, Maudie, that you are carrying on a . . . a liaison with a gentleman of the district and we have brought you here to tell you that it must stop at once. Don't you know that you might become pregnant again and be-sides—'

'It's nowt ter do wi' anyone else but me an' 'im so what—'

'Is he to marry you, Maudie? Has he promised to make you his wife?'

'Well, no, but 'e looks after me an' if I get in family way—'

'He will throw you out and look around for another young fool to—'

' 'Ere, 'oo are yer callin'—'

'I happen to know the gentleman, you see, and believe me he is not only a cruel and uncaring gentleman but he has a habit of beating those he professes to care about. However if you promise not to see him again I will let you stay and make something of yourself here where you are safe and your child will—'

'Safe!' sneered Maudie. 'An' earnin' bloody three bob or less a week. Last night 'e give me—'

'Perhaps another child?'

'Well, I'm off ter see 'im an' tell 'im what yer said. 'E's an 'ouse bigger 'n this un an' 'e'll see me right.'

'No, he won't, Maudie. I happen to know, you see. He is my father and I lived with him for sixteen years. He is cruel, selfish and totally without scruples where women, or indeed any living creature, are concerned. When he tires of you he will discard you—'

'I'm not listenin' ter this.' Maudie turned away. She was not sure what 'scruples' were but the revelation that the man who gave her a few bob for doing exactly what he told her to do, who liked hurting her was this woman's father had come as a shock and she wasn't sure how this was to affect her future dealings with him. Perhaps she'd do better with the bloody cowman. But would the cowman, or indeed any labouring man, which was all she could hope for, buy her a lovely bonnet like the one Arty, as she called him, had done?

'What are you to do, Maudie?' the mistress asked her as she was halfway to the door. 'What are you to do about Jackie? Do you think he will take you in, even as a kitchen wench, with a child in your arms? Are you not aware that Ellie, who lives with us in the nursery with my own daughter, is his child? Yes, Ellen is Arthur Drummond's daughter. I brought her to live with us when his wife died.'

Maudie burst into tears, leaning against the door jamb. Yes, she had known that Ellie was Mrs Armstrong's half-sister but she had not been aware that Mrs Armstrong was Arty's daughter. She stood for perhaps thirty seconds, weeping desolately then, amazingly, she stiffened her back and turned to face her mistress and Kizzie, who had said not a word during the interview. Her face, though wet with tears, was still pretty, for Maudie was one of those fortunate women who could cry without the swelling eyes and running nose that afflicted others of their sex.

'Well, I'm off. I'm not stoppin' 'ere in this bloody convent where a lass can't even 'ave a bit o' fun or speak to a lad without—'

'A lad! Arthur Drummond is hardly a lad, Maudie. If you had been . . . been meeting one of the gardeners or a stable lad, a decent man, I would do all I could to see that you were . . . well, see you married with a cottage and—'

'A soddin' kid every year. No, bloody thanks. I'll fetch Jackie an' me things an' get over ter Arty's. 'E'll see me right, will Arty, an' yer can all go ter 'ell, especially that bitch Violet 'oo no doubt told yer all about me.'

With that she flounced from the room and they could hear her upstairs crashing about collecting her 'things', which were barely worth the carrying. They heard Meggie's protesting voice as Maudie apparently snatched the bawling Jackie from his comfortable little bed, then footsteps clattering down the stairs, along the passage and out of the back door.

It was the talk of the kitchen that night so that even Brooke, who had lived in a quiet, peaceful world where all he cared about was getting back on his feet, making love to his wife who loved him as he loved her, and being a proper father to the lovely child she had given him, was aware of the buzz that seemed to circulate about him. He and Charlotte had dined as they always did in front of the fire in their bedroom, a small table between them while Nellie served them. Mrs Groves believed that only by eating her well-cooked, delicious and nourishing food would the master recover his strength. With the spring and summer before him, her good food inside him and the wound in his thigh healing so well, by autumn he should be back in the saddle. They had eaten hearty vegetable soup, the vegetables picked only that morning, the stock come from the shin of beef that had been simmering for many hours, saddle of spring lamb, again with fresh vegetables, followed by a baked apple custard. They were drinking coffee while Charlotte searched her mind for the best way to bring up the exciting prospect of buying a motor car when Brooke broke through her reverie demanding to know what was wrong with Nellie who had twice dropped cutlery and seemed to be seething with some inner emotion.

'I'm that sorry, sir. We're all of a doo-dah in't kitchen what wi' that lass goin' off an' . . . well . . .' She glanced at her mistress, for they all knew where she had 'gone off' to and could she, a servant, bring up the subject of their mistress's shameless father?

Brooke looked at his wife, then back to Nellie. 'Thank you, Nellie, you can go now. Mrs Armstrong will pour the coffee.'

'Well?' was all he said.

She sighed and shook her head. 'It's true, my darling. I have had a failure at the Dower House. One of the girls has gone off the rails and . . .'

He leaned across the table and took hold of her hand. 'Come.' Just the one word and in an instant she was nestled on his knee, the only way they could 'love' one another at the moment. The only way they could get close, even fondle one another. They slept in the same bed now, for the nurse, no longer needed, was gone but when they were alone he often cradled her on his knee. Though he could barely move one leg his old 'John Thomas', as he often called it, still stirred at her closeness and somehow they managed a sort of love-making which they were prepared to make do with until he was more mobile.

'Tell me.'

'It's Maudie. She's been . . . well, I can hardly call it *dallying*, but she has been sneaking out to meet her lover. Dear God, what a word, for if there is one man who is incapable of *loving* it's him. She left this morning with the mistaken idea that he would take her in and well, I don't know what is in her silly mind but since he is a so-called "gentleman" he will have sent her off with a flea in her ear as the saying goes and God knows where she will finish up.'

'The gentleman?'

'My father.'

The body of a young woman, her baby in her arms, was found in the mere in the centre of Beggers Wood, discovered on his rounds two days later by Brooke's gamekeeper. Her body had somehow drifted to the side of the mere, half in and half out of the water as though at the last moment she had changed her mind about so drastic an action. She was a pretty little thing, or had been, for the animals had been at her and the gamekeeper brought up his breakfast in the bushes at the sight of her.

He ran to the nearest farm which happened to be Jack Emmerson's and between them, armed with one of Mrs Emmerson's blankets, they wrapped her and the baby in it and carried it back to Emmerson's place and put it tenderly in the barn. Mrs Emmerson, kindly soul that she was, would not have them in the house, she told them tearfully. The constable was summoned and with the help of Mrs Armstrong's servant, Kizzie Aspin, she was identified as Maudie – how strange they never knew her surname, was Kizzie's sad thought – the young woman who had once worked for Mrs Armstrong.

They all wept, even the servants in the kitchen at King's Meadow, for though she had been a naughty girl, she had not deserved to die, nor her boy with her, in that fashion. The mistress went mad and it was not until she was shut in with the master, who took charge of everything, that she was quietened.

He held her tightly in his arms, his lips against her hair, soothing her, murmuring to comfort her and to damp down the rage that twisted through her.

At last he spoke. 'The man is a bastard of the first order and though you know how I felt about the girls you took in, girls in the worst kind of trouble, I grant you that now, they did not deserve the fate of this poor child, *and her child*. You were right and I was wrong and I am sorry. But he must be dealt with and not by you. I'll ask him to call and see what he has to say. We are assuming it was your father . . .'

'He did to her what he used to do to me and the boys. Whipping us until the blood ran . . .'

'Sweet Jesus,' he whispered. 'Send Percy with a message that I wish to see him but, my dearest dear, please keep out of the way. Promise me . . . promise me.'

She promised.

# 22

The men had carried their master downstairs and placed him in front of the drawing room fire, for he had felt he would be at a disadvantage if he was to face up to Arthur Drummond in the bedroom he shared with his wife. He was at a disadvantage anyway since he was unable to move about and he felt that Drummond would take advantage of his immobility. He was, of course, dressed and there was no sign of the badly injured man he had been at Christmas apart from the lines of recent pain that were etched on his face. Doctor Chapman had told him that in a week or two he was going to try him on crutches and if he did well, perhaps just a walking stick. His muscles would be weak since he had been inactive for three months and there would be months of hard work ahead of him to get him back in shape. His wound was healed but in an awkward place. Each time he moved the newly healing flesh was pulled and so he must be patient. The doctor was of the opinion that had it not been for his devoted wife Brooke Armstrong would have given up long ago and fallen into a depression that would have felled him. He was an active man, an outdoor sort of a man, a man of strong will and resolution and, Wallace Chapman privately thought, a sensual man whose wife had found a way to satisfy his needs despite his present disability. And of course, he adored his baby daughter and was well on the way to becoming besotted with Arthur Drummond's neglected child as well. He had a lot to live for and he knew it, which was half the battle.

Arthur Drummond lounged in a deep and comfortable chair opposite Brooke, a brandy in one hand and a cigar in the other, an expression on his face that was hard to decipher. It spoke of arrogance, a certain superiority that indicated that he came from a better family than Armstrong's, that his breeding was clear where Brooke's background was merely that of industrialists, which was true for their vast wealth came from the manufacture of woollen cloth during the previous century. Arthur Drummond was not rich but his blood was that of the gentry class. Brooke wanted to stand up and smash his face in, knock his teeth down his throat, put his hands round his neck and throttle him and not just because of what he had done to his own beloved wife and her brothers but for the casual way in which he had taken up with the pretty child who lay in a coffin with her son in her arms, and had then turned her away from his door as though she had been a tinker begging for a farthing.

'It seems a long time since we met, Brooke, old man, considering we are related,' Drummond drawled, 'but then your accident excluded you from mixing with your friends. I do hope you are recovering. The hunting season will be over soon but I'm sure you and I—'

'I have not summoned you here to discuss hunting, Drummond, but to—'

'*Summoned* me here! I must say I take exception to your use of words, old chap. Your man said you had something of importance you wished to discuss with me and as you are unable to get about at the moment I rode over as soon as it was convenient for me to—'

'Will you be going to the funeral, Drummond?' Brooke's voice was icy and Arthur Drummond looked genuinely startled.

'Has someone died, old man? I was not aware—'

'You bastard. How you can sit there and pretend—'

Drummond rose to his feet, his face almost purple with rage. 'If you were not a cripple I would lift you from that chair and beat the living daylights out of you. I haven't the faintest notion what you are talking about but anyone who dares to call me—'

'You're not just a bastard, but a bloody murderer and I have half a mind to summon the police and accuse you of driving that poor girl to her death. You are—'

'What the bloody hell are you on about, man? Have you lost your mind?'

'Does the name Maudie ring any bells, Drummond? A pretty young girl who you took to your house and debauched, violated, whipped her until she bled and then—'

'*Maudie!* Do you mean that prostitute from your wife's brothel? The house of ill-repute as it is called hereabouts. She was nothing, the mother of an illegitimate child, a street-walker who was paid for her services and who took my fancy, as some of them do as I'm sure you must know. She made no resistance to my . . . er . . . demands but when she came to my door and insisted on seeing me, my servants told me, her bloody child in her arms, I told them to send her on her way. There are plenty more where she came from and the best of it with women such as her is that they don't mind what you do, or demand that they do as long as they get paid for it. By God, how you have the bloody nerve to summon me here to castigate me like some preacher and even to threaten me with the law is beyond belief. Do you think the police are going to believe that because some trollop chooses to kill herself – oh yes, I heard the gossip – they are going to suppose I had something to do with it? You must be mad.'

'Perhaps you are right, Drummond, but believe me you will not go unpunished. I shall blacken your name in this county so that no decent family will have you across their doorstep. Oh, I know you consider your pedigree is superior to mine but I am a very wealthy man. An influential man. Many of our friends, *your* friends, are in debt to me. I could destroy many a business if I chose and I do believe I might inform them that if they continue to entertain you or be entertained by you then they will go under. Do I make myself clear? Now get out of my house and if I see you again I will seriously injure you!'

Arthur Drummond grew very still, his face drained of all colour and his eyes pure slits of venom. They were the same colour as his chestnut hair but somehow they had faded to a pale muddied brown. Something glinted in them though, like some predatory fish swimming just below the surface of the water, but then he smiled and Brooke felt his blood turn to ice in his veins, for it was a satisfied smile that told him that Drummond had an ace up his sleeve that he was about to reveal. His quick thinking had flashed it before him and now, sneeringly, he produced it.

'Do that, old chap,' he said, almost genially, 'but before you do will you summon your nursemaid and tell her to get my daughter, my *baby* daughter ready to go home with her father. It is high time I made her acquaintance. I will find a decent nursemaid for her, one who will not indulge her as I am sure she is being indulged under your roof and then, when she is old enough, I will undertake her . . . education myself.' The threat was clear. 'It was good of Charlotte to look after her while I . . . grieved for my wife but now I think I am—'

The murderous roar reached every room in the house and in the kitchen every servant froze to a standstill, paralysed with dread. Mrs Groves, who had been making treacle toffee for Master Robbie and his friend, Tad Emmerson, reached out and dragged the pair of them into her arms, pressing their alarmed faces to her capacious bosom, while upstairs in the nursery Rosie sat down suddenly in the armchair in front of the fire then jumped to her feet and swept both protesting babies into her arms. Aisling, who had never met Arthur

Drummond and never seen the master except when she took his daughter Lucy and the little one who they were all beginning to think of as her sister down to see him, backed up against the window, for she was not unfamiliar with violence.

But it was Charlotte who had been listening at the foot of the stairs who was first to explode into the drawing room, just in time to stop her husband from doing his best to rise from his chair and fling himself at her father. In a moment she was across the room and was pressed against his struggling figure, forcing him to remain seated.

'Don't, darling, don't move. Do you want to pull your wound apart? Stay there.'

'Stay here?' he bellowed, while in the kitchen Mrs Dickinson made a sign to Nellie to fetch men from the yard. 'Stay here while this . . . this perverted bugger takes away our . . . your . . . the baby he abandoned three months ago? No doubt he will subject her to—'

'Sweetheart, my love. . .' With her back to her sneering father she put her arms about Brooke and held him down in his chair, terrified, not that he would do harm to her father but that he might undo all the good the doctors had achieved. She pressed her face to his, kissing him passionately, sitting almost in his lap but facing him and the man at her back actually began to laugh.

'Well, it seems I did well to marry you to this half a man, my dear. I see you have formed an attachment and before he became as he is gave him a child. But you also took my child and unless the pair of you do exactly what I tell you I will have *my* child back. Your husband has threatened me and I will not have it. *I will not have it!*'

At that moment John the gardener and Percy the groom entered the room in a furious rush, for from what Cook gabbled the master was in great danger but a hand from the man they knew as their mistress's father, a hand raised in derision, stopped them in their tracks and they waited, should they be wanted, for a sign from either the master or the mistress.

'Thank you, John, Percy, we shall not need you so . . . shut the door as you leave and, Percy, if you would be so good as to bring Mr Drummond's horse to the front of the house. He is just about to leave.'

If they were astonished to see the mistress apparently holding down the master they did not show it. They both glared at Mr Drummond who had a bad reputation in these parts and left the room.

'Well,' drawled Arthur Drummond, 'what is it to be? Shall I give you a day or two to think it over? Let me know as soon as possible so that I might, if it is necessary, engage a nurse for the child. Now, I must be off. I'm to dine with friends this evening and I believe we are to go to the opera though it is not really my preference. The music hall is more to my taste. Pretty girls, perhaps a game of cards and then . . . whatever, or *whoever* I might be in the mood for. Well, Brooke, you will get my drift, being a man of the world. So, I'll say good-day to you. By the way, did you call the child Ellen?' He smiled as he sauntered from the room.

It was a long time before they moved, then, slowly, like an old woman, Charlotte stood up and, holding her husband's hand, rang the bell. Nellie, her face ashen, crept into the room. She had no idea what was afoot but she knew it was bad. The master and mistress had each aged ten years since she had seen them earlier in the day, staring into some horror that had come upon them, the master's hand in that of the mistress.

'Ma'am?' she quavered.

'Ask two of the men to carry my husband up to our room, will you, Nellie, and . . . and . . .' She seemed to falter as though she did not know what to do next, so after waiting for a moment Nellie scuttled from the room.

'Two of yer are wanted,' she told the men who huddled at the back door. John and Percy flung themselves forward and were led into the drawing room by the distressed parlour-maid.

When they were at last back in their bedroom, Brooke frozen in his chair, she knelt at his feet, her head on his knee while his hand smoothed her hair, his gaze unseeing at the garden where for the first time there was no activity since all the men and the two boys who often rode their new bicycles – Christmas presents from Robbie's brother-in-law – up and down the long drive were all at the back, huddled together in dread. They were aware that Mrs Armstrong's father had made some threat. Why else would the master roar as he had done? He had been outraged, they were aware of that, too, but what the dickens could it be? For comfort they stayed together, sitting or standing about, drinking the strong tea Mrs Groves considered a heartener, debating what was amiss in quiet voices, and when Kizzie bustled into the kitchen she was stopped in her tracks by the silence and the frightened faces that turned to look at her.

'What's up?' she asked, but they only shook their heads sadly.

In the bedroom Charlotte stirred, looking up into Brooke's face then asked the same question but in different words.

'He wants Ellie, or rather he doesn't want her but he is using her to blackmail us into keeping quiet about the young girl who died.'

'Maudie?'

'Yes. I knew there was nothing I could do within the law to punish him so I told him I would have him ostracised in the county. I could, too. I have some powerful friends, many of whom are in my debt so he said, "Go ahead, but fetch my daughter from your nursery and I will take her home."'

'No, *no*!' she leapt to her feet and again the servants clutched at anything that would steady them, a chair, the solid table, each other, and Robbie, who, in his opinion, was now grown up as he was eight years old, buried his face in Mrs Groves's protective arms. He was to go to the grammar school in Wakefield in the autumn and Brooke, who he thought the world of now, was to pay for Tad to go with him. He didn't know what was happening but the shouts and now Charlie's screams frightened him to death. He knew his father had been here and in his terror he thought it might mean he was to go back to live with him.

'Now, now, Master Robbie, don't fret, chuck,' Mrs Groves murmured.

Upstairs, Brooke recited in a toneless voice what had happened between himself and Arthur Drummond, even his comment about the Dower House being a 'house of ill-repute' filled with prostitutes and their illegitimate offspring and therefore available to any man with the brass to help himself to one. He had 'helped himself' to Maudie, promising her God knows what and the result had been her death. And the implication was that if there was another of his daughter's girls he fancied he would do it all again. He felt no guilt, nor shame that the silly bitch had taken her own life and that of her child, driven to desperation by his denial of her and therefore could see no reason for Brooke to take any action.

A week later, with a face carved in stone, Brooke Armstrong agreed to Arthur Drummond leaving his younger daughter in his elder daughter's care for the time being, the inference being, though not spoken for there was no need, that should a breath of scandal touch him through Brooke's *machinations* the child would at once be taken back to her home with her father. Arthur Drummond also implied that now and again he might be short of a guinea or two and he was sure his old friend and son-in-law would help him out.

After he had ridden off, cock-a-hoop, Kizzie said bitterly, having been told the whole story, Charlotte wept in her husband's arms and Brooke felt the frustration of a man who had once been strong and invincible and who was now unable to protect those he loved.

'He shouldn't be allowed to get away with it,' Charlotte moaned. 'He killed Maudie as surely as if he had thrown her in the mere and held her under. And how are we going to defend the girls we have at the Dower House? They are ignorant working girls who will be in awe of a man of my father's class who takes an interest in them. They have been taught their place and to believe what the ruling classes tell them. But I cannot allow Ellie to be torn from us and given to her father. I would kill him first,' she raged while Brooke tried to soothe her.

'My sweetheart, I wouldn't let him.'

'But he is her father.'

'We will come to some arrangement.'

'You mean *buy* her.' Her voice was wild.

'If necessary, yes.'

'But it must be legally binding.'

'Darling, trust me,' he shushed her, cursing inwardly the bloody bull and not just the bull, which was only doing what was in his nature, but himself for his carelessness and his inability to deal with this chaos as he would like. What *would* he like? He knew what he wanted to do more than anything in the world, but since it was not possible to beat a man to pulp and get away with it he summoned his solicitor instead and after a long and protracted interview in which the intricacies of the law were discussed it was sadly agreed there was nothing to be done.

'Could I not adopt her?' he had asked hopefully, his wife clinging to his hand.

'Not unless he agrees to it, I'm afraid.'

'But he is cruel. My wife and her brothers could testify to that. He beat them all.'

'A man is allowed to chastise his children, Mr Armstrong. It is not against the law.'

'Then there is nothing . . .?'

The solicitor shook his head sorrowfully. He had heard of Arthur Drummond's supposed connection with the young girl who had taken her life and that of her child in the mere, and who had been buried only the day before and but for Brooke Armstrong's influence it would have been in a suicide's grave. Mrs Armstrong, her maid Miss Aspin and, strangely, Doctor Chapman had been the only mourners.

Wallace Chapman called the next day and sadly told Charlotte that he did not think he should bring any more girls to the Dower House. It might not be safe, especially for the thirteen-year-old who was recovering at his own home in his wife's care.

'With a man such as your father luring young women as he appears to think is his right, and as they are all ignorant and, though I do not like to say it, easily tempted, he has only to accost one and . . . well, I will say no more. You will know what I mean.'

Brooke brooded for days on his own inability to do 'bugger all' as he said coarsely to his wife, the only time he showed any sign of peace when he nursed the two babies on his knee. They were his joy, both of them, and so alike apart from the colour of their eyes they might have been sisters. As spring drifted into summer and they began to crawl they no longer wanted to be nursed but struggled to escape his loving grasp and explore the many things in the room. Brooke was now attempting to manage on his crutches and the day he stood up and took his first faltering steps was a day for champagne, he declared, and every member of his household must drink a glass. He could not manage the stairs but with the help of two of the men was carried down them and out into the sunshine. A rug was spread on the lawn and the babies placed on them but they were off before their parents, as they thought of themselves, had barely got settled and the gardeners were kept busy heading them off from the small lake and the flowerbeds, which were filled with lupins in every colour of the rainbow, French marigolds, sweet william, larkspur and stock. They scuttled about on their bottoms, since neither seemed to get the proper concept of crawling on hands and knees, their plump, dimpled hands reaching for anything that took their fancy: worms, daisies from the grass, great fat bumble bees lazily drinking from the blooms. They yelled furiously together, as they did everything, when they were placed in their perambulator. Aisling and Rosie were heard to complain that they might as well sit by the nursery fire as the master and mistress took over what they considered was their work but as Brooke said, if Drummond should take it into his head to intercept the two young maids while they were out alone and help himself to his own daughter, they would be too terrified to resist him. They both were aware of the danger, as were all the staff and the babies were always in view of one or two of the men.

They often drove the small pony and trap, which could easily be manoeuvred about the grounds, Brooke at the reins, travelling round the paddock to feed the horses with apples and lumps of sugar and down to the lake to throw bread for the ducks. Had it not been for the fear of her own father, Charlotte thought it was the happiest time of her life. Brooke was beginning to walk about the house unaided and was talking about getting a motor car! Their love-making was a joy to them both though they were careful not to exert too much pressure on Brooke's wound. Damn, bloody thing, he called it, as a sudden movement, of which there were many, for how the hell could you make love to your wife without a bit of energy, caused him agony. The only flaw in their idyllic days was the work at the Dower House which was slowly drawing to a halt.

Jenny and Kizzie did their best to keep the girls busy but with their own children growing and needing more supervision it seemed they were becoming restless, wanting to go into town, take the money they earned and enjoy themselves. They had all recovered from their experiences and like all young things tended to forget what they had gone through. Maudie's death had alarmed them and Kizzie had warned them to beware of the 'toff' who had lured her away, but again, being young and healthy they did not take a great deal of notice.

Charlotte and Brooke sat for hours during the unseasonably warm spring in the comfortable chairs put out for them on the terrace by the servants, watching Lucy and Ellie wrestle with one another on the newly mown grass, studying the motor magazine *Autocar*, discussing the merits of the Lanchester, the Daimler, the Mercedes and though neither of them, even Brooke, knew the first thing about the new mode of travel it appealed to them both and took their minds off the constant, quiet worry of Ellie Drummond.

'I wish we could change her name to Armstrong,' Brooke reflected one day out of the blue.

'He wouldn't allow it,' Charlotte answered flatly. 'It might give us an advantage over him. Tell me, has he asked you for anything yet? I mean money. I know you had a telephone call the other day but—'

'Yes.'

'A lot?'

'A hundred guineas. A gambling debt,' he said, 'and he'd seen a horse he liked the look of. A hunter, but he'd let me know . . .'

Charlotte put her hands to her face and bent her head. 'Dear God, can we live with this hanging over us, my love?' The two little girls, almost walking now, one determined to keep up with the other, were shouting in a language only they seemed to understand, falling down, getting to their feet, chasing the dogs on unsteady legs, laughing, showing their new teeth, rosy with the golden tint to their flesh from the summer sunshine. She groaned and Brooke held out his hand, drawing her from her chair to sit on his knee. Her arms were round his neck and the two babies began to stumble towards them to join in what they evidently saw as a game.

It was then that Johnson came from the house, a silver salver in his hand on which rested today's newly delivered third post. Still curled up on her husband's knee, the children swarming about them, what they had thought was almost unendurable proved not to be *almost* but absolute.

It was a letter from Arthur Drummond. It was couched in a polite and even gracious tone. He wished to invite both his daughters to take tea with him one afternoon at their own convenience, of course, as he wished to discuss something with Charlotte. If she could let him know by return he would be most obliged!

# 23

Brooke wanted to come with her but when she insisted that her father would prove awkward – which was a ridiculous word to describe how he would *really* react – he reluctantly allowed that if she took Todd to drive the carriage he would let her go alone with Ellie, then if she met with any difficulty at least she would have one of their own men to defend her. He was not quite sure what he meant by that but his instinct told him that Arthur Drummond could be a dangerous man to defy.

Mr Watson, the butler who answered Todd's sharp tat-tat on the door, was clearly astonished to find Miss Charlotte, a baby in her arms, standing on the doorstep.

'Miss Charlotte . . .' he stammered, then remembering who she now was, hastily changed it to, 'Mrs Armstrong, we were not told you were expected.'

'Were you not,' Charlotte answered crisply. 'My father asked me to call with . . . with his daughter so if you would tell him we are here I would be obliged.'

'Very well, madam; perhaps you would wait in the drawing room.'

'Thank you,' making her way through the familiar hallway.

'I'll be in't carriage, Mrs Armstrong,' Todd told her with a warning glance at the butler's retreating back, a remark that conveyed to her that she had only to shout or scream or make some commotion and he'd be inside the bloody house before that jumped-up butler could say, 'Aye up'.

'Thank you, Todd.'

Mr Watson made no other appearance and Charlotte was thankful to sit down on the sofa, her knees almost giving way beneath her, doing her best not to tremble. It was almost two years since she had been in this house and the very atmosphere seemed to be redolent with the terrible dread under which she and her brothers had lived. Ellie squirmed in her arms, a lively bundle at five months old, her vivid green eyes filled with curiosity as she peeped about her. Her little arms waved enthusiastically and she turned to smile up into Charlotte's face. She and Lucy seemed to have brought each other on in their development, one watching the other and then copying a movement, a sound, a concerted effort to sit up. She was lively and alert and smiling. It was May now, for Drummond had allowed a few weeks to pass before inviting his daughters to visit him.

Had it not been for her destination Charlotte would have enjoyed the short journey from King's Meadow to the Mount. It had rained during the night and the hedgerows and the wild flowers in the ditches and the newly burgeoning meadows were heavy with what appeared to be sparkling, diamond dewdrops. Primroses were still thick on the banks and many of the apple orchards attached to the cottages along the lane were in full bloom. The oak trees in the woodland through which the lane ran were showing the first signs of golden, bronze foliage. Cowslips, red campion and wild hyacinths shouted the approach of summer, the passing of spring, the flowers embroidering the newly green of the waving grasses, and as the horses clip-clopped along the lane, a robin, as though disturbed by their clatter, flew directly from the hedge over the carriage. It was mild, almost warm, a lovely day for a drive, but Charlotte's heart was heavy in her breast. It had been difficult to leave Lucy, who had never been parted from Ellie, and the baby had wailed disconsolately as Charlotte, with Ellie in her arms, had left the nursery. Brooke, rigid with disapproval and with a curious fear, had lifted her from her little bed and did his best to pacify her, but it was plain that both of them had been distressed at being left behind. Aisling and Rosie had hovered restlessly about the room, wondering when *they* were going to get a look-in as the mistress dressed Ellie and the master cradled his daughter, exchanging glances and raising their eyebrows, sighing with ill-concealed reproach.

'Ah, Charlotte, there you are.' A silky voice from the doorway startled her, for she had not heard him enter and both she and Ellie turned their heads in that direction. Charlotte had given Ellie an ivory teething ring attached to a rattle to amuse her as they waited, but the child dropped it and her bottom lip quivered as she studied the unknown man in the doorway. It was as though, young as she was, she felt something pitiless in him, which Charlotte told herself was ridiculous, but Ellie's eyes brimmed with tears and she turned her rosy face into Charlotte's breast.

'Not another cry-baby?' her father sighed. 'I seem to breed nothing but weaklings, but then—'

'She is only five months old, Father, and doesn't know you,' Charlotte stated icily, determined to protect the lovely child in her arms.

'Well, when she returns to her rightful place with her father she will soon learn control, though I must admit I was singularly unsuccessful with you and your brothers.'

Charlotte clutched Ellie to her with desperate arms. 'You cannot mean to bring her back here, Father. She is—'

'She is my daughter, Charlotte, but her future depends entirely on you. You have given her a good start but I can see you have been far too indulgent. In fact you have been a very naughty girl and you will remember that I am a great believer in punishment for naughty girls and boys!'

Dear sweet God, surely . . . *surely* he did not mean to . . .?

'Please, Father, please, I beg you . . .'

'Come along to my study, my dear, and we will discuss . . . No, leave the child. One of the maidservants will look after her while we . . . talk. I'll ring the bell for Palmer to take her to the nursery.'

'Let me keep her with me, Father. She knows me and will be afraid if we are parted. I am aware that she would be kind but I really would rather have her with me.'

'She will have to become used to being without you one day, Charlotte, so why?'

'Please don't take her away from people she knows and who love her.' She wanted to weep, to place Ellie on the sofa and get down on her knees and plead but her father merely smiled as he reached for the bell.

'Palmer will see to the child while you come with me to my study.'

He stood directly before her, no more than two feet away and she could clearly see the huge bulge that filled the front of his breeches and his face, as he smiled at her, was suffused with colour. He was breathing rapidly. A terror so great, so overwhelming, a thought that was so absolutely preposterous ran through her veins like a burning stream of molten lava, for it was in the study that she and her brothers had suffered not only pain and fear, but a humiliation too terrible to contemplate. And hers had been, as a young girl, the worst of all. She could hardly bear the memory of it so that even the word 'study' brought it all back, *and her father's present behaviour*!

'Can we not talk here, Father?' she appealed piteously. There was a knock at the door, which opened, and a parlour-maid slipped inside, bobbing a curtsey. They were all agog in the kitchen, for this was the first time Miss Charlotte had visited her father since her marriage. There was something funny going on, the girl was aware of that at once, but it was nothing to do with her, was it. Besides, they were all dying to get a scen at the babby who had been whisked away by Miss Charlotte when she was born and the poor little mite's mam had died. Funny goings-on in this house there had been and still were by the look of it.

Miss Charlotte turned to her with what seemed to her to be despair. 'Perhaps we could have some hot chocolate? Is that all right, Father?' turning back to the master.

'Of course, my dear. Now, Palmer, take the child.'

'No, Father, please, she will be frightened.'

'Take the child, Palmer,' Arthur Drummond told the confused parlour-maid.

'Where shall I tekk 'er, sir?'

'Anywhere, girl. The kitchen will do and then fetch hot chocolate for my daughter. My elder daughter. To my study.'

Palmer moved uncertainly across the carpet and reached smilingly for the baby who cowered back from her, then turned and clung round Miss Charlotte's neck like one of the baby monkeys she had seen clinging to its mother when she and her friend had gone on a day's outing to the zoo.

Palmer was startled when Miss Charlotte slapped her hands away to prevent her taking the child. She turned to look enquiringly at the master.

'Charlotte, allow Palmer to take the child to the kitchen where she will come to no harm. Otherwise I myself will take her to the nursery where I shall arrange for a nursemaid of my own choosing who will not be as . . . as tolerant as the girl who has charge of her at King's Meadow. You really are making a spectacle of yourself, my dear. You have my word she will not be harmed . . .' for by this time Charlotte, to Palmer's astonishment, had begun to weep. 'I feel more . . . more at ease in my study, Charlotte, rather than this drawing room which I always think of as a ladies' room.'

'Father . . .' Charlotte whispered piteously, eyeing the bulge in his breeches.

'Come, come, my dear. Hand the child to Palmer. Oh, and I think we will dispense with the chocolate, Palmer. Miss Charlotte and I have something we must talk about and do not wish to be interrupted.'

Ellie Drummond was returned to her sister an hour later, none the worse for her visit to the kitchen for the servants had made a great fuss of her. They were surprised by Miss Charlotte though. She seemed frozen, one could almost call it *stunned* and she walked stiffly as if she were in pain. Her face was like chalk but had a round spot of livid red on each cheekbone. Her eyes had a strange look about them as though she did not really see any of them and she trembled like the leaves on the aspen tree that grew on the edge of the woodland.

'She's a bonny little thing, Miss Charlotte,' Cook said pleasantly, then stepped back hastily as Miss Charlotte snatched the baby and clutched her to her chest.

'Ista all right, Miss Charlotte?' she asked kindly, for they all knew what a devil the master was but Miss Charlotte, without speaking, turned and ran, *ran*, mind you, through the kitchen door to the hallway and out of the front door giving Watson barely time to open it for her. She flung herself so fiercely down the steps that Todd put out a hand to steady her, almost lifting her and the distressed baby into the carriage. She sat, her face like a stone carving, and positively shouted to her coachman to take her home. Todd turned several times to look at her since she made no attempt to comfort the fretful child, which was not like her, and ignored his anxious concern which again was unlike her.

Brooke was hanging about in the hallway practising, he told Kizzie who was also hovering nearby, walking with his sticks, or rather *without* them, because he meant to be his old self again by summer. He was beginning to manage well now with his balance, though when Charlotte tore up the steps and into his arms he almost went head over heels.

She huddled into Brooke's arms and he held her firmly, murmuring endearments, words of comfort. It was as though he divined what he imagined had been done and said to her, the dirt and filth and nastiness with which she had been tarnished and wished his own sweet, clean love to wash it all away. He knew Drummond's perverse ways and what she and her brothers had suffered at his hands and though he wanted to saddle up Max and gallop over there and kill him, failing that, beat him to a bloody pulp, the sad fact was that he could do none of these things, not even saddle his own horse. He was only just learning to walk again and unless he preserved his strength and went at the pace the doctor advised the wound in his groin and thigh would never be completely healed. It was doing well. *He* was doing well. He could move about the estate in his wife's little gig, visit his farms, chat to his tenants, keep an eye on his properties, but unless he obeyed the doctor's orders he would never be as he was. He could only comfort his wife, love his wife, love the woman for whom he would gladly *give* his life.

'You shan't go again, my sweetheart. We will fight him through the courts and keep the child with us. He is not fit to . . .'

Charlotte shivered for several moments in his arms, the child wailing between them, then Kizzie was there, taking Ellie and shushing her as she made her way to the nursery.

It was then that the true strength and great heart of Charlotte Armstrong revealed themselves. She was a happy woman, or had been since she and Brooke had declared their love for one another. She was a kind woman, good-natured, easy to like, fun-loving and eager to please her household, but now her face was like that of a warrior queen, wrought in marble. Strong and resolute, older somehow than her eighteen years and it told her amazed husband that she was ready to fight. To fight the man who attacked them in the heart of her family. She had made a place for herself here at King's Meadow. Her husband's people, his servants and tenants admired and respected her, as she did them. She had a child, one her husband, whom she loved above all else, had given her, and another who needed her protection. Of her blood. Her half-sister. She had done her best as a child, a young girl and woman to protect her brothers and she had taken punishment that she had not deserved but this was the end of it. He would not beat her again. Her enemy! Her father! He would not savage her life as he intended doing. Today he had seen her weak and submissive, for she had thought this behaviour would protect her family, but what he had attempted today, and she could tell no one about it, except perhaps Kizzie, of the horror she had endured, had, instead of terrorising her, strengthened her, turned her into the woman she meant to be.

'Darling, my dearest darling,' she murmured against Brooke's chest, 'it is done now. We will be safe, for I shall not allow . . .'

Brooke held her away from him, looking down into her bright face, steadying himself against her, then, taking her arm, led her into the drawing room. He sat her down on the sofa and placed himself carefully beside her, cradling her in his arms after ringing the bell for Nellie. When she came trotting in, her face alight with anticipation, for they all knew where the mistress had been, he ordered coffee. There was a great fire roaring in the grate because though the day was mild he felt the cold, probably due to his lack of exercise, and after Nellie had gone, disappointed not to have anything to tell them in the kitchen, he and Charlotte sat quietly side by side, sipping their coffee, strangely at peace, calm, relaxed, unafraid, for though nothing had been said he knew Charlotte had won something today and would tell him when she was ready. He would defend her and the babies with his life but something told him she was able to defend herself with him beside her.

At last she spoke. 'I will not go again,' she said quietly, 'and neither will Ellie. He is never to put a foot on our land and the men will be warned to throw him off if he does. I thought we might arm them but that would not do for they are not men to kill another man. Besides, it will humiliate him more to be handled by those he believes are beneath him. To be turned off like a common trespasser, a tinker or a beggar, would be a worse punishment than to be shot. We will not let him interfere with our lives but everyone, all the servants, the men and the women must be warned. Particularly Aisling and Rosie who must at all times have one of the men on hand when they are in the garden or about the grounds, as he is quite likely to attempt an abduction of Ellie. We must speak to your lawyer and find a way to put an end to his threats. Brooke, I would stand up in court and describe in detail what he did to me and my brothers, particularly to me, details that would shock the society in which he moves. It would alienate them, turn them against him if they knew what he would do to this child if he had her. And what he wanted to do to me today. He is out of his mind, a pervert.

'We will talk to Wallace Chapman. He knows so much about the kind of men who abuse women and he might know of some way . . . Dear Lord, *anyone* . . . I don't care if it threatens to besmirch my character and cause a scandal that would rock the county but I will shout to the world of the evil this man has perpetrated. I am only sorry if it affects you, which it is bound to do. Oh, Brooke, we must remember poor little Maudie. He killed her as if he had choked the life out of her with his bare hands. I don't know what I was thinking of, going there today with some idea of making a compromise when he is . . . Brooke, hold me, hold me . . .' Which he did but at once she struggled to sit up. 'And you might as well accept that I shall go back to my neglected plans for the girls in the Dower House and will not take—'

Brooke began to laugh, the sound of it echoing through the half-open door and down the hall to the kitchen where they all began to smile and bang about with their tasks since it seemed all was to be well at King's Meadow.

'It is a tigress I married, a lioness with a heart as strong as any man's. My love, my sweet love, do you think after all you have brought into my life I would deny you your dream? By God, we'll work together to make your endeavour a success. Anything I can do . . . I am not without influence . . .'

'No, no, don't you see, sweetheart, this is *mine*. Oh, Brooke, I am not denigrating what you are offering but I want to carry through this thing I began with such an innocent heart. I believed that I only had to make up my mind to it and it would succeed but it got away from me. Lucy and Ellie and, more importantly, you, came first and I neglected those in the Dower House and the plans I had made to give those girls a worthwhile life. God, will you listen to me? I sound like one of those ladies who do "good works" simply because they have nothing else in their lives. But I have you now, and Lucy and Ellie who are of a far greater importance. Even so, I can't let them down. And they must be protected, for I fear my father will not stop with . . . with Maudie. He will get at me in any way he can.'

She burrowed her head into his shoulder, her hair brushing his chin and he held her more tightly since he feared for her. He was busy making plans of his own because though there were nine menservants employed at King's Meadow he doubted whether his butler would be of much use if it came to facing up to Arthur Drummond, and the rest, the groom, stable lad, gardeners, all had work to do and could not be expected to patrol the grounds in defence of the womenfolk, his own beloved wife included. His mind was busy as he cradled Charlotte in the strength of his arms and cursed his own bloody carelessness in dealing with Jack Emmerson's bull.

Had it not been for that and his own present weakness none of this would be happening. He would not have allowed Charlotte to go alone to that beast's house but having done so and guessing what had happened to her there, even now would be on his horse galloping to the Mount to *persuade* – smiling at his use of the word – Drummond to stay out of his and Charlotte's life. In fact, by now, Drummond might be such a bloody mess he would never again have the strength to bother any female!

Charlotte sighed and sat up. She smiled into his face then leaned to kiss him tenderly.

'It's a lovely day. Look at the sunshine . . .' and they both turned to look through the window. The long stretch of lawn that led down to the small lake had been threaded with wild daffodils which John and Ned had been careful to mow round. There were wallflowers spilling over in the beds, brilliant with colour, and Virginia stock just coming into their best. The lime trees that bordered the drive showed their pale green, heart-shaped leaves waiting for the flowers which did not dangle their delicate blossoms until July.

They walked slowly down the lime tree drive, Brooke leaning carefully on his one stick, his other arm through Charlotte's. John and Ned were busy on their knees weeding beside the lake, removing the clogged debris of the winter, not speaking much, for they were of a similar nature though there was thirty years' difference in their age. They stood immediately when they heard the approaching footsteps of their master and mistress, touching the peaks of their battered caps, smiling and ready to chat if they were spoken to.

'Everywhere looks very smart, John,' Brooke said. 'I particularly like the colours in the flowerbeds. Wallflowers, are they?'

'Aye, sir, I allus did like a bit o' colour meself.'

'You've done very well. Thank you.'

'Thank *you*, sir,' the older man said, nudging Ned who, though he had been at King's Meadow for years, was considered to be his apprentice.

'Aye, sir,' he mumbled, 'thank yer.'

When the master and mistress turned and began to stroll back to the house, the men resumed their kneeling position.

'I allus liked t' master,' John said. ' 'E tekks notice an' I'm that glad ter see 'im on 'is feet again. That's thanks ter't missis, I reckon.'

'Oh aye, why's that then?'

'Don't be gormless, lad, wouldn't she put any chap back on 'is feet. She's some daft ideas like that 'un wi' them lasses at Dower 'Ouse, but she's a good 'eart on 'er. I 'eard 'er old man's tryin' ter't get babby back but she'll not 'ave it. Anyroad, 'e'd 'ave ter get through me first.' He pulled viciously at a weed that was proving awkward.

'Me an' all.'

That night Charlotte and Brooke Armstrong made love as they had never done before. He was still somewhat encumbered by his injury. She undressed him carefully as he lay on his back on the bed, sliding her hands across his shoulders, bringing her palms slowly across his chest, feeling the springy hair and the soft indentations around his nipples which rose at her touch. She slipped down his body, paying particular attention to his thighs then up again until she reached his mouth. The kiss lasted for a long time and his hands now began the slow exploration of her naked body. He was more than ready, she could feel that, for was not the evidence pressed hard against her belly and she was ready too. He cupped her breasts and rubbed her nipples, groaning. Their breath was ragged as she guided him into the slippery cleft between her legs.

'Holy God . . .' he breathed, neither of them knowing that he had just impregnated her again.

'Indeed . . .' she quavered, unable to get her breath, collapsing on top of him, her quivering arms unable to hold her up any longer.

'Did I hurt you?' she mumbled into his breast and then lifted her head as he began to laugh.

'Aren't I supposed to ask *you* that, my lovely, lovely girl?'

There was silence for several minutes while they both dreamily contemplated what they had just accomplished.

'There's just one thing.'

'What?' Her voice was anxious.

'Can we do it again?'

# 24

The salesman at Alcock and Upton's Quality Carpets in Westgate was a tall, perfectly groomed gentleman who was reverence personified when Charlotte entered the premises. She was so obviously a lady and he provided carpets and rugs to the upper classes of which she was one. Her manner and her dress, which was elegant and appeared to his practised eye to be very expensive, proclaimed her to be the sort of customer he, as head salesman, always dealt with, leaving the lesser salesmen to the upper middle classes who were wealthy but not deserving of his attention. And her maid was also well, if not as expensively, dressed, as befitted a servant.

Charlotte had left the house with Brooke's reluctant comments – for had he not made her a promise – and under his disapproving gaze, though he did his best to conceal it since he had given her his blessing. She wore a high-necked, peach-coloured lace blouse with an ankle-length skirt in dove-grey watered silk. Over the blouse she wore what was known as a zouave jacket, in a shade to match her skirt. Her hat was wide-brimmed, decorated with a positive garden of peach-coloured silk roses. High-cut, kid shoes had replaced boots at the beginning of this new century and hers had been dyed to match her outfit. They had a pointed toe, a bar across the instep fastened by a button and two and a half inch Cuban heels.

Jenny, who accompanied her and carried their 'samples' in a large canvas bag, was similarly dressed in the fashion of the day but in a subdued deep blue with a white blouse, and her hat, the same shape but smaller than her mistress's was decorated with dainty white roses, also silk.

They both looked extremely attractive and their progress through the shop was watched by many admiring glances, and not just those of the gentlemen.

'Good morning, madam,' said the salesman, having noticed the uniformed coachman and smart carriage from which the ladies had alighted, and which was half blocking the road outside the shop window. He was almost running across the sumptuous carpet in his effort to assist her through the shop door and close it respectfully behind her. 'How may I assist you?'

He indicated an elegant velvet chair where she might seat herself, snapping his fingers at an underling to bring another for her companion.

'Good morning,' Charlotte replied, hoping to God he could not hear her heart going nineteen to the dozen beneath her lace blouse, nor see it literally lifting the material as it thumped erratically. 'I think it is more a case of how I can help *you*,' she answered, smiling brilliantly, while beside her Jenny sat frozen to the chair one of the men, who looked in her opinion like tailor's dummies, had brought for her.

The head salesman, to do him justice, did not allow the expression on his face to alter. He was used to dealing with every kind of lady, *ladies*, mind you, from the very rude who demanded his undivided attention, to the icily polite, many of them from noble families who imagined they were doing him a favour by even sitting on his chair.

'Madam?' he enquired.

'Perhaps I am speaking to the wrong gentleman.' Charlotte smiled. 'You are a salesman and I do not suppose you do the buying in this establishment or have anything to do with the manufacture of carpets and rugs. You *sell* what is on display here so perhaps you could direct me to the office of the gentleman who makes the decisions on what you sell.'

'Madam,' the salesman faltered.

'I'm sorry, you must understand I am ignorant of the correct procedure in these matters. Shall you bring the manager or take me and my assistant here' – turning to smile encouragingly at Jenny who looked as terrified as Charlotte felt though Charlotte did not let it show – 'to his office? I have something he might be interested in. You sell some magnificent carpets here and a few rugs, I see,' she said, glancing round her.

The salesman looked mortified. 'The manager is very busy at the moment, madam. I believe he has a representative from the Axminster manufacturer with him but if you would like to make an appointment to—'

'What is the manager's name, if you please?'

'Mr Martin, madam, but as I say . . .'

Charlotte's face was like marble, creamy and smooth and her vivid blue eyes froze to the hardness of the jewel to which they were likened. She had become instantly the well-bred and autocratic lady she had learned to be, mistress of her household, director of her servants, wife to one of Yorkshire's most powerful gentlemen and her expression told him she would not be obstructed by any man who had the temerity to stand against her.

'I will wait to see Mr Martin,' she said, rising with such alacrity he was forced to move hastily to one side.

Still he tried. 'Mr Martin is extremely busy, Mrs . . .?'

'Mrs Armstrong. Mrs Brooke Armstrong who wishes to discuss business with him, so if you would inform him that I am here I would be obliged. In the meanwhile my assistant and I will look round your shop to see what quality goods you supply,' just as though there were grave doubts in her mind as to whether they would be up to the standard she required. She turned imperiously on her heel to study the lesser salesmen and their customers who stared open-mouthed at her. Though she was quaking inside like one of Mrs Groves's delicious jellies, she lifted her chin and then turned back again to the salesman who was dithering at her back, uncertain as yet how to deal with this beautiful commanding woman.

'Well,' she said.

Still loth to give up his authority, which was absolute in this establishment, he did his best to meet her eye with the look that quailed salesmen and customers alike but Charlotte had decided that if she was to do business – which she had already achieved with the manager of the shoddy mill – she must stand up to these men who believed a woman's place was in the bedroom or the kitchen. At that moment a door at the back of the shop opened and two men appeared. They shook hands and one was beginning to make his way towards the door, the other to turn back to the office. The one who turned back caught the small altercation that appeared to be disturbing the calm of his magnificent premises and he hesitated, then, with a stately stride that denoted his place in the smooth running of Alcock and Upton, he crossed the magnificent carpet that had been especially hand-made in the Aubusson style for the shop and bowed to Charlotte, who was obviously a lady of some standing.

'Is there a problem, Mr Johnson?' he asked unctuously.

'This lady would like—'

'I am Mrs Brooke Armstrong,' Charlotte told him, 'and would be glad of a few minutes of your time, Mr Martin.'

'Mrs Armstrong, this is indeed a pleasure,' he said as he bowed again over her hand, his eyes approving her young beauty, but very respectfully. 'Will you not come into my office and perhaps a cup of tea might be in order. See to it, will you, Mr Johnson.'

Tea and biscuits were produced and for several minutes they were very civil with one another while Jenny sat in a discreet corner. He had been sorry to hear of Mr Armstrong's sad accident and was delighted to hear he was recovering, thinking she was here to place an order for one of his hand-made carpets which were much sought after by the upper classes in the area. Their designers were the very best in the land and the Classic collections, botanical, Savonnerie, the silk route, their Rhapsody could be created in any size or colour-ing, he was saying when Charlotte stopped his words in mid-sentence.

'I have not come here to buy but to sell, Mr Martin,' she interrupted him crisply. 'My . . . my staff produce the most beautiful rugs you have ever seen and Jenny here, who is our designer, has brought several samples to show you,' turning to Jenny who rose to her feet and opened the canvas bag.

Immediately Mr Martin's courteously admiring benevo-lence was wiped away and his smiling eyes turned cold. He was not sure whether this lovely woman was playing a joke on him or whether she was completely mad.

He leaned back in his chair. If she was who she said she was and there was no reason to doubt her, he could not afford to offend a landed gentleman like Brooke Armstrong who was one of the top men in Yorkshire, but at the same time what was a lady of her standing, married to a gentleman of Armstrong's class, doing, trying to sell rugs, for God's sake, to Alcock and Upton's?

'I'm sorry, Mrs Armstrong, I don't quite see what it is you want from me.'

Charlotte turned eagerly to Jenny who stepped forward and drew from the bag one of her exquisite rugs, the first made up into a wall hanging. It was of a meadow drifting with wild flowers, ox-eye daisies, yellow rattle, meadow thistle and knapweed and the vivid red of poppies. Jenny had seen it in a book in the library at the big house, and copied it, wondering as she did so who had been interested in wild flowers. She was not to know that Mr Armstrong's mother had been a passionate botanist and there was certainly a wealth of books from which Jenny chose her subjects.

She held up the wall hanging and for several breathless moments Mr Martin was silenced by its beauty then he recovered himself. He regarded her steadily as he leaned forward, putting his elbows on his desk. He fingered his chin as though considering what he should say and Charlotte held her breath. Jenny still held up the wall hanging but in her heart knew they were lost. Mr Martin's next words confirmed it.

'Well now, Mrs Armstrong, it was very kind of you to consider me and this firm for your . . . goods but we do not deal with – such things in our establishment. We only deal with the highest quality, in our carpets and rugs and in our customers. There is a lot of work, I am sure in producing such a thing—'

'You have not seen all our stock, Mr Martin.'

He stood up courteously. 'I'm sure it is as good as the rug . . . or wall hanging you have shown me. A hooked rug, is that what it is? The sort of thing to be found in the parlour of a cottage or . . . or . . .'

'Mr Martin, can you not see the workmanship?' Charlotte's voice was desperate but she did her best to keep up the façade she had adopted as she entered the shop.

'I can indeed, Mrs Armstrong, but it is not what our clientele want. We sell to—'

'I have a friend – I had perhaps better not mention her name but she is the wife of one of the leading men in Wakefield and she bought one.'

'Then perhaps she will recommend you to others of her kind. Or perhaps some other carpet shop in the town or in others, Huddersfield or . . . or . . . there are others, not quite as prestigious as we are who might . . . then there is the market in the Bull Ring but I cannot . . .'

Charlotte rose to her feet, her head high, her eyes a cold and clear blue and Mr Martin wondered what the hell a gentleman such as Brooke Armstrong was thinking of in allowing this exquisite creature to hawk herself and her wares round the town.

'I will take up no more of your time then, Mr Martin. I'm sure there are others who are not so' – she had been about to say *particular* as you but decided it didn't seem quite right – 'short-sighted as you.'

'Then I wish you good luck with them, Mrs Armstrong.' He sat down and picked up his pen, drawing a document towards him, the interview evidently at an end.

As Mr Martin said, there were other carpet showrooms in the town, in Huddersfield, in Barnsley, in Dewsbury. She perhaps had started too high up the ladder with Alcock and Upton and over the next few weeks she and Jenny were driven by the patient Todd from one town to another but it was the same wherever she went.

By now she was beginning to feel slightly unwell in the mornings and realised that she was indeed pregnant and that if Brooke knew he would stop her at once, but she could not give up until she had tried every outlet for her rugs and wall hangings which were beginning to pile up in the workshop.

'I think it is going to be the market, Jenny,' she said despondently as they drove home at the end of a gloriously sunny day in July. 'I feel that what you and the girls have produced is too good for a market stall but not good enough for a carpet showroom, even those at the lower end of trade, so I'm afraid we shall have to make enquiries on renting a stall.'

Jenny had matured in the almost two years she had lived at the Dower House. Her little girl was the most important thing in her life and the woman who had made it all possible, the child, the home, the work, was the second. She would always, for as long as she lived, be grateful to Charlotte Armstrong

who had fought tooth and nail to give a better life to the girls at
the Dower House. She had battled with her own husband,
with the society of which she was a part and the prejudices of
the world in which they lived, with men in business who she
needed to get her project started and with some of the girls she
sheltered who had proved wilful. There had been Ruth who
had abandoned her baby, Pearl, who was being brought up by
Kizzie's sister Megan. There had been poor Maudie who had
succumbed to the blandishments of Mrs Armstrong's wicked
father and had died for it, and now and again Cassie and Edna,
both as daft as a dormouse, grumbled that they were sick and
tired of living out here at the back of beyond and had no 'fun'
as they called it. They forgot that but for Mrs Armstrong they
would probably be working the streets, their children in an
orphanage. They could not see that if they got this business
working and were given a decent wage they might have their
own place, perhaps find and marry a decent chap. They were
not bad girls, just young and ignorant and now, with their fears
behind them, were restless and sometimes discontented. Violet
and Aisling, and herself, of course, were grateful for this
chance to better themselves and she felt that if they could
encourage Mrs Armstrong, who was beginning to flag, they
should make a go of it. Even if it was only on a market stall.

The carriage had stopped at the front of the house and
Todd had jumped down to help Mrs Armstrong to alight. He
stood patiently and waited but Jenny, with great compassion,
took Mrs Armstrong's hand as her mistress turned towards
her.

'Don't give up, lass,' she said, unaware of what she had
called her. 'Don't stop now. I know . . . I guessed tha's ter 'ave
another babby. Oh aye, I've said nowt ter anyone but I reckon
Kizzie knows. Tha'll not be able ter work fer long, not with this
business anyroad, an' tha'll need someone ter carry on. Let me
do it. I can go ter't market an' see about a stall an' me an'

Violet'll run it. We'll need a . . . a cart or summat ter tekk rugs an' I reckon Cassie an' Edna'll be made up ter get inter town. They're only bits o' kids an' need a change' – as though she herself were middle-aged – 'but I'll mekk sure they stay decent. Kizzie an' Meggie'll look after the kids an' . . . oh, please, Mrs Armstrong, don't give up. See, 'ere's the master come ter see what's up so if tha'll come across we can talk about it.'

It was true, Brooke was on the doorstep, a frown on his face, making it clear he wanted her to come inside at once. He had made it plain recently that he thought it was time she stopped traipsing around trying to find buyers for her rugs and Charlotte knew that the minute she told him she was with child again he would put his foot down and that would be that, but if Jenny would . . . if Jenny was *capable* of continuing, even in a small way and she, Charlotte, could oversee the running of it from home at least it would not be a total failure.

'Are you to sit in the carriage all day, Charlotte Armstrong?' Brooke demanded to know, walking unaided across the gravel path and glaring at her from the carriage door. But his eyes were soft, tender with his love and his enormous pride in her.

'No, my darling,' she said, for neither of them cared if the servants heard their endearments. 'I am just waiting for you to help me down and then I think I will have a rest and . . .'

At once a worried look crossed his face, for Charlotte never rested. He almost lifted her from the carriage and Todd hovered at his back, for the master was not totally recovered from his accident, though he thought he was. He could walk alone but could he carry the mistress at the same time?

'Bugger off, Todd. I can carry my wife so you take Jenny round to the Dower House and put the horses away. We may be some time, my wife and I . . .' smiling down into the equally smiling face of his wife.

'Yes, I think we need to be alone, sweetheart. We have something to discuss.'

'Have we? Nothing serious, I hope.'

'No, something you will like.'

Jenny and Todd exchanged a look, their own faces reflecting the delight that was all about them. Eeh, this was a grand place to work.

Toby Armstrong was born on a pleasant February day just after lunch, which was a lovely time to come into the world. The sun was shining, it was mild and the spring flowers were there to welcome him, a sunny day for a sunny baby, for so he proved, no trouble to anyone, not even his mother who gave birth to him as easily as peas are shelled, as Kizzie said. They had sent for Doctor Chapman at the first pang but the lad was already in his mother's arms, waiting only for the good doctor to cut the cord that bound him.

Charlotte sat up in bed, a bright blue ribbon tying back her tangled hair, a clean and very pretty nightgown slipping from her shoulders, demanding strawberries and cream from her besotted husband who would have reached the moon from the sky if she had asked him, and had it been night-time, he told her, kneeling by the bed with an arm wrapped round the two little girls, neither of whom were sure they cared for this intruder.

'Well, this is a pretty picture.' The doctor smiled but, having heard Charlotte's demand for strawberries and cream was not sure if this was a good idea. 'It seems I am too late to be the first to greet your son, Brooke,' for by this time Brooke and Charlotte were on first-name terms with Wallace and Emily. During Charlotte's pregnancy they had dined regularly at King's Meadow and their hospitality had been reciprocated. 'I think a little of your good Mrs Groves's broth would be more the thing, Charlotte.'

'Oh, fiddle-de-dee, I was in the greenhouse with John only yesterday and the strawberries were at their peak. And I'm sure Lucy and Ellie would like some too. Here, Brooke, take your son' – for Wallace had made short work of the umbilical cord – 'and let the girls come up here with their mama.'

In a flash the girls, both of them fourteen months old and talking nineteen to the dozen in their own well-understood language, were being cuddled by their mama as they both called her. Ellie was too young to understand that Charlotte was in fact her sister and when Lucy called Charlotte Mama, so did she.

Charlotte, as she spooned strawberries into the rosy, pursed mouths of the two toddlers who cuddled against her, looked back over the last six months which had seen a satisfactory outcome to her plans for the business she had set up. This was thanks to Jenny Todd, as she was now, for she and Todd had married and shared a small cottage at the back of the vegetable gardens with Rose, her daughter who was almost two years old, and their own baby they hoped to have some day. But Jenny was not prepared to sit at home and be a coachman's wife, which she told Todd in no uncertain terms. She had Mrs Armstrong's trust that she would run her project to employ homeless girls and manufacture the rugs which she was to sell on a market stall in Wakefield.

She and Violet, who was as dependable as Jenny, had taken the small gig, driven to Wakefield and sought out the superintendent of the market and arranged to rent a stall. They brooded over the dozens of rugs that had been made during the past eighteen months, trying to decide which would appeal to the women who did their shopping in the market and not the shops, which were much more expensive. On their first day, three weeks later, they were driven by Todd, this time on the flat cart borrowed from the garden at the back of the house, and had set out their stall, Todd helping them to arrange their goods to the best advantage and agreed a time when he should return to pick them up.

They had sold only two!

Later, Jenny and Charlotte wandered round what they called the warehouse where the rugs were stored and agonised over why only two of the rugs into which such a lot of work had gone, were sold.

'I think you should take your rugs, Jenny, the special ones you have made. They are the more eye-catching.'

'But a lot o' money, Mrs Armstrong. More than these housewives will want ter pay.'

'Then we will sell them cheaply. We need something to draw the women to the stall.'

'They can make t'cheap ones theirselves, tha' see, ma'am, so they—'

'But they can't manage those you make, Jenny, and surely when they see the beauty of them and at a price they can afford they will perhaps be persuaded to purchase the others. We have to get the pricing right, don't you see. Perhaps if you stayed at home and made your own with Violet's help, Cassie and Edna can work on the stall.'

It took four months to begin to show a profit and it was Jenny's creations that brought the housewives of Wakefield to their stall. It was enough to dampen Jenny and Violet's enthusiasm to see such workmanship sold at rock-bottom prices but by word of mouth and a desire to own such lovely rugs and wall hangings and have them adorn their own small cottages, it was noticeable that more and more women flocked to see what was on offer at the Rug Stall, as it was named, since Charlotte was aware that it would not do to have Brooke's name used in such an enterprise. Christmas helped, as their wares made lovely Christmas presents and Jenny noticed that the class of woman who frequented their stall had changed and not only working-class women but those of the middle classes stopped to study the colourful array of rugs on show.

Now Jenny was talking of renting a stall in Huddersfield where a similar market took place. And if a stall, why not a shop, a smart shop in Wakefield where the upper middle classes might take an interest, or even the gentry! An ambitious woman, Jenny had become, and an enterprising one and Charlotte was of the opinion she had done well to marry a gentle, easy-going man like Todd, Charlie Todd, as they realised he was called, who seemed not to mind what his lovely wife did. In the Dower House another young woman was employed to help with the children, one of Wallace Chapman's pregnant misfits who had taken shelter there. There was talk of a teacher for the children, of whom there were five, soon to be six when Hetty's baby was born. Charlotte had, with Brooke's reluctant consent, worked each day over at the Dower House, as she was what she called the accountant. She and Kizzie, in the early days of her pregnancy, drove over to Victoria Mills to instruct Mr Scales on the quality of the shoddy he sold them and since he had a telephone it was arranged that she would be in touch with him on the amount they would need. It would, as the small business grew, increase, and as she lay in a euphoric haze in her lovely bedroom, her son held tenderly in his father's arms and the two little girls drowsing beside her she pondered on how good life had been to her and how splendidly her venture was succeeding, with Jenny and Violet as enthusiastically involved as herself.

Her husband lifted his head from his contemplation of his son and smiled, mouthing the words, 'thank you'.

Kizzie saw it and smiled as she tidied the room after the short battle that had just taken place in the birth of Master Toby Armstrong, then, turning to the window, wondered idly who the man was who loitered at the edge of the small woodland.

# 25

A partition had been erected in the workroom in order to form an office for Jenny and Charlotte. With business beginning to grow and the need to keep accounts this was where Charlotte spent some part of each day. She had a telephone installed and meticulously recorded every penny spent and received for her goods, wages, transport charges and the cost of setting up the office itself. Desks, one each for her and Jenny, filing cabinets, samples of their rugs and wall hangings, books and illustrations from which Jenny created her designs and a fireplace built in which they kept a cheerful fire on cold days. There were a couple of armchairs and on the walls they hung several pieces of Jenny's designs. On a table under the window stood a lovely copper vase filled with a great bunch of hothouse roses, pink and cream and just coming into bloom. One window in the office looked out into the workroom and another overlooked the courtyard and the gate that led into the lane at the side of the property through which the shoddy was delivered. There was also a door that opened into the courtyard put there for some reason when the building had been used for other purposes.

Jenny's marriage had left an extra bedroom in the Dower House, while Aisling resided in the nursery with Rosie Hicks and the three children in their care. Of the other bedrooms, one bedroom was shared by Cassie and Anne, her daughter, another by Edna whose son, Arthur, was the same age as Anne, and the third by Meggie. Hetty, whose child was due any minute, lived in the attic space. With Meggie, who had been with them for two years now, in charge of the children while their mothers worked, Kizzie moved back to the big house and once more became a sort of general caretaker in overall charge of Charlotte's household, though she did not infringe on the duties of Mrs Dickinson. But it was generally accepted that, as Mrs Dickinson was getting on in years and would shortly be retiring to a small house in Harrogate which she would share with her sister, Kizzie would take over as housekeeper. She was always busy though it was never quite certain what she did. Mrs Dickinson ruled the maidservants and Mrs Groves was cook but whenever Charlotte needed her Kizzie was always there. Charlotte simply called her 'my friend'! There were three new girls in the workshop, girls from the village whose mothers were widows – men died young in the coal mines – and who were glad to let their daughters work with the lady of the manor up at King's Meadow. Josie Garth, Betty Hobson and Nellie Sidebottom came from Miss Seddon's school which had benefited vastly from Mrs Armstrong's benevolence. They were simple, country girls, not clever, but nimble with their fingers and had been recommended by Miss Seddon who had equally recommended Charlotte to their mothers as the need for more needlewomen grew.

Brooke was totally recovered now and even Wallace Chapman was pleased with the way in which his wound had healed, causing no permanent damage to his upper thigh. He had a very slight limp which Wallace said he thought would disappear altogether with exercise and he was back in the saddle with Arch's help. For the first few weeks, to his chagrin and in his opinion totally unnecessarily, Charlotte insisted that Arch went with him when he resumed his rounds of the farms on horseback. It was over a year since he had been attacked by Jack Emmerson's bull and the first time he visited the farm

Mrs Emmerson wept tears of joy, obliging him to dismount and sample her latest elderberry wine or perhaps a glass of ale. Jack and Mrs Emmerson had always felt they were to blame for Mr Armstrong's accident, but their landlord would have none of it, making light of his year's convalescence, laughing and making a joke of it all. And it hadn't stopped him from getting his lady wife with child, had it, though none of them spoke of it except Jack and his missis after he had gone. Eeh, he were a grand chap, were Mr Armstrong.

His other tenants, too, were overjoyed to see him back, insisting he sat in their kitchens and have a sip of this or that until he complained to Arch on the way home it was a good job Arch was along or he would have fallen off his bloody horse he felt so merry!

Charlotte was alone in the office, her head bent over one of her account books, her mind marvelling at their success, when the door from the courtyard opened and then closed again quietly. She heard the door open and close but she did not hear the key turn in the lock.

'I can't get over how well that stall in Wakefield is doing,' she remarked, not looking up. 'You and I will have to get over to Huddersfield soon, Jenny. When Hetty's baby arrives I shall see if she is willing to take it on. Perhaps Cassie or Edna could do it at first and Hetty go to Wakefield with one of them until she gets the hang of it. What d'you think?'

She lifted her head and smiled into the amused face of her father!

'Quite honestly, my dear, I don't give a damn what you do with those trollops you employ. I just want you to know I don't approve and my approval or disapproval could make a great deal of trouble for you. Yes, *you*, my dear. You must remember my disapproval and the punishment that went with it. Please, Charlotte, close your mouth, you look quite absurd with it hanging open like that. Did you think all those men you have lolling about the grounds would keep me from you? Oh, they were very responsible at first. Everywhere I went there was one of the louts on the lookout for intruders but as time goes by and nothing untoward happens they become careless and I'm sure that if I attempted to snatch back my young daughter I should have no trouble at all.'

He leaned his back against the door, lounging with his usual arrogance, his hands in his pockets, his mouth lifted in a contemptuous sneer.

Charlotte knew she must look foolish with her mouth hanging open, her pen poised in one hand, but she was so astonished she could not help it and wondered why she felt no fear. The blood had drained from her face and her mouth was so dry she could not speak, but after all there were men within shouting distance, for as she had crossed the gravel drive at the front of the house, no more than a stone's throw from where she now sat, she had seen John and Ned carefully pruning branches from a lime tree at the beginning of the mile-long drive. And there were five girls with their heads bent industriously over their work in the workshop.

Charlotte sighed as though at the tantrums of a naughty child and Arthur Drummond's face hardened. 'Father, I don't know how you got in here but please leave by the same way. You know you can do nothing to harm the children, or your daughter. Ellie is—'

'Ellie, as you call her, is my daughter. Child of my wife's body and put there by me. She is mine, legally, and no court on earth would take her away from the good home she would have with me. You have no rights over her, nor has that opinionated husband of yours. Oh, I know he has consulted a lawyer, but so have I. But it need not come to that, my dear. I just want to . . . to be friends with you again.' His voice was silky with menace. 'To be admitted into your circle, though it has come to my notice that you shun good society these days.

They tell me they never see you, the Ackroyds and the Dentons, but it has not gone unnoticed that Wallace Chapman and his wife have become . . . intimate with you. But that is no concern of mine. *You* are, Charlotte, if you get my meaning. I saw the boys at Christmas riding in the woods, by the way. They are growing into fine young men, I see. Henry at Cambridge and William in his last year at Barton Meade so I have been told. You have done well with *my* children, Charlotte, and are to be congratulated. But I would like to remind you that I can put a stop to this charade any time I feel like it.'

He smiled at her and moved across the office in a way she remembered from her days as a child and a young girl and there was no doubt in her mind what he had in *his*! She didn't know what form it would take but it was all there in his manner and the way his eyes glowed hotly as they ran over her. He would not force her – *force her to do what, for God's sake*? He had no need, had he? She would go along with whatever he asked of her and go willingly. He had only to mention Ellie or even his sons and the fight would be over. She could defy him. She could tell Brooke, who would probably kill him and the constables would come and take him away and he would hang and . . . Sweet Jesus . . . Oh, dear, dear God, this was her father, *her father*, threatening that if she did not submit to . . . to whatever his foul mind had in store for her he would destroy his family, as there was no doubt that not only would Ellie suffer but also his sons who were still minors and must do as he said. They could fight, she and Brooke, but then Brooke would be in danger.

She tried to outface him. Her lion heart pumped hot blood through her body and she stood up, her expression as contemptuous as his. Her face was the colour of pipe clay and her eyes a brilliant blue as madness took over and if she had had a knife, or even the letter opener that was usually on her desk there was the distinct possibility she would have sliced it into his body. She stiffened her back, lifted her head challengingly and glared at him.

'What do you want from me?' she spat at him.

'Come now, daughter, is it too much to expect some show of affection for your father? I would find it most enjoyable to meet you now and again in the . . . say in the woods now that the summer is coming and the weather will allow us to . . . to . . .'

Here he spoke words of such obscenity, such odious, scarcely understood grossness that Charlotte felt her senses begin to slip away as he smeared her with filth and she could only think she was mistaken. She must be. He could not possibly mean what he was saying, but then she remembered the girls who had crept into her house to escape the wickedness, the lewdness, the *abuse* their own fathers had offered them. They bore children their fathers had forced upon them. And had not her own father, this man who taunted her, had he not always been perverted in his treatment of herself? He had beaten her on her bare buttocks as she stood with her drawers round her ankles, her skirts pushed up about her waist. She supposed he had treated his wives, her mother and the dead mother of the happy little girl growing up in the nursery beside her own children, in the same way. He was depraved and for some reason his depravity was directed at Charlotte Armstrong, his own child. He must have access to almost any woman he wanted, for he was a handsome, well-connected man with a few bob in his pocket as they said in the north. And there were whores, pretty ones who would be pleased to accommodate his perversions, but for some reason he was after her. He did not want his baby daughter back as she meant nothing to him and his sons, especially the two older boys, were young men now and would not be as pliable as they had been three years ago.

But from somewhere she found her strength and all the girls in the other room looked up, startled, as their mistress shouted something, they couldn't hear what, at the man who stood before her.

'Get off my property, you loathsome creature, you beast, and don't come back or my husband will shoot you where you stand when I tell him what you have just said to me. Self-defence it will be called and he will not be punished—'

'Will he not, my dear?' Arthur Drummond's smile was lazy.

'And if he doesn't kill you I will. I will defend my children—'

'Really, Charlotte, how dramatic you are. I am not threatening your children. I just want us to be friends as once we were.'

'We're not friends and never, never will be.' The memory of their last encounter nearly a year ago now was vivid in her mind and she felt a violent need to vomit as her stomach churned. Then he had abused her as he had done before she married Brooke, *punishing* her for some malevolent thing that wriggled like a worm in his damaged mind. She couldn't even remember what he had said to her, for she had simply turned off her own awareness and allowed him to beat her, but just for a moment his hands, without the cane, had smoothed across her bare flesh and his breathing, which had already been harsh, quickened and it was from that, and *for* that he wanted her.

'Well, my dear, we shall see about that. Look out for me in the woods or indeed anywhere I wish to go. You will need eyes in the back of your head, my love, if you are to avoid your loving father.'

With a suddenness that startled her, he turned his back on her, unlocked the door and slipped through it, making his way across the yard to the gate that led into the lane. He had said nothing more but then did he need to? Even if she avoided the woods, the walks, the lanes, the meadows where she, Aisling and Rosie liked to take the children, would she ever feel safe again? And not only for herself but Brooke, her servants, the girls who worked for her and trusted her. The three new girls went home at night to their families in the village and since they were simple, innocent, trusting girls might he not wheedle one of them . . . Oh, dear God, what was she to do?

An hour later Kizzie found her curled up in a corner of the house, her husband's house, so lately a place of refuge, love and happiness, high in the roof where all the furniture bought by previous Armstrong wives and discarded by others was neatly stored. She had hidden herself deep in a small recess made by a tall chiffonier and a wardrobe from another time. She was the colour of a mushroom and she was shivering though the day was warm.

Had Kizzie not gone up to the attic to retrieve a small set of drawers that she remembered and which would do nicely for the new girl's bedroom, they would have grown worried as to the whereabouts of the mistress who had not been seen since first thing that morning. Hetty's baby was due any day and she would need somewhere to keep the new baby's garments, tiny things saved from the previous babies born at the Dower House. Kizzie was sure the drawers had been put into the attic and if she found them she would get a couple of the men to fetch them down and carry them over to the Dower House.

Instead she found Charlotte. For a moment she was dumbstruck by the sight of her young mistress – who *was* her mistress despite Miss Charlotte's declaration that Kizzie was her friend – weeping silently but in a way that said she was heartbroken, in the overhang of the roof.

'Lass, lass, what is it?' She pushed her way through the conglomeration of old furniture as quickly as she could, kneeling down to sweep Charlotte into her loving arms. 'What tha' doin' up 'ere cryin' tha' eyes out? What's up, chuck? 'As someone 'urt thi' 'cos if they 'ave they'll 'ave me ter deal with. Tell us, lass, what's up? Nay, give over, tell Kizzie. Tha' know what they say, a trouble shared's a trouble 'alved. See, come 'ere ter Kizzie. Wipe tha' eyes, blow tha' nose an' tell us what's up. There, there, I'm 'ere, tha's all right . . .'

She rocked the distraught woman to and fro in the way a mother rocks a hurt child and after a while Charlotte was calm enough to speak.

'I don't . . . know what to . . . do, Kizzie,' she got out between sobs and hiccups. 'He'll never let go . . . and I'm frightened . . . not just for me . . . though that is terrifying enough . . . but for . . . for the children . . . Brooke . . . even my brothers . . . he'll destroy . . . them unless I . . . Oh, sweet Jesus Christ, watch over me and . . . and those I love . . . Kizzie . . . Kizzie . . .' She began to moan, throwing her head back in despair and Kizzie had a hard job to hold on to her but she did, gripping her in arms of steel, arms of protective love.

'Tha' faither?' For who else could have such an effect on this young woman, this brave and resourceful young woman who had been in her care for almost ten years. 'Tha've seen 'im?'

'Yes, he caught me in the office. I don't know how . . . the men have been . . . but I suppose after all this . . . this time they thought he had given up. Dear Lord, how little they know him and how careless I myself have become. He simply came up the lane, in through the side gate and seeing I was alone came into the office.'

'What did 'e want?'

'Me . . .' Charlotte began to whimper, a frail piteous whimper that nearly broke Kizzie's heart. 'He wants me to . . .' She hid her face in Kizzie's shoulder as though ashamed to show it. 'I am to be his . . . *friend*! He wants us to be friends. He wants to use me . . . use me . . .' Her voice began to rise hysterically.

'Hush, lass . . . hush, my lass, dost think I'd let 'im? Dost think Mr Armstrong'd let 'im?'

'No . . . *No*, Kizzie.' Her voice rose to a scream and in the stable yard the dogs rose to their feet. With the acute hearing of animals they heard it though the human ear could detect no sound.

'What's up wi' you lot?' Percy asked them, pausing from the tender grooming he was giving the master's horse. They remained restless and it was a while before they settled uneasily in a sunny corner of the yard, the four of them in a jumbled heap, their ears swivelling, their eyes watchful.

'The master must know, lass,' Kizzie told her gently. ''E must be warned ter be on't lookout, an' men an' all.'

'Don't you see, if Brooke knew he'd go over to the Mount and beat my father senseless. He might even kill him. Nothing would contain him.'

''E could tekk some o't men wi' 'im.'

'And do what with them?'

'Nay, see to it 'e can do nowt ter any woman again.'

Charlotte was no longer listening. She was aware as Kizzie was not, being an ill-educated woman, that her father had right on his side as far as his children were concerned. Perhaps not *right*, for no father was allowed to treat his children as he had done, but the law would uphold him in his demand to supervise the upbringing of his own children. To have his sons and his baby daughter under his roof. Perhaps Henry might escape him, being almost a man and at Cambridge, but the others, if he said they must, would be brought home under his protection. He would bring the might of the law to bear and she and Brooke would be helpless.

She stood up and brushed down her creased and dusty skirt and Kizzie did the same.

'Where tha' goin?' Kizzie asked her suspiciously. ''Cos wherever it is I'm goin wi' thi'. Unless the master is by tha' side I'm stickin' to thi' like a burr. An' I'm tekkin' no arguin' sitha'. An' no matter what tha' say I'm warnin' t'men ter be on't lookout. Them bairns'll stop in't nursery.'

'What about the boys?'

'Nay, cannot tha' go over there and tell 'em? They're big lads an' the teachers'll listen ter thi' if tha' was ter let on.'

'Robbie is only nine and if—'

' 'Teacher'll watch out fer 'im.'

'And the girls?'

'What girls?' Kizzie was genuinely puzzled.

'He threatened the girls as well as me. Remember Maudie? Josie, Betty and Nellie walk home at night on their own.'

'One o't men can go wi' 'em.'

'And how do you mean to keep all this secrecy from Brooke? Do you think he will not notice the extra precautions?'

Kizzie sank down on to a small stool that had been discarded by some Armstrong lady who had decided it was not fit to grace her drawing room and put her head in her hands and groaned. Then she lifted it, a curious look on her face and stood up again, squaring her shoulders and, baring her teeth and hissing like some feline creature defending her young, took Charlotte by the shoulders.

'Lass, my dear lass, tha've not ter worry over this. There's many a farmer what's got good reason ter resent tha' pa. Me mam an' pa 'ad a crop o' barley what were ter mekk family a few bob until bloody Drummond an' 'is pals were out 'untin' an' rode through it one day an' ruined the lot. A tenant farmer what's 'ad a crop spoiled can do nowt ter stop it. 'Appen summat can be—' She bit off her words, conscious that Charlotte was watching her questioningly but with a loving smile she put her arms about the young woman who was as a daughter to her though there were no more than four years between them. 'Stay close ter't'ouse an' mekk sure when them bairns go inter't garden John or Ned're close by. Now' – giving them both a shake – 'let's get down them stairs an' 'ave us a nice hot drink. The master'll be 'ome soon so go an' pretty tha'self up. An' tha's not ter worry. D'yer 'ear?'

'I'll do my best, Kizzie, but—'

'No buts, d'yer 'ear?'

The three brawny men, armed with nothing but their own fists, working men by the look of them, with the wide, muscled shoulders of those who are used to manual labour, crouched in the undergrowth at the very edge of Beggers Wood. It was almost two in the morning and there was a moon darting in and out of the clouds that raced across the sky with enough light for them to see should anyone be coming along the lane. They had been waiting for a long time and were thankful that it was a mild night.

They heard the approach of the horse first, its hooves chinking against the occasional stone, and at once they were more alert, waiting for one of them to give the signal. When it came they crept from the bushes into the lane and stood shoulder to shoulder as the horse and rider came towards them. The man on the horse was momentarily astonished but not afraid, since he was a man who was afraid of nothing.

'What's this, lads?' he said smilingly. 'I've nothing on me worth stealing because I lost it all on the cards this evening so you'd best go about your business and let me go about mine.'

He kicked his heels into his horse's sides, prepared to move on, but one of the men leaped forward and grabbed the bridle while the other two pulled the rider from the saddle. The horse was left to make its own terrified way to its stable while the three men systematically began their task of mangling and mauling the shrieking man on the ground, their fists striking in unison, on and on until they had reduced him to a bundle of bleeding rags. There was none of the usual bloodlust that prevails when men beat each other, just a cool, precise, almost rhythmic landing of fist or boot on flesh, and though the man on the ground had drawn up his knees to his chest trying to save his eyes and his teeth, he lay there as one dead. Blood poured from his nose, one cheek was gashed to the bone, both eyes were closed and would certainly be black by morning, his leg was damaged and by the way he breathed his ribs were surely broken.

It was several hours before he was discovered. His stable lad had long since gone to bed, for the master's horse was accustomed to being left to stand in the yard when the master fell off it and made his way to his own bed.

The three men were at their labours the next morning, for April was ploughing time and the farmers for whom they worked were ready to plant their crops. None of them had a mark on him, placid men who would help a toddling child to its feet, pat a dog with a gentle hand, ask a small girl the name of her doll, ordinary men who had given a helping hand to another, decent men who could not abide an injustice.

# 26

The news did not reach Charlotte and Brooke until they were about to sit down to their evening meal. The servants had been highly excited and not a bit sorry when they heard of it, for none of them gave a tinker's toss whether the mistress's father died or not. Had not the whole household been in a state of constant terror for many months because of his diabolical threats against his own children, keeping each and every one of them looking fearfully over their shoulder in case the devil should be there ready to snatch back the lovely child in the nursery who every single one of them adored? And what about poor Maudie who, even if she was a naughty girl and had an illegitimate child, had died because of him? Oh, he hadn't killed her with his own two hands, they knew that, but he'd apparently driven her to take her own life and that of her innocent child. The mistress and them boys had been terrified of him so good riddance to him if he actually died from his injuries.

It was Malachy O'Brien, the gardener at the Mount who was on friendly terms with John Dudley, the Armstrongs' head gardener, who brought the news of the attack on his master. They exchanged gardening tips with one another and had been known to share a pint at the local pub in the village. He was bringing John some cuttings in exchange for some new seed potatoes he and John thought might do well. He was pressed to sit down and drink a mug of tea while he described to them the state of his master's injuries.

Kizzie was the one who told Charlotte and Brooke. They were surprised when she burst into the dining room, for they had been expecting Johnson, the butler. Brooke had been through a trying time with Charlotte during the hour they had spent dressing for dinner and in the drawing room and was looking like thunder, since she would not tell him what was wrong.

'There's something bothering you, my sweetheart, and I want to know what it is,' he wheedled her. *At first.* Then he became more and more belligerent as she became more and more obstinate, swearing that there was nothing wrong, she had a bit of a headache, that was all.

'Stuff and bloody nonsense. Don't you think by now I don't know when you have a headache or . . . the other . . . your monthly thing and you don't act as though it's the end of the damn world then. But you look like death.'

'I'll wear some rouge if you think I look so ghastly.'

'Don't be so bloody ridiculous. I'm your husband. I love you. I love you so much, being without you would be an agony I couldn't abide and I can't bear to think there is something troubling you and you can't or won't tell me. Bugger it, Charlotte, don't—'

He was clawing her heart to rags and at that very moment Kizzie burst into the room and they both turned in amazement to look at her. But it was to Charlotte that she spoke.

'Tha' pa's badly,' was all she said but her eyes gleamed with what looked seriously like triumph.

'What's the matter with him?' Brooke asked, but without much interest, for the mention of his wife's father was anathema to him.

Charlotte stood up slowly, pushing back her chair. She knew that whatever it was that Kizzie was trying to tell her was good news and that . . . that somehow . . . somehow Kizzie had a hand in it. Brooke watched Charlotte. He had a trick of wiping all expression from his face when he wished to and since he was an intelligent man he was aware that something had happened concerning Arthur Drummond and the threats he had made almost a year ago and that Kizzie was telling Charlotte that she need not trouble herself with it any more. He too stood up.

'What happened to him?' he said quietly.

'Someone thrashed 'im. Injured 'im real bad or so Malachy ses. Malachy's gardener at t' Mount an' 'e come round ter speak ter John Dudley about summat ter do wi't garden an' 'e told us what 'appened. 'E were found this mornin'. 'Is 'orse come 'ome wi'out 'im so they searched fer 'im an' found 'im in't lane beside Beggers Wood. An' God bless them what done it, I say. A devil 'e were an' deserved all 'e got.'

Kizzie was getting carried away with herself and Charlotte knew that if she didn't stop her telling what had happened, whatever it was would all come out. Not that there was any fear Brooke could do anything about it for it was, apparently, already done. And that had been what she dreaded almost as much as the things her father had threatened. Brooke was not involved! That was all that mattered for the moment *and*, for the moment her father was out of action. She had no idea how badly he was injured but if it kept him at home for a few weeks it would give her and Kizzie time to decide what they were to do to protect the children, and her staff, and, of course, herself from the damage he would inflict if he did not get his way.

But Brooke was not satisfied. 'What exactly do you mean by that remark, Kizzie? I am aware that Drummond warned me and Charlotte that he would take Ellie from us if . . . if we did not . . . he wanted money, he said, but why should he terrify you and Charlotte? You say bless whoever has done this to the man and that he was a devil who deserved what he got. So, what evils has he promised both of you that you should be relieved he is now . . . well, we don't know what he has suffered but it might be—'

'I 'ope 'e's crippled, so I do and I'm not ashamed ter admit it.'

'Has he hurt you, Kizzie?' Brooke said softly, but he was looking at Charlotte as he said it.

'Nay, not me but—'

'Who, Kizzie, if not you? Perhaps my wife, the children?'

'Us all know what 'e did ter Maudie. Promised 'er all sorts an' then turned 'er away. Them girls is all at risk, sir, 'specially them what go 'ome at night. An' then there's bairns . . .'

'The outside men will guard them.'

'It didn't stop 'im comin' in at back yard and forcin'—' She stopped abruptly and put up her hand to cover her mouth, for she suddenly realised in her fear of Arthur Drummond and her joy at what had been done to him she was saying far too much.

'When was this, Kizzie?' There were sounds from the kitchen as Johnson prepared to serve the first course of the splendid dinner Mrs Groves, as always, had just cooked. Dusk had fallen, for it was almost the end of the day and from beyond the window came the sounds of birds settling sleepily in the trees. The three babies were all peacefully asleep in the nursery, cherished by Aisling and Rosie, after Lucy and Ellie, watched by a wide-eyed and fascinated Toby, propped on Rosie's lap, had played a game of squealing piglets with the master.

One of the dogs was barking at the back of the house but it did not alarm anyone now that that bastard was fastened to his bed. Malachy had not known the complete extent of his master's injuries except that the doctor had been there most of the day and a nurse was in attendance and would be night and day.

Kizzie looked at Charlotte and shrugged helplessly. Was she to lie to the master or was Charlotte to tell her husband the truth? Kizzie had been so delighted with the success of her scheme to incapacitate Arthur Drummond she had let her tongue run away with her. Her three brothers, who were mild men, big men but with a goodness in them that could not stand cruelty to the weak and helpless, had done their job well. They thought the world of Kizzie and of Mrs Armstrong who helped out anyone in need and Mr Armstrong was a decent man who looked after his tenants like their mam and pa. It was only a few acres of scrub they rented at the edge of Mr Armstrong's property but Mam and Pa had worked all hours God sent to make it worthwhile and only last autumn the bugger up at the Mount had led his hunt across their land and ruined the harvest. The lads no longer lived at home, all of them finding work on neighbouring farms, married men with children, but they were glad of the chance to pay the sod back. They'd not done as much damage as they thought he deserved but, by Gow, he'd not sit on a horse for many months nor manage the journey to town to gamble away the money he was demanding from Mr Armstrong. If he'd got it. They were simple folk who knew nothing of the doings of the gentry but their Kizzie had told them that Drummond was trying to blackmail Mr Armstrong and terrify her mistress. It had been enough.

Charlotte sighed and sat down heavily on a dining chair, putting her elbows on the table and her head in her hands. Kizzie quietly left the room and as she entered the kitchen told Mr Johnson he had best wait until the bell rang before serving the master and mistress with dinner.

Brooke sat down beside his wife and put an arm about her shoulders, pulling her into the circle of his arms. He tucked her head beneath his chin and waited for a moment before he spoke.

'Tell me, my darling.'

So she did, from the moment her father had silently entered her office until he slipped away unseen, leaving nothing out. She told him of her and her brothers' childhood and the punishments they had received at his hands. The beatings, the anger and cruelty, the isolation, the terror he had instilled into them so that finally Brooke began to understand why Robbie Drummond had been as he was. This woman, who had been only a girl then, had defended him and that was why he clung to her. The boys would probably bear unseen scars for the rest of their lives but at least they were recovering thanks to Charlotte and to himself, he supposed. So Charlotte had married him to get her brothers away from their father. That was what he must face now and he did. But he was sure in her love and in the love of the two children she had given him. She had surrounded him with care when he was hurt. He was sure of her devotion and was at peace in the happy home she had created. In his heart he knew where love was and his senses told him that he had nothing to fear. She loved him as he loved her.

There was silence for several minutes. Inside Brooke Armstrong a great volcano was slowly coming to life and creeping up his body until it could find the outlet it needed to erupt. But there was none, was there? All that needed to be done, for the moment, had been done by men who Kizzie knew, of that he was sure. She had three brothers, big chaps, but with the sense not to overdo it, who surely must be the perpetrators of this crime, for crime it was, and when Drummond was recovered Brooke himself would see that his family and those who sheltered beneath his roof, including the young women who worked for his wife, were safe.

'Come, my love, let me take you to bed. Let me make love with you. First we will have some champagne; yes, a celebration, for if ever a woman needed her life celebrated it is my wife. You're a bloody brave woman, Charlotte Armstrong, and when I get you to bed we will drink to our life together, to the future which I promise will hold no more fears for you or your brothers, or the children up in the nursery.'

The agent turned the key in the lock and opened the door of the empty shop with a flourish that implied this was one of the finest buildings in Wakefield. It was, in fact, quite dreadful. There was a double-fronted bay window from which the paint had peeled almost to the bare wood and the door, when it was opened, had shrieked in protest.

'Just needs a bit of oil,' Mr Whitehead, the agent, murmured optimistically, pushing the door against the rubbish that was piled behind it. The filth on the floor was thick and even, undisturbed for months, and cobwebs were draped like lace from corner to corner. But the actual shop area was large with plenty of room for what Charlotte had in mind. There was a door at the back of the room that led into another, equally large, and then another behind that with a sink, a fireplace and a big cast-iron range, plenty of cupboards and in the centre a table so big it had evidently been too cumbersome to remove. It was a kitchen, in fact, where a meal might be made, where tea could be brewed or perhaps coffee, or hot chocolate, or even a glass of wine poured, since the type of establishment Charlotte envisaged would be prepared to serve whatever the customer asked for while they perused her goods. At the back of the kitchen a door led to steps going down to a yard and a back gate.

'Wonderful . . . wonderful,' Charlotte said.

Stairs, again appallingly dirty, went up to a landing on to which two enormous rooms opened, but what appealed to Charlotte were the unusually large windows which let in a great deal of light in every room. She turned to Jenny with a satisfied expression on her face.

'This will do very nicely. Don't you agree, Jenny?'

\*     \*     \*

It was a time of great peace and content that summer, which Charlotte had thought she would never know again. Apart from a sprinkling of rain at night, it would be dry and sunny until the beginning of October. Brooke rode out unaccompanied every day to oversee his little kingdom, completely recovered now, though he would stay well away from bulls in future, he told Jack Emmerson.

But it was his wife's happiness that brought him the most pleasure and despite himself he found he was beginning to enjoy becoming involved with the venture she had started with two or three battered young women almost three years ago. First there was Jenny who had been turned away from the kitchen door at King's Meadow but who had been found by Charlotte and against the wishes and with the total disapproval of the other servants, she had given her and her unborn child a home in the Dower House. And from Jenny's clever fingers came the first creation that was to be the start of his wife's fast growing business.

They were at dinner several months after Arthur Drummond had been attacked on his own land. He was, of course, confined to his home with a broken collar bone, several fractured ribs, a great deal of bruising and a leg with a compound fracture which prevented him from climbing on a horse for many months. It had been rumoured that the break in his leg might necessitate amputation but Wallace Chapman had managed to save it, though Drummond had raged at being attended by his daughter's physician. Finally his own sense of self-preservation prevailed and he dismissed old Doctor Dutfield who would chop off a limb even if it was only bruised and was beginning to recover though it would be many months before he was up and about again.

So all at King's Meadow let out their breaths, relaxed and resumed their daily routine.

'You know the premises at the Dower House are becoming woefully small,' Charlotte said, spooning Mrs Groves's rich soup delicately into her mouth. 'I have an . . . well, it came to me that if we had a bigger workshop we could employ more girls and . . . and . . .'

Brooke smiled, shaking his head as though in wonderment at his wife's agile brain but he said nothing, letting her flounder on until she came to the point of her deliberations. The soup was a consommé of Mrs Groves's own devising and there was a great leg of pork waiting to be carved on the sideboard. Johnson stood to attention with Nellie beside him, waiting to serve the next course, moving forward to refill his master's glass with the fine white wine he had chosen. It had been a dull day for once, threatening rain and the children had been restless, confined to the nursery. It was the end of August. Lucy and Ellie were twenty months old and were accustomed to toddling about the grounds with their two nurses, the dogs bounding along with them, running after poorly and inaccurately thrown balls – an activity that the little girls delighted in. They tripped and tumbled and laughed and picked themselves up, fending off Taddy's enthusiastic attentions, for he was still only a young dog. The gardeners who were never far away watched indulgently, ready to run and pick up a fallen child while Toby, six months old and sitting up, yelled his displeasure at not being able to join in. He had begun to crawl and could see no reason why he should be confined to his perambulator.

But today Aisling, Rosie and Charlotte had been at their wits' end with three bored children who were used to the outside world, the attention and adoration of the servants, and it was a relief finally to get them into their small beds and cot and have a breather, praying that tomorrow would be fine.

'I want to start a new . . . a new line, Brooke,' Charlotte said abruptly. 'And I think it might be helpful if you were to . . .'

'You want my help?' Brooke did his best not to allow his smile to deepen. He had got the measure of his Charlotte by now and knew he would never tame her. By which he meant she would never be as other wives were. And did he want her to be? She never neglected her children, or him for that matter. She was always at the table when he was and in their bed she was as passionate and eager as he was. She loved him and showed her love in the most intimate way, sometimes embarrassing the servants with her attentions! To himself, of course. But she would not entertain those people she thought fools and nincompoops, which was how she saw the Dentons and the Parkers and the Pickfords, though she seemed friendly enough with Patsy Ackroyd who called every few weeks and who she said made her laugh. Society had stopped inviting the Armstrongs to their own dinner parties, balls and garden parties, to their tennis parties and on the outings they took *en masse* during the summer months.

'Jenny and I went into Wakefield yesterday and looked at a vacant shop in the Bull Ring. We are making rugs by the dozen and selling them on the market stalls in Wakefield and Huddersfield but I think we ought to be . . . well, why can't we have a shop in which to sell our goods? And . . .' She hesitated, placing her elbows on the table and cupping her chin in her hands. She looked unbelievably lovely in the soft lamplight. Her hair was carelessly arranged in a tumble of curls and tied with satin ribbons to match her gown of hyacinth blue, which slipped to one side off her silky white shoulder, revealing the top of one breast and as she leaned forward to speak to him he could almost see her almond nipple. He felt his manhood stir and for a moment was diverted by what he would do with her when he got her to bed, then he cleared his throat feeling quite breathless.

'Yes?' he managed to say, but he was beginning to grin now and Charlotte laughed for she knew she would win.

'Carpets. Why not carpets, or carpeting which is the correct term for floor coverings? There are Jacquard looms which make carpet weaving easier and, of course, being in the centre of the woollen trade in Yorkshire we shall make it our business to find the best supplier. There is a new phenomenon of wide-width carpet, or broadloom. All we need is a weaving loom and, of course, hand-made carpets are particularly sought after. The shop will need a great deal of money spent on it to bring it up to the standard Jenny and I need, and Jenny, of course, would be in charge. I have been reading about machinery and if you will purchase that motor car we have talked about we will be able to get about and make enquiries on how to start. And then I thought why stop at carpets and rugs? Bedspreads. Or quilts. I've heard that a young woman has created a bedspread with a hand-crafted pattern by sewing together thick pieces of cotton with a running stitch. No, please, don't ask me how it was done for I'm no seamstress, but it was apparently stitched on to unbleached linen, clipping the ends of the yarn so it would fluff out. It would have to be carefully looked into—'

'Whoa, whoa, darling girl, you are stunning me with your enthusiasm; quilts, carpets, motor cars – whatever next?'

'Oh, Brooke.' She stood up eagerly and moved round the table to sit in his lap and Johnson and Nellie didn't know where to look so, prudently, they edged out of the dining room and fled to the kitchen where Nellie was bursting to tell the others what she and the butler had overheard. But not until Mr Johnson had chivvied Mrs Groves into the small house-keeper's parlour and shut the door could she impart the news that the mistress was going into business in a big way with a shop in the Bull Ring and the master was to buy a motor car which he had been threatening to do for a long time and what were Percy and Arch, who looked after the stables, to do then?

It was almost Christmas when the shop finally opened and they had all become used to the glittering machine that either stood in the stable yard or was housed in a disused stable to the side of the stables where the horses remained, to the great relief of Percy and Arch who had thought they would be out of a job when the monster arrived. It was called by the grand name of a Mercedes-Simplex and the master thought it was big enough and was suitable for a family with three children to accommodate, plus their nurses! It had a hood that could be raised in inclement weather, and was embellished with a great deal of gleaming brass which Todd, who had been promoted to chauffaur and taught to drive by Jack Ackroyd's chauffeur spent a lot of time buffing to perfection. Percy and Arch disdained even to go near it and grumbled incessantly that the beast frightened their horses.

Charlotte had insisted that their new venture was to be open for Christmas and a sign on the window announced the date. But what a mammoth task it turned out to be. First the premises had to be cleaned which needed three women to scrub it from attic to cellar. There turned out to be a boiler in the cellar which, when it was stripped, cleaned and put together again, would provide hot water. Rotting floorboards and door frames were replaced, walls, ceilings, window frames were painted; and advertisements appeared in the local newspapers to announce the opening of the Carpet Shop, the name Charlotte and Jenny had decided upon. It was simple and said it all, Charlotte told Brooke in the nest of their deep bed where each night, after they had made love to the satisfaction, indeed repletion of both, they discussed what was turning out to be a joint venture. Much to Brooke's surprise, he had begun to catch Charlotte's enthusiasm as he drove her and Jenny from place to place, such as Axminster where superb carpets were manufactured, Kidderminster where Brussels carpeting was made and Halifax which was the home of the Wilton. Brussels carpets were made up so that the pile was left looped or *bouclé* and Brooke told his dearest love that his head was spinning with it all; he was amazed by how she not only absorbed the information like a sponge but retained it so that when she was in the shop she could give instructions to the girls who were already employed there about what they would be selling.

'By God, I fell on my feet when I married you, my sweetheart,' he told her. 'We shall be millionaires before we know it,' he said as they stood in the centre of the Bull Ring next to the recently erected statue of Queen Victoria and admired the Carpet Shop the day before it opened.

It was what could only be called elegant, though some of those who wandered past just to get a look considered it plain. Charlotte had fitted out one whole window as a drawing room with some good furniture brought from King's Meadow. The carpet was a silvery grey with a design of pale pink roses in each corner, and the electric light fittings in delicate wrought iron were the work of a craftsman Charlotte had found. On the back wall, which had been papered to look like linen and painted white, hung two of Jenny's wall hangings, framed to look like paintings. A final touch, echoing the carpet were the hothouse roses in crystal vases, again brought from King's Meadow. The whole effect was stunning. The display caused quite a bottleneck as folk stopped to gawp, as did Brooke's Mercedes, parked in front of the shop, which gathered a crowd about it.

Trams rattled past, for the electric tramway had recently started operating and the Bull Ring was busy and bustling with carriages, riders on horseback, bicycles and delivery wagons. A row of horse-drawn cabs waited in line for custom, the horses with weary heads hanging down, some with nose bags munching patiently. Charlotte was enchanted, since it seemed she had chosen the right spot for her young business enterprise.

There were many smart carriages bearing ladies on a shopping expedition, all with their hoods down, for it was a sunny day though cold, all except one which was closed. In it crouched a man in a tall top hat who stared with venom at Charlotte and Brooke as they crossed to the pavement in front of the shop, arms linked, laughing up at each other. The man's lips curled and he whispered something to himself before rapping smartly on the roof to tell his coachman to get a move on!

# 27

It was intensely cold but bright. The hoar frost was so thik on the lawn the gardeners' feet sank an inch into it as though it were a layer of snow and their breath hung in a hazy cloud about their heads. The trees were black and deep maroon against the sun, a round pink disc hanging motionless behind them, but every branch of the trees and every twig on the bushes were outlined in a silvery white tracery against the pale pink of the winter sky. Masses of red berries hung on the holly bushes and the birds hovered waiting for the coast to be clear before they descended on the feast. The sun was palely beaming and the grass, crisp and stiff, was tinted a pale pink. The cold hurt your chest as you breathed and Charlotte wondered whether it would be wise to take the children out in such a biting chill. She herself was well wrapped up in a fleece-lined jacket and an ankle-length heavy woollen skirt and she wore her riding breeches underneath, as well as stout boots and thick woollen stockings. Round her neck was wound a hand-knitted scarf worked for one of the boys by Kizzie. She wore no hat as she sauntered down to where John and Ned were contemplating the frozen ground with gloomy expressions. They turned when they heard her approach and whipped off their caps.

'No digging today I shouldn't think, John. The ground is as hard as a rock.'

'Aye, tha's right there, Mrs Armitage. Me an' Ned was thinkin' o' puttin' in the celery at back o't'ouse in't rows we got ready a few weeks back but us'll not get us spades inter't ground terday, I reckon. An't bairns'll be stuck indoors, I shouldn't wonder.'

Taddy, who had followed the men from the back of the house, leaped about her skirts, his tail going nineteen to the dozen, then he began to forage under the holly bushes, following some scent his keen nose had picked up, probably that of a fox who had crept out in the night. Chickens were kept in a hen coop at the rear of the vegetable gardens but they were secure in their well-built abode and the fox would have gone hungry. Nevertheless the young dog chased off on his trail.

'Well, I should stay cosy in the kitchens if I were you, men,' Charlotte told them and they nodded smilingly, though they could not see themselves getting under the feet of the maids. There would be indoor jobs to be done in the workshop, which was where they finally headed.

Percy was surprised when the missis appeared by the stable door where he and Arch were mucking out and with a bright 'good morning' she walked by, stroking and patting the soft noses of the horses who peered curiously over their stall doors. Magic whickered a welcome, nudging her shoulder and the men watched her with as much interest as the horses.

'I think I'll take her out today, Percy, if you'll saddle her up for me,' she began, but he protested at once.

'Nay, ma'am, not in this weather. Ground's that 'ard if tha' fell tha' could be 'urt bad, not ter mention Magic. Break 'er leg tha' could an' tha' know what would 'appen then. When a 'orse breaks a leg there's only one way . . .' His voice was anguished, for Percy loved horses. A horse could be talked to and would respond. A horse was intelligent and all those in his care were well looked after, treated with affection, and even if he had to fight the mistress he'd not let her take out the mare in today's weather.

Charlotte sighed. 'You're right, Percy, I don't know what I was thinking of. I'll wait until the thaw comes but it's . . . well, never mind. Sorry, Magic, I know you're as restless as me and would love a gallop.'

Percy sighed with relief. 'Good lass,' he said, forgetting he was speaking to the wife of his master, or perhaps he was talking to the mare.

Charlotte wandered from the stable and across the yard. It was Sunday. The shop was closed, the girls who lived in the Dower House were all ensconced by the fire enjoying their day of rest, nursing their children or, those, like Jenny, who wanted their offspring to have a better childhood than they had had, were reading to them, or teaching them to read for themselves. Rose, Jenny's daughter and the eldest, was already identifying the letters of the alphabet and in the small cottage which she and her mother shared with Todd, was nestling on her new father's knee, while in the bedroom Jenny was giving birth to Todd's son.

Up in the nursery Lucy, Ellie and Toby were enjoying a game of lions and tigers that Brooke had invented in which he hid under the plush tablecloth that covered the nursery table and then pounced out roaring while the children screamed hysterically, not sure whether to be frightened or delighted. Toby was barely aware of what they were doing but joined in enthusiastically. He had pulled himself up on to unsteady legs a week or so ago and was walking after a fashion. Charlotte had left them to it, raising her eyebrows at the two nursemaids as though to say she'd had enough and without Kizzie to chide her, had dressed in her warmest clothes and ventured out, calling to Mrs Groves as she went through the kitchen that she was just going to get a breath of fresh air.

'Daft besom,' Mrs Groves murmured as the door closed. 'She wants to stay where it's warm on a day like this.' Nobody disagreed!

Charlotte opened the gate and sauntered down to the empty paddock, her mind brimming with the steady progress made by the Carpet Shop. They were busy from first light until early evening. She had purchased from the Wilton manufacturers several carpets to start her off, having them made to Jenny's design, and showed them on a special display in the shop. Every week the window was changed with a new carpet and furniture filched from King's Meadow, one week a dining room, the next a drawing room or even a bedroom. In the second window she and Jenny had draped the beautiful hand-made quilts which, quite by accident, Josie Garth, who lived in the village and took the new tram each morning into Wake-field, mentioned casually that her grandmother made. Her grandmother, who had been making quilts since she was a girl, not only made them by hand but designed them too. Each quilt required many small pieces of material of every colour imaginable which were carefully pieced together with a run-ning stitch into patterns of breathtaking beauty and sewn on to a backing, beginning at the middle and working outwards. Charlotte was now providing her with the materials needed and Josie's grandmother was delighted to be paid for work that she loved. She had often sold her quilts, of course, since they were much in demand but now she had a ready market, sitting by her fire in her cosy cottage and patiently working to the designs Jenny passed on to her.

Charlotte sauntered beside the paddock then, picking up her pace as it was not a day for sauntering, tramped briskly into the denuded woodland known as Beggers Wood. It was quite enchanting. The sun was stronger now, highlighting the frozen trees to a fairyland of white and silver, still, silent, apart from an occasional crack as a frozen strand of bracken snapped. Tracks indicated where the fox had ventured, prob-ably the one Taddy had scented and as though she had conjured him up with her thought, there was Taddy, frolicking by her side, stopping to sniff the frozen air, one paw raised, then rushing on ahead, his nose to the ground.

Suddenly he stopped and began to growl, his muzzle lifting back from his teeth. She moved towards him, startled, for what could be hidden in this frozen woodland to alarm him? When the man stepped out from behind a group of lacy saplings she froze, then backed away nervously. The sun silhouetted him against the dazzling frost-laden branches and when she saw who it was she became quite still, like a young animal that senses a trap and she was deathly afraid.

'Well, daughter,' the man said, 'here we are at last. After all this time we meet again. You are well, I trust. You look quite blooming with your cheeks so pink and your eyes like blue stars. I must say—'

'What do you want?' She almost called him 'father', the habit of a lifetime hard to break. But he was no father to her or his sons, for a father was warm, loving, protective and not one such as this man. Her voice was as icy as the weather and though she feared him dreadfully, it was steady. She was furious with herself for venturing so far into what was a deserted fairyland with no one to hear should she cry out, but she would not let him see it. Taddy continued to snarl, his tail tucked between his legs, huddled against her skirt, wanting to protect his mistress but he was small, a young dog who was trying to be brave despite his fear.

'Now, Charlotte, is that the way to greet your loving father?' His smile was lazy but his dark brown eyes raked her from head to foot and his voice was thick with menace.

Her heart was thudding furiously but she managed a defiant answer.

'Loving father! When have you ever been that to me or your sons?' The memory of their last meeting was sharp in her mind. The implication of what he had said to her then rang still in her ears and she wanted to run, pick up her skirts and take to her heels in the direction of the house and safety but her pride would not allow it.

He sensed what she was thinking and smiled playfully. 'So at last we are alone and time to tell you exactly what you are to do or the consequences for you and that idiot husband of yours will not be pleasant. Tell me, how has that business of yours fared since last we met? It has been a long time, has it not, and I should think you imagined it was all over. Your punishment, I mean. Believe me it is not. Do you know where I have been these last nine months?' His teeth glinted between his lips, not in a smile this time but a rictus of venom. 'Do you, Charlotte? Well, let me tell you. I have been confined to my bed, to my house and all because of you. Oh, yes, I know it was you or that husband of yours who arranged for me to be beaten, to have my bones broken, to be confined to a wheel-chair then crutches. I have been unable to do all the things that make life pleasant. I cannot ride my horse, nor even get to my club and it is all due to you and—'

'No, no, you brought it on yourself with your perverted ideas and by your threats to take Ellie to live with you and treat her as you treated us, my brothers and myself. You are cruel and—'

'You have no idea how cruel I can be, daughter . . .' And it was then that Charlotte realised that her father had slipped over some invisible line between viciousness and into mad-ness. His eyes continued to flicker over her and a fleck of white frothed at the corners of his mouth. He was sweating and his face was scarlet with some inner rage. It was then she noticed that he leaned heavily on a walking stick. He saw her eyes move and he laughed as though at a huge joke. 'Oh yes, you would easily outstrip me if you bolted for it but there are other times as I grow stronger. I have a man who comes in each day, funnily enough recommended by your Doctor Chapman, who massages and manipulates me and I grow stronger weekly.

Strange, is it not, that if you had not insisted that he was the better man I might still be confined to the house by that old fool who first attended me. Life is ironic, is it not, Charlotte?'

He smiled benignly as though they were discussing the state of the weather, then made a sudden lunge and at her side Taddy backed away, turned and fled in the direction they had come.

Arthur Drummond shook his head as though at some puzzle. 'Perhaps you had better keep a braver dog by your side when you venture out and those girls of yours had better watch their backs.'

Charlotte stood before him, her loveliness illuminated by the sunlight and the reflection from the frost that hung from every tree and sparkled on every stalk of sleeping bracken. Her hair, a tawny gold and silver, lay down her back, unconfined and streaked by the light, her startlingly blue eyes glinted and her skin, touched by the cold, was rose at her cheeks and as flawless as porcelain. Her beauty had matured since she had married Brooke and become the mother of two children, three if you counted Ellie. She was desperately afraid and it passed snake-like through her mind that it might be the best thing to allow this madman who was her father to have his way with her. It might protect the others, her beloved children, the girls who worked so hard for her, *their* children and even Brooke, for this man was capable of anything. All these months he had brooded on what had been done to him and what he would do to exact revenge and now it was to begin again.

Just as suddenly as he had appeared he turned and vanished between the trees. For several minutes she stared at the spot where he had been, beginning to tremble, not realising how rigid she had kept herself, the trembling spreading and spreading until she shook like an aspen tree. Then she turned and her legs flashing in a gathering of speed she ran in the direction of the house. But she could not enter the kitchen because the

servants would know that something had happened to her
while she had been out. The men in the stable yard would stare
in astonishment, for how was she to contain herself and act
normally as though nothing out of the ordinary had happened
to her? And what about Brooke? He would sense at once what
had happened, or that *something* had and would shake it out of
her and before she could stop him would gallop over to the
Mount, probably taking a couple of their men with him, and
beat her father to pulp. Perhaps kill him and end up in gaol.
Dear God . . . Dear sweet Jesus, what am I to do? God in
heaven, what am I to do?

Without coherent thought she found herself at the door of
Jenny and Todd's cottage – and Kizzie. Who else was she to
turn to but the woman who had loved her, guarded her,
comforted her, held her while she wept, followed her since
she was ten years old, guided her through girlhood and
brought her to the safe harbourage of her marriage to
Brooke? And was still there, still shielding her back, ready
to die for her.

Without knocking she burst into the warmth and sanity of
the cottage where Todd, his pipe between his teeth, his face
beaming with joy, was seated by the fire holding his son who
was thirty minutes old. He turned to Charlotte and so absorbed was he with his own delight and thankfulness that he
did not seem to notice his mistress's agitation. Leaning against
him was Jenny's daughter Rose, gazing down at her new
brother with little interest, for she had been surrounded by
babies all her young life.

'See, missis, we've got us a lad. A little lad not half an hour
since. By Gow, I never thought I'd see't day when—'

'Where's Kizzie? I must see Kizzie.'

At this most special moment of his life, Todd, who at forty-
two had given up all hope of ever being a father, never mind
marrying a pretty lass like Jenny, looked at the mistress

affronted, for she was never anything but kind and thoughtful with her servants.

'Why, she's upstairs tendin' ter Jenny. She only 'ad babby 'alf an 'our since an'—'

'I must see her. At once. Oh, dear Lord, I must see her. I don't think I can . . .'

Todd began to realise that there was something badly wrong with the mistress and though he would have liked proudly to display the bundle in his arms he stood up and moved to the bottom of the stairs that led directly into the neat kitchen.

'I'll go—'

'No, I'll go. Oh, I'm sorry, Todd, I'm pleased you have a son but really, I cannot . . .'

And before Todd could put out a hand to stop her she was halfway up the stairs, but Kizzie had heard the voices below. She stood at the top, a big bowl in her hands which apparently contained the cloths, sheets and all the paraphernalia of birth that she meant to put in the boiler at the big house. Jenny was comfortable and was sitting up in bed sipping a cup of tea and waiting for her husband to bring their son up for his first feed at her breast which was already brimming with milk. It had been an easy birth, it being her second, and she wanted Rose to come first and sit beside her, for there was no sorrier sight than a first child being pushed out by a second.

'What's up, lass?' Kizzie asked, but one look at Charlotte's face made her hurry down the stairs, indicate with a nod that Todd, the baby and Rose were to go up, put down her basin and, when Todd and Rose had scuttled upstairs, draw Charlotte to the fire.

Charlotte sank into the chair just vacated by Todd and put her head in her hands.

'Oh, Kizzie . . . Kizzie, what am I to do?'

'It's 'im, in't it? No other bugger would upset thi' like this. What 'appened?'

'He was in the wood. He's recovered, you see. He walks on a stick but he's up and about and it won't be long before—'

'What did 'e say?'

'What he's always said but this time he wants revenge for what has happened to him. He thinks Brooke put those men on to him but the irony of it is, it's Wallace Chapman who is healing him. I asked him to help my father and now it seems he has and far from being grateful he says the time has come for my "punishment". He threatened the children, Brooke, the girls at the Dower House and . . . Kizzie, I think he is insane. Really insane. I believe if he had not still been forced to walk with a stick and could have caught me I might have been . . . I think he means to . . . *rape me.*' The last two words were spoken in a whisper.

'Nay, lass, nay, not tha' own father,' Kizzie protested. ''Appen beat thi' or . . . no man rapes 'is own daughter.'

'What about the girls who have come to us bearing the child their fathers gave them?'

'Nay, lass. Lass, 'e wouldn't.'

'I do believe I would give in to him if I had just myself to consider but I'm afraid for my children, and Brooke. Kizzie . . . Kizzie, what am I to do?' She began to weep broken-heartedly. In one swift movement Kizzie was kneeling at her feet, her arms tight round her, shushing her tenderly and it was obvious from the expression on her face that she would kill the monster who threatened this young woman before she allowed him to touch a hair of her head.

'Tha've got ter tell master, child. Tha' can't manage this on tha' own. 'E needs lockin' in't Lunatic Asylum off Eastmoor. Master's got a lot of influence. A charge could be . . . well, if 'e were ter speak ter someone, tell 'im truth.'

'My father is a respected member of society, Kizzie. Who would believe it? None of his friends, I can assure you. They would think Brooke was the one who needed locking up for his preposterous suggestion.'

'I'd tell 'im an't servants at t'Mount. They knew as 'ow 'e used ter beat thi' an' them lads.'

'But they are servants, Kizzie. Of the lower classes. I'm sorry, but that is how they would be perceived and anyway, my father would probably bribe . . . or dismiss them without a reference, or he would frighten them.'

Kizzie stood up, her strong jaw thrust out. She squared her shoulders and picked up her bowl, moving to the bottom of the stairs. 'I'm tekkin' this lot up ter't'ouse, Todd,' she shouted. 'If tha' want owt nip over. Can tha' manage, d'yer think? Or shall I send one o't girl's over?'

Todd appeared at the head of the stairs. 'Nay lass, ta. Tha's bin grand. Us'll manage. Little lad's 'avin' a right good feed. Us're callin' 'im Edward after t'King. Thanks again, Kizzie. Tha're a grand lass an' if there's owt I can do fer thi' tha's only ter ask.' He hurried back to his family.

'Someone's 'appy, anyroad,' Kizzie muttered then moved back to Charlotte. 'Come on, chuck. Let's get thi' 'ome.'

Charlotte was in her bed; after a cup of hot chocolate into which Kizzie had poured a good swig of brandy, exhausted, she had fallen asleep at once. Kizzie debated whether to send for Doctor Chapman but decided against it, as it would mean that there would be somebody else for them to worry about. The doctor might think it his duty to interrogate Arthur Drummond, perhaps take Kizzie's tale to the police and then where would they be? This must be settled in the family which meant the master and herself. Charlotte was in such a state she was not capable, at least at the moment, of making any decision. She was terrified, willing to do anything, even offering herself as a martyr to protect her family, and until she was stronger, more in control of her keen mind which knew that it would be impossible, she must be kept out of it. Kizzie had no idea what the master could do, or *would* do but, like Charlotte, he might do something that would throw them all into a deep black hole from which they might never be able to climb. She wasn't sure she even knew what she meant by that but nonetheless he must be told. Besides which, if Charlotte didn't tell him he would know at once that something was wrong. They were too close, this husband and wife. They had grown together into a happy family unit over the last two years, what with their own children – so fragile and vulnerable – and the lovely child who was part of it, Drummond's own child, who was a pawn in this horrific game of cat and mouse the devil was playing. Someone would suffer. They would *all* suffer in one way or another and she must speak to the master who was the only one who could protect them all.

Kizzie knocked on his study door where a curious Nellie had told her he had gone. They had all been curious in the kitchen, staring with open mouths as she and Miss Charlotte had staggered through, she almost carrying Miss Charlotte. Mrs Groves had even gone so far as to hold out a hand and say, 'Eeh, whatever's wrong?' but she and Miss Charlotte had continued through the kitchen and up the stairs where she had put her young mistress to bed.

'A hot chocolate fer't mistress,' she had thrown over her shoulder as she went by, and then when the chocolate arrived, had slipped down to the drawing room and poured in the brandy with a heavy hand. She watched patiently until Charlotte had drunk it down, satisfied it would keep her mistress asleep for at least a couple of hours.

Brooke looked up and smiled as she entered. He looked rumpled, his hair all over the place after his energetic play with the children. Even Toby had not been left out, for at almost twelve months he was a sturdy toddler and had been thrown high in the air by his father to the consternation of the two nursemaids.

'Kizzie, I was just going to try and—'

'Can tha' spare a minnit, sir?' she began politely. She didn't bob a curtsey as the other maids might have. She never had!

'Of course, what is it? Nothing serious, I hope.' He brushed back his thick hair and smiled.

'Oh yes, sir, very serious.'

'Sit down, lass.'

# 28

She was dreaming. There was a man holding her: her father. He leered into her face and she thought he was going to say something like, 'I've got you now,' and she started to struggle and tried to scream but the voice kept saying, 'I've got you, you're safe now, my precious love, I've got you.' And she was in Brooke's arms and he was holding her close, his lips covering her face with kisses and she thought she felt something wet and warm on her cheeks and suddenly she was safe. Safe from the horrors that had overwhelmed her, from the worry, from the fear, for Brooke would take it all from her, tell her what she was to do. She was in her own bed, drenched in sweat and shivering, but it was all right because Brooke was here to safeguard her and her family and the girls and their children. Not only would he share it with her but he would make it right, take it from her. She was loved, protected; she didn't know how he would do it but she was not alone.

'Why didn't you tell me, you daft, sweet, lovely, brave woman? Did you think I would let that man touch a hair on your head, or that of our children? You're safe now, my sweetness, and always will be . . .'

She sat up and pushed him away yet at the same time held on to him, for this dear man who was her life, the love of her heart, would never allow harm to come to her; but she was incensed that someone had told him when she meant to keep it from him for his own safety and who could it be but Kizzie!

'I'll give that woman the rounds of the kitchen when I see her. I told her in confidence—'

'Did you think that woman, as you call her, would let you shoulder this on your own, you addle-pated creature? She can do nothing since she is, as our social equals would have it, of the working classes, the lower classes and therefore would have no notice taken of her. They, the police, or whoever she went to, would not believe her, for she is in their eyes a person of no consequence, but *I am*. I'll have to have a – all right, *we'll* have to put our heads together and work out a plan that will render your mad father helpless. First I intend to employ several men, men who will patrol the—'

'I thought we were to decide this together, Brooke Armstrong.' She flung herself out of bed and stormed across the bedroom, the filmy nightdress Kizzie had put her in, the only kind she wore, clinging to her still sweaty body and Brooke watched her with growing attention. He could see her nipples dark against the fabric and the triangle at the base of her belly and as she flared past him he caught her to him and dragged her into his arms. For a moment she nestled up to him as he began to kiss her shoulder and push the nightdress down to reveal her breast but though she longed to respond, for his touch still thrilled her, she pushed him away angrily.

'You're not taking this seriously, Brooke. I dare not let the children or . . .'

Suddenly he was grim-faced. He put her gently on the bed and walked away to stare out of the window at the frosted garden beyond. There was no one in sight as it was too cold for the gardeners to put a spade in the ground. He could see smoke wisping from the Dower House chimneys and as he watched, the wrought-iron gate that let into the wall opened and Kizzie hurried through it. She was well wrapped up even for the short walk to the front door of the house and he realised that she had been to check on the young women and their children who lived there. They were vulnerable since there was a gate at the back into the lane and anybody, meaning Arthur Drummond, could easily slip in as he had done last year. Not at the present moment, it seemed, for he could not do much harm with a weak leg but when he was totally recovered there would be nothing to stop him from riding up to the gate, tethering his horse in the lane and frightening the life out of whoever was there. He would wait until all the mothers, Charlotte's employees, were at work, either in the workshop across the yard, at the stalls in the market or at the shop in Wakefield. Megan was in charge of the children while their mothers worked, three of them and the new girl. A man must be posted to guard them and several others to patrol the grounds. Men with guns. In the meanwhile he would make it his business to have a word with the inspector, or even the chief constable of Yorkshire who were both known to him and knew him as a responsible citizen who was not mad. Many people, however, would think he was out of his mind, since Drummond was well known, liked even, a member of what passed for the upper classes in the area. And what about Wallace Chapman? Could he help? He had been attending Drummond ever since his "accident" and might perhaps have noticed signs of, if not insanity, then eccentricity, a tendency to instability. He and Wallace respected one another and surely if he told the whole terrible story of how Drummond had treated his children, particularly Charlotte, and then this last episode, he might have some advice, even some solution, or at least back up Brooke in his hopes to get Drummond committed. Yes, that was what he wanted, to have Arthur Drummond put away where he could harm no one.

Charlotte was dressing and he watched her as she put on a grey, ankle-length gored skirt, a white high-necked shirt, a wide leather belt that reduced her neat waist to nothing and a warm cardigan with deep pockets in the same colour as the skirt. She twisted her waist-length hair into a knot at the crown of her head and thrust pins in it, which held it precariously. Her sleep and the knowledge that she was no longer alone in this dreadful experience had put a rose in her cheek and she lifted her chin, squared her shoulders in a gesture that tore at his heart it was so brave.

'I'm ready,' she said, for anything, her attitude said, and held out her hand to him, which he took. He raised it to his lips and kissed her knuckles tenderly.

'God, how I love you,' he murmured, his lips still to her hand, his silver-grey eyes soft as velvet.

The servants were not surprised when three large, unsmiling men appeared at the kitchen door a few days later, each carrying a gun broken across his arm. The master had told the servants to expect them and here they were. They had ridden up on the horses Mr Armstrong had supplied them with and they were to ride the perimeter of his land, through his woodland, across his bit of moorland, patrolling the paths and gardens and even the farmlands, though they had been given instructions that they were not to interfere with the farm tenants. At the back of each man stood a dog, not big, nor ferocious, even allowing the stable lads to pat them but they were alert, their ears pricked and it was clear they would be the first to sense any danger lurking in the undergrowth.

'How about a hot drink, lads?' Mrs Groves asked nervously.

'Ta, that'd be grand, misshiss, but us've got ter get ter work, so quick as tha' like.'

The maids eyed the men appreciatively, for though they were tough-looking characters they were also extremely polite, young and not bad-looking. Arch and Percy, who had come from the stable block to inspect these chaps, worried they might upset their own animals, approved of the steady way they held their horses and kept their dogs in check.

While the men, identified as Denton, Mitchell, or Mitch, he said, and Hooper, drank their enormous mugs of strong, sweet tea, the way all the servants, especially the men, liked it, standing just outside the kitchen door, Percy and Arch did their best to question them. Denton, who was obviously the spokesman, told them briefly, and with a note in his voice that said he was unwilling to be interrogated, that Mr Armstrong had given instructions to *their* employer who ran an agency in town, that this property and all its occupants were to be guarded.

'Anyone what can't hidentify 'imself, or 'oo doesn't work on one of farms 'ere is ter be 'eld until Mr Armstrong can vouch fer 'im. Right, lads, let's go.' He swung himself on to his horse, called to his dog who went by the name of Gypsy or Gyp and set off smartly out of the yard. He was followed by Mitch and Hooper with their animals. They could hear him giving instruction to the other two and, splitting up, they went off in different directions.

'Well, I must say that's made me feel right safe wi' them three about,' Katie, the laundry-maid informed the others. 'Every time I were peggin' out I allus felt I were bein' watched.'

The weeks went by and Hetty's child was born, called Albert after the first son of the King. She had wanted to call him Thomas after her pa who was the one who had raped her in the first place and Charlotte and Kizzie marvelled at the minds of these girls who could name a child after such a wicked man. Megan, who could not be expected to manage six babies, some of them toddlers, was given a helper in the shape of another of her sisters, their Peggy. Jenny, now recovered from the birth of Edward, was back at work in the shop in the Bull Ring and all was running smoothly in the Dower House, the workshop and the big house and with Denton, Mitch and Hooper quietly protecting his property Brooke resumed his own rounds of the farms.

While Max plodded slowly along the lane that led to Jack Emmerson's farm Brooke ruminated on the conversation he had had with Wallace Chapman on the subject of Arthur Drummond. Wallace had been plainly shocked.

'Are you telling me that for years Drummond beat his children with a cane and, I can hardly believe it, forced Charlotte to . . . to bare herself and struck her naked skin in what was a perverted—'

'I am and they were all terrified of him. I know, though it has turned out well – you can see how Charlotte and I are – that is why she married me. To get her brothers away from him. You have no idea how the youngest was when he first came to us. A pathetic, frightened little boy who would not let Charlotte out of his sight. They have done well but eighteen months ago, just after Charlotte started her scheme, one of the girls you brought to the Dower House was tempted by Drummond to his place and . . . well, she thought he was genuine and when he turned her away she drowned herself and her baby.'

'Maudie?'

'I believe that was her name,' Brooke replied grimly, then was ashamed of himself for not remembering what the poor child had been called.

'And the attack on Drummond?'

'I'm not certain but I think . . . you will not speak of this to anyone, you must promise me.'

'Of course.'

'It was three of Kizzie's brothers. They did not hurt him enough to cripple him for good but they thought that he would give up and leave us alone. He threatens to take Ellie, his daughter, from us and we cannot, naturally, allow that. Not after what he did to his other children.'

'Indeed, and now he is—'

'He says he will take her as I suppose he legally can, unless Charlotte . . .'

'Yes?'

'Acts as his whore.'

He remembered Wallace's face when he said this. It drained of all colour and his mouth fell open in horror. They had been in Brooke's study where Brooke had asked the doctor to call, drinking coffee and talking of this and that until it was clear from Wallace's expression that he was a busy man and would be glad if Brooke said what he had to say.

'I just cannot believe that a man could treat . . .'

'Wallace, you of all people know what men can do to their children. We have some of them in our care at the Dower House. Maudie was one and though he did not kill her with his own hands he drove her to her death. He waylaid Charlotte in the wood and threatened her and but for the fact he was still walking with a stick and is not yet nimble enough to catch her I believe he might have attacked her there and then. He calls it *punishment,* though only God knows why! The girls Charlotte employs are also in danger and that is why I have three men with guns protecting the womenfolk on my property. And the children, of course. We are quite a large household and have men who would give their lives to keep the women and children safe, but they are only gardeners and grooms and not men versed in fisticuffs. So, you see, you have put Drummond back on his feet and though, of course, you are not to blame for this I am hoping you might be able to help me. Shall I go to the police or would they think me mad? I know I have influence but then so has he and who would believe that a man in his position, who surely has access to women by the score, willing women, wants his own daughter! I believe he is insane, perverted, deranged, his mind twisted and in my opinion should be put away. But I haven't the faintest idea how to go about it. It needs a medical man, someone expert in the field of – what do doctors call it? – psychiatry to examine him.'

He remembered Wallace's measured reply.

'Brooke, there is nothing I would like more than to help you but I'm afraid it needs more than your word, or even Charlotte's. You and she say he has threatened you but are there any witnesses? He would deny everything and I can only say that while I was attending him he was perfectly normal, or appeared so. He swore he had no idea who had attacked him, or why. He was not robbed and seemed totally rational, perplexed, and said he could only presume that someone had a grudge of some sort against him though he could not think of one.'

'The servants at the Mount would say he beat his children.'

'Yes, but a man cannot be arrested for that.'

'And Kizzie who has been with Charlotte since Charlotte's mother died knows.'

'Only because Charlotte told her. Dear God, Brooke, I would give anything to help you out of this awful predicament.'

'You believe me?'

'Of course. Why would you or Charlotte make up such a tale? I did not know Drummond before his accident so I have nothing with which to compare him and he seemed . . . appeared to be merely a victim of an attack.'

'So there is nothing you can do?'

'Well, I can consult a colleague and ask his opinion but I hold out no hope. I'm sorry, Brooke. He sounds abnormal, perverted and, naturally, should he attack Charlotte it would be a different case altogether.'

'So we have to wait until he attacks her before he can be . . . and then there is the question of Ellie. He could drive up here tomorrow and take her out of the nursery.'

Wallace had reiterated his promise to talk to the doctor in charge of the lunatic asylum in Wakefield, leaving Brooke totally dissatisfied.

He nodded at one of the men who were patrolling his grounds before entering Jack Emmerson's yard where he dismounted and rapped on the door with his riding crop.

He was out in the top field, his wife told Brooke, bobbing an awkward curtsey but if Mr Armstrong would come in she would pour him a glass of ale and how was Mrs Armstrong and those lovely bairns and she was sorry she hadn't seen them about lately. But then all the tenants knew of the threat that hung over the Armstrong family though none of them was awfully sure what or who it was that threatened them. No wonder they kept the children close to the house.

He politely refused the glass of ale, touched the peak of his cap with his riding whip and, getting back on his horse, continued his rounds of his tenants. Cec Eveleigh with the help of his eldest son was ploughing in farmyard manure in readiness for his crop of turnips and swedes and though he stopped for a chat with his landlord he kept his eye on his lad who was not as adept with the plough as he was. It was evident he was keen to get back to the work in hand. Davy Nicholson of Bluebell Farm was lifting an enormous bag of seeds on to a cart in preparation for sowing.

'Seen them chaps on 'orses ridin' about, Mr Armstrong. Guns an' all . . .' obviously longing to know what that was all about, since it must be serious if his landlord engaged them. 'Keen they be an' mekk sure as tha' 'ave a right ter be there. Frightened the life outer my missus first time. Is it foxes, sir?'

But Brooke merely smiled and shook his head, touching Max's side and riding on.

'Summat very fishy goin' on,' Davy told his missus that night as he tucked in to the tasty stew she put before him. 'An' I'd like ter know what the 'ell it is.'

'Well, it's nowt ter do wi us, Davy Nicholson, so get them vittles inside tha'. I've some parkin fer afters and I've opened a jar o' me plums.'

Jeff Killen at Foxworth, which was a pretty, half-timbered farm with a small orchard between it and the lane, and whose wife had a reputation for the best cheese, butter and eggs in Yorkshire, was drinking a mug of tea, leaning against his stable yard wall and surveying the load of turnips that was to go into a great slatted rack at the back of an empty stable.

'Mornin' sir,' he remarked, 'an' a good 'un it is too.'

'You look busy, Jeff.'

'Aye, sir, I'm mekkin sure come next winter I've feed fer me beasts. Hay yield looks good but tha' can never be sure.'

'Good thinking, Jeff. It's best to look ahead,' wishing he could look ahead to the months that were to come and that bastard recovering daily from the beating he had received. Denton, one of the men who patrolled his estate, had reported to him that he had seen a man walking the lane that led up beside the kitchen garden. Not on Brooke's property, of course, so Denton could not order him off or threaten him with his rifle and he was doing nothing but walk steadily towards Birks Wood where he vanished under the trees.

'A gentleman, Denton, or a working man off to a job?'

'I'd say a gentleman, sir, by the clothes 'e wore an' 'e'd good boots on 'is feet.'

So he was still there, the man who was in the back of everybody's mind but whom no one talked about, pretending that the problem – what a weak word for this fear that hung over them – had gone away.

Nothing else demanded his immediate attention. His tenants knew they could come to him if in need or for advice. Not that he was a farmer. Soldiering had been his career but since his father died and he had resigned his commission he had found he took a growing interest in what had been left in his hands.

He cantered into the stable yard, leaping from his horse in a way that gave him a great deal of satisfaction. He had once thought he would never be the same again after that damn bull gored him but thanks to Wallace and Charlotte, firmly believing that she had been the pivotal point of his recovery, he was himself again.

Percy ran to take Max from him. Brooke heard a great deal of laughter and barking over the roof of the house and with a smile he walked round to the front where the children were rolling about on the lawn with the dogs, even old Dottie doing her best to take part in the fun. Aisling and Rosie watched them indulgently and at the end of the garden where the woodland began, so did John Dudley and Ned Phelps, leaning on their hoes and smiling. Lucy and Ellie were both almost two and a half now and Toby fifteen months and walking, or rather running about steadily doing his best to keep up with the two little girls. They were well guarded, he knew that, but this couldn't go on for ever. How many months, years even, before Drummond struck at his family? For Ellie was as much Brooke's daughter now as Lucy. He loved them all equally and his wife was the most precious thing in his life. She was in Wakefield now at her shop. She would be smiling at her customers, the number growing with every passing month, for her carpets were unique and her rugs much sought after. She had a knack of . . . well, he could only call it *dressing* her windows so that they tempted ladies to come inside and then come back with their husbands. Of course, they were all wealthy but those with less money in their pockets could buy exactly the same rugs made in the warehouse across the yard from the Dower House, on the market stalls she rented at Hudderfield, Wakefield and Dewsbury and the designs, brought forth by Jenny with ingenuity and flair, which, she said herself, she hadn't even known she possessed, sold out by the end of the day. Jenny and Charlotte were to be seen with their heads together discussing the possibility of selling carpets on the stalls and if he knew his Charlotte, which he did by now, the idea would be made to work!

Charlotte at that moment was in the workroom at the Carpet Shop leaning over the enormous table on which Jenny's designs were spread out. When the weather was frosty at the beginning of the year Jenny had braved the weather and, sitting in the porch of the big house, had drawn and painted in the most delicate strokes, the silver, white and black world of the ice-coated garden. There were touches of brown and maroon where the sun lit a patch of frozen soil, a shadow of a bush, an icicle hanging from the branch of a tree and with her usual dexterity with a hook had created a rag rug from the painting. She painted poppies now, hyacinths, crocus, wild flowers as they sprang into life, watercolours with the paints Charlotte provided. She then sketched out her design on to hessian, including colours to be used, with a soft pencil. The hessian was folded into quarters to find the central point, fixed to a frame and the hooking began, using rags in dozens of colours. These carpets were becoming a 'must-have' among the ladies who were Charlotte's customers.

Josie, who had been arranging a quilt in a lovely fall of colours over a plain balloon-backed chair, popped her head round the door and they both turned to look enquiringly at her.

'You're wanted in't shop, Mrs Armstrong. There's a customer 'oo can't decide over a chair he fancies or—'

'We don't sell furniture, Josie. You know that. What is in the shop is for display purposes only. Can't you tell him or get Mr Joseph to deal with him? I'm busy with—'

'I told him that, ma'am, an' so did Mr Joseph but he ses he wants to speak to the owner. He's really taken to that chair, the one I were just about to drape this quilt over.'

All the girls who worked in the shop, adept now at displaying what was for sale, wore a pale grey dress with demure white collars and cuffs, very professional, and were proud not only of their jobs and the position they had achieved, but their children who were being taught to read and write and do sums and when the time came would go to the school in the village. They had bettered themselves, thanks to Doctor Chapman and Mrs Armstrong, and they were made up with it, and the doctor and their mistress were accorded the positions of gods!

The man stood with his back to the door, gazing out of the window at the bustle in the Bull Ring but even so she knew who it was.

Her father turned as she stood in the doorway of the workroom. He looked very smart in his morning coat, a single-breasted waistcoat and striped trousers. He had a pristine white handkerchief in his breast pocket to match his linen collar and carried a silk top hat.

'Good morning, Charlotte. This girl seems to be simple and the salesman incompetent. Your staff do not give me the service I demand so I thought you might be able to help me.'

He smiled smoothly.

# 29

Her heart pounded so hard she thought it might run out of control and stop beating. She wondered at the back of her mind why, in all this storm that had them at its centre she and Brooke had not considered the shop as a place of hazard. But then it was in the middle of a busy shopping area with hundreds of people passing to and fro and there were five employees in the building, though what good the rather effeminate Mr Joseph would be in such an emergency she could not imagine. Good at his job of salesman. The ladies liked him, for he had a certain manner that was civil without being subservient and he very definitely knew his carpets! She sat down in the chair her father wanted to purchase and waited.

'My dear Charlotte. I was passing so I thought I would pop in and have a look at my daughter's new enterprise and very smart it is too. And busy . . .' for the shop was filled with customers, some of them just browsing, others discussing their requirements with Mr Joseph. She would have to expand soon if things continued to grow as they were, she had told Brooke only last night, secure in the knowledge that she was safe from this ogre who had haunted her life for so many years.

'I was interested in the very chair you are sitting in, Charlotte, but that girl who is as "daft as a dormouse" as they say in these parts, seemed to think—'

'We don't sell furniture,' Charlotte snapped, 'and she told you so. Now if that is all, I have work to do.' She stood up but he merely smiled and took a step towards her. To her own annoyance she took a step back.

'Very well, but since I am here I thought it would be pleasant if we had a little chat. I would so like us to be friends, you know.'

'Friends! You and I will never be friends.'

'Charlotte, really!'

'I haven't the time to—'

'I find your attitude displeasing, Charlotte,' he told her, still smiling, 'and you know when I become displeased you are always punished so I would be glad—'

'Get out of my shop or I shall call a constable. There is always one about the Bull Ring and if—'

'And accuse me of what, my dear?' His expression had turned dangerous and his eyes a deep muddy brown. 'I am here merely to invite you to step across the way and have a coffee with me in the Griffin Hotel. It has a very respectable lounge where a lady and gentleman may sit and chat without inter-ruption. You will be perfectly safe, my dear. Oh, yes, I have seen those men who patrol your husband's estate and so far I have made no attempt to cross the boundary so to speak. But you may have noticed' – here he held out his arms – 'that I no longer use a walking stick. Indeed I can even mount my horse thanks to the excellent man your Doctor Chapman recom-mended to me. I have seen the children playing, *my* daughter with them and I must say she is growing into a very attractive little girl. I am quite taken with her and I'm sure if she came to live with me she would feel the same about her father. So, perhaps you might like to discuss this over a coffee. I am actually on my way to see my lawyer and meet Sir Clive Parker who, you may remember, is my dead wife's father. In fact the grandfather of Ellen, or Ellie as I believe you call her. He and I have discussed the matter and though he has no wish to take her on he would like to see his granddaughter and tells me he—'

Charlotte put out a hand and grasped the back of the chair, defeated. 'I'll get my hat and coat,' she said.

Brooke took the telephone receiver from Mr Johnson's hand then held it away from his ear as a shrill voice gabbled so hysterically and so incoherently that he could not make out who it was or what she was saying. It was obviously a woman.

'Slow down, slow down, I can't understand what you are telling me.'

'Sir . . . gabble . . . gabble . . . come at once . . . mistress . . .'

'Who is this?' he snapped, instantly alert.

'Jenny . . . Jenny, sir . . . an' 'e's tekken 'er.'

'Jenny, for God's sake, woman, who? What the bloody hell are you saying?'

'Mrs Armstrong, sir, 'er pa come in . . .' In her distress Jenny had reverted to the way of speaking she had done her best to eliminate, copying her mistress. ''E's took 'er ter the Griffin 'Otel, she said ter tell tha', fer a coffee.'

'*A coffee!*'

'Telephone master ter come at once, she sed ter tell tha' . . .'

Brooke didn't even put the receiver back on the hook. Alarming all the servants to the extent that Nellie dropped a pan of soup all over the freshly scrubbed kitchen floor, he flew to the back door, ran to the garage and jumped into the Mercedes, shouting to Percy to give the starting handle a swing. 'In fact, get in and come with me. I might need you,' he told the startled groom.

'But I'm in me muck—' Percy protested, for he had been mucking out the stables.

'It doesn't matter. Get in.'

The journey from King's Meadow frightened poor Percy to death, as the master drove at an incredible sixty miles an hour racing along winding country roads through Middlestown,

Horbury and thundering into Wakefield at such a rate folk on
the pavements jumped hastily back in alarm. He screamed to a
halt outside the Griffin Hotel, flinging poor Percy back in his
seat, not even turning off the engine and leaving the motor
parked askew at the front door. He ricocheted into the hotel,
dodging guests and causing them to move hastily aside and
porters the same, shouting after him to watch what he was
doing.

'The coffee lounge, where the hell's the coffee lounge?' he
yelled at a waiter and when the man pointed a wavering hand
he raced towards the open door with Percy, who had no idea
what the devil was up, in close pursuit.

She was sitting opposite her father, her face drawn, her eyes
dead, leaning back in her chair with a cup of untouched coffee
on the table before her while Arthur Drummond, leaning
slightly forward with his elbows on the table, talked to her,
expecting no answer, it seemed. He was not holding a conversation so much as giving her orders.

Brooke's roar of outrage lifted every head in the room and
several ladies squeaked.

In two strides he was across the room, those drinking coffee
at the small tables cowering back in terror, for they thought he
must be an escaped lunatic. Grabbing Arthur Drummond by
the scruff of his neck, he hauled him to his feet, drew back his
fist and hit him squarely on his chin. Drummond landed on his
back, fortunately between two tables, and their occupants,
ladies having coffee after an hour's shopping, began to scream.
But Brooke wasn't satisfied. He wanted Drummond to stand
up and allow him to hit him again and again, so when he did
not he dragged him to his feet and struck him once more, this
time on his nose which immediately spouted a great gout of
blood.

Charlotte, who for several moments had been paralysed
with shock and fear, stood up, her chair crashing backwards

into the chair occupied by a lady whose bonnet fell over her face with the impact. She was screaming Brooke's name and attempting to get hold of him, for if no one stopped him he would surely kill her father. Percy, who had followed his master into the hotel, spreading dung on the luxurious carpet in the entrance hall, leaped across the room and tried to get a grip of his other arm, the one that the mistress could not reach. The room was in uproar. Several waiters were doing their babbling best to restore order and the manager, when he arrived on the scene, could not believe his eyes.

'Sir!' he was shouting to no avail, for it was obvious that the gentleman attacking the second gentleman was just that, a gentleman. In fact he recognised him as the wealthy and influential landowner Mr Brooke Armstrong and the one he was doing his best to smash to pieces was another, though not so wealthy nor so influential. There was a working man with muck on his boots and a lady screaming Mr Armstrong's name and everyone in the coffee lounge was either shrieking – the ladies – or protesting loudly that they had never seen anything like it in their lives.

'I shall send for the constable,' he cried, doing his best with the man in working clothes to hold back Mr Armstrong, but by now it seemed the white-hot rage that was consuming Mr Armstrong, whatever it was about, was cooling, owing to his wife, the one who owned the Carpet Shop across the Bull Ring, dragging him, soothing him, pleading with him to come away or he would be arrested.

Dazed and bleeding, the second gentleman was helped to his feet, his face a mask of hatred. The thought passed through the manager's mind that if the look directed at Mr Armstrong by the bloodstained gentleman had been hurled at him he would have been exceedingly frightened. His lip was curled back in a snarl, rather like that of a wolf ready to attack. He could barely stand and a couple of waiters held him, one on each arm, for though he was the one who had been attacked there seemed to be a chance he might retaliate.

'Gentlemen, gentlemen, I beg you,' the manager began, but Arthur Drummond, who had been taken completely by surprise by Brooke's appearance and attack – in fact he had been feeling particularly jubilant at his own success in cowing Charlotte – was in a rage so great he almost hit the man who held him. She had agreed to visit him at her old home, or 'call on him' as he had put it, in the manner of their class, but they both knew exactly what that entailed. She would persuade her husband to dine with him and to invite him to dine at King's Meadow. They were to put on a front to ensure that their mutual friends would be made to realise that their feud had been forgotten. They were to be 'friends' in fact, and he would rather enjoy riding with her on her husband's acres, he had told her and if her husband proved awkward then Charlotte was to let him know that Ellie would at once be brought back to live with him at the Mount. And then there was the question of his own grandchildren: what were their names? Ah yes, Lucy and Toby. He might like to have them brought over to the Mount now and again, just to make sure Charlotte was not allowing them to become undisciplined. She had been known to be indulgent with her brothers, particularly Robert. He wanted all this to be plain to them both so that when he kept his appointment with his lawyer he could tell him that all was now settled. Sir Clive could visit his granddaughter whenever he wished, either at the Mount or at King's Meadow. All he wanted in return for this perfectly reasonable request was that Charlotte and he would be friends again!

It was at that moment Brooke Armstrong had slammed across the coffee lounge and, if Arthur was not mistaken, broken some of his teeth.

'I want this man arrested,' he hissed through his bleeding lips, taking the white napkin the manager held out to him and putting it to his face. 'I think I have enough witnesses to prove that I was sitting here talking peacefully to my daughter when he—'

'*My wife!*' Brook bellowed. 'And I dare say he would not be willing to repeat what he was saying to her. *Demanding* of her. He is a bastard, a bloody pervert . . .'

'Brooke, darling, please . . .' Charlotte was doing her best to draw him away from the shocked and silently staring crowd of onlookers, some of the ladies beginning to whimper, for in their sheltered lives they were not accustomed to hearing such language nor to seeing such violence. Brooke wanted nothing more than to have another go at smashing Drummond's face in but the touch of his wife's hand, the sound of her voice calmed him and he was not to know that she was beginning to regret the telephone call she had asked Jenny to make. But she had been fearful of what her father might do: lure her into his carriage which waited outside the shop, or drag her some-where down a ginnel at the back of . . . God knew he was mad enough, and she had panicked. And now look what had happened!

She had been prepared to agree to anything her father demanded of her, no matter how humiliating. She had sat and listened to his whispered ultimatums, nodding her head as though she were willing to give in to them. She had kept her eyes averted so that he would not see the loathing in them and the growing, secret determination to deny him what he wanted. She would *never* become his 'friend' – dear sweet Jesus, she knew exactly what that meant – she would never, *never* give Ellie over to him nor let him have any input on how she reared her own children even if she had to persuade Brooke to move away and hide these precious children from him. Her own brothers had come for Christmas as they had done ever since she had married Brooke and though they appeared to have overcome their strict, no, cruel upbringing she would not under any circumstances permit her own children, nor his, to be treated as she and her brothers had been. He would never be allowed across her doorstep and she would not *call* on him at the Mount, she vowed silently. Sir Clive, if he wished it, though he had shown no sign of it so far, might come and visit his granddaughter at King's Meadow. Besides, she knew Brooke would agree to none of his demands. He'd kill him first. Dear God in heaven, help me, help me . . .

Brooke allowed his wife to draw him away. He was nearly out of his mind with fury but was sensible enough to know that if the manager called the police they would be forced to make some sort of enquiry. He might be taken to the police station and where would that leave Charlotte and the children? Unprotected, that's what!

'Come, darling, come,' Charlotte was murmuring softly as though she wanted no one but him to hear. Her father was still shrieking that he would have justice but he too was beginning to realise that this public display of his family's affairs was doing his own cause no good. He wanted Charlotte to fall in with what he had whispered in her ear but not for the whole world – their world – to know about it.

Reluctantly but quietly, much to the relief of the manager, Mr Armstrong let himself be led across the lounge and through the entrance hall into the street. Holding her tightly to him he crossed the Bull Ring and entered the Carpet Shop. Percy followed respectfully, wondering what the hell was to happen next. The motor stood idling by the front door of the hotel, the engine still running, surrounded by a group of awed spectators, small boys trying to get up the courage to touch the shining machine, a policeman moving slowly towards them, for the sight of one of these incredible machines impressed them all. Not many were seen in these parts. Obviously whoever owned it would not like a bunch of youngsters climbing all over it; besides, it was causing a bit of a traffic hold-up.

'We won't be long, Constable,' Brooke said firmly from the doorway then, turning to Charlotte, told her to get her hat and coat.

'I've got them on.'

'Right then, whatever else you may want to take home.'

'I'm not going home, Brooke. He—'

'You are coming home, Charlotte, and you are staying there until this bloody matter is resolved. Hurry up, or the constable will—'

'I can't just leave.'

'You can and you will. You will stay where you are safe under the protection of the men I employ. I was mad to let you come here,' sweeping his arm round the shop as though they were in the wilds of the new world surrounded by savages. 'No wonder he just walked in and forced you to accompany him wherever he fancied taking you. Thank God it was only into the coffee lounge. God alone knows what you would have done if he had demanded you get in his carriage.' His voice almost broke and he took her roughly in his arms to the embarrassment of Jenny and Mr Joseph. 'My darling, do you know how precious you are to me, how fine. I love the very bones of you, and our children, and if I have to keep the lot of you safe by chaining you in the cellar I'll do it. Now then, come home.'

Still she resisted. 'Jenny cannot manage here on her own.' Her face was muffled against his chest. 'I cannot run it from—'

'Then we'll shut the blasted place. I mean it, Charlotte. I've allowed it because—'

She dragged herself out of his sheltering arms, her face bright with indignant pride. '*Allowed* it! Brooke, Queen Victoria is dead. Women are fighting for the vote. We are independent or wish to be and most have husbands who are in charge of them as though they were children who could not decide for themselves. My love' – as he pulled away from her, as indignant as she was – 'you are not one of them and I know it is only this present danger that made you speak as you did, but I cannot just close the shop and—'

'Charlotte, how can you ask me to let my wife be threatened as your father threatens you? He is not in his right mind, you know that, and is unstable and the devil knows what he will do next. The children are not safe even in the confines of the garden. The men do their best but he is unpredictable, clever in his own mad way and I dare not, *will not* take the chance that he will trap you in Wakefield. I have nothing with which to go to the law in order to protect you. He is, so far as they know, a respectable, law-abiding citizen and it is your word only—'

'And Kizzie's.'

'Kizzie is not of his class and her word would not count against his. You must see that.'

She sighed and turned away. 'Very well, I will stay at home and do my best to keep the place running under Jenny's guidance. We can communicate by telephone if there are any problems and Mr Joseph is experienced in the manufacture of carpets. He will do the buying, I suppose, but . . .'

She turned and moved towards the small, glassed office at the back of the shop to which Jenny and Mr Joseph had tactfully removed themselves. She spoke to them briefly and though Brooke could not hear what she said he could see them turn to look at one another in consternation. Then briefly they nodded. Charlotte returned to him and with obvious reluctance took his hand and moved with him out of the shop and into the Mercedes. Percy had not dared to climb into it as he waited for his master and mistress but stood at attention as though guarding it from the slack-jawed onlookers who were not only astonished by the machine but by him, who looked what he was. A working man who was more used to mucking out stables than riding in a motor car.

Thankfully he climbed into the back seat when told to do so by Mr Armstrong and with great relief, at least on his part, they headed for home.

It worked in a fashion. Charlotte spent some time in the workshop at the Dower House, for Wallace Chapman continued to send abused and injured girls to her, most of them for a rest before moving on.

'I have no space for any more, Wallace,' she told him, 'nor the work. I can give them some place to recover from their injuries, that I promise, but unless I extend the roof space in the workshop there is not room for them all. Kizzie keeps them busy and Miss Seddon at the village school is always glad of a bit of help, though without pay, I'm afraid. I know they will probably return to their profession . . . oh, really, it is too awful what men do to women and what women put up with. D'you know I've half a mind to join the Huddersfield branch of the Women's Suffrage Society. Women's suffrage knows that the lot of women will not improve until politicians are made accountable to a female electorate—'

'Whoa, whoa.' Wallace laughed. 'You sound like my wife and if you feel as you do why don't you come to one of her meetings? Someone like you could have much influence with a husband as liberal as yours.'

'I didn't know she had one. A meeting, I mean.'

'Well, she doesn't approve of a militant organisation like Mrs Pankhurst's, at least not at the moment but they seem to be getting nowhere whatever their beliefs. Anyway, this isn't solving your problem, which is that of your father's determination to disrupt your life as much as possible.'

'If there was something you could do . . .'

'I never see him now, my dear. He has recovered from his
. . . er, injuries and no longer needs my attention.' He stood up
and made his way towards the door. He had been checking on
Hetty and her newborn son and he liked to look in on all the
girls who had passed through his hands.

'What you do for these young women is very worthwhile,
Charlotte. I know it must seem like a drop in the ocean to you,
as it does to me, but it is all we can do. Now, I must go. I am
due at the Clayton. I have a colleague interested in neurology –
medicine of the mind, he calls it – or a new word, schizo-
phrenia. I believe it means a mind that is split but I am no
expert in the field. Now if there is anything I can do let me
know.'

She sat for an hour in the drawing room after Wallace had
gone, pondering on the possibility that what he had said might
have some bearing on the state of her father's mind. He
seemed perfectly normal to other people, to his friends, those
with whom he dined, but he had this fixation on her, his own
daughter which, if they had known of it, they would not
believe.

She stood up and moved to the window to look at the
children and the dogs romping on the lawn under the watchful
eye of two gardeners and one of the men who carried rifles
broken over their arms. He was almost hidden on the edge of
the treeline beyond the lake, since he did not wish to frighten
the children who were not really old enough to understand
anyway. Toby was walking quite steadily now but without
taking his eyes from the ground so that he would not miss the
smallest object. A daisy, a beetle, a scurrying line of ants, a
coloured stone, any of which would stop him and instantly
absorb his baby interest. As she watched he crouched down,
his head between his plump knees, then, leaning forward, he
trapped whatever it was between his thumb and finger. His
tongue protruded from his mouth and as babies had done

from the beginning of time he put whatever it was in his mouth. Aisling let out a cry and ran forward, picking up the child, for he had been known to crunch a snail between his teeth. Prising open his mouth, much against his will, she scraped it out, ignoring his indignant cries. Taddy bounded exuberantly across the grass and ran full tilt into Aisling and knocked her and Toby over but they were both laughing by now and when she stood up the nursemaid threw Toby into the air and caught him expertly, then ran down the garden followed by Lucy and Ellie, begging to be told what it was Toby had eaten this time.

Her babies, her precious jewels, the bright stars in the sky of her life, her sunshine, the centre, with her husband, of her whole life, and that bugger of a man, the man who had given *her* life, was doing his twisted best to destroy it all.

She would kill him first!

# 30

The dry-stone walls meandered along both sides of the deserted lane, a focus of wildlife and a delight to the eye. Everywhere was a variation of form and colour and the walls themselves were a symbol of the passage of the seasons, the symphony of green mosses and lichens that mark the end of winter but in the summer are progressively submerged by a rising tide of growth. Sweet cecily, fragrant with the scent of aniseed, standing waist-high, almost blocking the sunken verges at each side with full green foliage and luxuriant blossoms, unlike any other white flower. Hedge parsley, dock and nettle, succeeded in the autumn by meadow cranesbill, ragwort, foxglove and willowherb. Others flourished on the stones themselves, like stonecrop and feverfew, a boon to the arthritic, it was said, but it was not any of these that the woman sought. She was tall, wide-shouldered, with bright nut-brown hair that glowed in the sunlight, bending forward as she walked, peering into the damp ditches and at last she found what she was seeking. The vivid yellow of the lesser celandine! Picking a great bunch of the pretty flower she placed it carefully in a canvas bag and, turning, sauntered back the way she had come until she came to a cottage. She passed through the white gate and entered the kitchen at the back of the cottage.

'Are yer there, Mam?' she called but there was no one at home. At once she began to strip the fresh leaves and stems from the plants she had gathered, put them in an old pan that she had brought with her in the bag, added a pint of water and, placing the pan on the fire, brought it to the boil. Leaving it for just one minute she snatched it from the fire and poured the decoction into a jar that she took from her pocket. She slipped the pan and the jar into the bag that had contained the plants and left the cottage, walking quickly towards her workplace. Before she got there she looked about her for several moments to make sure she was unobserved, then, fetching a small trowel from her pocket, she dug a fairly deep hole, buried the pan and hurried on until she reached her destination.

Everyone agreed that Toby was a little so-and-so, bless him. Take your eyes off him for a minute and he was off, his sturdy legs carrying him incredible distances, usually with one of the dogs at his heels, for they seemed to regard him as part of their pack and to be protected. They were the same with the little girls, of course, but Lucy and Ellie were not quite so adventurous, happily playing on the lawn with their dolls, old Ginger and Dottie panting at their side, their tongues lolling out, their eyes closing and opening, keeping an eye on them as Aisling and Rosie did. Taddy, for once, lay with them in the warmth.

This day Charlotte was sitting in a basket chair, Ellie and Lucy curled against her as she read from a book of nursery rhymes which they loved, but which bored or were probably not understood by Toby.

> Blow, wind, blow! And go, mill, go!
> That the miller may grind his corn;
> That the baker may take it
> And into bread make it,
> And send us some hot in the morn.

'That's for our breakfast, you see, my darlings, when we make toast.'

'Winter has come, Mama,' they begged. 'Say winter . . .'

'Very well, but this must be the last.'

> Cold and raw the north wind doth blow,
> Bleak in the morning early,
> All the hills are covered with snow,
> And winter's now come fairly.

'Will we play in the snow, Mama?'

'Yes, my darling, when the winter comes, but now it's time for tea.'

John and Ned were deadheading the roses and for several minutes none of them noticed that Toby and Floss had vanished, but as Charlotte lifted her head to call to her son her heart missed a beat for he was nowhere in sight. But then was that not typical of the engaging toddler who was everybody's friend? He had been known to escape from the nursery, slide down the stairs on his plump bottom and make his way to the kitchen where a great fuss was made of him. They all loved him, indulged him and were always pleased to see him, which he knew, the little tinker!

She stood up so abruptly both little girls spilled to the grass, protesting loudly. 'John, where's Toby? Is he with you?' But she could see he was not, wondering at her own foolishness.

The gardener looked about him and Ned moved slowly towards the lake. ' 'Appen 'e's gone round t'back, ma'am. I'll run an' see.' And run he did at such a speed that the three dogs who had leaped to their feet, alert at once to the panic, could not keep up with him!

Brooke was out doing the rounds of the estate, calling at each farm as was his custom, but the rest of them, even overweight Mrs Groves, ran about like ants spilled from an anthill, getting in each other's way, searching the same place twice. Ned, who was young and strong, plunged into the lake, wading up to his waist, brushing aside the reeds and lily pads, causing the ducks to protest loudly.

Charlotte's face was like bleached bone and her eyes stared into the terror that had haunted her for years now and when his voice called out she put out a hand to steady herself on John's shoulder, not at all surprised.

'Is this who you're looking for?' it said. 'He wandered through the wood on to my property and, since he is my grandson, I took the liberty of engaging him in conversation. I told him he was to call me Grandfather but he didn't seem to understand. In fact he reminds me strongly of Robert.'

The child cowered away from the man who held him and the moment he saw Charlotte he held out his arms to her.

'Mama . . . Mama,' he quavered, straining towards her and with a cry she leaped forward and would have taken him but her father shook his head pleasantly.

'I think not, Charlotte. I'll bring him inside, since he appears to have wet himself, just like Robert used to do, and will need his nurse's attention.'

'I'll run fer't master,' John murmured in her ear but she turned on him like a wild cat so that he cowered back.

'You will not. You will not. It's what he wants. And my husband would kill him. Stop where you are, John, and tell the other men that if one of them goes for my husband he will be dismissed on the spot.'

'But lass . . . lass,' whispered John, almost in tears, for the mistress and the children were obviously very frightened.

'Come inside, Father, and bring my son. Aisling, take Master Toby from Mr Drummond . . .'

'*Inside,* Charlotte, where I would be glad of a word and perhaps refreshments before that ruffian you call husband returns.'

'Very well.'

They moved into the hallway, Toby crying piteously for his mother who had, for the first time in his young life, let him down. The two little girls were whimpering against the skirts of the nursemaids who lifted them into comforting arms while the mistress and her father, watched by the others, entered the drawing room.

'May I have my son, please?' Charlotte asked tonelessly.

'In a moment.' Arthur Drummond sat down, the boy on his knee, and Charlotte did the same.

'May I offer you a brandy?'

'I think a cup of hot chocolate, if I may. It's a bit early for spirits, even for me.'

'I'll ring the bell.'

Nellie answered, bobbing a curtsey or two and then disappeared rapidly.

'She wants chocolate,' she said to the distressed servants who stood about as though not knowing what exactly they should do, or why they were so frightened since Master Toby had been returned safe and unhurt.

But before she had even finished the sentence Kizzie was busy with milk and setting the tray even though it was not her job. 'I'll do it,' she said in a strange voice, pushing Tess to one side. They were all so demoralised they meekly stepped away, their minds dwelling on the man who had their baby, the man of whom they were all deadly afraid.

In the drawing room Arthur Drummond was reproving his daughter, who watched him like some small animal caught in the deadly stare of a cobra. Her mind was blank with no thought in it except now and then the dart of something ominous like a shark in black waters. Her eyes were fastened on her son who, just as Robert had once done, had fallen into a still, almost shocked state. All his life he had been protected, loved by everyone around him but young as he was he appeared to recognise that he was in the presence of evil.

'May I have my son, please, Father? He is afraid since he does not know you.'

'And whose fault is that, my dear?' He planted a dry kiss on the boy's rounded cheek, which was more frightening than a smack. The boy flinched. 'I expected a call from you, Charlotte, perhaps one of apology after that nasty scene in the hotel. Your husband is a lout, really he is, and how he ever became accepted in a gentleman's world is beyond me. But still, I am not concerned with him. I saw him ride off in that arrogant way of his so, with this lad here, I took the opportunity to call. I think it is very responsible of me to bring him home, do you not think so, Charlotte? He might have been hurt in that wood all alone. You should take more care of him. Now, since he is wet and I believe he smells' – a disgusted look came over his face – 'you may take him off me and perhaps send him to be changed.'

There was a quiet knock on the door and Kizzie entered carrying a tray set with an immaculate white cloth and two cups of chocolate. She placed the tray on a small table, then she put one cup on its saucer on a smaller table she drew up beside her former master.

'Would you like a sip of Grandfather's chocolate, boy?' Arthur Drummond asked but the boy strained away and, suddenly losing interest, Drummond almost threw him at his mother.

'I'll take him, Mrs Armstrong,' Kizzie said calmly, scooping the boy up into her arms and almost running from the room. 'He needs changing.'

She was so relieved to see her frightened little son rushed from the room in arms that he loved it did not occur to her to wonder why Kizzie had brought in the chocolate instead of Nellie. Kizzie was housekeeper now, in charge of the others; she ran Charlotte's home, among her other duties at the Dower House, but then, like the other servants, their fear for Toby's safety had probably sent them all into a spin and Kizzie would be the first to bring order!

'Now then, daughter, when may I expect a visit from you?

Not with the children if you don't mind. We will leave that for later. I thought it would be . . . pleasant for us to be alone for an hour or two, catch up, so to speak.' He smiled his wolfish smile, sipping his chocolate and watching her with the same candid expression that said he had nothing in mind other than a return of their supposed former affectionate relationship. Charlotte felt sick, as though her own chocolate, which she did her best to get down, were choking her but she sat with her back as straight as a ruler, for she would not show the desperation she felt. She longed for Brooke to come home and share this torment with her but at the same time she listened in terror for the sound of Max's hooves on the gravel drive beyond the window. She could hear the trill of a meadowlark high in the heavens before it fell in its daredevil swoop to its nest somewhere on the estate. The voices of John and Ned, Ned having changed into dry clothes, came through the open window, low and cautious and obviously not far away. Keeping close in case she should need them. Her servants were all around her, the men ready to fight for her safety, the housemaids too, no doubt, as she knew they were fond of her but there was nothing to be done. Nothing. This man held all the cards and he would have his will of her, his smiling face said.

'Well, my pet, shall we say tomorrow for coffee? I am usually ready about eleven then we can . . . talk until lunch-time; in fact it would be pleasant if you could take luncheon with me and we could resume our conversation in the after-noon. I'm sure we must have plenty to talk about and I am free all day. One thing, I should not tell your husband of . . . our reconciliation if I were you. He might not understand. Make up some excuse about calling on friends, that is if you have any.'

He finished his chocolate and stood up and so did she.

'About eleven then. Perhaps you could ride over. No need

to disturb your coachman, or have you a gig of your own? Yes, then perhaps that would be convenient for you. And I should like to see you in one of your elegant morning gowns. So much more feminine than riding gear, don't you think?'

He seemed to find nothing wanting in her lack of response but let himself out, striding across the lawn and, as she watched, paralysed, barely able to walk to the window to see him go, he disappeared into the trees. The two gardeners stood to watch him, then turned to one another with the relaxed attitude of 'good riddance to bad rubbish'!

Kizzie must have heard the front door open and close, for the next minute she entered the drawing room and without a word put her arms about Charlotte and held her as she began to shake. Her teeth chattered and she clamped her lips together but strangely Kizzie was calm, patting her back then holding her away for a moment to look into her face.

'Don't fret, my lass,' she murmured, then kissed her cheek.

'Kizzie . . . oh, Kizzie . . .'

'Tha're not ter fret, my lamb. Dost understand? Everything'll be all right. Now go an' play wi't bairns, give that Toby a cuddle fer 'e needs 'is mam.'

She did as she was told, curiously comforted, but even so, how could Kizzie tell her not to fret when the devil himself was about to make her his plaything?

The children were clamorous in their childish pleasure when she strode into the nursery and Toby ran to her with his arms flung wide, lapsing into the babble of three months ago before he had begun to speak more clearly. He was cross with her, he said, in words only she and the nursemaids understood, for letting that man kiss him, but she held him close, in fact she managed to hold all three of them on her lap as she sat on the floor and the nursemaids watched and understood. The lad, and the little girls would never again be let out of sight until that man was behind bars, they all told one another in the kitchen,

That evening as she and Brooke sat at dinner she did her best to appear her usual self, asking him about his day, laughing at his description of the antics of Davy Nicholson's new calves who were as playful as kittens, marvelling at what promised to be a bumper harvest, but it was an effort and she thought he had begun to notice her forced merriment.

'What's up?' he asked abruptly when they were sitting in the drawing room where they took their coffee.

'What d'you mean, my love?'

'You seem . . . preoccupied. Oh, I know it is hard for you to keep in touch with the Carpet Shop through Jenny and by means of the telephone but hopefully it won't be for long. Surely your father will see that he is beating his head against a brick wall and give up. If only some woman would come along, like Ellie's mother, who would keep him occupied. Or perhaps when the hunting season begins he will be too busy to bother us. Let's hope they make him Master.'

'Yes, let's hope so.'

Brooke looked down at her where she nestled in the crook of his arm. 'You know I would never allow him to harm you, or the children. You must know how much I love you, my sweetheart. I would kill him with my bare hands without a qualm if he stepped foot on this estate and so would the men. I would take my chances with the law, in fact.'

'No, no, let it be, darling.' She had prayed to some being who must exist somewhere that the children, when he went up to play with them before bedtime, would not tell him of the stranger who had come into their small world that day. Toby might try to say something but Brooke wouldn't really be able to understand his infant chatter, not like she and the nursemaids did, and the girls had not really been involved. But the terrible strain it imposed on her, and the servants who were bewildered by the way her father acted, was beginning to tell on them all. Of the servants, only Kizzie seemed calm, even unmoved.

Suddenly she turned in his arms and clung to him passionately, for only in his goodness and love could she find any peace.

'Take me to bed, Brooke,' she whispered.

'What, now?' He was laughing as it was still full daylight outside. 'Mind you, dearest girl, I'm not averse—'

'Take me to bed. Tell me of the heart . . . tell me of love,' by which she meant, in her own mind and body and soul, in contrast to the filth with which her father coated her.

The servants nodded sagely but were accustomed to their master and mistress slipping to their bedroom early and Mrs Groves said wisely to Kizzie that there'd be another on the way soon. They went upstairs with their arms about one another and into their own private, candlelit space where he made love to her with a tenderness that made her weep, but when he asked her why, kissing away her tears, she shook her head wordlessly.

'Our life is so beautiful,' was all she would say and when he slept with his head on her breast, she prayed again, pleading in silent sorrow for release.

They were awakened in the dark of the night by the piercing shrill of the telephone and though Mr Johnson, whose job it was, usually answered it, Brooke jerked awake, he didn't know why. None of his tenants had a telephone, besides which, if they had one, what on earth would they ring about at this time of night?

'I'd better answer it. Johnson wouldn't know what the hell to do and anyway it's bound to be for me. It might be Wallace with one of his waifs.' He pulled on his dressing gown and Charlotte had a moment to think that his naked body was quite beautiful in the soft glow of the candles before he galloped downstairs.

It was Wallace.

'Brooke, I'll come at once to the point. I'm at the Mount and I'm sorry to say . . . or perhaps not sorry, but in a bit of a quandary on how to tell you . . .'

Brooke felt a small shiver creep down his spine as though a feather had outlined the bones of it. Somehow, later, he could never understand why, he knew what Wallace was going to say and his heart was filled with a mad desire to shout with joy but was instantly ashamed of it. Then again he was not, for this was an answer to his and his beloved and unique wife's prayers.

'Drummond?'

'Yes, Drummond's dead.'

'Really?'

'Yes, really.'

'What caused it?' doing his best to keep the triumph from his voice.

'I'm not sure and of course there will be an inquest as there is on any sudden, unexpected death, but it looks like a heart attack. That is what I shall say, anyway.'

'Thank you.' When he said it Brooke wondered why. It was as if Wallace, and he himself, although he had nothing to do with it, knew there was more to it than was immediately obvious. But then what did he care? The man deserved to die for the wickedness, the pain and fear he had inflicted, not just on Charlotte but on all his children.

'Thank you, Wallace. Let me know if . . . well, if we are wanted for anything. Perhaps Charlotte and I should ride over?'

'There is no need unless you wish to pay your respects.'

Brooke laughed in great amusement. Pay their respects! He couldn't wait to get back upstairs and break the wonderful, miraculous news that her father was gone. That their lives could now be lived out in peace. That their children could roam their small world, ride their ponies when the time came, without fear. That he and Charlotte could *allow* them to roam without the terror that had stalked them for years.

He was somehow not surprised when he replaced the receiver and turned to go back to his wife to find Kizzie at his back. She was wrapped in a white shawl over her night-gown and she was smiling in a strange but loving way.

'Not bad news, I hope, sir?'

'No, Kizzie, the best.'

The inquest took several weeks to be concluded, with a verdict that Arthur Drummond had died from a heart attack, con-firmed by the evidence of the respected Doctor Chapman. The funeral was attended by dozens of the gentry, all packed into the small church where Charlotte and Brooke were married. The Armstrongs, though a strange pair, she with her shop and the girls she had taken into her life and he because he allowed it, were, after all, gentry, both of them from their social strata. The funny thing was they both appeared quite cheerful in an odd sort of way. Charlotte didn't even wear the long veil of mourning that one would expect and her face was serene. Their servants and those from the Mount were all there at the back of the church but there was none of that gloom and dolour that one associated with a death. It seemed that Charlotte had found positions for all her dead father's servants and there was talk of her old home being sold. They went back to King's Meadow where, to their consternation, *champagne* was served.

'I do hope we will see more of you now, Charlotte,' Patsy Ackroyd told her, 'if you can spare time from your many activities. I quite envy you, really I do. That shop of yours seems to go from strength to strength even though I heard you are not there as much as you used to be.'

'No, I have a very good manageress now. Jenny Todd. She

is married to our coachman and my girls are all very competent so I shall probably spend more time with my children.
And my husband.'

'You . . . you love him, don't you?' It was said enviously.

'More than life.'

They had all gone, mouthing their polite farewells and sadness
at the passing of such a dear friend and much loved father,
holding Charlotte's hand, and shaking Brooke's.

Charlotte and Brooke stood on the terrace under the porch,
then as the last motor car and carriage disappeared down the
shaded drive, he put his arm about her shoulder and she
leaned her head against him.

They smiled at one another in perfect understanding of how
things would be and he dropped a kiss on her hair. Kizzie, who
stood in the hallway behind them, smoothed down her immaculate black skirt, rattling the chatelaine at her waist that
proclaimed her position in the house. She too smiled, turning
to the kitchen where her staff were already clearing up after the
reception.

On the terrace Charlotte and Brooke were gazing with
dreaming eyes at their garden.

'Do you know how much I love you?'

'Oh, yes, thank you.'

'Thank you?' He looked down into her upturned face in
astonishment. 'What is there to thank me for?'

'For bringing me to this. This peace, this place, this world of
ours.'

The sunshine washed the front of the house and the lovingly
cared-for garden with golden-edged brilliance and as though
they had been waiting for this moment of release from some
malignant situation, John and Ned sauntered round the corner
of the house, Ned trundling a wheelbarrow, laughing at something one of them had said. When they saw their master and

mistress, they stopped abruptly and put a respectful finger to their caps. Though they had not entirely understood the intricacies of it they knew a great cloud had been lifted from this home.

They were followed by Aisling with Lucy and Ellie, running and skipping, Lucy trying to do cartwheels, and Toby tumbling about the lawn on his as yet unsteady legs. The dogs were with them, four of them circling the children protectively. Taddy, with his nose to the ground, was following some scent made by a creature that had meandered across it during the night.

The gardeners watched them all indulgently, neglecting the task they were about to perform, and the children's parents did the same.

'Let's go for a walk,' Brooke said suddenly.

'Oh, let's. Down through the wood to where we met.'

He took her hand and they ran together like their own children, unnoticed, round to the side of the house, past the vegetable gardens, the greenhouses and the paddock, ignoring the welcoming whinnies of the horses. They reached the woodland, turning for a moment to see if anyone had noticed them, then vanished into the green tunnel beneath the motionless canopy of trees. They ran lightly across the soft bed of grass and wood anemones until they reached the thicket that guarded the glade where she had fallen beneath the hooves of Brooke's horse.

'I think I loved you even then,' he said, drawing her down into the wide spreading roots of an oak tree, 'and I wanted to do this.'

They made love with tender thankfulness, watched only by a squirrel who was busy about his own business and as they lay tranquilly afterwards she told him she was pregnant again.

'That was quick.' He laughed. 'Twenty minutes must be a

record.'

She turned in his arms and laid her head on his bare chest, for they were divested of most of their clothing. 'It doesn't take long,' she murmured. 'Not where love is.'

Fecundi